THE

CHILDREN

OF LOT

Montag Press 978-0-9822809-7-3
Cover art © 2013 Grey Matter
Cover design © 2013 Sam Cowan
Author photo © 2013 Lauren Vickery

Montag Press Team:
Project Editor – Mari Schwarzer
Layout & E-Book Designer – Sam Cowan
Managing Director – Charlie Franco

A Montag Press Book
www.montagpress.com
Montag Press
536 E. 8th Street
Davis CA, 95616 USA

Montag Press, the burning book with the hatchet cover, the skewed word mark and the portrayal of the long-suffering fireman mascot are trademarks of Montag Press.

Printed & Digitally Originated in the United States of America
10 9 8 7 6 5 4 3 2 1

THE
CHILDREN
OF LOT

VIC KERRY

MONTAG

DEDICATION

To my parents, Lacy and Phyllis. He taught me how to tell a story, and she encourages me to tell them. I love you both.

Vic Kerry

ACKNOWLEDGEMENTS

Whew! I've got a lot of people to acknowledge, so dear reader, bear with me. This book came about as a long intensive labor. I would like to say of love, but that would be a lie. Many hours, weeks, months, and years went into writing this. I would say blood, but that wouldn't be the case unless you count that lost by the characters inhabiting these pages.

I need to recognize the faculty, staff, students, and alumni of Seton Hill University's writing popular fiction graduate program. This program is an asset to the popular fiction publishing industry, and the faculty, students, staff, and alumni work their hardest to help out their fellow writers. To my family (mother, Gran, Gramps, Laura, and Jim) who provided support as I harrowed though this task. Here's to Marlene, Amanda, Steven, Heather, Matthew, and Magan for allowing me make them characters in this book, and then do with them what I would. A special thanks needs to be given to Dr. Kaycia Vansickle and Kathleen Williams, CNRP for the advice they gave me concerning the expression of genetic abnormalities that might occur with inbreeding, and to Hope Kohler, DMA for advice about vocalizations.

I say three cheers to my critique partners who read this book from the very beginning to the very end. They are: Kim, Rhonda, Paul, Craig, Elsa, Dave, and Kristin. (Even though she wasn't my critique partner then, she is now, Leadie.) I'm going to thank my wife in this part as well. She had to deal with me while writing this more than anyone else, and she provided important critiquing as well. Thanks, I love you.

My mentors who really helped shape this book are going to get their own paragraph. Scott A. Johnson is a wonderful writer and very good mentor. His sense of horror and humor are only bounded by his fascination with kumquats. Thank you my mean girl mentor. Michael Arnzen loves the uncanny and is a twisted man. That is why I was so happy when I freaked him out just a little bit (not as much as I have led people to believe however). He made me wrangle in the free association story that Scott let me run wild with. Help from both of these fantastic writers made this story what it is.

To the staff at Montag Press, thank you. A special thanks to Mari for editing this and forcing me to make the improvements it needed.

A memorial paragraph. I lost several people close to me during the writing of this book. My father passed away right after I completed the first draft. Although he didn't teach me to write, he taught me how to tell a story. My uncle, Alan, passed toward the end of things. Lastly, my best friend and first fan, departed this life while I edited, waiting for publication. J.B. would have liked this.

Lastly, Thanks to you the reader. What would a writer be without readers?

Thanks.

Darkly,
Vic Kerry

1

For God commanded, saying,
Honour thy father and mother.

MATTHEW 15:4

SUZANNE CLAY FELT TRAPPED between her green metal desk and the back wall of her office. A stack of tardy slips from two weeks ago lay awaiting her signature. She hated signing them. If the school board would just get her a vice principal, she could spend more of her time monitoring teachers and checking on school improvement, but the school system didn't have money for one so she did what had to be done without complaining. She moved the stack of thin pink pages onto the blotter in front of her. The Bic rolled out her signature in smooth black ink.

The afternoon sun, shining through her office window, warmed her back too much. She reached behind her, barely turning her chair, and flipped on the oscillating fan she kept on a small metal filing cabinet beside her desk. The artificial wind blew her brown hair and fluttered the papers on her desk. She put her thumb on the edge of the next tardy slip as she signed her name, looping the *L* with the tail of her *Y*. *A rubber stamp would be nice, too,* she thought. If the state hadn't cut the money to teachers this year, she would have bought one. The cage-covered clock over the door ticked down to 3:00 P.M. The bell would ring soon, and her day would be over. This gave her a little solace as the fifth slip landed on the signed pile. The day had been quiet. Another slip signed away.

Suzanne's phone buzzed. A slight crackle came over the small speaker.

"Principal Clay," the secretary said.

"Yes." A bland answer tagged with another bland signature.

"Mr. Lovell is here. He's got a problem."

Suzanne looked at the time. Only fifteen minutes remained. She'd almost beaten the clock.

"Send him in." It came out as a huff.

Her door opened, and Lovell stepped inside. He wore his square-tailed shirt untucked from his trousers. The pattern on the shirt alternated turquoise and white checks. Suzanne didn't like his casual appearance, but she let it go. Lovell looked cute in untucked square-tailed shirts, but not as good as in polo shirts. He smiled at her and placed his hand on her desk.

"Where's the student?" Suzanne asked.

"Sitting in the office with the secretary."

"School's almost out so we've got to get to the point quickly. What's happened?"

"You know Rachel Hassle, don't you?"

"The little red-haired girl with all the freckles and wide set eyes. She rides bus 38. Not the brightest, as I remember from her testing."

"That's her."

"Warren, I'd love to play twenty questions with you, but we're running out of time, and believe it or not, I'm a busy lady. So, if you could, get to the point."

"I caught her fondling one of my students."

Suzanne looked up from a tardy slip. Her mouth fell slack. She became aware of it and snapped her jaws shut. "Who?"

"Eric Bryce. His parents are the ones—"

She stopped Lovell. "I know who they are. I think every principal in the county knows them. Are you sure that's what you saw? Maybe she was just fanning her hand near him or something."

"She had *it* in her hand. I can describe it if I need to."

Suzanne slung her head in slow motion to show her frustration. "Do you have both of them?"

"Just her. I didn't think putting them together would be a good idea."

"Send her in."

Lovell opened the door. He beckoned entrance by waggling his index and middle finger together, something else that bothered Suzanne, but he told her that he'd learned to do that during his time in the army. A short girl covered with reddish brown freckles on her arms and smaller versions on her neck entered the room. Her head hung low, and stringy red hair covered her face. She stepped past Lovell and sat in a chair in front of Suzanne. She never looked up.

"Mr. Lovell, please step outside and get Ms. Dodge. I think we might need her. Also, get the secretary to write a note to Eric's parents and tell them I need to meet with them tomorrow morning, and that I'll call them tonight."

Suzanne noticed that Rachel looked up when she said Eric's name. Lovell stepped out of the room and pulled the door closed. Suzanne smiled at Rachel.

"There's no need to be scared, Rachel. I'm your friend. Mr. Lovell said some things that bothered me though."

Rachel nodded as Lovell returned with a short spindly woman. Her auburn hair rested in a tight knot on top of her head. Gray lines streaked her hair and the roots were nearly all gray. She wore glasses that hung from her neck by a beaded lanyard. Ghosts of freckles haunted her skin beneath caramel makeup. She sat in a chair by Rachel. Lovell closed the door and leaned against it.

"Okay Rachel, this is Ms. Dodge. She's our counselor. She's going to sit in and help us out some more."

The girl lifted her head and looked at the counselor. Suzanne felt a flutter rise in her. It seemed that Ms. Dodge and Rachel might have instant rapport or that they already knew each other.

"Do you know why you had to come in here to talk with us?" Ms. Dodge asked in her cool, controlled voice.

Rachel nodded her head. The greasy red hair bobbed up and down. Suzanne hoped she had a few baby wipes left in her drawer. She saw the streaks the girl's nasty hair left on her vinyl chair. The first mistake she had made as an administrator was to have cloth chairs. The first dirty parent to visit her had left a permanent grease streak. Vinyl made cleanup much easier.

"All right, Rachel, why?" Suzanne asked.

"Because of what Eric and me was doing."

The words fell flat from the girl's mouth like rocks tumbling to the floor. Little emotion pushed the words forward. The frankness of the statement made Suzanne uneasy. She felt a twinge of disgust in her stomach; anxiety and nausea with a bit of churning thrown in for good measure.

"And what was that?" Suzanne continued her questioning.

"I was seeing if he worked."

Lovell cleared his throat. Suzanne knew he tried to hide a snicker. She flashed him a rough look. The girl's comment must have caught him off guard because his expression back was one of amused disgust.

"Do you need to get some water, Mr. Lovell?" asked Ms. Dodge. "That sounds like a mean cough you have."

"No, I'm alright. Just a frog in my throat."

"What do you mean about finding out if he worked?" Suzanne forced this question out. The words seemed to have barbs, and they cut into her throat as she spoke.

"I had to see if he was a complete man. He ain't no use to me if he ain't whole." Rachel made no attempt at subtlety. She talked like she had nothing to hide.

"Why do you need to know that?" Lovell asked.

Rachel looked up at him. "Because I'm a complete woman, and I have to find the one. Eric told me he was the one, but I had to check. Ain't worth my time to waste with a boy."

"What are you talking about?" Lovell asked, not bothering to hide the confusion in his voice. "You're not making any sense."

Rachel huffed. "I need a man because I'm a woman."

To Suzanne, Rachel seemed to be spouting rehearsed rhetoric like a preacher reciting the Lord's Prayer.

"And what does that mean?" Suzanne asked.

"She means that she is able to bear children," Ms. Dodge said. "She's telling you that she wants to have a baby and that she was checking to see if Eric was able to give her a baby."

"Thank you, Ms. Dodge, but I wanted to hear that from her."

"Well, you were acting like you had no idea what was going on," Ms. Dodge said, straightening up in her chair until it appeared she had a board strapped to her back. "I thought maybe you might not understand how country people talk. It is simpler and at the same time very complex. I didn't mean anything by it. I just thought I was helping." She grinned a small, vicious smile in the bless-your-heart kind of way.

"I'm hardly from the city," Suzanne narrowed her eyes in irritation. "I grew up down in Reform, but that's neither here nor there. We'll talk a little bit later, Ms. Dodge." Suzanne turned her attention to the girl. "You realize that you can't do that in school, don't you?"

Rachel nodded her head.

"So, you know that I have to punish you for this. You can't just go around touching boys in inappropriate ways because you want a baby."

Rachel nodded again. She turned her head back to the floor. The stringy orange hair covered her face. Suzanne reached into her desk drawer. She brought out a two-ply document; she scribbled on it, and twirled her signature at the bottom. The top sheet made a gummy tearing noise as she pulled it apart from the yellow under-copy.

"Take this to your parents. It tells them that you'll be going to the alternative school tomorrow. They'll have to take you there, so the directions are on the bottom."

Suzanne handed the white page to Rachel, who took it her little hand. The bell rang, and the girl hopped to her feet. She rushed the door, but Lovell continued to block it.

"Mr. Lovell, please escort her to bus 38 so she can get home," said Suzanne. "Rachel, take time at home tonight and while you are at alt school to think about what you did."

The girl nodded then followed her teacher out the door. Ms. Dodge sat up straight in her chair and crossed her hands over her lap. Her face became pointed and sharp. Suzanne looked into her eyes. She knew the counselor loved to intimidate people, but not today. Suzanne hoped upon hope that Ms. Dodge would finally cash in her chips and retire before too much longer. The counselor had been at her post too long and felt she was the cock of walk.

"Have a seat in the front office, please. I'll call for you when I get off the phone with Dr. Cortland at the alt school."

Ms. Dodge cleared her throat, stood, and left the room. She closed the door hard behind her. Suzanne flinched even though she expected Ms. Dodge to slam the door. The principal's number at the alt school was on speed dial number 4, and it took Suzanne one push of the button and a few rings until the gravelly voice of Dr. Cortland rumbled over the receiver.

"Jimmy, this is Suzanne over at Marquisville Middle. I've got one for you tomorrow."

"Hadn't had one from you in a while."

"We've only been in school a few weeks. You can't expect me to send people on the first day."

"Why not, others do. So what you got?"

"A fourteen year-old girl, in seventh grade special ed. She got caught giving another classmate a hand job in class. So, you'll want to keep her isolated, and checked often."

"Hand job? I haven't had one of those in a while."

"A little too much information, Dr. Cortland."

The gravelly voice laughed. "No, I meant someone here for that. Freudian slip, I suppose. All right, so what's this girly's name?"

"Rachel Hassle."

"Hassle. That name sounds familiar. Have I ever had her here before?"

"Not to my knowledge, but she might have come when she was in elementary school."

"I don't know. Just something about that name makes me think I should know it. But I reckon I'll see her tomorrow. Don't be a stranger now, Suzanne."

"I won't, Jimmy. Do a good job with her."

Suzanne hung up the phone. She took the yellow referral sheet and stuck in into the fax machine. It hissed and made digital pops as the paper slid through and went to the Kosciusko County Alternative School. The yellow paper then went into the file in a large metal filing cabinet for the current year's referral. Suzanne walked out of her office to the waiting area. Ms. Dodge sat behind the secretary's desk. The grinding of an emery board over fingernails greeted Suzanne even when the counselor didn't look up.

"Why did you do that, Ms. Dodge?" Suzanne asked, leaning against the doorjamb.

"Do what?" The emery board shifted to the pinky.

"Answer that question. I was trying to see how much that girl actually understood."

"She's in special ed, Ms. Clay. How much do you *think* she knows?" Ms. Dodge's voice grated as much as the grinding of the emery board.

"I don't know. That's why I asked. Just because someone is in special education doesn't mean they're totally ignorant. Don't ever do that again, or I'll make sure to write you up."

The emery board moved to the other hand starting with the pinky. The sinister smile from earlier again sneered from Ms. Dodge's face. "I'll keep that in mind. I just figured someone of your quality of professionalism would be familiar with her case."

Suzanne moved from the door and grabbed the counselor's arm. She jerked the emery board away and flung it on the desk.

"I don't think you get it, Ms. Dodge. I'm the principal here, and that makes me your boss. Not the other way around. You'll do what I tell you to do. I'm not going to have you disrespect me anymore like you did last year." She let go of her wrist. "You can go, and make sure you call and report this to child services."

Ms. Dodge stood with a huff and a roll of her eyes. "I know my job, Ms. Clay. I'll call them just as soon as I get into my office." As Ms. Dodge walked out of the room, Suzanne pulled her door shut. She turned to leave when Lovell popped in.

"You want me to be with you when you call Eric's folks?" he asked.

Suzanne flipped the lights off and walked out the main office's door forcing Lovell into the hall.

"I was going to call them from my house."

"I can come over there. I've got a good rapport with them. It might help to smooth the issue over."

Suzanne noticed the dimples in Lovell's cheeks. She had a thing for men with cheek dimples, on both ends. Dimples got her into more trouble than anything she could think of. She'd been hoping he would make a move for a while. Those dimples had drifted into her daydreams and nighttime thoughts more than once since she'd met him.

"I don't think so, but thanks for trying to help." She didn't want to decline, but thought it more professional than jumping at the opportunity on school grounds. That and she didn't want to seem too excited about the prospect of him coming over.

Lovell shrugged his shoulders. "I could even bring over something to eat."

Suzanne smiled. "The only take-out you can get around here is a Jack's hamburger or pizza. I eat at Jack's too much, and pizza gives me heartburn."

She wished he didn't have such pretty eyes. Pretty eyes and dimples were kryptonite to her superhero principal alter ego. She felt that stony veneer beginning to crack.

"I could cook something."

Suzanne chuckled and patted Lovell on the shoulder. It felt hard and well muscled. "You're coming off desperate, Warren. Maybe next time." She gave him a smirk, and walked out of the school.

Suzanne swung her hips so her walk had a sexy sashay. She knew Lovell would stand in the door watching her. His dimples were so cute. Maybe she should let him come over when she called the Bryces. They were the most difficult parents she'd ever dealt with, and if he did have a rapport with them, then it might help.

Suzanne turned around just as she stepped out from under the front awning. Sure enough, Lovell still stared at her from the doorway. She waved him out.

"Yeah?" he asked.

"I've got some cube steak thawing in the fridge. Why don't you come by about five o'clock and help me call after all. We'll eat supper after that. If you like cube steak, of course."

"I don't like it that much. How about I pick up some take out from the China Dragon? If that's okay?"

She grinned liked she'd just been asked to the homecoming dance but tried to hide it. "Sounds better than cube steak. Just make sure you get some egg drop soup, and of course fortune cookies."

"Fortune cookies and egg drop soup by five o'clock." He nodded. "See you then."

Five o'clock neared and Suzanne opened the door after hearing a few short knocks. Lovell stood on the porch, holding out a bottle of wine. A paper bag with the red serpentine logo balanced in the bend of his other arm. He'd changed into an orange polo shirt. It was tucked in letting his pectoral muscles bulge out. Suzanne smiled and took the wine from him.

"Red," he said, stepping inside. "I don't know what goes with fortune cookies and egg drop soup, but I like red wine best."

Suzanne stepped from her foyer into the living room. She turned back to look at him. "You should have just brought beer. It would've been fine."

He followed her as she walked through the open archway into the kitchen. "I was out. In all honesty, that was the only booze I had in my house."

Suzanne sat the bottle on the counter above the dishwasher. She reached up and took down two wineglasses. Lovell did the honors of unscrewing the top off the wine. He poured it into both glasses, careful not to drip onto the counter.

"I guess supper's ready, but I thought we'd better call the Bryces before we ate," Suzanne said, sipping wine.

"If we've got to," Lovell said.

"I've got a speaker function on my portable phone. Let's do this at the table."

Suzanne led Lovell from the small kitchen to the dining room just adjacent. There was an archway between the rooms much like the one from the living room to the kitchen. Suzanne sat at the head of the table and Lovell beside her. After a deep breath and a momentary pause, they began to dial.

Suzanne switched to tea after her second glass of wine. She would have liked to have kept going. Eric's parents were less than understanding. Lovell kept drinking until only a sliver of the bottle was left. He looked a little glassy-eyed.

"That Mr. Bryce is one rough dude." Lovell slurred a little. "I wonder if he's been a drill sergeant at some point."

"Maybe they got some of the yelling done tonight, so we don't have to deal with that tomorrow." Suzanne thought about another glass of the hard stuff but didn't want to risk waking up with a wine headache. It would be a lot harder to deal with the Bryces with a sword of Napa Valley dangling over her head.

"Maybe so."

The television jabbered with the commentary of a documentary on VH1. It had been little more than background static until the conversation lulled.

"They don't make music like they used to," Lovell said. "What happened to Metallica?"

Suzanne grinned. "I'm pretty sure they just released a new album. I think they were even nominated for a Grammy last year."

"Shows you how much I keep up with it," he said.

"I try to stay up on the music. It helps with relating to the kids," Suzanne said. "Although you're right, they don't make them like they used to."

"Bon Jovi," Lovell said.

"Huh?"

"I was just thinking what my first concert was. It was Bon Jovi. I was sixteen and can't believe my old man let me go. He was a strict one. It rocked. I rounded the bases for the first time that night."

"Charming," Suzanne said. She licked her bottom lip. Her thoughts drifted to thinking about the thirty-something Lovell getting laid listening to Bon Jovi.

"What was your first?"

"None of your business, Mr. Lovell."

"Concert."

"Oh." Suzanne grinned. "Bush. Gavin Rosdale was so fine."

"Give me a break."

"It's better than Bon Jovi. When you were sixteen, they were kind of washed up weren't they?"

"No, they'd just brought out a new album."

Suzanne cocked an eyebrow up at him. Lovell grinned. His dimples deepened. She knew those were going to get her into trouble.

"All right, maybe they were a little past it, but they still rocked."

"I bet you had a mullet," Suzanne said. "Great big, long one and you probably wore t-shirts with the sleeves cut off."

"I didn't have the mullet then, and I quit wearing those kinds of tee shirts in the ninth grade."

"I figured that or you wouldn't have gotten laid at sixteen." Suzanne felt a little giddy.

"Yeah, my style had improved by then." He slid closer to her. "Much like now."

They eased toward each other. Suzanne closed her eyes and let her lips part ever so slightly. Their lips almost met when her phone rang. Suzanne opened her eyes. She felt for her phone on the armrest of the sofa. It rang twice before she got a hold of it. The caller ID told her the number was unknown. She rolled her eyes as she answered.

"Hello."

"You don't have Prince Albert in a can do you? If you do you better let him out."

The line went to the disconnect buzzing. She tossed the phone on the floor and huffed.

"I get one of those at least once a night," she said.

"Heavy breather?"

"No, just some punk kids making stupid crank calls. That one asked if I had Prince Albert in a can."

"I'm surprised he knew what Prince Albert in a can was," Lovell said.

"His parents probably told him. I'm pretty sure I've gotten crank calls from parents before too." She stood up. "Don't ever become a principal, Warren." She gave him her hand. "It's getting late. I need to get to bed."

Lovell stood up still holding her hand. Suzanne led him

to the door. She opened it, and he stepped onto the porch. The night air was cool.

"Thanks for coming over and making that call with me," Suzanne said.

"No problem."

"Thanks for dinner too."

Lovell snapped his fingers as if remembering something. "We forgot these." His hand went into his pocket and pulled out the cellophane packages of two crushed fortune cookies. "I put them in my pocket after we ate. I guess they got crunched."

Suzanne took hers, tearing open the packaging. Bits of the cookie fell to the floor. She slipped her fingers into the plastic and took out the slip of paper with her fortune on it.

"You are a goddess," she read.

"Never argue with a fortune cookie," Lovell said. "I bet you'd look good riding naked on a clam."

"Maybe you should let me drive you home. I think you're a little too buzzed to be driving," Suzanne said, as little pins started to prick around inside of her.

"I'm fine. I was just telling the truth. You don't have to have a wine buzz to know that you are . . . well you know." He arched an eyebrow up, and walked off the porch.

Suzanne watched him to his car, and then closed the door. Something down inside her felt like she was sixteen again. She reached to flick the light off as the telephone rang. She walked back to where she'd left it on the couch, noticing that the caller ID displayed a string of zeros. Suzanne huffed and hit the green talk button.

"She will have known men, and in knowing them, will be

the mother of many." The voice seemed purposefully strained to sound like an old person.

"Who is this?"

"And one that she will know before the time will be a soldier and fighter for the side of good chosen by God through his prophet."

Suzanne hit the red off button. The pins poking deep inside her changed to ice crystals. She locked the door, the deadbolt, and even the safety chain over the door. Tonight the living room light would burn all night.

2

Thou preparest
a table before me
in the presence
of mine enemies.

PSALMS 23:5

SUZANNE DRUMMED HER FINGERS on the top of her desk. The sun glared through the window and on her black blouse heating up the thick cotton. The color didn't help in keeping cool, but it gave an air of authority. Suzanne needed to look as authoritative as possible today.

Ms. Dodge walked into the office. Her hair lay on her shoulders, and her makeup looked softer than usual. She would take a gentle approach with the Bryces while Suzanne took the hard one.

"Eric's parents are in my office," Ms. Dodge said in even tones.

Suzanne nodded and stood from behind her desk. She wore her highest heels and towered over Ms. Dodge. Her brown trousers broke above the top of her shoes and flared out just enough to be stylish but not enough to be trendy. The Bryces would not be able to accuse her of unprofessional dress as a principal, as they had when she was a teacher. She followed Ms. Dodge out into the main office, turning the thermostat down as she walked past. She was already hot but would be overheating by the end of the meeting. Unlike her car, a little water in the radiator wouldn't keep her from redlining; she'd need her office as cold as she could get it to cool back down after dealing with these parents.

The counselor's office was across the hall. Lovell waited for them outside the closed door. Suzanne's heels clicked as she crossed the tile hallway to Ms. Dodge's room.

"How are you this morning, Mr. Lovell?" Suzanne asked.

"Fine." He rubbed his hand behind his neck.

The outfit worked. Every time she wore her highest heels men seemed unnerved. Suzanne felt a surge of superiority. Lovell's slightly glassy eyes told her a small hangover might be responsible for his nervousness as well. She smiled as the counselor's door opened and she spotted Mr. and Mrs. Bryce seated on the opposite side of a sturdy wooden table. Ms. Dodge entered first, followed by Mr. Lovell, and Suzanne pulled the door closed as she stepped in. The room's temperature cooled her off some, and the sweat on her back chilled her. She nodded to Eric's parents as she sat down. They stared back, chilling her more than the air conditioning ever could.

"How are you doing today, Mr. and Mrs. Bryce?" Suzanne asked. "I'm sorry we have to meet like this."

"Knock it off, *Miss* Clay," Mr. Bryce said, flushing red. "We know why we're here, so there's no need for the niceties. Don't think that smiling and batting your eyes is going to keep us from going to the school board about this."

"Mr. Bryce, I promise you that I was not batting my eyes or smiling to keep you from doing anything. We have a serious problem, and we've got to deal with it."

Mr. Bryce pounded his clenched on the table. "You mean, *ya'll* have a serious problem, and you want us to roll over."

"Now honey, simmer down." Mrs. Bryce placed her hand on his arm.

"Shut up." His words were almost a hiss. "I told you to stay out of it."

"I promise that no one is asking anyone to roll over," Ms. Dodge said. "We don't want you to feel like we are pressuring you into anything. We need to get this straightened out though."

"If you people had Eric in the right class with the right kind of kids and teacher, this wouldn't have happened."

"Wait a minute, Will," Lovell said. Suzanne cringed when Lovell called parents by their first names. Professionalism kept you on formal terms with them; plus, if you were too familiar with parents they might expect favors. "You've seen Eric's test scores. Let's not blame this on something like that."

Bryce leaned over the table at Lovell. His face remained flushed, and his fists stayed clenched. "So, *Warren*, who or what are we going to blame this on?"

Mr. Bryce slammed his fist on the table again. His wife flinched and made a small move to touch him but stopped. The tension in the room seemed tight enough to twang if struck. Suzanne cleared her throat.

"Let's settle down," Suzanne said. "Things are getting a little heated."

"I want to know," Mr. Bryce said, sitting back down.

Lovell shrugged. "I don't know, hormones, curiosity, being a thirteen-year-old boy with a girl who wants to touch him." He made a hand motion to Mr. Bryce. "Come on, we've all been in that boat."

"Speak for yourself," Mr. Bryce said. "I have never had any retard try to touch me."

"That's not the point," Lovell said.

"Then what is it?"

"The point is that no one should be engaging in sexual activity in the school," Ms. Dodge said. "The fact that it has happened is disturbing. Nothing like this has ever happened at this school for the fifteen years I've been here. We've always had excellent administrators who've kept this from happening." She grimaced just enough to be noticeable.

"Had," Mr. Bryce said.

"Still have," Ms. Dodge said in a strained tone and a forced smile.

Suzanne felt the sting from Ms. Dodge's body language. Slamming the emery board down yesterday wasn't such a smart idea in hindsight. "I think a lot of things failed these two kids, not just the administration. Has Eric ever had issues like this before?"

"Oh no, no, no." Mrs. Bryce shook her head. "He never even acts interested in girls or sex. Will always has some smutty picture on the television, and Eric just goes right on playing his PSP or Gameboy. He never gives it notice."

"I thought I told you to shut up," Mr. Bryce said.

The tension tightened a little more, and Suzanne felt the invisible wires about to snap and hurt someone. She cleared her throat again and turned, smiling, to Ms. Dodge.

"Why don't we bring Eric in and ask him about this?" Suzanne said. "Do you think you can get him for us, Ms. Dodge?"

Ms. Dodge nodded her head. Her ruddy brown hair bounced about her shoulders. She stood up and walked to the door.

"Good, now we'll get to the bottom of this crap, and you

will see how my boy shouldn't be in any special ed. class with a bunch of skanky retardos."

"Mr. Bryce, I understand that you are upset, but try not to call our children *retardos*. We should all try to be as adult as possible," Suzanne said.

The door opened, and Ms. Dodge guided a boy, short for his age, in front of her. His hair curled at the long ends over his deep gray eyes. He pushed his chestnut bangs up as he walked in. His cheeks and upper lip carried a heavy peach fuzz shadow. Suzanne thought he looked about nine if not for that. Ms. Dodge closed the door behind her. Mrs. Bryce patted her hand on the chair beside her. The boy looked over at Lovell then at Suzanne.

"It's okay, Eric," Lovell said. "Go sit by your momma."

"It's fine," Suzanne added. "We're just here to talk. Nothing bad is going to happen." *Hopefully*.

Eric walked around the far end of the table behind Ms. Dodge and pressed himself against the wall to stay out of his father's grip as he passed. Mr. Bryce kept his hands on the table, letting the boy pass. Eric sat down beside his mother, who wrapped her arm around his shoulder and toyed with his hair. She smiled at him then up at Suzanne, who saw a sad pride in that smile. Suzanne felt sorry for Mrs. Bryce.

"How are you doing today, Eric?" Suzanne asked.

"F-fine." Eric's voice reverberated with deep bass, much deeper than she had expected. "How are you?"

"I'm doing well, thank you. You're certainly polite."

Mrs. Bryce screwed her eyes up and grinned, letting small wrinkles gather around the edges of her mouth. "I insist on that. My baby isn't going to be rude."

"What?" Mr. Bryce said. "You think that so-called retards can't be polite?"

Anger rose from the depths of Suzanne's being. Her neck started to heat up even more than it had been. She cleared her throat. "No one said anything about that. I thought we were going to quit using that word and act more like adults, Mr. Bryce."

"You said that. I didn't agree to anything."

"Plus, language like that doesn't exactly boost Eric up either," Lovell said.

"Neither does leaving him in a room with a bunch of drooling sex perverts."

"Mr. Bryce, you've said quite enough," Ms. Dodge said.

The words were heavy and forced out like a swing of a sledgehammer. Everyone looked at her. Control of the meeting seemed to be coming back to their side now. Suzanne liked that.

"Are you t-talking about Rachel?" Eric said.

"That's why we're here," Ms. Dodge said. "To talk about what happened with you and Rachel."

"She d-doesn't drool."

"You're right. She doesn't," Lovell said, "but why did she and you do what you did?"

Eric looked down at his feet. Suzanne saw a blush growing across his tanned cheeks. They became apple red. He looked up with his eyes only, first at Suzanne and then at his mother.

"She's my girlfriend," he whispered to the table.

"Your girlfriend? Don't be stupid," Mr. Bryce said. "You can't have a girlfriend because these people say you're retarded."

"No one has said that, Mr. Bryce." Suzanne slapped her palm on the tabletop. "No one here has called anyone a *retard* except you."

"Eric." Ms. Dodge said. "Do you think what you and Rachel did was wrong?"

Suzanne looked over at Ms. Dodge. *How can she stay so focused despite this irritating man?* Ms. Dodge's eyes seemed to dance with an impish joy like she'd heard Suzanne's thoughts.

Eric looked Ms. Dodge in the eye. "No, we were doing what boyfriends and girlfriends do."

"How do you know what they do, honey?" Mrs. Bryce asked. "You've never had a girlfriend."

"That's what they do in Daddy's movies, and he said those people were girlfriend and boyfriend."

"I knew it was those smut movies," Mrs. Bryce said. "I told you that you were giving him ideas."

"Shut up, Sally. This hasn't got anything to do with that. It has to do with these people not having my boy in the right class and letting any piece of filth walk in this school and rape whoever they want to."

"Mr. Bryce," Suzanne said, fuming but trying to control her tone of voice. "You are out of line. No one has raped anyone at this school, and as far as the placement of Eric is concerned, that is decided by the school board not here."

"And I assure you that I've seen the scores and Eric is in the best place he can be for his education," Ms. Dodge said.

"He does really well with extra help. He's started to stutter less. Now he just does it on words starting with T's and hard D sounds with occasional slips," Lovell added. "Isn't that so, Eric?"

"I don't care. If the school board is where I need to take this up at, then that's where I'll do it." Mr. Bryce grabbed his wife by the arm. He jerked her to her feet. "We're leaving and we're taking our kid with us. We'll see you at the board with the superintendent."

The Bryce family walked out. The mother and son dragged by the father. Suzanne tried to stand before they stormed out, but didn't have the time. She caught herself halfway then plopped down as Mr. Bryce slammed the door. The crack of wood on wood rang through her head. She huffed.

"That went super," Lovell said, rubbing his temples.

"It went exactly like I expected," Suzanne said. "So what do you think, Ms. Dodge?"

"I think I need to call Dr. Larson down at the board," Ms. Dodge said, "and let him know about what's going to be blowing in his door."

"Do that then," Suzanne said. "We're going to need all the help we can get on this one."

Suzanne settled into her office chair after lunch. She took her lipstick out of the top desk drawer and applied it. Her reflection in the small mirror on her desk showed her lips deep red and moist. The air-conditioner cooled the room so no sweat rolled down her back. After the morning meeting, she was happy for that. It had been a long time since she had such an uncomfortable meeting. She sighed.

Her phone rang. It brought her back to the tension of the day. She grabbed it up before the second ring. "Ms. Clay,

Marquisville Middle School."

"Suzanne, this is Jimmy. That Hassle girl didn't show up for school today. Is she there?"

"No," Suzanne said. "I'd have brought her to you if she'd shown up here. Are you sure she's not there?"

Suzanne heard Jimmy humming on the other end and the shuffling of a few pages.

"I just got the roll, and she's not on it."

"And you've got no idea why?"

Jimmy snorted on the other end. "It's not my job to have an idea about that. I'm just giving you a courtesy call so you can check it out. She might've been sick or something. Let me know if you find out anything."

The phone clicked, and the empty tone hummed into Suzanne's ears. She set the receiver on the cradle. She flipped to the *H*s in her student Rolodex. The other administrators laughed at her for keeping two paper and ink Rolodexes instead of a computer. Suzanne reminded them that computers crashed taking all their information with them. Her way kept things in a separate, tangible place and was just as mobile. She found Rachel's entry. The address was for a place outside town. The phone number was a string of zeros. *Leg work.* Suzanne hated the leg work. There was nothing worse than way-out country folks who couldn't afford or didn't believe in telephones let alone something even better like e-mail.

"Mrs. Norris," she said, holding down the intercom button on the phone. "Please have Ms. Dodge and Mr. Lovell come to my office as soon as the bell rings."

If she had to go to this little girl's house, she was taking them with her. All of their heads rested on the chopping

block over this incident, but she always believed three heads
were better than one.

3

When the unclean spirit
is gone out of a man,
he walketh through dry places,
seeking rest;
and finding none, he saith,
I will return unto my house
from whence I came out

LUKE 11:24

SUZANNE STEPPED OUT OF Lovell's Ford Taurus into the humidity of an October afternoon in the Heart of Dixie. She wished she'd changed clothes before coming out here. The house's driveway was red dirt, and puffs of dust circled Suzanne's feet as she walked to the front of the car. No one came to meet them.

The house stood three stories high with whitewash peeling from the wooden siding like bark off a birch tree. The porch floor hung at eye level and covered the whole front of the house. Old wooden columns with dirty cracked paint held up the porch's ceiling that doubled as the floor of the second-story veranda. Suzanne imagined that a tattered and rundown Scarlet O'Hara might sashay out of the louvered French doors that opened onto the porch. Instead, an orange tabby with ribs showing like a furry xylophone dashed across the porch and jumped onto a bench at the far end. It curled up and began licking its scraggly underside.

"That's a fine welcome," Lovell said.

Suzanne looked at him as he leaned against the open driver's side door. He hung half in and half out of the car. He grinned at her, forming dimples at the edge of his curled lips. Suzanne smiled back. She had to; the smell of the place left a small lump in her throat. The air hung heavy with the smell of rotting vegetables and animal dung, a sweet scent that you only smelled in places out in the country. She wondered how one family might make that much of a stink. It even seemed like the smell of human waste mingled in the air. Suzanne wondered if they still used an outhouse.

The car door behind her slammed, and Ms. Dodge cleared her throat. "Maybe you should blow the horn, Mr. Lovell."

"I thought that might be rude," Lovell said. "Maybe we should just walk up there and knock."

Suzanne looked at the house again. A curtain in an upper floor window moved back together. Whoever lived here knew they were there. She hesitated and stared at the window. A faint outline of a human face seemed to stare back. It reminded her of a ghost story she heard as a kid, about a man staring out from a window. Ghosts weren't real to her, and she would need more than cold spots and flickering lights at night to make her believe. The smell of the red dust filled her nostrils, and a cool breeze came up from the hollows while the face in the window stared down and made Suzanne feel spooks all around her.

"Blow the horn, but just toot it," Suzanne said. "It won't seem rude."

"I think that we should walk up there," Lovell said.

"Just blow the horn." Suzanne whirled to face him, letting the staring face in the window slip away.

The car gave two friendly toots. They echoed off the house and through the hollows, leading back to the main road three miles away. Sound carried a long way in the autumn. A haunted hoot from a dove answered back from somewhere beside the house. Suzanne looked up at the window where the face stared from, and though the curtains moved again this time no ghostly face stared back. The silence passed slowly as the dove still trilled in the distance. Suzanne looked toward the bird's lonesome cry. A path led around the corner of the house.

"Maybe we're at the wrong place," Lovell said.

"This matches the address," Ms. Dodge said.

"It looks like no one has lived here since the Civil War or at least since Sweet Charlotte died," he said.

"I don't know if Rachel lives here, but someone's been staring at us through that window up there. It looks like the driveway goes around this house. Maybe they live out back," Suzanne said.

"Which window?" Ms. Dodge asked.

Suzanne pointed to a window at the edge of the second story veranda. The window stood empty and dark.

"There's nothing there now," Ms. Dodge said. "Blow the horn again, Mr. Lovell."

He reached inside to blow the horn again when a high-pitched squeal screamed out from behind the house. It echoed out like an explosion. The sound made Suzanne's head throb. She covered her ears with her hands and noticed that Lovell did the same thing.

"What is that?" she asked.

"Sounds like a pig in pain," Ms. Dodge yelled over the noise that now included what sounded like several people chanting.

Before Suzanne could ask what would cause that much noise, a hulking man with flaming red hair ran from around the house opposite the side with the path. He held his meaty hands over his ears. The muscles in his arms flexed with the strain to keep his palms pressed as tight to his ears as he could. A fine carpet of orange hair covered his arms, and a beard hung to his chest. He gave them no notice but leapt up three steps at a time to the porch and slunk onto one of the benches. The pig squeal grew louder and more intense. The ginger lump of the man on the porch let out a long sharp whistle like that of a train. All the other noise from behind the house grew rhythmic, pulsing like drumbeats. Suzanne readied herself to yell to see if the man was okay. He seemed to be foaming at the mouth and slinging the froth as he shook his head. She lowered her hands from her ears when an old bent man hobbled around the house the same way the huge man had come. He leaned on a gnarled cane and stopped in his tracks when he saw Suzanne and the others. His fingers touched his forehead in a salute. The squealing and chanting reached the point that Suzanne thought she wouldn't be able to hear a gunshot, but she did. A loud pop rang out as the squeal died away into the thin echo of distance. The pulsing of voices chopped off without a single leftover note.

"Howdy," the old man said, once the echo faded away. "Can I help ye folks?"

"Is he okay?" Suzanne pointed to the man on the porch.

"Esau? He's fine. He can't stand no loud noises. Like a ruined dog that one is." The old man leaned on his cane and turned his attention to Esau. "Boy, get on back there and help them fix up that hog. Ya know they'll hack its head all to pieces, and I want some good souse out of it. No tellin' what that dasted 'Grippa do to it either."

Esau looked up at the old man. He jabbed his thumb to his chest and shook his head while fanning his fingers in and out.

"I know you can't stand no loud noises, but ain't no reason to be acting like some gun-shy hound dog. Now, get around there and keep them from hacking that pig head up."

Esau nodded, stood up, and ran to the end of the porch. He leapt down and made his way around the house. The old man started toward them. Suzanne stepped up to meet him with her hand extended.

"Are you Mr. Hassle?" she asked.

"I am *a* Mr. Hassle."

"Are you Rachel Hassle's grandfather?" Suzanne asked.

"No." He took her hand and shook it. His palm felt hard and callused. "I'm her daddy. Daddy Sol to be exact." His eyes stared out like two peridots set deep into his skull.

"Well, you're the gentleman we need to speak to." Suzanne flourished her hand to Lovell and Ms. Dodge. A flurry of butterflies flittered in her stomach. "I'm Ms. Clay, the principal at Rachel's school, and this is Ms. Dodge and Mr. Lovell, the counselor and Rachel's teacher."

"Y'all sent me that letter yesterday about Rachel getting into trouble with that boy." Solomon nodded his head and started toward the porch. He beckoned for them to follow. Suzanne and the others obliged. He sat down on a bench to the right of the French doors. Suzanne, Lovell, and Ms. Dodge sat on the bench to the left.

"We came out today, Mr. Hassle, to find out why Rachel didn't go to the alternative school," Ms. Dodge said.

The sound of singing rose from behind the house. The

cadence sounded like a hymn to Suzanne, a hymn she vaguely recognized.

"Ye can call me Solomon." He tapped his cane on the warped floorboards and hummed a bar of the song before continuing, distractedly. "Ain't got no way to get her to that school. If the school bus doesn't pick her up, then I can't get her nowhere."

"Do you need to go back there and tend to your hog, Solomon?" Suzanne asked. "We could go back with you."

"Ain't nothing back there ye folks need to see." He leaned on his stick and gave Ms. Dodge an almost amorous look. "Like I was sayin', I ain't got no way to get the girl there."

"You don't have a vehicle of some kind?" Lovell asked.

"Of course, I've got an old pick-up truck, but it ain't up to driving out to Leesville to that school. If ye want my girl in school, y'all need to provide her a ride."

"We can't do that. There isn't a bus that runs to the alternative school. The county can't afford it," Suzanne said. "Plus having to get the student there is part of the punishment."

"And I can't drive her there either. So I guess y'all just have to take her back to yer school."

"We can't do that. Don't you know what she did?" Suzanne asked.

Solomon screwed his pale green eyes into his cavernous eye sockets. "She was playing with a boy. Don't reckon nothing's wrong with that."

"What do you mean?" Lovell asked. "I can think of a few reasons why it was wrong."

Solomon whipped his old gray head around. The freckles stuck out from his wrinkles so clearly that it was easy to see the resemblance between him and Rachel. His easygoing expression hardened, and his humming quit. "Why? Was the boy a Yankee?"

"Not that I know of, but that's not one of the bad reasons," Lovell said.

"It'd be bad enough." Solomon relaxed. He started humming the tune with the singing from the back of the house and eventually started mumbling with the words. "Shall we gather at the river? The beautiful, beautiful river." He smiled. "Pretty song ain't it?"

Suzanne looked quizzically at Lovell. Did people really sing church hymns when they killed a hog?

"It's one of my favorites," Ms. Dodge said. "I've loved it ever since I was a little girl."

"Can't stand it. My daddy made me sing it all the time. It was one of his favorite songs," Lovell said.

"We always start out the hog dressing with it," Solomon said. "Then we move on to others."

"Is that normal?" Suzanne asked.

"For us, a hog killin' is like meetin' God hisself. We get closer to God by eatin' his creatures."

Suzanne reached into her trouser pocket and brought out her slim red cell phone. She flipped the lid up. To her amazement, the LED screen showed enough bars of signal to make a call. She needed a distraction. As Solomon talked about drawing nearer to God through pig dressing, the singers in the back switched to a song she definitely knew: *Nearer my God to Thee*.

"I'm going to talk to Dr. Larson and see if we can't get an exception for that bus," she said.

The phone rang, and the superintendent picked up. Suzanne stood and walked to the edge of the porch. Static crackled over the receiver.

"What can I do for you, Suzanne?" Dr. Larson asked.

"Rachel Hassle. I know Ms. Dodge talked to you about this, but we need a bus to take her the alternative school. Her family can't get her there."

Dr. Larson hissed through his teeth. "I don't think we can swing that. Money's tight right now."

"I can't have her back at the school, and she has to be educated. It's the law."

"I know, but I think even the President would make an exception here."

Suzanne shook her head as if she stood before her boss. "What do you mean?"

"Those Hassles are a bunch of freaks. They're lucky we let them go to any of our schools. It's just better if you let that girl drop on out and stay with her family up there on that hill."

"But sir."

"That's my answer, Suzanne. Take it or leave it."

The line went dead. Suzanne flipped her phone closed. She walked back to the others as she slid it back into her pocket. Ms. Dodge and Lovell looked at her. Solomon rested his whiskered chin on his stick. All their eyes asked the question before any of them voiced it.

"We can't get a bus to take her to the alternative school," Suzanne said.

"So what are y'all going to do?" Solomon leaned until his crooked back touched the wood of the bench. "Law says my girl's got to go to school."

"We'll let her back into our school."

"Suzanne, are you nuts?" Lovell asked. "What about Eric's parents?"

"Like Solomon says, Rachel has to go to school. We can't deny her an education. We'll just make accommodations. We'll put her in an alternative classroom on our campus. Maybe you can look after her, Ms. Dodge?"

"I think I can. I agree that we can't let her not go to school."

Solomon clapped his hands together. "That's just fine and dandy. I'm happy to hear it. Maybe one of my young'uns will finally finish school."

"Maybe so," Suzanne said.

"Yes, indeedy, lemon squeezy." Solomon popped his tongue against his lips.

Suzanne saw the small yellow nubs of teeth, and for the first time she whiffed the burning odor of this breath. Whatever teeth hid in the back of his mouth must be blackened nubs. She motioned for Lovell and Ms. Dodge to get up and tried to cover her nose with a fake rub. It felt awkward, but the others took the hint and stood.

"Mr. Hassle, we'll see Rachel tomorrow. Expect her bus at the usual time."

"That's just plain old excellent." He clambered to his feet. As Suzanne and the others stepped down from the porch, he continued. "Just how many in her class are Yankees?"

Suzanne turned to look back at Solomon. "I don't know." She couldn't keep the surprise and confusion from her voice. "I've never had that question asked. Why?"

"Can't stand them Yankees. They the reason we like we

are. I don't need them making things more complicated than they already is."

Suzanne nodded. "I'll keep that in mind. We'll be seeing you, Mr. Hassle."

"Hopefully now that ye know where we live, y'all won't be a stranger." Solomon gave a hearty wave like Granny on *The Beverly Hillbillies*. "Ifin' y'all come back tomorrow, we'll have fresh souse meat."

"That sounds tempting, but I think I'll pass," Suzanne said.

"Don't know what ye're missing. By the way, Miss Clay, ye got any children?"

Suzanne stared at him. "No. I'm not married."

"Well, can ye have any?"

"That is a very inappropriate question, Mr. Hassle."

"Just wonderin'. Ye've got good child bearin' hips. Be a pity if you wasted that God-given gift. Heaven knows our family could use some built like ye."

Suzanne worked up a small grimace of a smile. She nodded and followed the others to the car and climbed in. The car felt cool as the air blew from the vents. Suzanne hadn't noticed how hot she had gotten while chatting with Solomon. He waved at them as they backed around to leave. Suzanne looked back to the second story window and saw Rachel's small pale face staring back at her. The girl grinned, and Suzanne felt that nothing could be creepier than that. At least no ghost haunted the place though, she thought.

"That was strange, wasn't it?" Lovell said.

Suzanne looked over at him. His bangs stuck to his

forehead in sweaty tendrils. "Yeah, especially all that stuff about Yankees, and did you hear him talking about my hips?"

"What about that singing from around back?" Lovell asked. "How many do you reckon live up there?"

"It sounded like a whole church congregation singing," Suzanne said. "I know they can't all live in that one house. There have to be others around behind it."

"Some country folks still blame everything on the Yankees and the Civil War," Ms. Dodge said as if she had only heard the first part of the conversation. "Us Southerners are just like that."

"I've lived my whole life in Alabama, Ms. Dodge. I think I qualify as a Southerner," Suzanne said, "and I've never blamed anything on the Yankees."

"I meant from this area. That's just a common thing. Don't pay it any attention."

"What about my hips?" Suzanne said.

"I think he might have been flirting with you. He is quite a stud," Lovell said.

"Mr. Lovell, he is the parent of one of our children. You shouldn't make light of him. It's very unprofessional," Ms. Dodge said.

"I'm sorry, Becky. I was only joking."

"It was in poor taste," Ms. Dodge said. "They are all a bit touched. You of all people should recognize that."

"How do you know so much about them?" Suzanne asked.

"The Hassles have always lived here. I went to school with some of Solomon's other children."

"How many does he have?" Lovell asked.

"I don't know. Dozens. They are all inbred. That's the

reason that he said his family could use some women that were able to have children. They've inbred so long that they're all about sterile," Ms. Dodge said.

Suzanne stared out the window as they descended the hill back to the main road. She tried to pay it no mind, but butterflies still fluttered in her stomach. She wondered if Rachel could have children because she was looking for a whole boy. The girl gave her the creeps, but she agreed to take the girl, and she would. Rachel had to be taught.

"Ms. Dodge, Rachel will be with you in your office tomorrow morning, and Warren, get something together for her to do," Suzanne said.

"You still think it's a smart thing to keep Rachel at school?" Lovell asked.

"She has to be educated," Suzanne said.

Ms. Dodge pressed her knees into the back of Suzanne's seat. "I agree."

"What about Eric's parents? If they find out, we're up to our necks in it." Lovell turned to Suzanne, placing one hand below his chin.

Suzanne thought about Rachel staring down at her from that window. In memory, the girl grimaced like a gargoyle. The butterflies that fluttered around inside her gave way to the icy feeling she'd gotten last night when that strange call came in.

"I think that we may already be in that deep anyway." She wriggled in her seat so that Ms. Dodge's knees no longer put undue pressure on her kidneys.

The others said nothing, and she watched the high weeds along the dusty driveway blur past. For a reason she couldn't put her finger on, everything seemed like some long faded Polaroid. That didn't help the icy grasp on her spine any.

4

She shall find the savior
of our people and thus save them.
Her job shall be
to bring about the prophecy.

BOOK OF LOT 3:13

RACHEL RESTED HER HEAD on a desk in Suzanne's office. Her greasy red hair splayed out over the sides of the gray plastic top, and her thin, freckled arms lay limp. Suzanne thought she looked as if someone bludgeoned her from behind but without the blood. She would have worried if the girl's shoulders didn't rise and fall in rhythm with her breathing.

Naptime wasn't part of the special ed. curriculum, but Rachel couldn't go to P.E, which she had at this time, so Suzanne gave her a break by letting the girl nap during the period. It gave Suzanne time to do actual principal work instead of baby-sitting.

Everything fell apart shortly after the buses arrived when Ms. Dodge called complaining of stomach trouble. So Suzanne bucked up and planted Rachel in her office with the assignments Lovell gave her to do. It included a mixture of multiplication, sentence writing, and reading comprehension.

Suzanne turned back to her computer screen. The black cursor blinked at her from the mostly white document screen. All she'd typed so far was the address of the superintendent's office, and 'Dear.' The words to tell him about keeping the girl in an alternative class on her campus wouldn't come. If Eric's parent's found out about it, she might lose her job and never get another one. She glanced back at Rachel who moved her legs in small spastic motions and made a whimper. Dogs did the same thing when they dreamed. Even dogs were teachable. Guilt pulled a knot down in her stomach. No child could be shoved into the category of unteachable. Even Helen Keller learned to talk and finished college.

"Of course, Rachel's not deaf and blind, and you're not Annie Sullivan," Suzanne whispered as she started to type out her letter to the board of education. Helen Keller would make an appearance in the memo, though, as an example.

Rachel scuffled some more and made another whimper. Suzanne looked up from her work, but the girl still napped. A tap came on the door, and the secretary stuck her head in.

"Ms. Clay, sorry to bother you, but Mrs. Tittle has a problem in her classroom."

"Can it wait? I'm in the middle of writing a letter to the board of education."

"Two of her kids got into a fight, and one knocked the other's tooth out."

Suzanne pushed back from her desk and stood. She grabbed her paddle that hung on the wall near her door. The outer office seemed cooler than hers, but it always heated up as soon as the sun moved overhead. A glance over her shoulder found Rachel still asleep. Suzanne closed the door, letting the latch click.

"Keep an eye on her," Suzanne said. "This shouldn't take me but a minute."

She shoved her paddle in the waistband of her pants behind her back and headed out of the office. The junction toward the sixth grade hall where Mrs. Tittle's class could be heard rooting for the different brawlers was right past Ms. Dodge's office. She turned at the water fountain and headed toward the fight.

Before she got to Mrs. Tittle's door, the cheering and cajoling stopped. She swept into the classroom. Mrs. Tittle, a small mousy woman, held Bryan Simmons back in her chair with one hand on his chest. His nose bled. Mr. Thom, the effeminate aide, held back Wayne Forman, a meaty boy with a split lip. His mouth hung open, and Suzanne saw that he'd lost the tooth and apparently the fight.

"What happened here?" she asked.

Both boys started to blame the other at the same time. Some of the class started to add their accounts as well. Suzanne put her fingers in her mouth and whistled. The shrill sound split the air and quieted the room. She whipped out her paddle.

"I don't care," she said. "Haul Wayne into the hall. I'll be back for you in a minute, Mr. Simmons."

Mr. Thom tugged at Wayne's arm, and they both went into the hall. Wayne took the normal position. This wasn't the first time this year that he'd gotten a paddling from Suzanne. He put his hands on the wall and spread his legs as he poked his large butt out. Suzanne grabbed the waistband of his pants and lifted him as best she could to his tiptoes. She swung and made contact three times. Mr. Thom took Wayne back inside the classroom. He brought Bryan out. Suzanne did the same for him, but had to explain the position because he'd never been in trouble. He and Mr. Thom went back into the classroom. Suzanne poked her head back inside.

"Let Mr. Thom call their parents to come and get them, and I'll make sure they are suspended for a couple of days," Suzanne said.

"But Ms. Clay," Mrs. Tittle started to protest.

Suzanne knew she'd just broken half a dozen board of education rules about punishment, but at least a dozen broken rules already slept in her office in the form of Rachel Hassle. "I'm sorry, but I've left more important business in my office."

Suzanne opened the filing cabinet nearest the door to her office to get out two suspension sheets. The secretary took lunch with the seventh grade. The bell for their lunch had just rung as Suzanne started up the hall. She wasn't worried about Rachel still being there. The girl wouldn't have been alone for long. Suzanne's hip bumped her office door, and it swung open.

"Rachel, did you open that door?" Suzanne asked, flipping through the filing cabinet looking for the forms.

No one answered back. Suzanne grabbed the two forms and turned to enter her office. She cast her eyes to the empty desk in the corner where Rachel had been napping. Only a greasy spot rested on the desk's work surface. Suzanne stepped inside and looked in all the corners for the girl but found nothing. She closed the door and looked behind it. Rachel wasn't there either.

"Shoot!"

Suzanne flung the papers and paddle onto her desk. The sound of the wooden top of the desk meeting the paddle popped like thunder. She hurried out of the office, leaving her door wide open and ran down the hall to the nearest girl's restroom. A few seventh-grade girls filed out after stopping on their way to lunch. Suzanne grabbed one by the shoulder.

"Was there anyone else in there?" she asked.

"I don't think so," answered the girl. "But a few of the stalls were closed."

Suzanne pushed open the door. The musty smell of the bathroom rushed in her face. One of the faucets dripped and echoed through the room. She leaned over to look under the stall doors. No feet touched the tile.

"Anyone in here?" Her voice echoed off the walls, and no one replied.

She turned and hurried back into the hall. All the seventh graders had gone to the lunchroom now, leaving the hall empty. Only the muffled sound of teachers giving assignments hummed in the hall as Suzanne made her way towards the special education classroom. The door to the library stood ajar. She poked her head inside, but the librarian was teaching a group of eighth graders about the difference between the Dewey decimal system and the Library of Congress system for filing books.

"Ms. Clay?" Lovell's voice came from behind her.

Suzanne pulled her head out of the library. "I was just heading to your classroom. Where are your students?"

"I was just going to get them from the gym. P.E. is about to end. Why?"

"I had to deal with a discipline issue, and Rachel left my office after Mrs. Norris went to lunch," Suzanne said in one long breath.

"You don't think she'll try to find Eric, do you?"

"Do you want to take the chance? If his parents even find out she's in the building, we're up to our necks in it."

Lovell jogged up the hall. "Let's get to the gym."

Suzanne followed walking fast, heels clicking down the hall like a manic typewriter printing out a dire warning. They rounded the corner of the back hall to the steps that led to the gymnasium. The double doors flew open, and the special ed. students filed out in a broken line.

Suzanne recognized them all. Before becoming the principal, this had been her class. Ty Arthur, tall and lanky, came out first. He smiled at Suzanne as he came down the steps.

"Ty, is Eric in line with you?" she asked him.

"He was in class." Ty spoke deep and slow. He focused on getting each word out.

"Did Rachel Hassle come to gym class?" asked Lovell.

Ty thought hard. He screwed his eyes up to the top of his sockets. "I don't remember seeing her, but I was playing basketball." He smiled. "We won, Ms. Clay."

"That's great." Suzanne patted him on his damp back where sweat had seeped though his shirt.

Ty walked down the hall back toward his classroom. Lovell stood on his tiptoes looking through the door to the end of the line. Several other special ed. students filed past Suzanne. Each waved as they passed. Still neither Eric nor Rachel emerged from the gym.

"I don't see either of them," Lovell said.

Suzanne pushed past Lovell into the gym. The pot-bellied coach pushed Magan Harrison in her electric wheelchair across the carpeted basketball court toward the door. The girl smiled as her head lobbed back and forth.

"Hi, Ms. Clay," she said with a strong clear voice. "How are you?"

"I'm fine sweetie, but I need to talk to Coach Alderman real quick. Can you drive yourself out of here? Mr. Lovell is at the door." Suzanne bounced on her toes, hoping Magan would get the hint that she was in a hurry.

"Sure thing." Magan used a spastic full body jerk to get her hand on the joystick that drove her chair. She pushed it forward, and the small framed wheelchair scooted off to the low hum of the battery motor. Suzanne didn't wait for Magan to get past her before moving on to the coach.

Coach Alderman put his hands on his hips, "What do you need?"

"Was Eric Bryce in class today?"

Alderman pushed his maroon and white baseball cap up and scratched the bald head underneath. "Yeah, but he had to go to the bathroom before class ended." He cleaned his ear out while he thought. Suzanne bulged and bubbled underneath her skin ready to burst, though her coach didn't seem to realize it. "Come to think of it, he didn't come back."

"What about Rachel Hassle?"

"No, haven't seen her. I thought she was in the alternative school."

"Thank you, Coach."

Suzanne hurried out of the gym. Lovell waited on her at the bottom of the small steps leading from the gym. She didn't stop but headed to the nearest boy's restroom. He followed. Suzanne shoved the door open and stormed in. Several seventh grade boys whirled around from in front of the sink. They checked their flies quickly to make sure they were zipped up.

"What are you doing?" Lovell barged in after her.

"They're in a bathroom." Suzanne bent over to look under the only stall in this bathroom. She saw nothing. "Come on."

Suzanne and Lovell hurried out of the bathroom and down the back hall to the next boy's room. She pushed the door open and let Lovell go in first.

"The coast is clear," he said.

Suzanne walked in. The restroom smelled heavily of sweat and old urine. The only stall's door was closed. It was a wide wheelchair accessible door. Suzanne and Lovell looked at each other. Small breathy sounds came from the other side of the locked door.

"I'm going to give you until the count of three to unlock that door and come out," Suzanne said in a clipped assertive tone.

Behind the door scrambling noises echoed out along with faster tighter panting. Suzanne pointed for Lovell to kick the door open. He drew back on one leg and slammed his other foot into the door. The wood cracked. Another kick snapped the door free. It swung open. Suzanne caught a glimpse of Eric tugging his jeans up. Lovell reached into the stall and pulled Eric out by his shoulder. The boy fumbled until his pants were fastened. Suzanne stepped into the stall. Rachel sat on the top lid of the toilet. She tugged her skirt down. Suzanne grabbed her by the arm and jerked her to her feet.

"What were you doing?" Suzanne voice was strong, but she felt queasy about what she'd just witnessed.

"I think you know," Lovell said.

"Doin' my job." Rachel flattened her skirt down. "Daddy told me to."

"What?" Suzanne's voice echoed through the bathroom. "Come on, we're getting to the bottom of this."

She dragged Rachel out of the bathroom. Lovell pulled Eric along behind him. Suzanne felt a ball of rage pressing against her chest. The bitter taste of bile surged to her tongue. She squeezed Rachel's wrist tighter and twisted it a bit as she pulled the girl around the corner by the gym into the main hallway.

"You're hurting me," Rachel said.

"Don't say anything," Suzanne said. "I don't want to hear it."

"Get that girl's parents in here, right now," Mr. Bryce yelled. He flailed his arms over his head while he stood in front of the window in Ms. Dodge's office.

Suzanne sat across from him. "I told you. They don't have a telephone."

"What kind of people don't have a telephone nowadays?" Mr. Bryce clasped his hands on the back of his neck. "I'll tell you what kind. The same kind that let their whore daughters have sex with little boys in the school bathrooms."

"Please, sit down. You're only working yourself up more," Suzanne said.

"How about this? I keep standing, and you shut up."

"I don't think that's very productive, Will," Lovell said.

Lovell sat beside Suzanne, keeping his hands flat on the table. Suzanne clenched hers on the arms of her chair. Her knuckles ached. She'd expected Eric's parents to be angry, but Mr. Bryce seemed ready to burst.

"Why was this girl back in school, anyway?" asked Mrs. Bryce. "I thought she was going to the alternative school."

"Don't answer that." Mr. Bryce pointed at Suzanne. "Let me guess. These people can't afford a telephone, so I'm sure they can't afford to drive their no-good kid to the alternative school."

"That's what happened," Lovell said. "We went to their house. These people are very poor, Will."

"Quit saying my name every time you address me, Warren." Mr. Bryce punctuated the sentence with his finger. "It's not making things smoother, Warren. It's ticking me off worse, *Warren.*"

"Enough." Suzanne stood. Her chair screeched across the floor as it pushed out. She put her hands flat on the table and leaned toward the Bryces. "I made the decision to bring Rachel here for alternative study. She can't get to the alternative school, and she can't not be educated. Check it out, Mr. Bryce; it's a law. I promise you that."

"You can't make an exception for a retard, like her?" Mr. Bryce asked.

"Especially not for mentally challenged students." Suzanne felt flushed. "I made a mistake. This is going to rest on my shoulders, but I've had enough of all this bickering."

"Oh no, you haven't. I want that girl's family in here now. I'm not going to say it again."

"We've addressed this," Lovell said.

"Yes, dear, let's just take it up with board," Mrs. Bryce said.

"I told you not to second-guess me." Mr. Bryce turned on

his wife. "I'm not going to be satisfied until I get to look this Hassle man in the eye."

The door creaked open. Suzanne and the others turned their attention to it. Solomon stood framed in the doorway as the door finished swinging open. He leaned on his gnarled walking stick and stroked his hand through his white beard. A smile crossed his crusty lips showing his yellow nubs of teeth. The room filled with the sour smell of old sweat and dirty hair.

Suzanne straightened up, smoothing her clothes and looked at Mr. Bryce. His mouth hung limp as he stared at Solomon.

"Mr. and Mrs. Bryce, meet Mr. Solomon Hassle, Rachel's father," Suzanne said.

"Her father?" Mrs. Bryce surprise popped out with every syllable.

"That's right. She's my girl. That woman in the office told me there was a meeting about her over here. What has she done now?"

"I'll tell you what we're talking about. Your whore of a daughter raped my son in a bathroom." Mr. Bryce came around the table toward Solomon. "I want to know what you are going to do about it, old man."

"Are ya threatening me? I don't take kindly to that."

Solomon leaned forward on his gnarled stick. The deep sockets where his peridot eyes lived widened so Suzanne thought they might pop out. The loose skin around his neck tightened and veins stood out. His blanched skin rouged as his cracked white lips snarled.

"What are you going to do about it, geezer?"

"Both of you stop it," Suzanne said. "This is not going to solve anything."

"I'm tired of your guff," Mr. Bryce said to her. "I'm handling this myself."

Solomon whistled a sharp tone as Mr. Bryce advanced with two large steps, his chest poked out and his fists clenched. Before Suzanne could step between them, Esau's huge frame pushed his father out of the way. Mr. Bryce tried to square off with him, but Esau sent Mr. Bryce stumbling backwards and crashing over a chair. The brute reached down and lifted Mr. Bryce up by the front of his shirt. His feet dangled inches from the floor. Esau shook him, and the cloth of Mr. Bryce's shirt ripped.

"Take care of him, my boy," Solomon said.

5

Let nothing stand in thy way.
The prophecy must be fulfilled
Or thy people shall perish
like those of Sodom

BOOK OF LOT 3:19

SUZANNE REACHED TO GRAB Esau's arm, but someone pulled her by the shoulder. She tumbled over backwards onto the floor and slid under the table. The tabletop popped and bent downward as Mr. Bryce was thrown on top of it. She covered her head with her arms to keep the table from bashing her in the face as it fell. How the table didn't crack in two and fall on her, Suzanne didn't know. She peeked through her fingers as a body rolled off the tabletop and thudded to the floor. Mr. Bryce lay crumpled there with his eyes rolled up in their sockets revealing only the whites. Suzanne crawled from under the table as Esau tossed a chair out of his way and against the wall. The back of the chair split and fell free. Gray plaster crumbled from the wall exposing the cinderblock behind it. Mrs. Bryce screamed a long shrill scream and pounded on Esau's muscled shoulder. He shoved her aside and cupped his meaty hands over his ears. Suzanne watched her topple to the floor.

"Stop this!" Suzanne slammed her hand on the table.

A hot ache rose from her palm to her elbow, but the sound stopped Esau. He looked at her with a blank, dull stare. His mouth fell slack showing only a few teeth. He looked back to Solomon for his orders. Suzanne looked at the old man too.

"That'll do, boy," Solomon said. "He's learnt his lesson."

The old man toddled to the chair at the head of the table and sat down. Suzanne looked at him, and he smiled back with an almost jovial smile. Esau straightened up and sat down. He clasped his hammy hands in front of him. One of his knuckles was raw and bloody.

Solomon opened his hands as if he were about to pray over a meal. "Let us talk."

Mr. Bryce sat up, the top of his head sticking up above the table. His wife helped him to his feet. Suzanne grabbed his other arm and helped him to a chair opposite the Hassles.

"Please sit there, until we can get you some help, Mr. Bryce." Suzanne turned her attention to Lovell. "Warren, please call an ambulance."

"I think I should stay," he said.

Suzanne looked at Mr. Bryce who sat in a chair flopped out like a scarecrow that had just survived a tornado, and she looked at the Hassles who now sat with their hands clasped in front of them. Mr. Bryce drew in short breaths and grimaced with each one. He held his hand on his side as he did this.

"I think I've got it," she said.

"Are you crazy?" Mrs. Bryce asked. "These men are insane."

"We ain't crazy," Solomon said. "We just live by the book."

"What book? You can't mean the *Bible*," Mrs. Bryce said.

"And why not? An eye for an eye and a tooth for a tooth. Yer husband attacked me for no cause. I's an old man, nigh around eighty-four. Should I let him beat me down?"

"You shouldn't have let your . . . freak of a son beat my husband down."

"Enough." Suzanne stressed the statement by horizontally slicing the air with flattened palms. She saw that Mr. Bryce tried to rally some strength to come out of his dazed state. He clenched his side and slumped back over. "This is getting us nowhere. Just like fighting did. Now, let's see if we can be civil."

Suzanne looked at the Hassles. They still sat with their hands clasped in front of them. She looked to the Bryces. Mr. Bryce blinked hard. Small droplets of sweat beaded on his forehead. Mrs. Bryce wiped them away with her hand and wiped her hand on her lap. Suzanne became aware of the sweat beading on her own forehead. A cold droplet rolled down the back of her neck. Neither of the Hassles had a drop of sweat on his face, though a deep pungent smell wafted from them. Suzanne thought it smelled like a mixture of mud and cooked onions. She figured the Hassles always smell like they just finished cooking some onion-laden mud pies. After being at their house, she thought they were lucky to not smell like pig's blood. Then Suzanne thought the stench bore undertones of shorn copper as well. She tacked that up to letting her mind run away with her.

"Are y'all Yankees?" Solomon eyed them suspiciously.

"Yankees?" Mrs. Bryce spoke the word like it made her dirty. "What does that have to do with anything?"

"I thought it might explain y'all's rudeness," Solomon said.

"It doesn't matter if they are or aren't Yankees." Suzanne felt a drop of sweat roll down her back.

"But it does. It does," Solomon said. "Ye see, no Hassle has had dealings with the blue bellies since, well my great-grand daddy talked to the angel."

Suzanne studied the old man. Had he said what she heard? She looked at the Bryces for confirmation. Even as dazed as Mr. Bryce was, Suzanne recognized the expression of subdued astonishment. Before anyone could respond to Solomon's comment, Lovell walked back into the room. He looked around and grinned as if he were working for tips.

"We'll have an ambulance here in a few minutes." Lovell looked at Esau, who still sat with his hands folded in front of him.

Solomon leaned on his cane as the paramedics tended to Mr. Bryce. Esau stayed in his seat and twiddled his plump meaty thumbs like a bored child. Suzanne stood in the hall watching all the commotion of the EMTs through the open door. Several of the eighth graders took special interest in the flashing red lights of the ambulance. They had to be shooed from the administration hall to their lunch break. Suzanne moved out of the way as the paramedics pushed Mr. Bryce out on a stretcher.

"I think he's got some broken ribs," one of the EMTs said.

Rusty Cardiff, the chief deputy sheriff, followed the EMTs out of the room. He held a small notepad in his hand. Mrs. Bryce came out with him. Suzanne didn't know why the sheriff's department always sent Rusty out to handle school problems. He sauntered as if his feet were caught up in molasses. Suzanne called it the "sheriff's sashay" every time she dealt with him.

"So do you two want to press charges against the Hassles, ma'am?" He licked the tip on the short golf pencil he held.

"What do you think, honey?" Mrs. Bryce asked her husband as the EMTs wheeled him out.

Suzanne watched Mr. Bryce eye Solomon. He appeared to size him up as if getting ready to jump down off the gurney and fight him again. Mr. Bryce put his raised head back down on the pillow and closed his eyes.

"It's not worth it," he said. "What would they do to him?"

"Are you sure about that?" Lovell asked, opening the doors for the EMTs.

"Yeah," Mr. Bryce said.

"We've got more important things to worry about," Mrs. Bryce said.

The EMTs pushed the gurney out to the ambulance, and Lovell let the doors close. Rusty put his stub of a pencil back into his top pocket. The pad followed. He took Suzanne by the arm and moved her away from the door.

"Do *you* want to press charges against the Hassles?"

"If the Bryces don't want to bother with it, then no," Suzanne said. "I prefer to just do some damage control."

"That's a relief." Rusty pushed his brown ball cap up on his head revealing that his forehead had grown long due to balding. "The last thing the sheriff wanted was to stir up the stink with those freaks. You best get them out of here before they cause you some real trouble, because they're very likely to."

"What do you mean 'real trouble?'" Lovell's voice dropped in pitch, his brows knitted together. "They just broke a man's ribs and a couple of chairs."

"Trust me. Those folks can cause a lot more trouble than just breaking some ribs. They're all inbred and nutty. Ain't no telling what they might do. I've had some bad personal run-ins with them myself. Don't trust them any farther than I can throw 'em. I say get rid of them as soon as you can, and get that girl of theirs expelled as quickly as you can."

"Thank you, Rusty," Suzanne said. His skinny frame with a pot belly always made her think of a small town sheriff's deputy. "But running this school is my job. I happen to think that everyone deserves an education no matter how backward they might be or seem."

"It's your problem then." Rusty tapped the bill of his cap with his fingers. "Good day, ma'am. Sir."

Suzanne turned back to the counselor's office. Solomon stood outside the door looking at her. A yellow slip of paper hung from his dirty fingers. He smiled like a greedy opossum caught in a trash can.

"I almost forgot I have a telephone number for ya," Solomon said, waving the slip of paper. "It ain't mine, but a family member who can come get Rachel if need be."

Suzanne took it. The number was written in a heavy black ink and judging by the waviness of the lettering by an unsteady hand. "I'll put it in my Rolodex when I go back to my office." She folded and put it in her pocket. "If you two are ready, Mr. Lovell and I will escort you to your car."

"We ain't quite ready to go yet. I'd like to see my daughter's classroom if that be okay."

Suzanne looked to Lovell for his answer. He shrugged his shoulders with a blank stare on his face. She hated not being able to read people's thoughts.

"Are there any students in your classroom right now, Mr. Lovell?" Suzanne asked.

"No, they should still be at lunch for a few more minutes."

"Then take Mr. Hassle and his son to your classroom. They can get Rachel's stuff and assignments for a few days of work. I think that she should stay out of school until the end of this week, doing work at home. Maybe I can figure out some way of getting her to the alternative school after that. You two can go ahead and take her home when you leave."

"I thank ye, miss." Solomon still smiled. "I wished everyone was as nice as ye."

"Thank you." Suzanne forced it to sound sincere.

Lovell waited for Esau to come out of the room, and then escorted the Hassles to his classroom. Suzanne watched them all the way down the hall until they turned the corner at the far end. She wished she could hold the lunch bell a few minutes extra so she could get those people out of her school before the other students saw them. As she walked into her office, the secretary looked up. Stress had plowed deep furrows on her forehead.

"Dr. Larson's on line one for you."

Suzanne reached over the desk and picked up the receiver. "What do you need, Dr. Larson?"

"I just got a call from Sally Bryce. She tells me that her son and a girl got caught having sex in a bathroom today. Is this the same girl you tried to get me to bus to the alternative school?"

"Yes."

"Seems like we've got a problem, Ms. Clay, a big problem. They've threatened to sue, and I don't think we've got a chance in the world. I want you and that special ed teacher here at six tonight. We're having an emergency meeting with the board to decide what's going to happen."

"I'll let him know." Her throat tightened so that she had to force words out.

Suzanne didn't have time to say good bye. Dr. Larson slammed his receiver down, and the line went dead. She eased the receiver back to the cradle. Her eyes burned. They always started to burn when she needed to cry. The problem was she couldn't figure out what kind of tears they were. She thought they came from fear, and that didn't sit well with her. Until she met the Hassles, Suzanne thought she wasn't afraid of people. She could be wrong though. The old man remained eerily calm as his son raged out. He almost seemed to enjoy it like men at a cockfight enjoyed watching roosters peck each other to death. His belief in the "old eye for an eye" made him seem even more malignant. Solomon might really pluck out an eye if he had to. Suzanne imagined him tossing her eyeball into grinder with the head meat from a hog as they made souse meat.

"The eyeballs give it the real flavor," he would say. "Vengeance is mine sayeth the Lord."

Watered down versions of Solomon Hassle had been enough for her to quit going to church years ago. She shook his image out of her head and went into her office to calm down. Her heart still beat quicker than she liked it to. Lovell burst into the room. He looked flushed and ready to fight.

"What is it?" Suzanne asked. Her heart seemed to rev up more.

Lovell clenched and eased his fists. "I've got to get some of this battle energy out."

"What are you talking about?"

"Ever since I got back from Afghanistan I get this way

when people argue or try and fight. Even when the kids do it. I get so full of pent up energy I think I'll pop or hit something." He paused. "Or someone."

"Do you need to go home for the rest of the day?" Suzanne asked.

"No, I just need to run or do some kind of high-energy activity. It'll burn off the stress."

"Take an hour. I'll sit with your class," Suzanne said.

"Thanks." Lovell jogged out the office door.

"Warren," Suzanne called after him. "We've got to meet with the board tonight. Thought you might need to know that now so you can burn off some extra energy."

The main glass door slammed, rattling the panes. Suzanne looked at her secretary. She felt raw anger bubbling inside her. If this woman had just done her job, no one would be in this mess.

"I'm sorry," Mrs. Norris said, as if sensing Suzanne's thoughts. "Those Hassles scare me. They always have."

"What do you mean?" Suzanne sat on the edge of the spare desk in the room, arms crossed.

"We had a few in school when I went—Zachariah and Haggai, or some Bible name. They always stank and tried to have sex with the girls, even in elementary school," she said. "Finally they dropped out."

"Why would they do that?"

Mrs. Norris looked from side to side as if to make sure no one heard her. She leaned in close to Suzanne. "Some people believe they have a cult where they have sex with each other and make sacrifices."

"What kind of sacrifices?" Suzanne asked, feeling like a kid around a campfire, but also burning with a real desire to know. The thought of the squealing pig and all the chanting from her visit rang out in her head.

The secretary shrugged her shoulders. "It's according to who you talk to. Some say Yankees because supposedly during the Civil War the Hassles were wealthy slave owners, and when the slaves were freed they became poor. Some folks say hogs, and others say anyone who causes them trouble. I've even heard they steal children like a bunch of Gypsies."

Suzanne chuckled. "This is starting to sound like a campfire story. Next you'll be telling me that one of them has a hook and kills high school kids making out on lonely roads."

Mrs. Norris gave Suzanne sideways look. "Don't be silly. If they all act like those two I went to school with, they'd just watch and you know," she got close to Suzanne again, "play with themselves."

Suzanne shook her head. "This is too much. I've got to go sit in with Mr. Lovell's class. Just take messages for any calls I might get."

Suzanne got up and left the office. The idea of the Hassles making sacrifices while having wild orgies with one another almost made her laugh again. Then she remembered all the noise when they visited yesterday. A group of them were singing hymns after slaughtering the hog.

"Nobody's *that* crazy," she murmured, turning the corner by the gym.

6

The time of prophecy is nigh.

BOOK OF LOT 17:9

THE STRAIGHT METAL CHAIRS set up in the council chambers felt cold and harsh against Suzanne's backside. It seemed the board and Dr. Larson wanted her and her employees to be uncomfortable. Lovell shifted in his seat then crossed his leg. He uncrossed that leg and turned sideways. Then he stood and turned the chair backwards, straddling it like one of their students might do.

"What's taking them so long?" he asked. "If they're going to fire us, just do it, but don't torture us like this."

The door at the back of the hall opened. Suzanne turned around. Ms. Dodge scurried down the side of the room to them. She wore denim slacks and a red sweater. The freckles on her caramel face looked dark brown without any makeup to smooth them away. Suzanne had never seen her wearing street clothes. They never associated with each other outside school. Ms. Dodge flopped down in the chair beside Lovell. It screeched on the tile as it slid from her momentum. She pushed her hair up out of her face and caught her breath.

"I'm not late, am I?"

"I didn't even know you were supposed to be here," Suzanne said, "but no, you're not late."

"I promise you that I didn't know until just a few minutes ago," Ms. Dodge said, "or I wouldn't have shown up like this."

Suzanne looked her over. Ms. Dodge shifted a bit and tugged at her clothes. Suzanne could tell she was uncomfortable and felt scrutinized.

The door behind the desk opened. Dr. Larson stepped in carrying a black three-ring binder. His tie hung loose around his fleshy neck, the fluorescents reflecting off his bald scalp. He sat at the far end of the desk with a small huff. A little brass placard announced this as his seat. The five members of the school board walked in behind him. Each sat behind his or her own brass placard. They all looked like they had been given as much notice as Ms. Dodge had. Charlie Mullaly still had on his UPS uniform and board president Cindy Bird kept her hair up in a baby blue babushka. The bristle hair rollers left their outline on the silky material.

"Ms. Dodge, Mr. Lovell, and Principal Clay, thank you for coming to this meeting with such limited notice," Bird said, smiling.

"We all know why we're here," Dr. Larson said. "So let's get down to it."

Ms. Dodge put her hand up like a child waiting to ask to go to the bathroom. "I don't know why I am. You said I needed to get here because of something with the Hassle girl. I was absent from school today."

"The gist of it is that Principal Clay allowed," Bird looked at her notes. "Rachel Hassle to attend school despite having sent her to alternative school. The girl found Eric Bryce and had sexual relations with him in a restroom. When the Bryces came to the school, Rachel's family assaulted Mr. Bryce."

"He ended up with several broken ribs and a collapsed lung," Dr. Larson added. "He's in the hospital right now. We're going to be lucky not to have to give these people a fortune in a settlement."

"I protest." Suzanne stood to let her legs warm up a bit. "William Bryce attacked Rachel's elderly father first. His very large and obviously mentally deficient son then assaulted Mr. Bryce. I'm sorry he's so injured, but he did that to himself."

"Yes," Bird said, "but if that girl hadn't been in school then there would have been no confrontation at all."

Suzanne felt the flush of rage building over her body. She clenched her fists at her side. "Rachel's family couldn't afford to drive her to the alternative school, and Dr. Larson said that we couldn't bus her. The girl has to be educated. What would you have done?"

"Expelled her," Charlie said, "and let Walker or Fayette County deal with her."

"If they couldn't get her up to Leesville for alternative school, what makes you think that they'd be able to get her to Oakman or Berry?" Lovell asked.

"All they would have to do is make it to a rendezvous point with that system's bus." Calm oozed through Bird's voice. "It's that simple, when you take a moment and think about it."

Suzanne let her fist flatten out and sat down. The board looked at them with set jaws and frowns. Bird's eyebrows arched up almost to the point of cartoonish exaggeration. Lovell and Ms. Dodge kept their lips thread thin. The only friendly expression was Dr. Larson's poker face. His lips bore a half sneer-half glower. It made the edges of his mouth turn up just a tick. Suzanne hated when neutral was a positive thing.

"The board discussed this before coming into session," Bird said. "We came to a unanimous decision about how to handle this situation. Dr. Larson, will you please do the difficult job?"

Dr. Larson nodded, keeping his poker face as neutral as Sweden. He took a manila folder from Bird and opened it. Suzanne saw the results had been typed on goldenrod paper. Goldenrod was used in personnel files.

"Ms. Suzanne Clay, because you let Rachel Hassle attend an alternative program on your campus, you bear the brunt of this," Dr. Larson said. "As soon as a new principal can be assigned to your school, you will be dismissed."

"But I'm tenured," Suzanne protested.

"I don't think the state department of education would care, seeing as how you allowed children to have sex in your school and nearly got a parent killed. Not to mention how much money Kosciusko County is going to lose when the boy's parents sue the school for your behavior," Bird said. "Trust me— we've already talked to our legal counsel about this."

"Trust *me*— I'll be talking with mine," Suzanne answered.

"Mr. Warren Lovell," Dr. Larson ignored Suzanne. "You were aware of the alternative plans for the Hassle girl, but didn't make special accommodations to keep Eric Bryce safe. At the end of this semester, you will be put on unpaid leave until next school year when you will be reassigned to another school."

Lovell made no protest. He nodded. Suzanne saw his hands bouncing up and down on his knees. He kept opening and closing his fists. He had the battle feelings coming over him just like that afternoon. Suzanne hoped he wouldn't burst before they could get out of the chambers.

"Finally, Ms. Rebecca Dodge. You weren't present at school today, but you had prior knowledge of Ms. Clay's arrangements. You did nothing to change it. At the end of the school year you will be asked to retire, seeing as how you have more than 25 years in the system or be reassigned to another location and made a classroom teacher again." Dr. Larson closed the folder. "You have the right to appeal this to the state board of education within two weeks. Thank you."

Dr. Larson and the school board stood.

"This is outrageous," Suzanne jumped to her feet. "I have tenure in this county. You can't just throw me aside like the wadded up minutes from your last meeting."

"Ms. Clay, we said that you could appeal this decision," Bird said.

"To who? The state board? That's not going to help much, is it?"

"All I can say is that you have the right to appeal our decision," Bird repeated as she and the other members of the board began to file out.

Ms. Dodge stood and shook her head. "I'm going home and taking a long bath."

"That doesn't sound bad," Suzanne said.

Lovell pumped his fists. "I'm going to the gym, before I do something stupid."

Suzanne looked at him. He trembled with anger. She thought he was a man on the edge of snapping. "Need some company? I could do with a run myself."

"That'll be fine."

The treadmills pointed into the weight area of the gym. Suzanne ran as hard as she could on the conveyor belt. The music blared over the speakers throughout the gym. She could hear it over the machine's motor and her own footfalls. The manager sat in a small office by the door. He watched Motorcross racing on TV. Suzanne watched Lovell on the leg press machine. He pushed at least three hundred pounds up with his legs. His face turned purple as he did so.

Lovell had ridden with her to her house so she could change. He kept his own gym clothes in his car. He said that he never knew when he would go for a workout. Suzanne tried to keep things conservative but interesting. She wore her shorts a little shorter than usual to show off her legs, but made sure to wear a t-shirt over her sports bra.

A stitch tore across Suzanne's side. She bent over as she cranked the speed down on the treadmill. Her sprint downgraded to a light jog. Then she went down to a quick walk. The pain in her side subsided, and Suzanne straightened back up. Lovell moved to the leg extension machine. She watched his quads bulge out as he flexed them, and she imagined his thighs could do things that no other man she'd known could do. Lovell grimaced as his extended his legs. The dimples popped out in his cheeks. Suzanne slowed the treadmill to the lowest setting and got off it. She grabbed a towel from a stack on the sign in desk. She wiped her face as she walked to Lovell. He grunted as he lifted the weights.

"You about ready to go?" she asked. "I think I've done myself in."

He watched her as he finished his reps. Sweat glistened on his face. Suzanne could the see the crease of his pectoral muscles through his shirt that stuck to his body. He slid off the machine, and started putting the weight plates back on their rack.

"I think I've burned off enough energy." Lovell eyed her. She could feel his eyes. "I could use a drink though. You wouldn't have any of that wine left from the other night would you?"

"I might have something."

Suzanne flopped down at her small dining room table. Lovell sat opposite of her. A half-empty bottle of apple schnapps sat between them. Suzanne opened the bottle and poured some into a shot glass bearing the saying, "Show us your boobs. Mardi Gras 2003." She slid the bottle over to Lovell who filled his Hooters shot glass. He raised it and tipped it toward Suzanne in a toast. They both tossed the alcohol back and slammed the small glasses onto the table. Lovell coughed.

"How long have you had that stuff?" he asked.

"It's been opened since Christmas before last, I think." Suzanne smiled. "Not too strong for you I hope?"

"The problem with schnapps is I don't drink it too often, and the longer its opened the harder it gets to drink." Lovell poured another and slammed it. He grimaced. "I have to say I like your taste in shot glasses."

Suzanne turned her Mardi Gras glass to her face and smiled. "I have a whole collection of them."

"Really?" Lovell slugged another dose of apple liquor. "Wouldn't figure that was your type of souvenir. I'd expect something a little more Martha Stewart like little spoons or thimbles. "

Suzanne poured another and sipped it. Schnapps snuck up on her too often when drinking it, but she did love it. "They're not really mine. They belonged to an ex-boyfriend. When we broke up, he never got them back. I keep them around as a reminder of bad decisions and the horrors that come from them."

Lovell reached for the bottle, but didn't pour any. "I think I better pace myself. I'm feeling a little warm already."

"Schnapps'll sneak up on you."

"So what kind of horrors did that old boyfriend leave you with?"

"Have you ever wondered why I wear tights instead of sheer panty hose when I wear skirts?"

"I've never noticed anything except how good your legs look," Lovell bit his lip and shook his head. "Sorry about that."

Suzanne laughed. "That's okay. I know you look at my legs, Warren. Here's the reason."

She stood and walked to Lovell. She pushed down her sock to reveal the name *Bruce* tattooed in old English script on her ankle. Lovell touched it and traced the letters with his finger. He slid the tip of his index finger up her leg and took her hand. His touch felt soft and tender. Suzanne felt the schnapps warm in her stomach, making her feel warm and fuzzy elsewhere. Lovell stood and took both her hands in his. He pulled her close. His breath felt hot on her neck, and the smell of apple filled her nose.

"You're very sexy, Ms. Clay."

"You're drunk, Mr. Lovell."

"All the better, that way I don't think about getting fired."

"Oh."

Lovell moved in to kiss Suzanne. Her anticipation parted her lips and extended her tongue to the edge of her teeth. They met in a tender mixture of passion and liquor. She eased down onto his lap. He slid his hand up her back. Suzanne felt Lovell pulling her shirt over her head. She let him. Their kiss broke apart long enough for him to toss her shirt on the floor, and for her to start lifting his over his head.

He smelled manly—a mixture of salty sweat and natural musk. Suzanne nuzzled her face on his chest and started kissing his neck. Lovell positioned her so she straddled him. They began to kiss again. This time they made sloppy kisses like kids making out for the first time. Suzanne felt Lovell's callused and warm hands slide inside her sports bra and over her breast. Her nipples went erect. Something she sat on started to do the same thing. A slight gasp of excitement escaped her lips, as Lovell brushed over her areolas with his thumb. She started to grind her hips ever so slightly.

The phone sang out, bringing her focus back to the room and the realization that she was with her employee. Suzanne broke away and grabbed the phone hanging on the wall just inside the door between the kitchen and dining room. She tugged her bra down to hide her excitement.

"Hello."

The line crackled like water had run into the outside jack. A loud hum and another crackle sounded.

"Suzanne Clay." A clipped husky female voice said.

"This is she."

"Suzanne Clay. She will be liken to earthen pots ready to fill with seed."

"Who is this? I'm getting tired of these stupid calls."

Lovell walked to her. "What is it?"

Suzanne tried to wave him away. He pressed his ear against the phone as well. She felt the extra heat of his hot lobe and flush of his excited skin against hers.

"Salvation will sprout from those seeds, thus is prophecy."

The disconnect signal hummed before Suzanne could say anything.

Suzanne glanced at the caller ID box. The location read: Marquisville Middle School. The number matched her office extension.

"What the?" she said. "That call came from my office."

The phone rang again. She waited for the call ID to flash up. The call came from the sheriff's department. Lovell snatched the phone before she could.

"What?" he said.

Suzanne wrenched the phone from him. She listened to the dispatcher stammer for a moment.

"Excuse him," Suzanne said. "I just got a disturbing crank call."

"Are you Principal Clay?" the dispatcher asked with a smoker's voice.

"Yes."

"You need to get down to the school. Someone's broken in. We just got the alarm call, and officers are on the way."

"I'll be there in a minute."

Suzanne slammed the phone on the cradle. She walked into the dining room and grabbed her shirt from the floor. She pulled it over her head and snatched her keys from the pegged holder.

"What's happening?" asked Lovell.

"Someone's broken into the school. That call really did come from my office."

7

When I see the blood,
I will pass
I will pass over you

AMERICAN HYMN

RUSTY CARDIFF STOOD BY the administrative entrance to the school building. His ball cap sat back on his head revealing how far his forehead went up before meeting actual hair. As she parked in her assigned space, Suzanne noticed his shirttail hung out at the back and his gun belt cinched it down. He had his hands on his hips. The cherry-red end of his cigarette burned from the newly lit tip.

"Remember to say as little as possible," Suzanne whispered to Lovell. "Otherwise he'll know you've been drinking."

She walked to the deputy. "So what do you know?" she asked.

"Nothing so far. All the doors and windows are locked, and not a single pane of glass is broken."

"So how do you know someone broke in? The alarm could've malfunctioned?"

"If you look inside the door there, you can see why I'm sure someone broke in." Rusty pointed to the double glass doors that entered the school by the main office.

Suzanne walked over and looked in. Papers, chairs, desks, and other hard to identify school items littered the hallway between the office and the gym door. The bright cheerful paper that hung on the bulletin boards flanking the corridor hung in tatters like flags following a battle. Suzanne jiggled the doors. They clanked but didn't open.

Lovell stopped beside her. He stared inside. "Looks a like a bomb went off or something."

"Have you been drinking, Mr. Lovell?" Rusty blew Camel smoke between Suzanne and Lovell.

"Yes, he has, and he isn't driving or anything to that effect," Suzanne said.

She dug into her pocket and brought out her keys. With a quick jab and twist, the doors opened, and the cool air from the school blew into their faces. Suzanne welcomed the gush of air. It sent the cigarette smoke the other way. Second-hand smoke always gave her a vicious headache.

"I don't reckon that you've got a good alibi to where you were when this happened, Mr. Lovell?" Rusty asked.

"He does." Suzanne kept her words clipped and tight. "He was with me drinking apple schnapps. We had a bad evening."

"I could arrest you both for public intox."

Suzanne turned on the deputy. "If you're going to act like Barney Fife, Deputy Cardiff, I suggest getting back to Andy and Aunt Bea and letting me get to the bottom of what happened to my school. If you want to help me and the school board out, then let's get down to business."

"I'm sorry. Let's figure out what happened here," Rusty stepped into the school with his cigarette still dangling from his lips.

Lovell snatched the Camel out of the deputy's mouth and tossed it onto the sidewalk. Rusty turned to him, his fingers drumming the top of his leather handcuff holder. Suzanne knew he was itching to draw those steel puppies out and slap them on somebody.

"No smoking in a school building," Lovell said. "Even after hours."

Rusty nodded begrudgingly and walked deeper into the building. Suzanne followed. She flipped on all the hallway lights. The entire corridor filled with the bluish humming light the fluorescents provided. Things looked worse in the light. A ruddy brown substance streaked both walls of the hallway all the way to the end. A strong smell of feces rose on the air the farther they walked down the hall.

"It smells like pig crap in here," Rusty said. "You reckon that's what's on the wall?"

Suzanne stared at the gritty-looking streaks. She put her face close to it, but not close enough to touch it. A whiff of air didn't seem to increase the stench any.

"I don't think the smell is coming from the wall," she said.

Lovell grabbed a broken ruler off the floor and scraped at the stuff. A bit of the ruddy filth came off onto the ruler. He examined it.

"I think I know what it is, and it's not pig flop," Lovell moved some of the substance with his fingers. "It's salt putty with mud or something like that mixed in. We made a batch of this a couple of weeks ago in class. We built mountains out of it then painted them green."

"It's good to know our intruders weren't sick enough to smear feces everywhere," Suzanne said.

"I found the smell." Rusty held up a metal bucket. "It's full of liquefied pig crap. This stuff's been sitting someplace for a while to get in this state. I'm going to get it out of here and see if it'll make this place smell better."

He walked past Suzanne. The smell wafting past brought the schnapps surging to the top of her throat. A large exaggerated swallow sent it back to her stomach. She watched Rusty leave the building then started shuffling through the litter in the hallway. The papers were from several different classrooms as were the desks. Seventh-grade math tests mingled with eighth-grade literature tests. All the doors down the hall were closed, and none looked like they had been forced. Lovell jiggled the handles of a few. They were locked.

"I don't think whoever did this had time for all this damage from the time of the crank call to when the alarm sounded," Lovell said.

"Of course not," she answered. "They either were hidden in the school and after I left they came out and started doing the damage, or they had a key and a code to the alarm."

"The alarm would've gone off if they had started walking around after it was set," Lovell said.

"I didn't think about that. You should go check your room. I'm going to see about the office."

As Suzanne unlocked her door, Rusty walked back inside the building. He wiped his hands on his uniform pants and smiled at her. For the first time, she noticed his yellow nicotine-stained teeth. After four years of living in the place, she realized most all the locals who had teeth wore cigarette smiles. She decided that yellow must be the official color for teeth in Marquisville. Suzanne grinned back and eased the door open.

"Deputy Cardiff, before we got the call about the school, I got a strange call. My caller ID said it was from my office. Would you mind standing by, just in case the caller is still here?"

"No problem." Rusty undid the strap over the top of his .9 mm. He stood in draw stance as Suzanne slipped inside the front office.

She flipped on the lights. Nothing seemed disturbed. The light on the alarm system alternated blinks from green to red. It meant the alarm had been tripped at the keypad. Suzanne flipped the plastic cover off the keypad and deactivated the system. The light blinked to red and held steady.

"Rusty, the alarm was tripped at the keypad," Suzanne pointed to the mechanism.

"An inside job?"

"That's for you to figure out. I'm just telling you what I know."

Rusty looked the keypad over. "Well I won't be dusting for prints. Yours will be the most recent, and I watched you disarm the system."

"I didn't think about that. Sorry."

Suzanne walked to her office door. Pry marks scarred the wood of the doorjamb. The door hung slack like a bored student's jaw. No light shone through the gap, not even from the desk lamp Suzanne always left on.

She pushed the door, and it swung open. With the light borrowed from the other office, the damage from the break-in revealed itself. Suzanne flipped on the overhead light. Everything looked turned over and mishandled. The desk set aside for Rachel lay upturned. The special ed. textbooks lay in torn bits here and there as did Suzanne's tardy slips. Red ink pooled on her desk. Broken blue pens oozed their lifeblood on the Navajo rug she'd bought on vacation in Arizona. The leather of her office chair grinned at her with slash marks. The

Norman Rockwell print that hung over her filing cabinet was hung upside down with more of the salt putty caked on it. Most of the picture was obscured by the orange-brown muck.

"Is everything okay, Ms. Clay?" Rusty asked.

"No. As you can see, my office is completely trashed."

Rusty whistled through his teeth as he took in the mess. "They did a humdinger of a job in here. Is there anything missing?"

"How could I tell? Have you looked at this office? There's stuff everywhere."

Suzanne slapped her hand on her desk and into a puddle of red ink. She grimaced and wiped her hand down her work-out shorts not worrying about a stain.

"Jeeze, they did a job in here," Lovell said, coming into the office.

Suzanne was glad he came in when he did. She stifled back her frustration and the burning in her eyes faded. A nod in agreement was all she responded with.

"How about your classroom?"

"Nothing ransacked or anything. The only thing is my folder of permission slips for Friday's field trip is missing. I had it locked up in my desk."

"So your desk had been jimmied opened?" Rusty asked.

"No, I'm pretty sure I forgot to lock it this evening."

"The Hassles," Suzanne said. "Do you think that it might have been Solomon and his son that did this?"

Rusty put his gun away. "How would they get in without breaking a window or jimmying a door?"

"You said the intruders would have to have hidden in the school or had a key," Lovell said. "I escorted Solomon and

Esau out myself, and I don't think the school board would give them a key."

"There's a broken window in the girl's locker room. It can't be locked," Suzanne said.

Rusty ran a hand over his stubbly cheeks. "Since it looks like an inside job, someone else must have known."

"I didn't know about it," Lovell said. "Who else would?"

"The coach, of course, and probably a janitor. Some kids might have discovered it as well." Suzanne stared hard at an empty place on her desk. "My Rolodex, it's gone. I keep it right there."

She pointed to empty area on her desk. A black Rolodex stuffed full of address cards sat in a smaller pool of red ink beside the empty space.

"What's that?" Rusty asked.

"That's my general Rolodex. The student Rolodex with their phone numbers and addresses is the one missing."

"Are you sure it didn't get thrown around with the rest of all this stuff?" Lovell asked.

"If you threw a Rolodex, all the cards would fly out of it. The floor would have name cards all over it. I've not seen a single one. I would've noticed that for sure."

"I think it confirms the Hassles couldn't have been the intruders. Why would they need a Rolodex? They don't even have a phone," Lovell said.

"It might explain why they didn't take the computer though," Suzanne pointed out. "I don't remember seeing any electrical lines at their house either."

"The Hassles are a bunch of retards," Rusty said. "They ain't smart enough to do something like this. It was kids; I guarantee. No-good little punks."

"Kids would link to the crank calls you've been getting, Suzanne."

She shook her head. "It still doesn't explain how the alarm was set off at the keypad. No students know that code, only teachers and staff."

"A staff member's kid?" Lovell asked.

"Let's see if Ms. Dodge's office was broken in." Suzanne said.

She pushed past Rusty and Lovell into the front office and then into the hallway. Suzanne unlocked Ms. Dodge's office door and threw it open. From the light that spilled in from the hallway, the office looked similar to Suzanne's own, chairs lay on the floor, papers strewn everywhere, and a large pool of red ink on the large conference table. A sickening smell crept from the room. It mixed pig manure, dust, and blood into a strange perfume. The light flickered on.

It illuminated the horror of the room. Large letters written in the salt putty spread across the back wall, and the puddle of ink on the table didn't come from Bic ballpoints but from the veins of some animal. The blood pooled darker than any ink. Two more buckets rested on the table, but the manure contents were splattered the floor. Suzanne sighed long and wavering. From behind, Rusty whistled through his teeth again.

"We're dealing with a sicko here," he said. "Blood, pig crap, salt mud."

"The savior is found. The prophecy begins with a feast of salt," Lovell read the message scrawled on the wall.

"Do you have any idea who would do this if it's not the Hassles?" Suzanne asked. "The person who called me used almost the same words."

"Like I said those Hassles are too dumb to write, much less scribble something like that. It was Satanists." Rusty said with a full confident speech.

"Devil worshipers?" Lovell sounded surprised. "I thought I was supposed to be the drunk one. There's no such thing. Preachers came up with that in '80's to keep kids from listening to heavy metal."

"Laugh if you want to, but we've had trouble every now and again with them. The last time was couple of years ago a bunch of high school kids decided to worship the devil by sticking firecrackers inside of dogs. Killed a few folks' pets, but that was it."

"So go get those guys," Suzanne said.

"Can't really do that. Two of them joined the army. One died in Iraq, and I think the other is stationed in Germany. The girl's in county lockup for prostitution and manufacturing methamphetamine."

"So do you know any other Satanists?" Lovell asked.

"I'll get the word out," Rusty said, "before they do any more animal sacrificing. They might even hit a church next."

"I'm going to get on the phone and call all the teachers," Suzanne said. "I'll have to cancel school. Then I'll call Dr. Larson, and see what he wants us to do."

"You can't clean up anything yet," Rusty said.

"I'm not going to. You and the other deputies are going to have to investigate. I guess there's nothing else for us to do tonight." She looked at Lovell. "Do you mind giving Mr. Lovell a ride home, Deputy Cardiff? I'm going to be here a while."

"I don't see why not. Come on, boy."

Lovell stepped out of Ms. Dodge's office. He followed

Rusty out of the school building. Suzanne locked the door behind them. She closed up the counselor's office and went to the main office to start calling the teachers.

Suzanne hung up with Dr. Larson as the bell rang out through the school. It did that every fifty minutes night and day even in the summer. The system was old and too expensive to change, so it kept doing it. No one usually heard it after 8 pm, but tonight the 10:50 bell had an audience. She almost applauded its loud tinny ring.

Dr. Larson became angry when he heard what happened, especially when he was told that nothing had been damaged to get in.

"So you're saying it was an inside job, Ms. Clay," he had said.

"I'm not saying anything. I'm just telling you the facts."

"Somebody might think that you and Mr. Lovell did this because we fired you."

"I don't care how mad I got about that, I've never been mad enough to pour blood on a table and fling pig crap around. I don't even understand that part. Really, who slings pig crap around?"

The superintendent made her madder with those accusations than he had by firing her for doing her job. Suzanne's head started to ache from the base of her skull up toward her forehead. She needed to go home and sleep. Everything would be waiting for her tomorrow, and probably smelling worse. She stood to leave.

"Going so soon?" Ms. Dodge asked.

Suzanne jumped. She hadn't heard the door open. "Why are you here?"

"I came to see the damage. Impressive isn't it?"

"Not exactly what I was thinking, but it was thorough," Suzanne said.

"They did a real doozie on my room, didn't they?"

"Yeah."

"I really came by to tell you about Eric Bryce."

"What about him couldn't wait until tomorrow?"

"He's run away. Rusty didn't want to call because he said you'd be busy calling the teachers and such. So I just came over."

"Are they sure he ran away?" Suzanne felt the headache throb worse.

"Rusty said he left a note talking about seeing his girlfriend. Mrs. Bryce is livid."

"I bet. What are we supposed to do?"

Ms. Dodge shook her head, "Nothing. We can't do anything. I thought you would want to know."

"Thank you, Ms. Dodge."

"Call me Becky. I think we've been through enough now for first names, Suzanne."

"Thank you, Becky. I don't know why we've never called each other by first names."

Ms. Dodge smiled a sheepish grin, "Because I didn't like you when you started here. Now that doesn't matter."

"Well at least you're honest. I'm ready to go now. It's been a rough night." Suzanne pushed past the counselor.

"I'll lock up. I'm going to look around a little more, if that's okay."

Suzanne rubbed her temples. "Fine, but be careful. Deputy Cardiff thinks that Satanists might have done this."

"He thinks Satanists do everything."

Suzanne gave Ms. Dodge a strange look.

"What? Rusty got real big into heavy metal during the '80's. His mother and preacher scared it out of him by filling his head full that devil worshipers were everywhere and looking to sacrifice virgins. He became the biggest Pat Boone fan you'd ever seen after that."

"Still, be careful."

Suzanne pushed the front door open. It locked behind her. She crawled into her car and headed home. The events of the evening had a sobering effect on her.

8

For thy love
is better than wine

SONG OF SOLOMON 1:2

STEAM STILL FLOATED BETWEEN her small bathroom and bedroom when Suzanne turned out her bed-side lamp. She lay on her side with her legs curled almost to her stomach, with the covers tucked to her chin. The room felt chilly when she got out of the shower, and she'd already shivered too much for one day.

The air conditioner hummed from the hallway as the air rushed into the intake. The switch-over to heat would come in just a few weeks or at least heat at night. As she lay trying to clear her mind so she could sleep, Suzanne thought about how strange it was to live in Alabama. Sometimes in the year you had to run the air conditioner in the daytime to keep cool but the heat in the evening to keep warm. Then there were the times when the air conditioner ran just to keep down the humidity because the temperature was okay. Thinking about the weather did the trick. Suzanne drifted off to sleep as the cooling system clicked off.

The door bell rang. Suzanne heard it somewhere deep in her mind. The simple ding-dong made her aware that she was sleeping. It kept singing out until she roused herself to respond. The only light in the room spilled in from the street lamp just outside the window. Suzanne got to her feet and headed to the bedroom door. The bell rang again now with an anxious pace. She scurried down the hallway.

"I'm coming!"

The doorbell quit ringing. She paused at the entrance into the living room. Two narrow windows flanked the front door. Privacy curtains hung over both windows, but shadows silhouetted on them when someone stood on the porch. Suzanne saw nothing, and the bell didn't ring again. She unlocked the dead bolt and turned the tab on the doorknob. The door opened a few inches before the safety chain caught it. Suzanne flipped on the porch light and stuck her eye to the crack. She scanned back and forth, but no one stood on the porch.

"A fine night for ding-dong-ditch," Suzanne said to the dark porch.

The clock on the DVD player showed 1:00 AM in glowing green numbers. Suzanne undid the safety chain and stepped onto the porch. A slight breeze blew the hem of her gown that stuck out from under her robe, tickling her thigh. She looked around the yard. No one seemed to be hiding in the shadows, and there were no shrubs to crouch behind. She turned to go back in.

"There you are," Lovell said from behind her.

Suzanne screamed out, spinning around as he jumped onto the porch. He carried her Rolodex in one hand and a brown manila envelope in the other.

"What do you mean scaring me like that?" Suzanne grabbed her Rolodex from him.

"I didn't mean to, but when you didn't answer the door, I got worried. I was walking around to try to find your bedroom window so I could check on you."

"Let's get in before we wake up the neighbors."

Lovell walked in first. Suzanne followed. A push from her foot closed the door, and a flicking motion turned the lock tab on the doorknob. Suzanne walked back through her living room, through the kitchen and into her dining room. She laid the Rolodex on her table beside the still-opened bottle of schnapps and Lovell's dirty shot glass. She turned the lights on and gathered the glasses and liquor. They all went into the kitchen sink. The schnapps turned over, and the smell of booze permeated the room as it leaked from the bottle down the drain. Suzanne looked out the small kitchen window while running water in the sink. The view of the street showed nothing unusual. Her neighbor's Ford Escort sat in front of his driveway, and his garbage cans lay overturned on the lawn like they had been since garbage day. Suzanne's hand slipped off the faucet handle, and her knuckles banged the metal sink.

"Are you okay?" Lovell asked, stepping into the kitchen from the living room.

"Nothing's right. Teaching is supposed to be easy."

"No it's not."

"Well," she turned to look into Lovell's gray eyes. "It's not supposed to be filled with creepy games like this."

"I'll give you that."

He walked away into the next room. Suzanne followed him as he sat down at the dining room table. He opened the envelope and started flipping through the permission slips. Suzanne sat and watched him over the top of her Rolodex. He shook his head at her.

"Nothing's missing. Every permission slip is here."

"What about Rachel?"

"She never brought one back. I figured her family couldn't afford for her to go to the aquarium."

"Everything is normal with my Rolodex except for this."

Suzanne slid a small white card to Lovell. He picked it up and examined it, flipping it over and over in his fingers.

"I don't see anything."

"It was placed backwards in the Rolodex, but you wouldn't be able to tell that from the card."

Suzanne got up and walked to his side. Lovell looked like he just pulled on a pair of jeans crumpled in the corner of his bedroom. His knee stuck out of a hole in the denim and his t-shirt had Mr. Rogers on it. It read: "You're special!" *Indeed.* Some stubble stuck up from his cheeks and chin. The light caught the highlights in it. He looked rustic, and Suzanne made sure to let her hand touch his as she reached for the card. She took it from him, and he looked up at her.

"Look here."

Suzanne flipped the index card over to the back. A rusty smudge tipped the top of the card. It was in the shape of half circle. She pointed it out to Lovell.

"What do you think it is?" he asked.

"A bloody thumbprint."

"But there's no fingerprint on it. Do you think the person wore a glove?"

Suzanne took his hand and pulled his thumb up. She pressed the top of it to the stain on the card. Although the tip of his thumb was thinner than the mark, they had the same general shape. "A glove would be pointier at the end than this. Look." She pointed out a crease crossing the print. "That's part of the thumbprint, not a flaw in the paper."

Lovell took the Rolodex card. He stared at the stain. "It's still not a fingerprint though. It could be anything."

He handed the card back to Suzanne. She made sure to touch his hand again. Lovell had long fingers. A few freckles dotted the flesh between knuckles. Suzanne thought his hands were sexy. She had a thing for hands and couldn't explain it.

"I read something about a family who didn't have fingerprints. The pads of their fingers just had calluses on them. They showed a series of prints taken from that family, and they looked like that." She popped the stain with her finger.

"So find out which family that was, and we have our thieves."

"Not quite what I meant. I mean another person could have that disease or abnormality or whatever it is."

"I knew that was too easy." Lovell stood up. "Well, unless there is something else. I'm tired. I think I'll head home."

He walked to the kitchen and started toward the living room. Suzanne followed. He got to the door and opened it. She leaned on the door jamb.

"You going to be okay?" he asked.

Suzanne let her robe fall open enough for Lovell to see the skin of her shoulder. "I guess so. I probably won't sleep any tonight. It's so creepy."

"Do you want me stay? I can sleep on the couch."

"It might help."

Lovell smiled. He stepped back into the house. Suzanne closed the door behind him. They walked into the living room. Lovell flopped down on the sofa.

"I'll get you a pillow and a blanket. Just make yourself comfortable."

She went to the hall closet and pulled down an old quilt she'd bought at a yard sale when she moved to Marquisville. It was green with orange butterflies sewn on it. She kept all the extra pillows on her bed and walked to get one. A lacy sham covered the thin pillow. Lovell would end up with a checker pattern on his face, but she thought that might be cute. Suzanne walked back through the kitchen holding the pillow in one hand and with the quilt draped over her arm. When she stepped into the living room, Lovell stood facing her. He wore nothing but his boxers and a smile. She stopped short and tried to cut her eyes away. His chest looked firm and a dusting of reddish hair covered it and his tight belly. He walked to her with smooth fluid steps and took the pillow and quilt, tossing them to the floor.

"You said to make myself at home," he said.

"I didn't mean quite *that* at home."

"You don't seem to mind."

Lovell pulled the belt of Suzanne's robe. It opened to reveal her thin silky nightdress. The robe slid down her arms, and she let it fall to the floor. Lovell's long fingers wrapped around her waist and slid to her breast. His lips pressed to her neck, and he nibbled. She shuddered as his hands cupped her breasts. His fingers ran toward her nipple which already stood erect. Before she knew what was happening, Suzanne felt the straps of her nightdress fall off her shoulders. She stood with her naked body pressed against his. They kissed, and she felt safe with him.

Lovell spread the quilt out on the floor and laid her down on it. He lay beside her, hugging her close with his strong arms. He was hard all over. They kissed some more before he pulled her on top of him, using his athletic thighs to her advantage.

Glass shattered and metal popped. Suzanne sat up from a dead sleep on the floor of her living room. Lovell put his hand on her shoulder and tried to force her to lie down. She brushed him off and clambered to her feet. Now, she could hear water spraying. The light from the living room showed into the kitchen. In the dim light and over the bar that separated the two rooms, she saw water spurting up from her sink faucet. Suzanne scooped her robe up and pulled it on as she dashed into the kitchen. She flicked on the overhead fluorescent. Slivers of glass reflected the light, sparkling on the floor like glitter had been spilled everywhere. In the middle of all the glittery mess, a gray cinder block sat baptized in the water spewing from the broken faucet as if it were a fountain in Rome.

"What's going on?" Lovell said from the living room, undoubtedly still lying on the floor.

"Someone threw a cinder block through my window. It's busted the faucet, and just look."

"Huh?" His voice clung to the cobwebs of sleep.

Suzanne didn't bother trying to answer him. She stepped up on the cider block to keep the glass from grinding into her bare feet so she could reach the faucet and try to turn it off. The water hitting the cinder block started to splash on the top of her right foot. It scalded. Suzanne pulled her foot up and toppled to the floor. Bits of the broken glass stabbed through the terrycloth robe into the soft flesh of her butt. She yelled out as her head hit the cabinet door on the bar.

"What is it?" Based upon the movement of his voice, Suzanne could tell Lovell had jumped up and moved to the kitchen.

She saw him round the doorway to the kitchen, his feet bare and body naked. Suzanne pushed herself up and slid her back against the cabinets. The shards of glass pricked the palms of her hands.

"Stop. There's glass all over the floor."

Lovell screeched to a halt just short of the glistening splinters of glass. He looked the floor over, and then held his hand out to help Suzanne up. She shook her head.

"I'll get glass all in my feet." She brushed the glass from her hands. Small specks of blood beaded on her red palms. The floor pooled with the quickly cooling water. An occasional stray drop from the faucet geyser hit her bare foot, leaving a red mark. "Go into the closet next to the bathroom. The hot water heater is there. Turn off the valves."

Lovell ran out of the room. Suzanne heard him knock into the walls down her narrow hall to the bathroom as he hurried to stop the water. She heard the door to the closet jerk open and then the water spurting from the sink died to a bubbling then to nothing. Lovell walked back in with a towel from the linen closet wrapped around his waist. He tossed her a pair of old mottled blue flip-flops she kept in the linen closet. She snagged them in the air and slipped them on her feet. The strap of the right thong made the scalded top of her foot sing out, but Suzanne struggled to her feet. She stepped on the glass. It crunched a little, but she knew it mostly bore into the rubber soles of her shoes.

"Are you okay?" Lovell asked.

"I've got a bit of a bump on my head, and a few scratches, but no worse for wear. How about you?" Suzanne pointed to red blotch above his navel. "Did you get scalded?"

Lovell looked down and rubbed the place. "That's just a birth mark. Are you sure you're okay?"

"I'm mostly worried about how that got in here." She nodded toward the cinder block in her floor.

She grabbed the cement block and dragged it closer to her. Old spider webs hung in the square holes she had her hands in. Nothing crawled on her though and that was a good thing. Lovell reached past her and lifted it up and over. On the underside written in dark black letters was Luke 17:32.

"What does that mean?" Suzanne asked.

"It's a Bible verse."

"I know that, but what does that verse say?"

"You're asking the wrong guy. I haven't been to church in years."

The top pane of glass in the kitchen window shattered as a rock flew in. Suzanne screamed as the small hunk of pavement skidded across the floor. Lovell tore out, running for the door. He slung it open and went to the porch. Suzanne followed, pulling the robe's belt tight around her waist. As she stepped onto the porch, she saw Lovell running down the sidewalk, shaking his fist and screaming curses at an old model green pick-up truck speeding down the street. He stopped as the truck rounded the corner at the end of the block. Suzanne saw some of the lights in her neighbors' homes light up. She motioned for Lovell to hurry back. The last thing she needed with everything else was her neighbors seeing a naked man wrapped in a towel running down the street from her house screaming and yelling. As he walked back, light from a street lamp illuminated the sweat glistening on his bare chest. The night trended toward a bit of humidity. Even though she knew it was the wrong thing, she thought about how he had made love to her. His strong arms embraced her, and he was firm and confident but gentle too. Lovell grabbed her hand and took it in his as they walked back on the porch.

"Who was it?" Suzanne asked.

Lovell walked into the house, then pulled the door closed after escorting her in.

"I couldn't tell. All I saw was some kids diving into the bed of that old Chevy. I couldn't tell who they were."

"Were they our kids?"

Lovell shrugged. "Like I said, I couldn't tell."

"Let's see if we can figure out another mystery then. I've got a Bible in my study."

"You go get it. I'm going to put some clothes on," said Lovell.

Suzanne walked through the wet and cluttered kitchen. Her flip-flops splashed water up her calves. She walked into the back spare bedroom she had made her office. A King James Version of the Bible sat on a shelf next to the collected works of Freud, and Strunk and White's *Elements of Style*. The Bible's golden lettering glittered to her that the words of Christ were in red. She pulled the black leather book off the shelf.

"What was that verse?" she yelled.

"Luke 17:32," Lovell said from behind her.

Suzanne yelped and almost dropped the book. The thin gilded pages fluttered as she regained her grasp on it. "Don't do that." She slapped him on his still bare chest. "After all this tonight, you could have a little sympathy."

"Sorry. So what does it say?"

Suzanne used the thumb index to open the Bible to Luke. She flipped until she reached the proper place. "Remember Lot's wife."

"What does that mean?"

Suzanne tossed her hand up casually. "I don't know. Isn't she the one that God turned into salt or something?"

"I told you it's been years since I went to church, but I remember somebody was turned into salt."

"I want to go back to the school," Suzanne said. "Something deep down inside me says that I just need to be there."

Lovell grinned and let the towel drop from around his waist. "I thought we might work off some more stress."

Suzanne's cheeks pulled up into the tiniest smile, but she shook her head. "I don't think so. Put on some clothes and you can go with me. I'm not sure I want to be there by myself."

His expression melted to a disappointed frown, and he nodded. She knew that going back to the school was the last thing he wanted to do. His face said more than that he was just disappointed by not having more sex. Uneasiness peaked out from his eyes. She figured the same thing might be sparkling in her own.

"Go on." She slapped him on his bare butt. "We've not got all night."

Lovell walked out of the room. She watched him, pulling the robe she wore tighter around her. Once he was gone, she walked across the hall into her bedroom to get dressed. Something comfortable was called for; today was going to be tough.

9

Remember Lot's wife

LUKE 17:32

SUZANNE SAT ON A church pew. The soft purple material of the cushion tickled her legs. Stained-glass light speckled everything as the outside street lamp shown through the windows. Church services ended hours before. Suzanne remembered that from a long time ago. She remembered everything, but the velvety feel of the pew cushion was real, as real as the man slipping through one of the doors that flanked the baptistery. Suzanne remembered him as a man, but now he seemed more of a boy.

Brother Bryan, the 22-year-old youth minister, sat down beside her. His sandy hair and blue eyes captivated her. Suzanne felt sixteen again. No, she *was* sixteen again and running on nothing but hormones and fear.

He touched her knee, then slid his hand higher and higher until he touched the upper part of her thigh. His hand bore small calluses that tickled. Suzanne broke out with goose bumps.

A sudden insight hit Suzanne as Brother Bryan began to take her. He had done this many times before with many other girls, not just in her congregation, but at all the ones he ministered and attended. She hadn't known that at the time. All she'd known then was Brother Bryan, with his gorgeous eyes and muscled body, loved only her. He told her so when he'd arranged the *rendezvous*.

Lightning streaked from the pulpit. It hit the pew Suzanne and Brother Bryan made love on. The wood cracked and split. The pew fell in two. Brother Bryan toppled backward, his naked body flailing through the strobe flashing of the tempest raging in the sanctuary. He fell into an inky abyss.

Suzanne watched, helpless to do anything. She wanted to scream, but when she did, thunder cracked and rumbled. The whole floor shook, and now she felt herself slipping from the fragments of the pew. Her feet slipped off, and she found herself falling into the same abyss Brother Bryan plummeted into.

The air blowing around her warmed her body. She became aware of her nudity. As the air rushed past, clothes like silk robes swaddled her. She kept falling, wanting to yell, but when her mouth opened, only thunder cracked. The lightning still flashed above in the distant cavern that was the church sanctuary. The air smelled less and less of the dusty hymnals in the pews and more like rain soaked dirt. The air cooled and even felt damp.

The silken garment the wind had woven around Suzanne suddenly felt harsh and itchy. She touched the toga, and burlap had replaced the silk. The smoky scene cleared away, and she stood in front of the Hassle's house. The pale yellow moonlight gave the old plantation house a jaundiced appearance. In the yellow glow, Suzanne saw a face staring down from the highest window just like the day she had visited. The face was different. She made out the features of Rachel glaring down at her. Rachel pointed to her. Somehow Suzanne could hear the girl's voice as if she stood next to her.

"That's her. She's the whore. See how she's covered with the blood," Rachel said in a liquid voice.

The door of the house burst open. Solomon charged out, followed by Esau and a multitude of red-haired men and women, none of which Suzanne recognized, but she knew they were all Solomon's children.

"Get the whore!" Rachel shouted from her window.

The hands of the Hassle family grasped Suzanne. They pawed at her burlap sack of a dress until she stood naked before them. Solomon walked around her so close she felt his hot breath on her neck. The burning smell of his rotten teeth wafted to her nose. His hard, callused hand touched the small of her back, slid to the buttocks, and squeezed.

"String her up, boys. This sow's sullied," Solomon said.

The gang dragged Suzanne from the front of the house to the back. She still felt Rachel looking at her from a high window. A lone sweet gum tree stood at the back next to the barbwire fence of a pasture. A sow, split open and devoid of internal organs hung from one large branch of the tree. Old pig's blood pooled at the base of the headless carcass.

"She squealed something fierce when we kilt her," Solomon said. "Ye reckon ye'll squeal as much when we string ya up?"

The crowd of Hassles snorted, themselves sounding like a herd of pigs. Then Suzanne saw what hung from the other large limb of the tree: a noose. She fought against them. They picked her up and slipped the noose around her neck. The hemp rope burned into the flesh of her neck.

"Maybe her head'll pop off, and we can make souse meat with it," Solomon said. "We'll have everything but the hog nuts."

The crowd chortled more. They even began to look like fattened hogs to Suzanne as she looked at them from the gallows made of two Hassle men holding her up.

"Let the whore go," Rachel cried from her window.

"Let her drop," Solomon said.

Suzanne felt the two men let go, and the sense of falling. The noose tightened, burning more into her neck. The rope became taut with a sharp jarring motion. Her ears echoed with the snorting laughter now sounding as if the crowd chanted "Remember Lot's wife." The words formed like smoke in front of her eyes, and Suzanne knew she was dying. As the rope snapped as tight as it would, she felt her body begin to slip away. Like watching a movie from the very first row, Suzanne saw her hanging naked body turn into salt, and crumble to the ground.

Her feet disintegrated, followed by her legs and torso. Then her neck disappeared leaving only her head to fall, which squeezed through the noose and joined the pile of salt on the ground.

Remember Lot's wife, echoed out as Solomon tossed handfuls of salt into the air and over his family. He baptized them with the salt that had been Suzanne. She saw it all as if floating away from everything. Suzanne felt safe as she drifted into the sky. As she looked down, Solomon glared up at her.

"No so fast, girly."

He reached up, his arm growing longer and longer until he grasped her disembodied spirit. She grabbed toward the sky as he pulled her to him. His mouth gaped open wide like a snake's mouth. Then he swallowed her. Suzanne screamed, but her words only echoed out through the cavern of Solomon's gut. She burned from digestive acids surrounding her, and salt rained down adding new injury to her wounds.

"Suzanne, are you all right?"

Suzanne startled awake and looked up to see Ms. Dodge framed in the office doorway.

"You're early," Ms. Dodge said.

"Well, I couldn't sleep with everything that's happened." Suzanne rubbed her stinging eyes.

"You sure you don't need to go home and try to get some sleep? You look like you've been ridden hard and put up wet."

"No, I'm fine." Suzanne yawned. "What time is it?"

"Six-thirty. I always get here at this time to get things ready for my day."

"But there's nothing to get ready for today."

Ms. Dodge smiled. "Old habits die hard."

"I got my Rolodex back and Warren got his missing permission slips returned."

"How?"

"Someone left them at his house. He brought them over to my place, and the strange thing was nothing was missing from them."

"That's strange." Ms. Dodge didn't sound the least concerned.

"Then someone in a green Chevy truck threw a cinder block through my kitchen window."

"Did you call the police?" She maintained her nonchalance.

"No, I figured I'd be seeing enough of them over the next few days that I would just tell Rusty or one of them then. I'd rather get this mystery about the school vandals dealt with before that. I think they might be the same anyway." Suzanne rubbed her eyes and imagined how dark and puffy they must look. "You go to church, don't you?"

"You could say that."

"Tell me about Lot's wife."

Ms. Dodge rubbed her chin in thought. "There's not much to tell. She and her husband and children lived in the city of Sodom. God told them to leave and not look back. She looked back and got turned into a pillar of salt."

"I thought that was her," Suzanne said.

"Why do you ask?"

"The cinder block that was thrown through my window had a Bible verse written on it that said, "Remember Lot's wife.'"

"That's sort of creepy, isn't it?" Ms. Dodge sounded in no way unnerved.

"What do you know about her husband, Lot?" Suzanne stood up from the secretary's chair and stretched her back.

"As much as is in the book of Genesis. He was Abraham's nephew who went to live in Sodom. After God told him to get out, he went to the mountains where his daughters slept with him and bore him children," Ms. Dodge said. "After that, he disappears."

"He had children with his daughters?" Suzanne's voice sounded a little disgusted.

"Yeah, they thought no one was left alive on earth, and they wanted their father to have heirs."

"Knock, knock," Lovell poked his head into the room.

"What's up?" Suzanne asked.

"I wasn't expecting Ms. Dodge to be here, but all the better. It'll give me another opinion about my question," Lovell said. "Do you think my class should still go on their field trip to the aquarium tomorrow?"

Suzanne sucked air through her teeth. "I don't know. School will probably stay canceled until sometime next week. Can you reschedule it?"

"No, I had to make the appointment the second day of school. They're booked until after Easter."

"What do you think, Becky? How do you think the parents will handle this?" Suzanne asked.

"I think it might be a good distraction for the students, but I think we should let the parents decide if they want their children to go or not," Ms. Dodge answered. Her voice was tinged with interest.

"I agree." Suzanne sat back into the creaking office chair the secretary had bought from K-mart during their last big blue light special. The particleboard of the seat pressed through the thin cushion. "Call all the parents you have a release for and see if they want their kids to go. Tell them that I'm going just for extra support."

"Do you want to go, Ms. Dodge?" Lovell asked.

Ms. Dodge jerked her head around so fast, Suzanne thought it might snap off. "No." The word came out like a chunk of iron. It was the first truly expressive comment she'd made so far.

"That's fine," Lovell said.

"I mean, someone should be here to help the cleanup crew and deputies with the investigations." Ms. Dodge looked at her watch. "I forgot to turn my oven off. I put a roast in and meant to take care of it before I left. I've got to run."

Ms. Dodge hurried out of the office. The main doors slammed shut as she apparently hurried from the building. Suzanne shook her head.

"That was weird. She said she wanted to get things started for the day."

"Maybe I scared her," Lovell said, playfully. "She might have felt all this sexual energy coming off me."

"Go on and call those parents. We've not got any more time for that kind of stuff right now." Suzanne waved her hand at him like a damsel waving a token handkerchief to a jousting knight.

Lovell grinned, showing off his prize dimples, and left. Suzanne turned back to the incident report she'd been trying to write before dozing off. Two sentences stared up at her, and the blankness of the page overwhelmed her.

The lunch bell rang, filling the empty hallways with its tinny clanging. Suzanne pushed the last batch of filing she needed to sign to one side. None of the teachers came to work today. Suzanne figured the fewer people running around while the deputies investigated, the better. The only problem was that the deputies had yet to show. With nothing left to sign, Suzanne decided to look at her office in the light of the day.

Suzanne stood and pushed the cheap desk chair back with her legs. It rolled across the tile and banged into the metal desk the secretary kept an old electric typewriter on. The dust of a year lay on the cover. Not a single key had been pushed since late last year. Suzanne shook her head at the outdated machine and walked to her office's door.

The inside of her office looked much the same as the night before. The ink pooled on her desk had started to dry around the edges, but the center of the pond remained as deep and viscous as ever. The blue ink on the rug had dried dark and almost black. Suzanne just stood in the doorway. She didn't want to walk in and disturb anything before the deputies got there, if they ever did. The sun from the window behind her desk caused a prism on the wall. Suzanne noticed that the heavy glass fleur-de-lis she won as teacher of the year in Choctaw County remained in one piece on her bookshelf. She smiled at it. The award showed what a good educator she was. She won it her first year out of college, and she would still be teaching there if she hadn't been pink-slipped because of not being tenured. Kosciusko County would never give her an award for excellence, especially since the school was in shambles. She sighed and reached to turn off the lights. A blue ink fingerprint stained the white wall next to the switch. Suzanne got so close to the print her nose almost touched the wall. She snapped her fingers and hurried into the outer office.

The intercom to the classrooms sat on a small wooden table beside the tardy and absent student filing cabinet. Suzanne grabbed the microphone and switched the toggle button for the special education classroom. The intercom system was almost as old as the bell system. A green light brightened over the number 45, the number for Lovell's classroom.

"Warren," Suzanne said into the mike.

"Yo?"

"Get up here, quick. I've got something to show you."

"Saw it last night."

"Stop that. I'm being serious; get up here."

Suzanne put the microphone back in its place and switched off the toggle button. She turned around to find Rusty poking his head into the office. A smear of barbecue sauce colored the corner of his mouth, and a half-smoked Camel rested behind his ear. He held his cap in his hand like a man creeping into church to ask for a hand out.

"It's about time you got here, Rusty," Suzanne said. "I've been waiting all morning."

"I have to sleep sometime, Principal Clay," he stood like one of her pupils who was about to get scolded.

"Drop that formal crap, Rusty, and put your hat back on. I don't want to stare at my reflection in your bald head. I've been up most of the night and reckon I don't look too good."

Rusty nodded and pulled his cap back on his head. He came all the way into the office. Suzanne flipped through the Rolodex that arrived back on her porch in the early morning. She found the card with the fingerprint on it and pulled it free of the plastic holder.

"Look at this." She handed it to Rusty with the print side up.

Rusty held it to his face. "It's a fingerprint."

"So you think it's a print too?"

"Of course, I can see the swirls."

Suzanne snatched the card from him. She looked at the maroon colored semicircle. Small, almost invisible, swirls cut through the color, but the crease she had seen last night was still there.

"It must have still been tacky when Warren touched it," she said. "I got my Rolodex back last night, and found that print, but there weren't swirls on it then."

"There are now. Maybe I should get some prints on Mr. Lovell."

"No, he was with me when the break in happened, and after I got the Rolodex." Suzanne put the card on her desk. "I know that he didn't toss a cinder block through my window last night."

"Someone did that? I can pick them up." Rusty wiped the barbecue sauce from the corner of his mouth. "Dang, Satanists."

"I don't know who for certain, all I know is that they drive an old green pick-up."

"A 1967 Chevy to be exact," Lovell said, walking into the room. "Nice for you show up, deputy."

"So, you saw someone in a 1967 green Chevy pick-up tossed a brick though Ms. Clay's window?" Rusty ignored Lovell's comment, but Suzanne could tell it was a strain to do so.

"It was a bed-load of kids," Lovell said. "I chased after them about half a block before they got enough speed on me."

"Why didn't you call us last night?" Rusty asked.

"Forgot," Suzanne said.

Lovell looked at Suzanne. "I think you said you had to show me something."

"Yeah, come look at this."

Suzanne escorted Lovell and Rusty into her office. She pointed to the blue fingerprints on the wall. Five oval-shaped blobs without swirls stained the drywall. Each of the blobs had a single crease across the middle.

"That looks like the stain on your Rolodex card," Lovell said.

"You mean that print you just showed me?" Rusty asked. "But there ain't any swirls."

"That's what I tried to tell you. The print didn't have a swirl until Warren touched it. The blood or whatever it was must have been tacky and left his print on the stain."

"I think I'll check out the rest of the building for more of those kinds of prints. If I find any, it will eliminate down suspects. There can't be that many people running around Marquisville without fingerprints," Rusty pulled out his note pad and pencil. He jotted something down.

"That's what I thought," Suzanne said. "I think I figured out one other thing too."

"What's that?"

"Kid's didn't do this," Suzanne said.

"How do you figure that?" Rusty asked.

"It's too clean for kids to have done it," Suzanne said.

"Pig crap slung everywhere is clean to you?" Rusty asked.

Suzanne shook her head. "I mean, kids would've torn the books up and destroyed teacher's grade books and personal property. None of that happened."

Rusty thought a moment and wrote some more in his notebook. "I didn't even think of that. You ought to become a police officer, Ms. Clay. You've got an eye for detail."

"Comes from being a principal. There's one other thing. I wish you'd talk to the Hassles. I just can't help but think they're part of this."

"I'm going to get with everybody." Rusty slipped out of the office like a man on a mission. "Even the Hassles if need be." His voice echoed back into the office.

Suzanne and Lovell stepped back into the outer office. She pulled her office door closed.

"Well, I called the parents about the field trip. About half think it's okay to go," Lovell said.

"So you think the van will do it?"

He shook his head. "One of the kids is Magan. We'll need the wheelchair accessible bus."

"I'll call Jack and tell him he's taking us to the aquarium."

Lovell grinned. "The kids'll be happy; they love Jack."

The phone chirped. Suzanne bent over the desk, letting her shirt ride up her side to give Lovell a bit of a show. She pushed the speakerphone button.

"Marquisville Middle School. Principal Clay speaking."

"The time of the prophecy is near. Remember Lot's wife," a croaky female voice said. "The children will bring about the new age."

"Who is this?" Suzanne answered, but the other line clicked. The disconnected sound hummed.

"I'll go and get Rusty. We need to tell him about this. Maybe he knows some secret way of tracing phone calls or something," Lovell said.

"Did that voice sound familiar to you?" Suzanne asked.

"Sounded like the caller from last night."

Suzanne felt that wasn't it. The voice almost seemed commonplace except for the added distortion.

"That's not it. I know that voice in some other way," she said. "Go get Rusty all the same."

10

Bringing in the sheaves,
Bringing in the sheaves
We shall come rejoicing,
bringing in the sheaves.

AMERICAN HYMN

SUZANNE PULLED INTO HER parking place by the school entrance. Only the half-sized bus and a few unfamiliar cars waited in the parking lot. Several parents and children stood under the awning at the entranceway. Lovell stood with them. He wore a maroon t-shirt with white writing on it. The front said, "Marquisville Middle School—Home of the Raccoons" and bore a white picture of the school's mascot, Bandit. He turned to talk to one of the parents and "Lovell" blared out in bold block lettering on his shoulders. Suzanne climbed out of her car and walked to the awning.

"Ms. Clay," Lovell said. "Everyone's almost here."

"Who's missing?" she asked.

"Magan's not gotten here yet, but she is usually a little late. It takes time to get her up and about," Lovell said.

"I like that t-shirt," Suzanne said.

"Good," Ty Arthur stood to the side of the other kids and parents. He smiled and reached into a cardboard box. "I've got you one, too."

He shook out a maroon t-shirt. The school's name and mascot smiled on the front. He turned it around to the backside, and "Clay" glared back in the same bold letter's as Lovell's shirt. Ty wadded the shirt into his fist and thrust it to

Suzanne. She took it and spread it out over her top.

"Thank you, Ty."

"No problem." He smiled and screwed his eyes up into his head. "Momma owns a t-shirt store. We made enough for everyone on the trip."

Suzanne then noticed that all the kids wore maroon t-shirts. She smiled at the fact that Ty had such a good idea.

"That way we're easy to find," Ty said.

"Because we all got the same shirts on," a petite girl said. Her hair was brown and in a pixie cut. "Ours just don't have our names on them."

"We didn't know who all was going, Marlene." Ty thought over each word before he spoke them.

"That's okay," Marlene's mom said with a thick New England accent. Suzanne thought they called it Downeast, but she wasn't sure. "No one expected t-shirts at all."

A large blue and white van pulled up to the awning and blew its horn. The melody played *Close to You*. The side door opened automatically, and Suzanne saw Magan sitting in her wheelchair fastened into position by two special seat belts. Her smiled beamed so bright it shined through the dimness of the van's passenger bay.

"I'm here," Magan said. "Sorry I'm late."

"No problem," Lovell said. "We wouldn't leave without you."

Suzanne folded her t-shirt over her arm. "I'm going to change into my shirt. That'll give Magan time to get out and into the bus."

"Sounds good," Lovell said. "Jack, crank her up."

Jack McAllen waved from the driver's side of the bus.

Suzanne saw the purple and black sleeve tattoo on his right arm. She never understood why people wanted something like that. Then she thought of the name scrolled on her ankle. She rubbed her foot over it and headed to the school's door. The bus' engine roared to life as she slipped into the school to change.

She left the office and stepped back under the awning. All the parents were gone, and the kids waved from the bus. Lovell sat behind Jack. Suzanne locked the door. Jack blew the horn. The students on the bus laughed, and she waved at them while walking to the open bus door. The familiar smell of a school bus washed over Suzanne as she took the big step up to it. The smell of rubber and vinyl seats mixed with the perfume of diesel fumes made her nostalgic for her days as a trumpet player in the marching band.

"You can sit back here by me, Principal Clay," Magan pointed to a lone seat beside her.

The girl's wheelchair was held in place by four nylon straps with metal clips on them sat against the back window. Each clip attached somewhere on her chair. Suzanne made her way down the short aisle and sat beside Magan.

"The only problem with sitting in the back," Magan said, "is that the ramp makes a lot noise."

Suzanne looked at the large metal grating that stood vertical to the right of the bus. A metal box with chains like those on a bicycle stood beside it. A red and green light was on top of the metal box. Currently the red beacon glowed. Suzanne expected the ride would be noisy, seeing at how loose the whole apparatus looked.

"Is everyone ready to go?" Jack yelled from the front.

The half dozen special ed students cheered back. Suzanne caught herself clapping too. There was nothing like taking a field trip, especially when the kids were this excited. It would help take her mind off the weirdness that had been happening. She needed that more than anything else.

Suzanne watched the road roll by out her window. They drove down what the locals called the Seven Swamp road. She hated this stretch of highway to Tuscaloosa. No shoulders flanked the road. The ribbon of asphalt ran on a built up causeway across a series of swamps that fed the Madiwapus River. She always imagined losing control of her car and veering off into the murky water where no one would find her. The off-key warbling of the students hummed around Suzanne. The name of the familiar tune and the words hid somewhere in her memory. Her fingers ached from gripping the seat in front of her.

"Are you okay?" Lovell asked.

Suzanne focused back on her surroundings in the bus. The children sang *Livin' on a Prayer*. Jack sang the loudest and most off-key.

"I was just daydreaming."

"Sure you weren't daymaring?"

"There's no such thing as that," Suzanne said. "Planning for the worst, yes, but daymaring, no."

"You ought to sing with us. I've noticed some of the kids looking back here at you expecting it. They look disappointed that you're not participating."

Suzanne looked at Magan, who swayed back and forth in her chair. She sang loud with a wide mouth and clenched eyes.

"They really look concerned."

The whine of the tires on the road quieted as the bus slowed down. Jack quit singing and held up his tattooed arm for the kids to stop too. Bon Jovi's greatest hits, the Marquisville version, ended with a few squeaky notes left in the air. The bus came to complete stop. Lovell turned and started back to the front.

"What's the matter, Jack?" he asked.

"There's a truck blocking the road," Jack said loud enough that Suzanne could hear him. "Look's like they're having some trouble."

Suzanne got up and made her way to the front of the bus. She patted each student she passed on the shoulder to let them know everything was okay. Lovell stood behind the driver's seat, and Suzanne paused beside him. She bent down to see out of the windshield. An old green pick-up sat cattycorner across the road. The hood stood up, and someone tinkered under it.

Jack reached for the door release. "I better see if they need help."

Suzanne clasped her hand over his to stop the door from opening. "Is that what I think it is, Warren?"

"That's it, the truck from the other night," Lovell replied.

"Get us out of here, Jack. Now," Suzanne let his hand go.

"I don't have a place to turn around," he answered.

"Drive backwards until you do." Suzanne couldn't keep her voice calm. She turned to head back down the aisle of the bus. "Kids we're going have to turn around and take another route. Don't worry though; we're still going to get to the aquarium."

The gears of the bus ground, and Suzanne had to catch her balance when the bus lurched back as Jack put the bus in reverse. She held onto the seat midway back as the bus picked up speed. They weaved a bit from side to side. She felt her gut cinch to.

"Not too fast there, Jack." She imagined the bus plunging into the swamp. The bus slowed and stopped. "But don't stop, either."

"Got to stop," Jack said loud enough for Suzanne to hear. "There's no place to go."

"Why?" Suzanne protested.

"Look out the back window," Lovell said.

Suzanne looked up. A log covered with muck and green slime had been pulled across the road. Her heart beat loudly enough for her to hear it over the kids' murmuring. Jack shifted gears to go forward again. The bus moved, and Suzanne tottered off balance as it pulled to the left lane. Lovell steadied her. His hand seemed firm and in command. She straightened up and peered out the window. All she could see were the trees set low in the swag below the road. The bus had to be stopped on the edge of the road embankment. The shoulder would undoubtedly drop off just past the wheels.

"All right, kids we're okay. Just a bit of a delay." Panic wanted to come out in her voice. Her nightmare of toppling off into the swamp seemed more likely than ever.

"Yeah, Mr. Jack and I are going to see what we can do about it," Lovell said.

"Do we have a CB?" Suzanne asked. "Cell phones don't work out here."

Before Lovell could turned to ask, something hard and heavy hit the right side of the bus. The children screamed, Lovell squatted down, and Suzanne twirled to look at where the blow came from. Another, heavier, blow rocked the bus to the left. The kids screamed more.

"Kids, settle down," Suzanne yelled, climbing over Ty to look out his window.

Three stout men stood outside the bus. One held a double-edged ax. The other two carried nothing. Each of the men had bright red hair and freckles all over them. The man with the ax looked up at Suzanne and smiled, a calm almost genial smile. His features were pleasant, with a strong, square jaw line and sparkling green eyes. He ran at the bus, swinging the ax over his head as he did. The blade hit the base of her window as he swung it down. The metal popped, and the ax blade stuck into the side of the bus.

"Everyone into the middle of the bus!" Suzanne yelled. "Get in the aisle and squat down or sit on your knees, and don't move until I tell you to."

"What about me?" Magan swung her head back and forth with spastic spurts.

"I'm coming." Suzanne hurried down the short aisle to the back of the bus. She crouched to keep her head as low as she could. Hands and rocks beat and pummeled the bus on both sides now. A spray of glass exploded behind Suzanne. Bits of it fell into her hair. Magan screamed. A thin line of blood rolled down the girl's cheek from a cut just under her eye. Suzanne got to Magan and unfastened the seatbelts that held the wheelchair in place. Suzanne took a moment to look out the other side of the bus. At least six red-haired men of different statures pummeled the bus with their fists or sticks. None looked angry, but instead like men in the middle of relaxing activity. A glance to the right side revealed that several more men had joined the attack.

"Roll on up to the middle," Suzanne told Magan. "You're going to be okay."

The girl pushed the joystick that moved her chair. It didn't move. "There's still a strap attached!" Magan said, with near panic in her voice.

Suzanne moved to release the missed strap just as the wheelchair ramp's door ripped open with a metallic tearing. A freckled hand reached in and groped at her. Red hair sprouted from the long fingers. They wrapped around her pant leg. Suzanne shook and kicked at the hand. Then it tightened around her ankle and tugged at her. She hit the floor hard. A sharp pain rose from the base of her spine.

"Warren! Somebody!"

She kicked at the hand, now with her other foot as well, but the strength of the man connected to the hand outmatched hers.

"Let the ramp down," Magan said, the words falsettoed with fright. "Just hit the green button, Ms. Clay."

In the struggle, Suzanne saw the glowing green button. She stretched as far as she could up the control panel and smashed it with the heel of her palm. The hydraulic-driven chain began to move, and the wheelchair ramp jerked into life. The chain hesitated, and the hydraulic motor strained. Suzanne felt the hand try to jerk her through the small gap between the bulkhead and the ramp. Then a sickening, wet pop sounded over the motor's whine. The pressure pulling against her stopped, and Suzanne scrambled to her feet. The lift eased down to its horizontal position. The man who had grabbed Suzanne lay on the ground a few feet from the ramp. A jet of blood shot into the air from the end of his arm. His hand, wrist, and bit of his arm were gone. Suzanne hit the green button again, and the ramp started to move back into its docking position.

As she began to hear the man with the gory arm scream, she looked at her leg. The hand and part of an arm still gripped her ankle. The elbow was shredded and splintered bones stuck out of it, yellow and bloody. The chain from the wheelchair lift had mangled the meat. Suzanne used her other foot to push the hand until it fell off. She kicked it like it was a roach. The numbness of shock washed over her as the children screamed louder and more blows rocked the bus to the side. She looked up and, through the softening vision of disbelief, saw Lovell tugging on the front door lever to get it closed. Jack's feet stuck up from over the metal wall that divided the front bench from the exit steps, then slipped away. Lovell popped the door lever shut and forced all his weight against it.

"Don't let them get in through the lift door," he yelled over the noise.

To Suzanne, his yell sounded like a whisper muffled in cotton. Everything seemed to fuzz over a bit: her hearing, her vision, her feelings. The door at the ramp slammed shut. Suzanne looked out the side. She saw the gang of goons lined up against the bus. They heaved against it, and the bus tilted to the left. The wheels hit hard back on the pavement. Her knees buckled, and she toppled to the floor. The hard rubber grooves dug into her knees. The bus horn blew. She saw Lovell struggle to his feet. The bus rocked back to the left. The momentum seemed ready to carry the bus over, but it landed back on its wheels.

"Ms. Clay, I'm still fastened by a strap," Magan yelled.

The terror in the girl's voice cleared Suzanne's head. She clambered back to the wheelchair and fumbled to unfasten the last strap. As her fingers probed for the release button, the bus reared up again, and this time continued over.

A strange feeling of vertigo overtook Suzanne. She remembered up-and-over rides at the fair. In a strange way, the giddy feeling of that machine washed over her. The right-side windows brightened as the sun beamed into them. The crashing and breaking of glass drowned out the kids' screaming. Bits of glass pummeled Suzanne's neck as she floated midair and slammed into the side of one of the seats.

Something grazed her hair. It felt hard and metallic. As the bus made another topsy-turvy motion, she realized Magan's wheelchair had barely missed pinning her against a seat while the bus rotated over. She felt the sensation of going airborne again as the bus made another revolution. The wheelchair pendulum swung away from her, leaving her free to bounce around the cabin. The bus finished rolling down the embankment. The top sank into the soft ground below the road. She landed on the ceiling between two seats. Bright lights sparkled in front of her yes. She struggled to shake it off.

"How is everyone?" she asked.

"I'm okay," Lovell answered.

Suzanne saw him pick himself up with his elbows from beneath the steering wheel's dashboard area. She started looking around at the kids. They moaned and grunted. Some started to stir around.

"How are you kids?" Suzanne asked.

"I think I'm hurt, bad," Magan struggled to speak.

Suzanne looked at the girl in the wheelchair. The black chair hung upside down by a single nylon strap. Magan's arm seemed to be pinned between it and the edge of a seat. Blood trickled from the girl's nose. Suzanne clambered to her feet and got closer to the chair. She tried to push the chair up, but it was too heavy.

"I need help," Suzanne strained against the wheelchair. "I can't get her down."

"We've got more problems than that," Lovell said.

Loud stomps rattled on the metal sides of the bus. The glass in the folding door shattered inward. The door was pulled to the side, and the red-haired man wielding the ax slid into the bus. The door at the ramp flopped open as well. Lovell started fighting with the intruder. Suzanne moved toward the ramp door. She crawled up the side as a crowbar broke the ramp. Another of the goons pushed the ramp up. A short, red haired man jumped into the bus like a rabid orangutan.

Suzanne saw the man with fiery red hair and freckled skin. His green eyes glared from deep in his sockets like jewels set into the eyes of an idol to a god of death. As soon as his feet hit the floor, he reached out for her and caught her with a strong grip.

"One of them's got me!" She pried at the green eyed monster's grasp.

The kids screamed. Suzanne struggled against her captor. She clawed at his face, drawing some blood. He roared and struck at her with a flattened palm. A sharp pain passed through her jaw as he made contact.

"Don't rough her up too much," the ax man said. "Daddy Sol wants them presentable."

"She done made me bleed, John Mark. Can't I just smack her around a little bit more?" the short Hassle said as he shored up his grip across Suzanne's chest.

"Ya can deal with Daddy Sol if ye do," John Mark said.

"All righty."

Suzanne wanted scream, but before she could, the short Hassle threw his hand over her mouth. She bit it hard. The taste of dirt and metal washed over her tongue. The little Hassle squealed and let her go. Without having to think twice about it, Suzanne ran down the length of the bus toward the front, but more men as wild as the two she dealt with had boarded the wreck. Each one of them grappled one of the kids. In the middle of all this, Esau loomed like a bad dream. He pointed toward Suzanne, but she realized his gaze went past her to Magan who still dangled upside down. The girl's screams had blended in with her own and all the other confusion going on aboard the bus. Suzanne turned to see John Mark pulling a knife out from his belt. He reached for the sole strap holding the wheel chair up.

"Help me!" Magan shrieked.

"No!" Suzanne rushed back toward the girl. All her terror wadded up in her gut.

It unfolded as the blade sliced through the nylon strap. Magan blurted out a last frantic scream as the chair fell. Suzanne stopped short as Magan and her chair came crashing down. The sound it made hitting the ceiling of the bus was like nothing Suzanne had ever heard—a meaty slam accompanied by metallic picks and boney cracks. The sight of a single white arm twisted at an unnatural angle from under the chair almost made Suzanne swoon.

"Get back a hold of that 'un, Levi," John Mark said. "I got to deal with the Yankee. Where's she at?"

The short Hassle grabbed Suzanne again. She forced the words up through the tightening in her throat. "We don't have any Yankees."

Suzanne looked at Esau, who shook his head in disagreement. He pulled on his beard and then ran his finger across his throat, the universal sign for killing. John Mark grabbed Suzanne's chin and pulled her face to him. His hands felt rough on her skin, but his eyes were like those of the rogue that stared out from a bodice-ripper novel. She felt a strange, gamy mixture of terror and attraction toward him.

"T'ain't goin' to ask ye again. Where's the Yankee?"

"What's a Yankee?" Marlene asked in her sweet New England tone. "I don't think we have anyone named Yankee."

"Thank ye, mightily, little Yankee," John Mark said and pushed past Suzanne and Levi to advance on the little girl.

"You will not hurt her." Suzanne jerked free.

She stepped into John Mark's path, fist clenched tightly and ready to fight for her life and the kids.

"Outta the way."

He knocked her aside. Suzanne lost her footing on some broken glass on the slick roof. She fell between two seats, and her head knocked against the side of the bus. Everything swam back and forth for a moment before her lights went out.

Suzanne blinked awake, but everything remained black. Her breath came back to her hot and sticky. She moved, but a rope tightened around her neck so she stayed still. Whimpers and low cries surrounded her. She sat in the bed of the idling Chevy.

"Who's there?" she asked.

"You're alive." Ty said in his drawn out way. "We thought they had killed you."

"Where are we?"

"In the back of a truck, still on the road."

Suzanne pushed up with her legs, and the rope around her neck dug in as she shifted. "Where's Mr. Lovell?"

"He's here with us, but I think he might be dead," Ty said. Suzanne didn't like that he kept his voice so calm. "They put that one who lost his hand on top of him."

Suzanne blinked hard. Tears seeped from them, partly from the dirt that scratched at her cornea, partly at the thought of Lovell being dead. A tight knot in her throat choked her. She set her teeth solid against each other until the knot slipped back down in her gut where she could manage it better. Numbness was a welcomed feeling when it came over her. At least with that in place, she wouldn't cry or whimper in front of the children. That was the last thing they needed. She needed to be their rock. Ropes tightened around her wrists as she tried to free her hands.

"What about Mr. Jack?"

Ty whispered. "They killed him, too."

Suzanne closed her eyes. She didn't know why, because nothing could be darker than the sack over her head. When she opened her eyes, a bit of dirt fell into one of them, and for the first time she noticed the musty, earthy smell of potatoes.

"Ty, can you get this sack off my head?"

The bright sunlight blinded Suzanne as the scratchy burlap sack cleared her head. Ty tossed it down beside him, and Suzanne took in the scene. Ty sat beside her with his long legs curled almost to his chin and his hands tied in front of him. She saw Amanda O'Mary slumped over and crying. Heather Summers sat beside Christopher Plum. Each tied to the other. As Ty had said, Lovell lay beneath the gray hulk of a man whose hand she had cut off. Lovell's face was turned to the wall of the truck bed.

"Where's Marlene?" Suzanne tried to keep from sounding frantic but feared that she failed to do so.

"Still in the bus," Ty said with his well-chosen diction.

Before Suzanne could say anything, the attackers started leaping in the bed of the truck. Two or three jumped on the fenders. Esau scurried from the side of the road where the bus had rolled off.

"I'm lightin' this thing up," John Mark yelled. "There's a car comin'. I can hears it."

Esau hurried past the bed of the truck. Suzanne heard him slam the driver's side door. She strained to see what was happening. The rope pulled and burned her neck. Smoke began to twirl from the bus. It rose high into the pale blue sky. Then a single tongue of flame lapped the air. The old pick-up roared to life. John Mark and Levi clambered up from the side of the road and jumped onto the truck. The rest of the

Hassle attackers climbed on as well. Several stood on the bumper, hanging onto the tailgate. A few more piled onto the fenders.

The blue exhaust floated into the truck bed with its acrid odor of gasoline. The gears ground, and the truck rolled forward. A short, impish looking man ran behind the truck. He jumped onto the bumper, clasped a hand on the tailgate, and waved his hand in a circle.

"Get going," he yelled in a high nasally voice.

Suzanne noticed that his lip split in two and that his teeth bucked out with a gap in them mirroring the gap in his lip. The truck sped up, forcing the hare-lipped imp to hold on with both hands to keep from falling off. Suzanne caught a glimpse of the bus as they sped down the road. The flames flared all around it, and the smell of burning petroleum wafted to her. No words came to her. She couldn't even cry out in anything more than babbles. Suzanne could remember Magan's twisted arm protruding from under the wheelchair. At least that little girl didn't have to burn alive and conscious. She hoped the Hassles killed Marlene before they burned them, but she doubted it.

A sharp horrible scream confirmed her doubts. The small girl's voice echoed through the hollows overtaking the noise of the truck. Suzanne had never heard anything like it. The closest she could compare it to was the sound of the pig squealing the day she'd been introduced to these subhuman Hassles. She was glad that the smell of the little girl roasting wouldn't waft to her. It was the sole solace of the situation because the children's faces did nothing but make things worse. The sheer look of innocent puzzlement forced the air out of her lungs like a sharp punch to the gut. Even worse was the smiling, laughing faces of the attackers. The hare-lip guffawed like a high-pitched donkey bray.

"Reckon Yankees sound lots like hogs, duttin' they?" he laughed.

John Mark sniffed at the air. "They smell like bacon too."

"Wish I could stay and watch," the harelip said.

Suzanne almost vomited right there. She forced herself not to by clenching her jaw as tight as she could. Nothing human could make such jokes about a dying child. Nothing. She focused all the mishmash of emotions inside her to portray the vision of strength to her kids. The truck took a sharp turn to the left and hit on a dirt causeway running through the swamp off the main road. Before she realized it, the truck with captives and captors rolled through big oaks with Spanish moss hanging from the branches like rotting flesh.

"Where are you taking us?" she yelled at the harelip.

"Don't ye worry none about that. Ye'll be findin' out soon enough," he answered, and gave a loud snorty laugh.

"Kids," Suzanne said loud enough for her students to hear but hopefully not enough for the captors. "I don't know what's going to happen, but I'm going to do everything I can to keep you safe."

The harelip kept guffawing, now sounding more and more like a goose. Suzanne closed her eyes again, preferring the darkness of her eyelids to the whizzing blur of greens and grays. The smell of the Hassles aided in the motion sickness that was developing. The scent of half-rotten cabbage, onions, and mud surrounded her. Occasionally, the pungent, ferric scent of blood would rise on the air as well. The mental images of Magan and Marlene in the bus slowly turning black rolled her stomach even more. She was going to be sick despite best efforts.

11

For destruction and violence
are before me;
and there is strife
and contention riseth up.

HABAKKUK 1:3 (ASV)

AFTER LISTENING TO THE kids sobbing for what seemed like hours, Suzanne opened her eyes. The truck bounced up and down, and the rope around her neck seared like rug burn. Her insides felt just as hot from all the friction of tumbling feelings of horror, pain, and disbelief. She could only imagine what floated around in the heads of her students. They couldn't understand things as she did, which must be far scarier than what she was experiencing. She had to do something. Suzanne opened her mouth to speak, but the only thing that came out was a tiny squeak only she could hear over the noise of the wind and the truck. She cleared her throat pushed down the thick lump blocking her ability to speak and tried again, focusing all the energy she could to project stability for her kids.

"Guys, let's sing to take our minds off what's happened," Suzanne said, ignoring the fact that their kidnappers surrounded them and the tiny quiver in her voice. "What do you want to sing?"

None of the kids answered. They kept sucking back sobs and snot. Suzanne looked to Ty, but he kept his head down. She could see the red rims around his eyes. No one wanted to sing, but she needed to keep control.

"You were singing *Livin' on a Prayer* in the bus, how about that?" There couldn't be more truth in that song title than right now. Suzanne would have prayed but was too terrified to even try.

Still the kids said nothing, so Suzanne started the song at the chorus, mainly because it was the only part she knew. The song had been popular when she was a kid, and she had no idea how this bunch knew it. She sang alone.

"You've got a pretty voice," the hare-lipped Hassle yelled over the rush of wind and roar of the V8. "Sounds like an angel, don't she, John Mark."

"Sure do," John Mark clung to the tailgate of the truck. Locks of flowing orange hair blew in all directions like flames trailing the truck. "She's about as pretty as one too. I even bet she feels like one on the inside."

He reached toward her, but his arms stopped well short of touching her face. Suzanne turned her head in disgust as best she could with the rope around her neck. The harelip snorted. "I guess she ain't interested in ye, purty boy."

"Hush your gab, 'Grippa, ain't like she got eyes for somethin' like you. Teeth bucked out of yer split lip," John Mark said.

"I'll split your lip, just as soon as we get home."

A thunderous bang issued from the rear window of the truck. The force of the blow bounced Suzanne forward causing the rope to tighten around her neck. A scratchy gasp escaped her, making her throat raw. The truck stopped, and Suzanne saw Esau get out of the cab. He jerked John Mark off the fender and shoved Agrippa to the ground. Esau grabbed them both by the front of their blue chambray shirts and pulled them to their feet. He nodded toward John Mark and let go of Agrippa long enough to pull on his beard.

"We's know what Daddy Sol said. Ain't none of them supposed to be touched except that gimpy one and the Yankee," John Mark said, as if reading Esau's mind.

Esau let them go. Agrippa angrily tugged at the front of his shirt. John Mark climbed onto the fender in submission. The hulky giant pointed to Agrippa's lip and then spread his finger apart. The hare-lip covered his mouth with his hand, looking very much like a chastised child. Then Esau turned to John Mark and made the same gesture. The handsome man hunched over letting his flowing hair fall over his face.

"I'd figure ye'd be madder than a wet hen at that woman. She killed yer brother. Pulled his hand clear off like it wasn't nothin'," Agrippa sneered after recovering.

Esau pointed to himself and then to Agrippa.

Agrippa nodded. "But Israel was yer twin."

Esau shook his head and pulled his beard. Then he pointed to Suzanne with his thumb. It was like a jab in the eye. She didn't like the gesture at all. It worried her even more than the fears for her and the children's safety.

"He said, it don't matter none. Daddy Sol will handle you," John Mark looked up at Suzanne with an evil little smile.

Esau turned to get back into the truck. He pointed to John Mark and Agrippa. His thumb poked into his chest and then he flicked his ears. Suzanne got the impression he was telling them he could hear very well. After all he heard over the noise of the truck and road, she figured he might be able to hear thoughts.

The giant Hassle climbed back into the truck and slammed the door. Suzanne eased herself back to relieve the pressure on her neck. Agrippa stepped back onto the bumper, looked at her and ran his tongue out between the gap in his lips. She kept her revulsion to herself. A lump of pure disgust settled midway in her gullet making her throat ache on top of burn. The truck roared to life again, and with the grinding of the gears the trip continued.

"Guys," Suzanne said, swallowing the knot of disgust and not caring if the Hassles heard her or not. "If you heard what John Mark said, they can't do anything else to us."

"Until we's get home," Agrippa said. "Then we's do whatever Daddy Sol says."

The kids stopped whimpering, but Suzanne began to worry more. Lovell laid beneath Israel, Solomon's son, who she'd killed. She was close enough to him to feel the warmth of Lovell's breath and knew he was unconscious, but alive. Even though she'd killed Israel trying to save her own life, Suzanne didn't know what Solomon might do, or let his *children* do to her or the kids.

As the truck kept rolling down the road kicking up dust, she felt the eyes of all the Hassles boring into her. Suzanne's lungs ached for breath as panic started to creep up her spine. The kids didn't need to see her lose it, but she had to get free. The ropes scraped at her wrists as she wrestled with the bindings to get loose, making sure to keep the movements small. The last thing any of them needed was for the Hassles to catch her. When she thought of the horrors that those red-haired beasts might do to them, her breath hitched inside of her. She stopped squirming with the ropes long enough to gulp down two quick breathes and then ease several long slow drinks of fresh air through her nose. The Hassles might control the situation, but she wouldn't allow herself to lose control of emotions, no matter how tightly panic coiled itself around her.

After what seemed like another hour of bouncing up and down on rutted roads, Suzanne felt the truck stop. Her butt tingled from numbness. The constant vibration and bumps had put it asleep a long time ago. The Hassles clambered off the fenders and bumper of the truck. The tailgate fell down with a metallic thud. John Mark and another of the red-headed kidnappers grabbed the ankles of the dead man lying atop Lovell. Even though Suzanne knew the dead body was Esau's twin, the two looked nothing alike. The dead man was long and lean with a small amount of hair on his visible body. Israel's body slid out of the truck's bed, and Suzanne heard a heavy meaty thump as his corpse hit the ground.

"What ya want us to do with Israel?" Agrippa asked Esau as he came around the side of the truck. Suzanne strained to see him.

The mountain of a man looked down at his dead brother with red-rimmed eyes setting off the deep green of the irises. He blinked hard, and then pointed off into the distance. Agrippa took Israel's body by the shoulders and hauled him up as high as he could. John Mark took the legs. The dead man swayed in the middle as the two carried him away. Esau grabbed Lovell by the ankles and dragged him half out of the truck. With a huff, he heaved the dead weight onto his shoulder. Esau jabbed his index finger at Levi then pulled on his beard. After this, the massive man waved his hand toward

Suzanne and the children and pointed toward a weathered shack.

"He's sayin' fer ye to get up and follow him. No funny business or ye'll get skinned alive," Levi said. "I's going to tell Daddy Sol, y'all's here."

Suzanne watched Esau as he walked back to the side where Ty sat. Lovell's head hung midway down the giant's torso. Esau patted Ty on the back and shoved his thumb into the air. The kids stood up. Suzanne could tell their legs had gone to sleep like her butt. They stretched them and padded to the back of the truck. Ty hopped down first and helped the others despite his tied hands. Esau stared at Suzanne. His eyes told her everything she needed to know. It was like he telepathically told her to get out too because Lovell wasn't getting any lighter.

"I'm still tied to the truck," Suzanne said, stretching out her neck to show the rope better.

Esau nodded and brought up a large-bladed knife from a belt holster. Suzanne felt the tip of the blade against her neck. Her stomach knotted in response. With a quick upward motion, the rope split in two and fell from her neck.

Suzanne touched the rope burns. Even the lightest touch sent shocks of pain up her neck. Esau jacked his thumb back into the air as if to say, *get out*.

Suzanne stood up. She stretched and clambered over the side of the truck. A glance at Lovell found his chest rising and falling against Esau. He *was* still alive, which was a relief. Esau put his free hand on her shoulder and pushed her toward the front of the truck. She looked up and saw a shack made of gray boards. A rusty tin roof sat atop of it. The door had a heavy chain and lock on it. It looked about twelve foot square with no visible window on the side Suzanne stared at.

"That's where we're going?" Suzanne eyed the building suspiciously.

Esau nodded his head and led the way.

The kids rested against the back wall of the small shack. Ty's legs stuck straight in front of him, taking up almost half of the floor space to the door. The boy had too much leg length for this shack, Suzanne thought, as she stood over Lovell. He lay on his back with his head resting on the hard packed dirt floor.

"It's hot in here," Amanda fanned with her hand.

Suzanne looked at her. The edges of the girl's bangs were wet, making her chestnut hair a shade darker. Sweat either beaded on the other kids' faces or slicked their hair down. Suzanne stepped over Lovell. A small shuttered window was in the wall to the left of the door. Nothing seemed to hold the shutter in place. She walked to the window and opened it up.

A waft of cool air hit her in the face. The smell of a working farm did as well. The afternoon light flooded the dark shack with its orange light. Suzanne could almost feel freedom in the beams. She reached her arm through the window. Her skin burned as she did so. Pulling her arm back, she noticed that it crossed over a latticework of barbed wire crisscrossing the window's opening. Her arm had two short parallel scratches down it.

"You didn't think they'd make it that easy did you?"

Suzanne turned. Lovell looked at her. He propped himself up on his elbows, but trembled from the effort.

"Lay back down," she said. "You might have a concussion or something. The last thing I need is you getting sick and vomiting everywhere."

"Is Mr. Lovell going to puke?" Heather asked. "If he is, I'll puke too. I can't stand the smell of puke."

"I'm fine, Heather. Ms. Clay is just being fussy," Lovell said, his voice showing exhaustion.

Suzanne stepped back across the room, dodging Ty's gangly legs, to Lovell's side. She knelt and pushed him back to the supine position.

"We can't take a chance like that. You were out for a long time."

"I already have a headache," Lovell said. "This hard dirt isn't helping anything."

Suzanne sat down beside him and crossed her legs Indian-style. Lovell lifted his head. She helped him turn so he could rest on her lap.

"Is that better?"

"Thank you," Lovell said.

"Ms. Clay, what are they going to do to us?" Chris asked.

"I don't know," Suzanne said, "but I won't let anything bad happen to you. I promise."

Comfort seemed to take over Chris' face. Suzanne was happy to see that, but she wasn't sure she could keep her word. She hadn't been able to stop them from being kidnapped.

"Did you hear that?" Chris whispered to Heather. "Ms. Clay said we're going to be okay."

Suzanne closed her eyes and leaned her head back, a mixture of shame and anxiety brimming. Now at least one of the kids had his hopes up, but when the Hassles came for them, Chris would be heartbroken and might not trust her from that point on.

"I didn't quite say that, Chris. I said I'll try to keep bad things from happening. I can't make promises that I'll be successful."

Chris nodded like he understood, but Suzanne doubted it. Of all the kids, she worried about him the most. He wasn't as bright as the others. The chain on the other side of the door rattled. Suzanne lifted Lovell's head and placed it on the ground. She popped to her feet with ease, an old cheerleading trick she could still use. The door opened, and Solomon stepped inside, leaning on his cane like he had a serious limp. He smiled at seeing them.

"After the looks of poor ole Israel, I figured y'all'd be torn to pieces," Solomon said.

Suzanne let a smirk of disgust cross her lips. "We aren't as good as we look."

"What's the matter with him?" Solomon said, pointing to Lovell with his walking stick.

"I think he might have a concussion," Suzanne said.

Lovell sat up, then stood. He wobbled a bit as he steadied himself. A step toward Solomon set him off balance again, but he recovered. "I'm just fine." He smiled at Solomon. "It's going to take more than a couple of your boys to keep me down. My truck got rolled over by an IED in Afghanistan. I had a serious concussion, but was fighting three days later. Esau isn't anything compared with that."

Solomon huffed a laughed. "Strong boy. I like that. Ye'll do well with us."

Suzanne eyed Lovell. He had a hard time keeping his balance. She walked to him and let him lean against her, just enough so Solomon shouldn't notice.

"If you've come to mock us, we can do without it," Suzanne shot daggers at Solomon as she spoke.

"I came to see how beat up y'all was." He eyed her neck. "Got a nasty rope burn, Ms. Clay." He looked Lovell up and down again. "Reckon, I'll send Haddie in here to ya'll." He whistled as if for a dog, and Esau stepped inside. "Go get yer Auntie Haddie. Tell her she gots some doctorin' to do."

Esau nodded and left. Solomon relaxed. He looked like he would fall if not propped up by his stick. His smile remained.

"Go ahead and lay back down, Mr. Lovell. You've proven to me that yer tough."

"I don't have to prove anything to you," Lovell said. "I'm going to sit down anyway."

Suzanne helped Lovell back to the floor, but she kept standing. A glance behind her found the kids still seated against the far wall. They looked scared but not terrified.

"What now?" she asked.

"Well, Haddie's goin' to look at yern and make sure nothing's wrong."

"Who is Haddie?" Lovell asked.

"The family nurse for right now," Solomon said. "She's getting a bit dotty in her old age, and she's always been contrary."

"And after she comes?" Suzanne asked.

"We start teachin' ye."

"Teaching us what?" Lovell asked skeptically.

"About our ways, and the plan of God and Father Lot," Solomon said. "Y'all's a big part of what's goin' happen. As soon as Rachel is with child, the new age begins. The last of days," Solomon said. His voice took on the pitch and cadence of a television evangelist.

"You kidnapped us for that?" Suzanne asked. Her mind raced just a little bit as panic tried to surge back inside her.

"No, y'all's here to help fulfill all the prophecy. Rachel's child alone cannot save our people. Father Lot said others had to be used to purify the blood."

"Are you going to kill us?" Heather squeaked, her brow knitted in worry.

"What good would that do?" Solomon said.

"As sacrifices, like Abraham did to Isaac," Heather responded.

Solomon laughed a long deep laugh that ended in a hacking cough. He broke something free from his lungs and hocked it onto the hard floor. Yellowy-orange phlegm pooled there. "No, God and Father Lot don't want no human sacrifices. That's why Abraham found that ram. We's goin' use y'all for somethin' else. I's glad that at least one of these young'uns knows somethin' of the book."

A bent woman came into the shack. She carried a black leather satchel the size of an overnight bag. Her gray hair rested on top of her head in a bun. The skin on her face folded in wrinkles with the largest ones disappearing into her mouth. Her sunken cheeks attested to her lack of teeth.

"So why'd ye call me in here?" she asked Solomon.

"These is our new family members. The boys might've roughed them up a bit. I need ye to check them out," Solomon said. He turned to Suzanne. "This is my sister, Hadassie."

"Hadassah," the old lady corrected, putting stress on the last syllable. "They don't all look that new, but I got it from here. Ye can go back to yer other business now."

She sat the black bag on the ground and pushed Solomon toward the door. He stepped out, and Esau started to close the door.

"Don't do that. I need the light," Hadassah said.

"I can't leave the door unlocked," Solomon answered. "They's might escape."

"Leave Esau, but keep that door opened," she ordered.

Solomon agreed with a huff and a glance towards Esau, who stepped up to block the exit. Hadassah went to the kids first. She squatted down beside Ty. He cowered away from her when she started to touch him on the neck and face. Suzanne told him to let her.

"You're a nurse?" Suzanne asked as Hadassah examined Heather.

"Not no formal one, no," she answered. "I did some care of the soldiers back in WWII."

"But Solomon said you were the family's nurse," Lovell said.

"I'm the closest they got. I keep everybody in the family runnin', 'ncludin' the animals." Hadassah walked from Chris to Suzanne.

The old woman's fingers felt cold on the hot skin of her neck. They prodded and probed over the rope burn. Hadassah put her face close to Suzanne's. She could smell the rank breath of the woman.

"I'm okay except for that rope burn," Suzanne said.

"I reckon so," Hadassah said. She moved to Lovell, who still sat on the ground. "What's yer problem?"

"Headache and nausea."

"Dizzy any?"

He nodded his agreement.

"Esau knocked ye on the head?"

Lovell nodded his agreement again, wincing with the movement. Hadassah nodded as well. She walked to her bag and took out a small pill bottle. Two small white tablets fell out into her hand. She gave them to Lovell.

"What are these? I'm not taking any strange drug from you people," he said.

"Ain't no strange pill," she said. "Not every Hassle on this hill's out to get ya."

Lovell let the tablets sit in his hand. He stared at them and then looked to the nurse.

"They's aspirin. Ain't goin' help with the nausea, but they'll stop the headache." She reached back into her bag and brought out two dried leaves. "Chew on these. They'll help quiet that stomach."

Lovell dry swallowed the two tablets. He grimaced as he chewed on the leaves. Suzanne looked back at Hadassah. The old woman fumbled inside her bag and closed it. She picked it up.

"I reckon that's all y'all need," Hadassah said. "Pity y'all ended up here at 'all."

"What do you mean?" Suzanne sensed the old woman had a secondary meaning.

Hadassah reached up to pull the door closed. Esau stepped up to block her.

"Get on back, boy," she said. "I's got to do some private doctorin'. Nobody needs to see these folks naked, especially ya."

Esau moved away, eyeing the old woman with a fierce stare as Hadassah closed the door. The room dimmed to the soft late afternoon glow through the window. Suzanne waited as Hadassah took her time turning back to them.

"Solomon's tryin' to bring about a prophecy what was never made by no angel," she said, hushed and with an air of anger. "Our family's plagued by barrenness. We've been that way for years."

"You can't have children?" Suzanne asked.

"Only a few of us can, but I ain't one, thank God."

"So what does that have to do with us?" Lovell asked.

"When animals get too much inbred blood in them, they's start throwin' problems into their young'uns. Sames true for men."

"You're really inbred?" Suzanne tried to hide her disgust.

"Every last one of us." Hadassah took a pink bottle from her bag. She handed it to Lovell. "Just remembered that I had some bismuth. It'll help that nausea better than them leaves."

"I'm okay." He handed her the bottle back.

The old woman shrugged her shoulders. "Suit yerself."

"Why kidnap us?" Suzanne asked.

"He's goin' have y'all bred to the ones who can has children. Y'all goin' purify the blood, so to speak."

"He's going to rape us?" Suzanne forgot the kids were in the room.

Heather whimpered out. Suzanne went to her and patted her on the head.

"He ain't goin' to call it that, but if he has to, then yes. Keepin' people trapped ain't nothing to him. He's been tryin' to bring about his prophecy for ages. Been keeping me here for years too. Might have had a normal life otherwise."

The door swung open, and Solomon stepped inside. His face bore a harsh look on it. "Ye done yet, Hadassie?"

"Just finishin' up." She looked at Lovell. "Ye best take it easy for a spell, or ye'll have more trouble with that head a hurtin'"

Hadassah nodded to Suzanne and walked passed Solomon. She didn't try to hide the look of contempt on her face as she passed him. He seemed to bare the same feelings for her.

"So you're going to rape us?" Suzanne asked, hand on her hip and head cocked in defiance.

"Is that what she told ya'll?" Solomon said with his face hardening more. "Ain't the case. Y'all are going to mate with my family to get rid of the bad blood. Father Lot foretold it to my great granddaddy through his angel."

"I refuse," Suzanne said, crossing her arms and shifting her feet.

"Lord's will be done. Nothin' can stop that."

"I'll try my best," Lovell said.

"Ye can't do nothin'. Yer gimpy from one run in with my boys. Another one'd kill ye."

A sharp knock cracked at the doorjamb. Solomon turned, and Suzanne saw John Mark carrying a plank with tin plates on it. A fat red haired woman followed him. She carried a string with tin cups hanging from it and a large tin pitcher. The first whiff of the food on the tin plates wafted to Suzanne.

It smelled good, which surprised her. Her stomach had been doing somersaults since the attack, but now she noticed how hungry she was. Her mouth even watered.

John Mark eased to a squat and sat the plank on the ground. The plates stayed in place the whole time. The fat woman shoved the pitcher to Esau, who stepped inside, then took a cup from the string. She handed them out to everyone. Each time she jabbed them like she meant to stab the person to death with the cup.

"Hold yer cup up if you want something to drink," she said in a baritone voice.

"What is it?" Chris asked. "I'm not allowed to drink coke."

"Ain't coke, boy. It's milk fresh from the cow's teat," the woman answered. "Like it or lump it."

The kids held out their cups. Suzanne waved for them to put their cups down before Esau could pour anything into them.

"How do we know you aren't going to poison us?" Suzanne asked.

"Why would I poison you? I just told ye about how we need ya'll, and that Father Lot hisself is protectin' y'a'll," Solomon said. "Go ahead young'uns and get ya some milk."

The kids held out their cups. Each one trembled as Esau tipped the pitcher and thick, creamy milk poured out. Suzanne took Lovell's cup and held it out with hers. Both were filled. She handed his back to him.

Heather spit the milk out. "This tastes funny."

"Yeah," Chris let his mouthful spill from his mouth and down the front of his face and shirt.

"Wipe your mouth," Lovell said, a grin peeking out, despite their situation.

Chris took the tail of his shirt and wiped the milk from his face.

"I guess y'all is used to that store-bought milk," Solomon said. "Well, that came straight from the cow's teat. It ain't going' to taste the same, but nothing's wrong with it. Ain't nothing wrong with this supper Sheba fixed for y'all either."

"Just the ham steak from that hog we kilt the other day that's all. Of course the freshest peas too." Sheba spoke with a sharp, acidic tone. Suzanne knew she wasn't happy about cooking for them. "Ways I see it, y'all should eat like the rest of us."

"Quiet yerself, Sheba." Solomon drew back his hand. "Or I'll give ye one right across the jowl. Ya ain't so fat that you wouldn't feel it, and don't think I won't just cause yer husband's a standing here neither."

Sheba backed out the door keeping her head low and avoiding eye contact with Solomon. John Mark sulked out as well. Esau tramped out the door, bending over to keep from hitting his head. Solomon hobbled back to the door.

"I promise ye's safe here. No one's going to do a thing to ya. That food's safe and so's the milk. I'll be back by 'n by."

Solomon walked out and pulled the door closed. The light in the room dwindled by half.

"I guess I'll play lunchroom lady," Suzanne said, moving to the plates.

"There aren't any forks," Ty said as he took a plate from Suzanne.

"Guess we'll eat with our fingers," she said.

"But they're nasty," Chris said. "Momma said don't eat with nasty hands."

"You're momma's not here, Chris. If you want to eat, you'll have to use dirty fingers. It won't kill you," Lovell said, sliding to sitting position.

Suzanne handed out all the plates, and then started to eat her own. Everything tasted even better than her own grandmother's cooking, but she still had to force the stuff down. Even if her grandmother had cooked the food, nothing would sit well on her stomach right now. She almost wished Hadassah had left her bottle of bismuth.

A pile of tin plates sat near the door of the shack. Six tin cups surrounded the pile. The glow of early evening left the room in a dusky light. Suzanne sat with her back against the far wall. She studied the window, the door, and the walls. The hard packed dirt floor seemed to end just at the base of the walls. Suzanne wondered how long it would take to dig out from under them. Lovell sat beside her. He rubbed the bridge of his nose.

"They did a job on me," he said. "I think I'll be sore for days."

"Do you think the kids are okay?"

Lovell looked at his students. They played tic-tac-toe in the dust of the floor. Suzanne noticed that they seemed to look to Ty as their leader. He seemed to be the most outgoing of them.

"I think they'll be fine as long as we stay strong," Lovell answered.

"Even after seeing Jack killed, and Magan and Marlene burned up?" Suzanne's throat tightened with memories of Magan dangling upside down, panic on her small face. The oily stench of diesel smoke seemed to circle around her again.

"They'll have some issues, but I meant okay for right now. I thought that's what you meant."

Suzanne stood up. She walked to the window. "I guess it was."

She looked out at the darkening woods. Sweet gum trees marked the boundary between the home place and the copse. Wild privet sprawled out from under the shade of the gums. The shrubs' evergreen leaves blocked the view into the thicket. Suzanne wished the barbed wire didn't crisscross the window. The odds of the group making out through the woods seemed better than waiting for what Solomon had coming. He promised no harm. The word rape must have been torn out of his dictionary, if Solomon thought it wasn't harm. Of course, Suzanne didn't trust him, much less his brood.

"Plannin' yer escape?" John Mark popped up from underneath the window like an adolescent boy trying to scare his crush.

Suzanne screamed and stumbled backward. Magan's killer snorted a high-pitched laugh. The lock on the door rattled and thudded to the ground. More light filled the room as the door swung open. Suzanne backed up against the wall as the kids scurried to her. Sheba stepped in carrying a silver serving tray. John Mark followed her.

"See y'all had no trouble eatin' those ham steaks," Sheba said, looking at the empty plates. "Or choking down that milk the young'un whined about."

"Thank you," Suzanne's heart still thumped from John Mark's surprise. "You're a good cook."

"Hear that Purty? I's a good cook." Sheba smacked John Mark on the back. "Ain't that gettin' there?"

"She's just as sweet as an angel." He flapped his hands like wings. "Y'ought to heared her singin' in the truck."

"Don't ye be gettin' no idees, Purty," Sheba said.

He and Sheba walked to the group. John Mark reached out and touched Heather's curls, and then brushed his hand over Amanda's rosy cheek, a lustful smile turning up his cheeks. Sheba cut her eyes at him and then stood in front of Lovell almost straddling him.

"I just can't wait 'til we get a crack at these pretty 'uns," John Mark stared straight at Suzanne. He ran his tongue out between his lips. "Solomon paired me with this 'un. Good at poppin' out the babies; ain't much to look at though." He glanced over at Sheba. "Man needs something to look at as well as rut."

"I told ye not to be getting' no idees."

Lovell struggled to get to his feet. Sheba put her foot on his chest and kept it there, letting the hem of her long skirt rest mid-calf. She tossed the silver tray to John Mark. He flicked his tongue at Suzanne again and walked to the empty plates.

Sheba pulled the tail of her blouse out of the waistband of her skirt. She lifted the shirt until her white cellulite-pocked belly fell free and jiggled it. "Ye best be glad I ain't birthin' babies no more, or I'd put a hurtin' on ye lil' man. Might still, to spite Purty over there." She pushed Lovell back down with her foot. He pulled his head as far from her as he could. Suzanne imagined if he had been a turtle, he would have hidden it in his shell.

John Mark piled the plates and cups on the tray. "Come on, Sheba. Daddy Sol be comin' around soon, and we don't want him to catch us with 'em."

The fat woman eyed Suzanne. The look was like an ice cube sliding down her spine. Sheba would like to kill her right then and there, Suzanne knew it.

"Best not do nothin' with my man," Sheba told Suzanne. "I'll make sure to get ye back. Ya hear me."

"Don't worry about that," Suzanne said, trying hard to keep the utter disgust and surprise out of her voice. The idea that these people thought that they might actually *want* to have sex with them almost dumbfounded her, even if John Mark exuded some rugged handsomeness with chiseled features and what appeared to be a well muscled body. Suzanne understood where the look she'd been given came from. Jealousy, in this case, really was a green eyed monster. For someone like Sheba, John Mark was the catch of a lifetime.

"Come on now, Sheba," John Mark said. "Daddy Sol ain't in no mood tonight."

Sheba nodded, and they walked outside. The door slammed shut, and the lock was secured. Suzanne let out a long sigh. She put her palm to her mouth to muffle the sob she knew would come. The children didn't need to hear that. John Mark's face appeared at the window again.

"Sleep well. Y'all be needin' it," he said and snorted a hearty laugh.

The child murderer's face stayed in Suzanne's mind. Religious prophecy wasn't driving him. He was horny. She didn't understand fanaticism, but she understood lust. Enough men in her life had made bad decisions following that emotion that she understood the power she had at her advantage. Her womanly wiles might come in handy. She just hoped that there was enough time.

12

Behold, I will send you
Elijah the prophet
before the coming of
the great and dreadful
day of the Lord

MALACHI 4:5

DARKNESS FILLED THE CABIN sometime after they ate supper. The darkness stifled Suzanne. Her lungs burned as if she'd been holding her breath too long. The darkness felt like drowning.

Suzanne felt Lovell beside her. His arm just touched hers. She heard his deep breathing, the breathing of sleep. Somewhere in the dark, one of the kids moved. They sounded like they slept too. She was the only one awake in cabin, maybe on the whole farm. Never before had Suzanne wanted to know the time so much. If she knew the minute and hour, things would be better. Her lungs would fill with oxygen and everything would dry up. She gasped for air, feeling like it was all she could do.

"Are you okay?" Lovell asked.

"You're awake?"

"I've just been resting my eyes is all," he said.

"As if I could see your eyes in this darkness." Suzanne took a long breath in through her mouth and let it out slowly through her nose as if she just took a drag off a cigarette. "It's drowning me."

"What's drowning you?" Lovell stirred beside her. Somehow she knew he was propped up on his elbows.

"The darkness. All of this. It's suffocating me." Suzanne put her hand on Lovell's.

"You can't drown in light," Lovell said. "You need to work on your metaphors."

Suzanne took her hand away. She felt her ire rise with the warm flushing of her face. "Do you think this is funny? Do you?" Lovell said nothing. "Well?"

"Of course not. I was just—"

"Just what, being an . . ." Suzanne thought of the kids against the wall lost in the stifling blackness. "A-hole?"

"Are you still drowning?"

"What?"

"Do you still feel like you're going to suffocate in this darkness?" Lovell asked with a calm voice.

"What kind of stupid question is that?" Suzanne felt her ability to maintain her anger slipping away. "I'm just about ready to start screaming."

"Then my job is finished," Lovell said.

Suzanne knew he was smiling. She felt the balance in the room shift as his lips curled up. He'd made her mad on purpose, so she wouldn't panic. Everything seemed to return to normal. Her breathing trimmed out, and her lungs quit burning.

"Where did you learn that trick, Mr. Lovell?" she said with a mixture of sarcasm and thankfulness.

"Around."

"Around where, your frat house?"

"Kandahar. If you want to talk about overwhelming, imagine this kind of darkness and feeling of dread along with mortar explosions and small arms fire zipping over your head. Sometimes the only way to not freak out was to get angry."

He whistled through his teeth making it sound like what Suzanne had heard bullets do in movies when they whizzed past someone's head. "I got good at ticking people off to save their lives." He made another bullet-whizzing whistle, and then a mock explosion. "You can thank me later."

"Wow, Mr. Lovell," Ty said. "You make good sound effects."

Lovell chuckled. "Thanks. I wish I didn't know how they sounded though. It means I got shot at."

"Cool," Ty said with a great amount of awe in the words. "Are you a war hero?"

Suzanne waited for Lovell to chuckle again and lie to them, but he paused a long time. She counted off in her head sixty-Mississippi. Still Lovell remained silent.

"Are you going to answer him?" she asked.

"No, Ty, I wasn't anything close to a hero." His voice sobered the mood again. "I'm sorry to disappoint you."

Suzanne heard the hidden pain in his voice and put her hand back on his. "That's okay. I feel a lot better knowing you're here with us. We've got a better chance of making it out of here with you around."

"Thank you." Some of the gaiety returned to Lovell's voice.

"Well, ain't that sweet?" The nasally voice of Agrippa came from the window, making Suzanne jump.

A thin beam of light flashed into the room. It was orange, and the smell of oily kerosene smoke filled the air. Suzanne saw the burning bus again in her mind's eye. Magan lay crushed under her wheelchair, and Marlene screamed as she burned to death. The light disappeared, and the door lock clanked. Two beams of the flame light entered the room as the door swung open. Agrippa and Esau stepped inside. The smell of onions and wet dogs filled the air. It mixed with the kerosene smoke into a powerful aroma.

"What do you want?" Lovell asked.

Suzanne felt him stand up beside her. She got to her feet as well.

"No need to square off, Warren," Solomon said as he stepped into the light from behind his sons. "We ain't here to fight."

"So what are you here for?" Suzanne asked.

"To be hospitable," he answered, long and drawled. "We can't be thought of as unpleasant hosts. If our Father Lot's uncle hadn't taken in those mysterious men, then none of us might be here at all."

"You don't make any sense, Mr. Hassle," Suzanne said. "You come in here hours ago and tell us you're going to rape us, and now, you're offering us hospitality?"

"We's offered nothin' but hospitality since y'all got here," Solomon punctuated his words with barely constrained anger.

"So you're bringing us king-size beds?" Lovell asked.

Agrippa snorted a laugh. "Ain't bringin' *ye* nothin'."

"Thank ya, 'Grippa. Ye've said enough already," Solomon slapped him across the face with enough force to make blood trickle from his lip. The old man seemed to quiver with pent up rage. "Our company's goin' to think we's all rude."

The hare-lip touched the blood and appeared to want to cradle his wound, but he didn't.

"Kidnapping people isn't usually considered friendly," Suzanne said.

"Ya keep usin' that *word*, Miss Clay," Solomon said, his nostrils flared in and out. "Ain't nobody been kidnapped. You's been brought here by God's will and the grace of our Father Lot. Now as part of that divine measure, you, Miss Clay, and the children are coming to the big house with my boys and me. We've got good rooms all set up for ya'll, and something a little special."

"What about Mr. Lovell? We're not going anywhere without him," Suzanne said.

"He'll be stayin' here, and yes, y'all's coming without him. I hate for somethin' ill to befall yer wards," Solomon squeezed his fist.

"I have a feeling your *little special something* is going to do that anyway," Suzanne said. "I demand you tell me what your intentions are toward me and my students."

"Ye ain't got no authority to be makin' demands of any-one, missy," Solomon said, loud and firm. "Ye ain't dealin' with Solomon Hassle on this one. You's dealin' with God Almighty, hisself, and ye best not forget that. He's made special arrangements for y'uns to be here. Nothin' goin' change that I'm afeared."

Suzanne felt trapped. Her mind started to activate all the symptoms of panic again. Her legs turned to lead, and a tinny quality started to enter everyone's voices.

"So we got us a deal?" Solomon asked, the rage seeming to seep from him.

Her answer danced in the back of her cavernous mind. It took an eternity for it to leave her parietal lobe and exit her mouth. "Yes."

"Good." Solomon's voice became jolly like a grandfather's

again. "Young'un's, y'all and Miss Clay come with us." He paused as Esau stepped out the door. "Somebody'll be around to deal with you later, Warren."

Suzanne sat in the large parlor of the big house. A kerosene lamp chandelier hung over a large plank table. The oily yellow light cast deep shadows over the room. Esau had spirited the kids up the stairs away from her. Solomon had made some polite chitchat then said he would come back in a few minutes. Agrippa had locked the doors from the outside, so she sat there waiting for someone to come in or something to happen.

The big house made noises of its own. The timbers groaned under foot, and upstairs the floorboards popped and creaked as people walked across them. The kerosene lamps hissed and sizzled. Someone coughed upstairs, not once but many times. It ended with a long hack that sounded like phlegm was brought up. Somewhere something whimpered. Suzanne didn't know if it was a dog or a human or something else. She didn't want to know.

The stinging odor of the kerosene smoke gave her a headache. The pain seared from her sinuses up behind her eyes and into her forehead. She wondered if the windows of her bedroom would be latticed with barbed wire. The size of the house, as she had seen it, promised that some nook or cranny of an escape route would show itself.

The windows in this room didn't seem to have anything over them except the louvered shutters. If they left her sitting here too much longer, Suzanne thought that she might try to get out one of those. The kids and Lovell would still be here, but she might get help to them faster without dragging them through the woods to get to the road. She twitched in her seat, antsy to toss her chair at the shutters and make her way out the broken window like the Indian at the end of *One Flew Over the Cuckoo's Nest*. The Hassles' house couldn't be considered too far from that place.

"Lookin' a bit antsy, Ms. Clay."

Solomon's voice from the shadows that edged the room drained all the hope Suzanne built up fantasizing about her escape. Her shoulders sank, and she sat still, staring at the walls and not saying anything back. He moved around in the darkness just at the edge of her vision. Only a passing shadow marked his movements. For some reason, Suzanne thought of the quote from *Macbeth* when the titular character finds out about his wife's death. *Life is but a walking shadow . . . A tale told by an idiot full of sound and fury.* Solomon was the walking shadow that strutted and fretted on the stage, but she was afraid he wasn't just going to pop out of existence when the lights came on like any other good shadow, and his sound and fury signified far more than nothing. He might be the embodiment of her death.

"Silence ain't goin' make me go away," Solomon said, stepping into the light.

He carried a red hardbound book with him. Suzanne could make out *The Bible* on the spine. The gold lettering had flaked off. He placed the book on the table before her.

"That's a Bible," he said.

"I'd never guessed," Suzanne wanted every word to sting.

"I didn't know if ye was familiar with one or not," Solomon pulled a chair out from beside her at the table and sat. "Ain't one of them like ya might have at yer church in the pew, though. This is a special Bible."

"Has it been blessed by you?"

"By God, hisself. This book is holier than any Bible, ye've ever seen. It's got the last testament in it. The last book of prophecy given to man by God."

"So it's got the *Book of Mormon* in it," Suzanne said.

A sharp stinging pain smacked her in the face. Her cheek tingled as she realized that Solomon had slapped her. He didn't even seem to move. With wide eyes and a knitted brow, she rubbed her jaw. It felt hot from the hit.

"God nor I won't stand for no sass mouth," Solomon said. His words sizzled with hate and fury. "That Bible has the *Book of Lot* in it, as given to my great-grand daddy by the angel, Hazariel."

He reached and flipped the book to the back. Suzanne took her hand away from her face as he did so, to prepare to block any more punches he might throw at her. Instead, he tapped his finger on a section of text that looked glued into the back of the Bible. The thick, pulpy paper looked old and yellowed. The words imprinted by an old typewriter. Some letters were only partially printed on the page because of an ink ribbon getting old. The very top of this pasted apocryphal text said: THE BOOK OF LOT.

"That's what you live by? That's why you've kidnapped me and the kids, and brought us up to this God-forsaken place?" Suzanne expected another hand to pop her for being blasphemous, but she couldn't hide her contempt and exasperation.

"How right ye is, and ye don't even know it." Solomon lowered and shook his head. The dandruff danced in the beams of kerosene light. "God is angry with us. We's been draggin' our feet too long. I seen the signs. I ignored them."

Suzanne almost felt sorry for him. He seemed on the verge of breaking down in real tears of anguish. Her hand went out on instinct to comfort him, but she brought it back to her almost as quickly.

"I waited a year after Rachel's time of blood to have her seek the savior. A year! God struck us not two months after her blood. He let the hill behind the house burn with fire from heaven, just like he warned in Amos. Still, I did nothing." Solomon nodded his head. His voice seemed on the verge of crying or roaring in rage. Suzanne wasn't sure which one, but each seemed just as frightening as the other. "I got the picture when He let our best barn be consumed not three months ago."

"Fire from heaven?" Suzanne said.

"A great storm came, and lightning hit a tree. The rest went from there."

"But storms happen all the time. I don't think that was a sign from God that you had to kidnap a bunch of special education students."

"Yer blasphemous tongue's goin' get ye in trouble." Anger rose in his voice. "God told through his prophecy that our family would be saved from the blight of blood when a daughter name Rachel found the savior. She did it."

"She had sex with a boy in a bathroom," Suzanne wanted to get the old man's ire up. "She just got her rocks off. Nothing holy or prophetic about that."

Solomon shot up. His chair toppled over backwards. "Whore of Babylon!" Spittle flew from his mouth. "As we speak a new member is nestled in Rachel's belly. So tis written in the book that after the seed is planted, God will send the one who will cleanse this family and the world. But that boy, the father, ain't the chosen one."

"So who is?" She pulled back startled but tried hard not to show how startled she was.

"Ye are, Miss Clay. Ye's to bring about the cleansing. From yer loins the new family will be born." Solomon lunged forward, jabbing his finger into Suzanne's chest. "In the past I tried to bring all this about before the time was right. I forgot that it was written, 'be not ignorant, God needs no mortal help.' I was ignorant to think I was doing the providence of God. It has caused me many pains. Now's different. I knows ye is the one."

"If I'm the one, why kidnap the kids?" Her body felt tight like a spring ready to pop.

"Takes more than one to cleanse the blood, so says the book. All must take the seed or spread it to cure our plague." Solomon let out a breath and seemed to loosen up a bit. "'Many plants can grow from many seeds planted in a few soils.'"

Suzanne stood to meet Solomon toe-to-toe. Anger welled up in her so much she felt like she could take him down without any help. No kook and his strange beliefs were going to get her or her kids molested.

"You're crazy and so is that book that your crazy granddaddy wrote."

Solomon's hand caught Suzanne under her jaw. The force of the blow toppled her backwards to the floor. Green and blue stars danced in her vision. He slapped the chair she sat in to the side, sliding across the floor before it smashed into the wall. The force splintered the wood. Suzanne stared, stunned by the strength of this once feeble-seeming man.

"You's protected from the rain of death that God's given us to bring on the unbelievers because ye and those young'uns are here to help the savior. Otherwise, I'd tear yer tongue out and shove it in your baby hole," Solomon said. He reached down and grabbed Suzanne by the wrist of the arm she held up to block him, jerking her to her feet. "I hope for yer sake, after ye read this book that ye come to an understanding with God and Father Lot. Otherwise, ye in for a rude awakening."

Solomon snatched the Bible from the table and shoved it into Suzanne's gut. She lost her breath from the blow.

"Believe ye me, ifin' that book didn't lay out exactly who ye are, I'd let the boys kill ye on that bus. Ye'll read all about how the chosen one will be the Whore of Babylon, the Harlot of the Kingdom of Clay foretold in a dream to Nebuchadnezzar. She'll have known many men, the last being a soldier." Solomon pushed the book deeper into her gut not allowing her to catch her breath. Her lungs began to burn. "Sound familiar?"

"The phone calls?" she croaked.

"We had to test ye according to the prophecy. We had to make sure ye'd do the right things when told of the words therein," he answered.

Suzanne closed her eyes against the lust for air, and the pressure on her abdomen subsided. Before she caught her breath again, the old man disappeared back into the darkness, ranting the whole time and slamming his fists into the walls.

She stood alone in the large room and listened to the heavy footsteps of someone coming in from behind her. She hoped that whoever it was wasn't about to kill her.

13

There's a book
which surpasses the sages,
And the glory
that gleams from its pages,
No splendor of earth
can outshine

HYMN

SUZANNE TOOK A DEEP breath and turned to face whoever came up behind her. Agrippa tramped in from the darkness. He walked flat-footed in heavy boots. Suzanne almost laughed at the relief of seeing the harelip instead of the giant.

"I thought Esau was sneaking up on me."

"I gets that sometimes, cause of these boots I wear. They make a lot of noise when I walk, 'specially on wooden floors."

Suzanne took notice of his footwear. His boots had three inch platforms as soles. She thought about how short he must have been without them. The argument he had at the truck when she and the others were kidnapped made sense. He was self-conscious of his height too.

"I guess Solomon's got you to show me to my room?"

Agrippa didn't answer. He stood illuminated by the lamps just at the edge of the shadows. His eyes squinted, and the tip of his tongue stuck out of the side of his mouth. Suzanne thought he was drooling like a dog about to eat something tasty. She moved backward. Another chair from the table she'd sat at scooted across the floor making a high-pitched screeching sound until it toppled to the floor. She pressed against the table, willing the whole thing to slide, but nothing moved except Agrippa who drew closer. He became more ravenous-looking with every step. His eyes widened. Lust gleamed in his shamrock eyes. The kerosene-lamplight flickered around in them making his intents even more known.

"You're taking me to my room, right?" Suzanne tried hard to not let her voice break from fear.

"Naw, we's goin' do this right here against the table."

Agrippa grabbed Suzanne and twisted her around to face the table. He pressed her down over a chair. The low wooden back dug into her rib cage just under her breasts. A rough, callused hand slid under her t-shirt and approached the latch on her bra. The other hand kept her pressed down against the chair. She put her hands on the tabletop and pushed up with all the effort she had. Nothing happened. She didn't have enough leverage. The one probing hand fumbled with the fastener of her bra.

"Too dumb to figure that out?" Suzanne asked. If she couldn't budge him off her, she'd get in whatever jabs she could.

"No matter of that."

Agrippa moved his hand to the front of her bra. He began pawing at her right breast, trying to free it from her lacy undergarment. Suzanne felt his hot breath on the back of her neck as he pressed in closer in his attempt to excavate her breast from her bra. He pressed into her so much that she felt the bulge of his lust against her leg.

Suzanne gave another thrust up with all her strength, as his callused hand pulled her breast free. Her effort did little, and his rough palm scratched over her nipple as he groped her.

"We's gonna have us a good time. I bet ye buck like real filly."

Agrippa pinched her nipple and twisted. Suzanne yelled from the pain. She wriggled her leg to get leverage and planted the heel of her foot into Agrippa's shin. The pressure against her back lifted, and the rough hand exited her shirt as he toppled over backward.

Suzanne straightened and twisted around. Agrippa lay on his back holding his smarting shin. She drew her foot back to kick him in his bulge, but before she could let it fly, Solomon came back into the room. His cane clicked quickly against the floorboards.

"What's goin' on in here?" he asked.

Suzanne paused with her foot behind her, panting from the struggle. She looked at Solomon and lowered her foot down to balance. "Ask your boy here."

"Ye heard me," Solomon said.

Agrippa said nothing. He kept his leg pulled close to him, and his mouth closed. Solomon whacked Agrippa's other shin with his cane. The crack of wood on bone echoed through the house.

"Answer me, boy. Don't act like yer stupider than what ye are."

"Wasn't nothing, Daddy Sol. We's just havin' some fun." Agrippa now favored his other leg.

"He wasn't doing anything more than you told him to," Suzanne said.

"Was he tryin' to know ye?"

"Yeah, he tried to rape me."

Solomon kicked Agrippa in the ribs. The younger Hassle yelped, and Solomon kicked him again.

"I's just tryin' to get the prophecy goin'," Agrippa began to cry.

"Ain't yer place to do that. Besides, this woman ain't for the likes of ye. She's got pure blood and ain't goin' to be mated to ye. One of ye cousins is good enough for that split-lipped blood that runs in yer veins." Solomon kicked Agrippa once more. "Get out of here before I have Esau get a hold of ye."

"Ain't goin' to do no such thing," Agrippa said. "I knows for a fact Esau's gettin' to do what I's tryin' for."

Solomon cracked the harelip across the shoulder with his cane. "I ain't tellin' ye again. Ya don't have to worry over Esau. He's doin' his part of the prophecy. The time ain't right for the chosen one yet. Even if it t'was, ye ain't no part of it."

Agrippa clambered to his feet and scuttled off into the darkness toward the back of the house as Solomon raised his cane for another blow. Suzanne didn't feel safe by any means, but she felt better. Solomon didn't seem the type who would try to rape her, but Agrippa said that Esau was.

"You promised nothing would happen to the kids." Suzanne reached into her shirt and put her breast back into her bra. She didn't want to risk enticing him, just in case. "Now I find out you're letting Esau rape them."

Solomon shook his head and looked liked a forlorn father disappointed with his prodigal daughter. "My word's my bond. Esau ain't doin' nothing to them young'uns. 'Grippa's just jealous of his older brothers. He's always been that way." He scratched at his beard and flakes danced down to the ground. "Now that Israel's dead, he probably expected to take his place. Ain't nobody who could take that'uns place. Ifin' he hadn't been no free bleeder, he'd still be here with us. I suppose it's just another of God's punishments for me." He shook his head. "I've been the patriarch a long time. I should know better."

Suzanne almost told the aged Hassle that she was sorry for his loss, but she remembered that *she* had killed Israel. Even more, she remembered that Esau was still out there doing something to someone.

"So what is Esau doing?"

Solomon looked at her for a few moments before answering, as if he was thinking of what to say. "Teachin' yer Mr. Lovell."

"Teaching him what?"

"Same as I's been tryin' to teach you, and what Jonathan's teachin' them young'uns, The Book of Lot and the prophecy of the Savior." Solomon took the Bible off the table and handed it to Suzanne. "Reckon you should read it fer yerself. Probably be better than me tryin' to explain it all to ye."

Suzanne took the book. The hardbound cover felt damp and warm, humid from the old man's hand. Solomon put his hand under her arm and pulled her toward him. She felt like pulling against him, but the touch didn't seem lustful or malicious. It seemed almost grandfatherly.

"I'm takin' ye to yer room. That way ye can read in some comfort."

Suzanne pulled her arm away from him but followed him up the creaking, popping stairs to the second floor. The hallway was dark except for flickering lamplight coming from a room at the far end. That's where they ended up, a decent sized room with a single window.

"I'll be checkin' on ye, by 'n by." He walked through the doorway. "The time of prophecy will come in three days after the Feast of Purification."

Solomon pulled the door to. Suzanne breathed in the stale, kerosene-perfumed air. She walked to the window and opened it. Barbed wire latticed the opening just like the window in the shack. The Hassles had thought of everything. The fresh air came in freely though, which helped relieve the weariness of the room.

Everything in her new cell seemed like it was out of some old movie. A ceramic washbasin and pitcher sat in a wooden rack against the far wall. A brass bedstead with what looked like a cotton-batting mattress rested against the wall opposite the window. A large washtub sat on the floor close to the window. A tall circle framework stood over the tub; a curtain hung from the top of the frame. A porcelain vase sat in the dark corner, almost unnoticeable, as any good chamber pot should be. The flickering light came from a lamp suspended from the ceiling too high for her to move without standing on something.

Suzanne turned the Bible over in her hands. She sat on the bed and turned to the back where the pulpy Book of Lot was pasted. Memories from her childhood played hide-and-seek with her as she tried to remember the story of Lot. She hoped not knowing it didn't matter as she started reading the section of the book.

Lot, the cousin of Abram, who was called Abraham by God, passed down this new prophecy to his children, the descendants of Lot. This seemed to be a dedication of some kind. Suzanne flipped to another section of the Bible. She fumbled with the pages until she came to the start of "Acts of the Apostles." No introduction started this book, just the first verse. She turned farther back. "Hosea" didn't have an introduction either. Her memory hadn't played her wrong. It seemed that no *real* books of the Bible had an introduction. She returned to the Book of Lot: *Ye are my children; ye are the children of Lot. Thou hath come from the loins of my flesh and the flesh of my daughters. Here be the generations.*

Suzanne began reading down the page. Ben-Ami started the list of begets. As she read, the names became more bizarre and harder to read until she came to the end of the genealogy. *Zebulun begat Earnest who in turn begat Thomas who had two sons Robert and William. Robert was struck down by the devil in the great war, but William was fruitful and multiplied. He begat Simon, Richard, and Charles. Richard the son of William received this prophecy for his good work fighting the evil of Satan in the great war. He was fruitful and multiplied. He bore Simeon, Ruben, Ahab, and Saul by his sister Maggie. By his daughter Laura, he begat Thaddeus, Adam, and Joseph.*

Suzanne put the book down. She rubbed her eyes. The Book of Lot seemed to encourage incest. A new fear crept up in her. She'd thought that Solomon was just blowing smoke, trying to play to some sick part of a person that lets people have freedom of religion, but this was serious. She fought down the urge to run out of the door and take on the whole bunch to keep her and the kids safe. Something made her start reading again.

And of these, Simeon begat Solomon, who became the preacher. Suzanne closed the book and sat it beside her on the bed. A lump formed in her throat. The last line of the genealogy had been written with a pencil in a shaky hand. It was the same shaky hand that had signed an excuse for Rachel. Solomon completed his family's genealogy. Suzanne knew that she

needed a plan to get out of there. She got up and walked to the
door. It was locked, and she was stuck for the night.

"I should sleep on it."

Suzanne pushed the Bible off the bed and lay down. Her
mind raced. After a long while playing out different escape
scenarios, she dozed off.

A sharp pain in her ribs woke Suzanne up. The light of morning shone into her eyes. It caused her to have green and red
floaters. She rubbed her eyes to clear them.

"Get up, woman," Agrippa's voice said with no sympathy.

Suzanne rolled over and saw the harelip staring down at
her. Nothing of his lecherous look remained. He had hate and
worry in his eyes, probably left over from his belittling by his
father last night. He grabbed her by the arm and jerked her
up. Suzanne got to her feet. The force made her shoulder hurt,
and his fingers kept digging into her bicep. It felt as if they
would pull the muscle from her bone.

"I'm up. Let me go. You're hurting me."

She hated to admit something like that to him, but she
had no choice. He let her go. She shook off the pressure that
still lingered after his vice-like grip subsided.

"What is your problem?" Suzanne asked.

"Daddy Sol told me to get ya up in a hurry. He also said ya
better keep yer mouth shut."

"I don't understand. Tell me what's going on, or I'm not
going to cooperate."

"Well, Miss Clay, Daddy Sol gave me special permission

to keep ya shut up any way I want."

Agrippa's face changed. Suzanne watched his eyes look her up and down. He stuck his tongue between the gap in his lip. His old lecherous look had returned. Suzanne felt the lust pulsing off the man. He kneaded the air with his hands as if he kneaded her breast again.

"All right. I'll cooperate."

"Good. Come with me, and don't try nothin' funny or," Agrippa looked her over again and grinned.

He pushed Suzanne in front of him as they walked through the door. Every door opening to the corridor stood wide open. The morning light shined in through the windows of those rooms. The hallway looked friendlier now with the new light. Suzanne didn't feel much comfort because every single room was empty. If the kids had been on this floor with her, Solomon had them moved earlier. She paused and tried to see into one of the rooms. Agrippa pushed hard on her shoulder.

"Keep movin'. We ain't got much time."

"Why not?"

"Ain't got to answer no questions." Agrippa shoved Suzanne hard enough that she stumbled forward.

She caught herself before she fell down. Agrippa grabbed her arm again. He squeezed hard, and she flinched. Now, Suzanne found herself not pushed down the remainder of the hall but pulled. He started down the grand staircase. Suzanne tumbled over her own feet as she started down.

"Slow down, or I'm going to fall," Suzanne said.

"Don't care. Ain't nothin' to me if ya do. Daddy Sol told me to get ya down to the cellar and that's what I'm going to do. I'll drag ye, carry ye, or ifin' I need to, hump ye down there." Agrippa kept tugging on her arm. He stepped onto the floor of the entranceway. "Daddy Sol said whatever it takes. I's good at causing pain, too."

Suzanne reached out and took hold of the railing and got her footing just before Agrippa gave her a stiff tug. She skipped the last step and landed hard on the floor of the entranceway.

"Just point the way, and I'll go," Suzanne said. "No more games, I promise."

"That might be the first sensible thing ye've did since ye got here," Solomon's voice came from behind the stairs.

He walked around to Suzanne's line of sight. She felt relief when he shooed Agrippa away.

"The steps to the cellar are right there." Solomon pointed to where he came from. "Ye'll find all yer young'uns down there waitin' for ye."

"Can I ask why we're being put into the cellar?" Suzanne asked.

"No ye can't. I ain't got time right now, but ye'll know soon enough," Solomon said.

He put his hand on Suzanne's shoulder and pushed her to the area under the stairs. She turned and walked toward the shadows. Her eyes adjusted to the darkness, and she saw a set of stairs disappearing into the floor. The front door burst open, and Esau charged in. A hammer dangled from a loop on his pants. The giant slammed his meaty index finger into his palm, twice.

"Get in that cellar," Solomon said, shoving Suzanne.

She stumbled and fell, scuttling into the shadows. Solomon turned and headed to the door. Esau followed him. Suzanne crawled to the edge of the grand staircase. She crouched there, trying to keep herself out of view if Solomon or Esau turned around.

Suzanne could hear the sound of a car pulling up to the house. The brakes squeaked a bit as the car stopped. Esau stood framed in the door. He glanced back over his shoulder. Suzanne shrunk down to let the risers of the stairs hide her. He turned back around, and she felt safe for the moment.

"Can I help ye?" Solomon said loud enough for Suzanne and whoever was in the car to hear.

Someone answered him back. Suzanne could tell it was a male voice but nothing else.

"Lookin' for a busload of young'uns?" Solomon apparently repeated back what was said to him. "Ain't seen no busload of nothin' come by here. How 'bout you, Esau?"

Esau shook his head.

Suzanne licked her lips. Someone had come to find them. She bounced on her heels. The porch steps creaked. Suzanne wished Esau wasn't blocking her view.

"Do you mind if I look around, mister?" The visitor's voice commanded authority, Suzanne thought.

"My name is Solomon Hassle, and I reckon ain't nothin' here for you to find, except me and my kinfolk."

Esau stepped back into the entranceway. Suzanne ducked back down. She pressed herself against the risers. Out of the corner of her eye, she watched Solomon walk in followed by a tall, black man in a gray and blue state trooper uniform. He took his hat off and held it at his side.

"What's up there?" he asked.

"Just bedrooms, mostly," Solomon answered.

"How many people live in this house?" The trooper stepped closer to Suzanne's side of the stairs.

"We's a big family. So big not all of us can stay in the house. We've got some places out back."

The trooper made a noise to say he was listening. He walked a step closer. Suzanne waited. The trooper took a baby step closer to where she hid. His free hand rested on the butt of his service-issue .9mm. She sprang up and turned full to face the trooper, throwing up her hands.

"I'm Suzanne Clay, principal of Marquisville Middle School," she shouted. "The kids are in the cellar."

"Shut her up!" Solomon roared.

Esau stepped toward her. He grabbed for her, but she moved away, his meaty hand grasping the hammer hanging from his pants. Suzanne moved to the trooper. He freed his pistol from the holster and turned on Solomon.

"I think you might have some explaining to do, Mr. Hassle," he said.

"I reckon I do," Solomon said. "Now let's not get all hot headed."

"Don't listen to him, officer," Suzanne said. "Shoot him. Shoot him before he can do anything."

A loud crack echoed across the entry hall. The trooper's hat fell free from his hand as he crumpled to the floor. Blood began to spread across the dusty hardwood planks. Suzanne looked at Solomon. He stood stone still. His lips disappeared into a thin line hidden in his mass of beard. The trooper's hand slapped her ankle, and she screamed. His whole body convulsed two more times before he lay still in his own seeping blood. His pistol lay at her feet. She bent down grasping for it not knowing if she could even use the thing.

"Stop her, boy," Solomon yelled.

As her fingers brushed the texture of the pistol's grip, Suzanne felt a crushing grasp on her shoulder. She saw Esau standing beside her. He held his hammer in his hand. A bit of dark red gore dripped from it. He smiled. The top of his front teeth were black. Esau nudged his head toward Suzanne, and he shook the gory tool at her. She looked at the old man as Esau forced her to stand upright again. His glower burned into her. A snarl curled his lip up.

"It's temptin' to let you bash her brains in, but toss her in the cellar with them young'uns. Then get 'Grippa, John Mark, and a few of the others to deal with this darkie and his car. Take it up the main road a stretch and make it look like he died in an accident. Use lots of fire, and don't let 'Grippa fool around with his body none. Remember it needs to look like an accident." Solomon kicked the trooper as he reached out and took Suzanne by the chin. "We's goin' to have us a real conversation, missy. You's goin' to regret ever doin' that."

Solomon let Suzanne's chin drop. Esau dragged her away from the trooper. The next thing she realized she was being tossed down a short flight of steps into a dark, dank root cellar. The whole room smelled earthy, and she could hear the whispers of her students.

"Are you all right, Miss Clay?" Ty's husky voice asked from the darkness.

Suzanne went to her knees. The dampness of the earth seeped through her pants. The room was so dark she couldn't make out her own hand hovering a few inches from face.

"No," she answered. There was no point in lying to them or keeping back her emotions. She started to cry. Her words were mixed with big stuttering breaths. "None of us are."

The sound of the trooper being dragged across the floor punctuated this statement, and a knot of guilt tightened in her stomach.

14

All who deny
that this is thy prophecy
and I am your father
Let them be flogged
for his transgressions.

BOOK OF LOT 1:34

THE CELLAR DOOR JERKED open and slammed against the floor above. The whole dirt pit, used as a cellar, filled with light. Suzanne stood hunched over. The ceiling was too low for her to stand up completely. She watched Esau lumber down the steps. He stopped before he had to bend in half to be in the cellar. He clicked his tongue and waved her to him.

"No, Miss Clay," Ty said. "He's not happy. He seems real mean."

Ty scurried between Suzanne and Esau. The brute stamped into the pit. His hulk bent almost in two, and his beard rested nearly to his waist. Esau pushed the boy back and huffed again.

"No," Ty balled his fists. "I'm not moving, and you aren't going to take Miss Clay." His words were slow and strained. "I mean it."

A noise rumbled up from the depths of Esau's gut. Suzanne felt the vibration like standing too close to the speakers at a concert. The noise turned into a heavy snort. A bull getting ready to charge came to Suzanne's mind. She put her hand on Ty's shoulder, both to calm herself and Ty.

"Don't, Ty. I'll go with him."

"No." The boy said the word with a force that seemed to equal the animal noise uttered from Esau.

The rattling bass of Esau's rumble turned into a sound that Suzanne didn't realize a human could make, something like a clucking of birds and the snorts of bull. It echoed around the musty dirt walls. The solid feel of Ty's shoulder disappeared from under Suzanne's hand. She felt a rush of wind and heard the boy's body slam against the wall. The next thing she became aware of was Esau's hand completely wrapping around her upper arm. The ruddy ogre tugged her forward. She tipped off her feet. The bulk of Esau and the strength of his stiff arm kept her upright as he hauled her up the cellar steps. He stared at her the whole time. His misty sea foam-colored eyes kept locked on hers.

Each stair smashed into Suzanne's knees. She grunted with each blow not able to keep it in. Esau made no sign of stopping his progress as he backed up the steps. Anything could await her at the top of the stairs. Solomon seemed more unstable than she could have imagined last night. A spark of terror shot through her as did raw anger that she was powerless to stop all this. She watched as he straightened up after reaching the main floor. The tendons in her shoulder strained up as Esau lifted her out the cellar by the arm he kept such a tight grasp on.

Needles and pins pricked the tips of her fingers. The evil stinging feeling intensified the tearing pain at Suzanne's shoulder. Just as she thought her arm would tear free, Esau slung her to the floor. She scooted across the dirty wooden planks on her unhurt shoulder and side. Her feet flailed above her, and she felt like she knew what a turtle toppling down a creek bank felt like. Her momentum stopped as she slammed into the leg of the dining table.

Little burst of pain stars dazzled Suzanne. Everything sang with the song of impact. There were no cartoon birds twirling around her head, but the noise was there. She almost laughed at the absurdity of thinking about *Looney Tunes* while the hulking monster of Esau slammed the cellar door down. Lost in her own delirium of the moment, Suzanne thought he even looked like the hairy orange creature that Bugs Bunny so often tricked.

"I'll love him and squeeze him," she said and laughed.

Esau turned his head and looked at her like a dog who hasn't understood his master's request.

The little firecracker explosions in front of her eyes fizzled away, and Suzanne saw the purple-cheeked Esau towering over her. She tried to get to her feet but couldn't. Nothing was real, she decided as the cartoonish brute pulled her up by both arms. Her right shoulder throbbed with pain, and she came back to herself. Bugs had turned left in Albuquerque, leaving her square on Hassle Mountain.

The world went topsy-turvy as Esau flung her over his shoulder. As her gut slammed into his meaty shoulder, the air pushed out. She snorted like getting caught up in a long snore. The need to inhale overtook her, but her muscles hadn't recovered for her to draw in air. Without that cool air, Suzanne couldn't even imagine beginning to fight back.

Esau began to walk. Suzanne felt like she was belly side over a horse in an old western. His shoulder moved up and down with a stride she would have expected from a horse. Her lungs started to work again, and she drew in a long gasp of air.

It wasn't cool like she had wished, but swarthy. The taste of sweat filled her mouth as if Esau's collar rested on her tongue. The flavor of his nasty hair even washed into her mouth. A gag came up but caught in her throat. She'd struggled too much for air to begin dry-heaving.

"Where are you taking me?" she gasped.

Esau swung around the corner from the dining room to the back hallway. Suzanne felt her hair brush past the wall. She just missed being smashed into the crumbling plaster. Fear clawed at Suzanne like never before. They were heading to the backyard. In her dream, the noose hung in the backyard. She had mulled over her dream of her death happening in that backyard, from that tree with that noose. Her fists beat against Esau's back. It felt like hitting lightly padded brick. The musculature of his frame barely pressed in with her blows. She started to kick her feet like a six-year-old having a tantrum. Her feet sunk into his soft belly and came out with an audible pop. Esau grabbed her by the ankle and sent her further over his back.

Now Suzanne's head bobbed at Esau's knee. She moved back just enough with each step to keep from ramming her nose into his legs. Her hair dangled to the ground. As the brute slammed through the back door, the rush of morning air took Suzanne by surprise. She hadn't anticipated it seeming so fresh and reviving. She didn't like being revived.

Panic gripped her. The base of her skull prickled with new psychic electricity.

"I'm going to die," she said to herself.

Esau stomped down the few steps to the yard. Finally, Suzanne's nose made contact with his shin. The whole tip went numb, and she felt the slow ooze of a nosebleed start. She could taste the flavor of blood in the back of her throat. The hard, grassless ground came into view as Suzanne felt Esau let go of her ankle. She crashed to the hard packed earth. Her shoulders popped as they slammed down. She somersaulted backward and came to rest against the flagstone foundation that held up the porch. The stars from a few moments before dazzled her again. This time she didn't feel anything like a cartoon character. She felt like a rag doll crumpled in the corner of a forgotten closet. Esau bent down so he could stare her in the face. His nostrils flared out, and his cheeks remained purple. The force of the wind he blew from his nose rippled the wild whiskers of his mustache.

"What are you going to do to me?" Suzanne whispered. Not only did she feel like a torn, ratty doll, she felt like that doll locked in the closet with the boogie man.

"Nothin." John Mark said, coming from the corner of the house.

"What?"

The stark answer in such a flat tone tumbled some clarity into her. Suzanne stirred, shifting up to a better sitting position. She finally wiped under her nose. With no surprise, a streak of bright red blood covered her finger.

"Nothing?"

"I ain't that Eric boy who's Rachel's man. I ain't stuttered," John Mark said with sarcasm that Suzanne would never have expected from this brood.

"Then why have I been dragged out here?"

"We's goin' to teach ye a lesson. That's what Daddy Sol said."

Suzanne pressed her aching shoulders into the hard stone foundation. A lesson from the Hassles wasn't one to come lightly.

"You're not going to do anything to the children to teach me, are you?"

"Daddy Sol told ya nothing bad would happen to them young'uns. If he says it, it's as good as gold," John Mark said. "Trust me, it's only him that's keeping me from ruttin' you like a buck."

"Then what?" Suzanne yelled. Where the boldness came from she had no idea, but she was suddenly on her feet as well. Her legs wobbled a bit, but she still stood and squared off with John Mark.

"Ye's a bit braver than I thought." John Mark looked at Esau's coy smile. "If he wasn't no Sodomite, he might like to father a brood with ye, hisself. Lot knows I'd jump at it in heartbeat."

"I's wishin' he weren't no Sodomite." Solomon's voice came around the corner of the house before Suzanne ever saw him. "Ye and Esau would make fine young'uns. As far as yer concerned, John Mark, ye've had yer run with Sheba, and made a decent brood. I'd thought yer good looks would've passed down the line. Suppose ye're a fluke."

Suzanne turned to see Solomon come around the corner leaning on his stick as he did. John Mark looked defeated by the old man's words. He must think highly of himself. Apparently, vanity was a trait the Hassles could possess as much as sarcasm. Her kidnappers surprised her more and more.

Agrippa followed him, holding the end of an old hemp rope. He held a rolled bullwhip in his other hand. As Agrippa's lead continued to draw out from the corner, Lovell appeared, attached to the rope by bound hands. His head hung down to his chest.

"No," Suzanne said. "No, no, no."

Solomon grabbed her by the arm. He sank the tips of his fingers deep into her skin. "No what?"

"You're not going to punish Warren because of me. I'm the one who tried to escape. I'm the one to punish."

Solomon let go of her arm. A jolly, uproarious laugh came from him. It echoed across the yard, then petered into a wheezy cough. "Don't be flatterin' yerself, Miss Clay. I ain't worried about what ye did. I's workin' on God's will. No darkie or no other man goin' to stop that."

Suzanne watched as Agrippa untied Lovell. He pulled her lover's arms up and bound them with the noose hanging from the tree. She saw his face. His left eye was bruised almost shut. His lip looked split. Lovell didn't try to look at her.

"John Mark said I was to be taught a lesson."

"Ya is," Solomon said. "This ain't no lesson about tryin' to escape though. I think my boy's done taught ye that by the look of yer nose."

Suzanne wiped another line of blood from her face. Agrippa pulled on the rope that formed the noose Lovell hung from. Lovell came to his tiptoes. Agrippa secured the rope again so Lovell would remain that way. Then he gave the bullwhip to Esau.

"Ye see, Miss Clay. The book given to our family tells us how to handle the unfaithful. We worked all night last night tryin' to show Lovell the way of my people. While ye slept snug in yer bed, we taught him. He wouldn't learn."

Agrippa pulled a knife from his belt. He took the tail of Lovell's shirt and sliced upward with the blade. The fabric fell away. Suzanne saw Lovell's white back with a few freckles spread over it. The muscles of his shoulders strained upward. His whole back seemed in a spasm.

"It is written Miss Clay, 'All who deny that this is thy prophecy and I am thy father let them be flogged for his transgressions.' Thus saith the word. Thus saith our whip."

Suzanne heard the bullwhip unroll. The tip hit the ground with a loll. She watched as Esau jerked it up. The leather cracked like thunder as he popped the whip behind him. Then the thin strip slit a line down Lovell's taut back. He screamed.

Another lick from the whip followed so closely that Suzanne couldn't recognize when it hit over the screaming. Now two bleeding lines crossed Lovell's back. As she watched, his back erupted with the slices of a cruel hatred. She remembered her nails leaving scratches of passion on its smooth skin. Those whiplashes almost burned on her own skin. They had only been intimate once, but it was one of those experiences that bonded two people together. That, or at least she had smoldered for a while for him. Now his pain was her pain.

When the whipping stopped after what seemed like hours to Suzanne, Lovell's back looked like a fillet of salmon, pink with scored flesh and oozing blood. His cries had stopped, but still lingered in Suzanne's ears. Her own sobs mingled with his pained echo.

When the rope around the tree was loosened, Lovell crumpled to the ground. He lay bleeding into the dirt. Agrippa took an old weathered length of sackcloth and laid it over Lovell's back.

"I hope ye's a fast learner, Miss Clay," Solomon said slow and with no emotion. "Be a shame to ruin *yer* pretty back."

"Can I help him?" She sucked up sobs.

"We know better than ye how to deal with that kind of wound. He'll be taken care of," Solomon said. "Believe it or not, I knows it ain't easy watchin' a dear one beaten, but it's for the best. Keep these words in your heart Miss Clay. 'Your Father Lot wills his people to live.'"

"Can I talk to him?" Suzanne asked.

Solomon nodded. She ran and fell to a knee beside Lovell. He kept his face to his chest. Streams of blood rolled off his shoulders and matted his chest hair to his skin. His swollen eye looked angry and purple. His good eye looked at her with a hollow, lost stare.

"I'm *so* sorry," she whispered. "I got you into this."

"No." Lovell's voice was cracked and strained. It told the story of his beating and sleepless night. "There's nothing to be sorry about." He coughed and winced. "Do like they say."

"What do you mean?"

"Do what Solomon wants. It's better than this." Another cough came out raspy and low. "Anything's better than getting . . . broken."

"Even rape is better?"

"Have sex with them and then it won't be rape." Lovell's stare told her that was what he meant. "Just consent to them."

"You're tougher than this," she said. "What about that soldier who served in Afghanistan?"

His eyes were weak. Pain beyond what she'd seen him receive looked out at her. "The Taliban just shot at us. Esau has changed me . . . forever." His eyes looked deep into hers and he whispered, "He's a monster, you know. A frustrated, angry perverted monster. Going against his wishes is pretty much impossible."

Suzanne closed her eyes and stood up. She understood what Agrippa meant after Solomon stopped him from raping her. Apparently, Esau knew ways of breaking even the strongest ones. Without opening her eyes, she walked back towards Solomon. When she felt his nearness, she opened her eyes again. They stung with new tears. Solomon grinned slightly.

"Did ye say what needed to be said?"

Suzanne nodded.

"Did ye hear what needed to be heard?"

Suzanne narrowed her eyes to slits. She would rather spit in the old man's face, but she nodded.

"Good." Solomon smiled showing his gaped and dirty teeth. He reached into his pocket and brought out a small glass bottle, containing a brown liquid that looked like tea. Small particles floated around in it. Solomon pulled the cork out with his teeth. "Drink this, Mr. Lovell."

Lovell looked at the old man. Suzanne willed him not to follow Solomon's orders, but he reached up with a hand trembling from pain and took the bottle. The liquid drained out quickly. Lovell gagged but swallowed the stuff.

"That's a good lad. Boys, take Mr. Lovell back to his shack. Have Haddie tend to him. When he's up to it, start back teachin' him."

"Was that poison?" Suzanne asked.

"Of course not. What would it benefit me to have him dead? What he took in was an elixir that will help him avoid more unneeded pain."

Suzanne watched John Mark and Agrippa help Lovell up. They did so almost gingerly. Solomon's hand rested on her shoulder. It felt like a tender caress.

"It ain't like we's offerin' somethin' so horrible." Solomon spoke softly as Agrippa and John Mark walked past with Lovell.

Lovell kept his head down and his back bowed as they walked away. The whole cloth laid on his back had turned dark crimson from his whipping wounds.

"I suppose ye read a copy of our Father's book?" Solomon asked.

"Yes." Suzanne watched Lovell until he and the two Hassles disappeared around the corner of the house.

"I think it would be well for you to spend the rest of yer day readin' it some more."

15

Yea, the night-monster
shall settle there,
and shall find her a place of rest.

ISAIAH 34:14 (ASV)

LOVELL'S WORDS KEPT REPEATING over and over in her head. How could she just give into the Hassles and let them rape her and the kids? Suzanne couldn't wrap her mind around how horrible one night alone with Esau was. It had been enough to make Lovell give up hope. He spent time fighting in Afghanistan just after the invasion. Physical strength wasn't an issue. He taught special education, so emotional fortitude shouldn't have been a problem either, but take away a man's power over himself and humiliate him would make even the strongest man break. Suzanne turned the Bible Solomon had given her over and over in her hands without realizing it.

The sound of the tumblers turning in the lock brought Suzanne back from her ruminations. The door swung open. Sheba walked in wearing a blue striped apron over her clothes. A large red patch of a different material was sewn on it. She carried a wooden bowl.

"Here ya go," Sheba shoved the bowl toward Suzanne.

Suzanne just stared at Sheba not moving.

"I ain't bringin' it any farther. Either get yer tail up, or I'll toss it on the floor."

"What is it?"

"Dinner. Fall vegetable soup."

Suzanne got up and took the bowl from Sheba. Kernels of corn floated on the red-orange surface of the vegetable broth. Green bits that looked like chopped up collard greens floated around in the soup.

"Somethin' the matter? Don't it suit yer tastes or ya wantin' another ham steak or maybe Purty?" Sheba said, hands on her hips.

"No, I'm thankful. I just didn't realize it was lunchtime already. Believe me I have no interest in John Mark."

Sheba snorted in derision and walked out the room. She pulled the door closed and locked it. Suzanne heard the large woman chortling down the hallway back to the stairs. The soup still steamed, but the smell was less than appealing. It smelled heavily of the cooked greens. One sip told Suzanne that it wasn't for her. She put the bowl down on the floor and took the Book of Lot up. She began to read it again.

It was raining outside. Suzanne heard the water dripping off her roof and into the bucket she kept under the eave near her bedroom window. She used the caught runoff to water her plants. They responded better to rain runoff than tap water. Suzanne wanted to open her eyes from her nap, but the pitter-patter made her drowsy.

Against all the protest her body gave, she opened her eyes, but the room was not her own. She found herself facing the plastered wall of the Hassles' old plantation house. The musty smell of the room filled her nostrils ten times worse than she remembered before dozing off. Suzanne rolled over to face the rest of the room and watch the rain. Bright sunshine glared through the window.

She sat up and let her feet touch the dusty floor. Not a single drop of rain fell outside, but she still heard the dripping. The steady rhythm still lulled her. Suzanne shook the grogginess from her head and stood. The room moved as she did. Not a vertigo movement that she would get after a long night with one too many fuzzy navels, but an elongation like a trick in a fun house mirror. The window became smaller and smaller as the wall shoved away from her, and the floor kept growing out.

Suzanne gave chase to the shrinking window but never got closer. Wind blew around her as if she sprinted, but everything stayed in place. The dripping, however, grew louder and faster. It sounded like tom-toms.

She stopped, and the room slammed on the brakes. The window slingshot back toward her. Suzanne held her hands in front of her to keep from being hit, but everything fit back into its proportions. The dripping shifted as well. Now the sound of liquid splattering on the floorboards came from behind her. Suzanne turned. A growing puddle of dark blood pooled on the floor just inches from her bed.

Suzanne followed the drip up to the ceiling. The corpse of the state trooper hung above her. One of his arms dangled toward her with a long rivulet of blood running down it and dripping to the floor. His eyes stared at her through white cataracts.

She screamed, but nothing came out. She tried to run, but stood still. Then the dead eyes blinked to life, and the corpse opened its mouth. Blood and salt gushed from it and splattered across Suzanne's face. She tried to block it, but it coated her. The taste of salty iron filled her mouth. She started choking.

Suzanne sat up in bed. Something sticky ran down her face. She brushed it with her hands trying to get it off. Expecting to find the salt and blood mixture the dead trooper vomited on her, Suzanne instead found the thin broth from the fall soup she hadn't eaten.

"Ifin' it ain't good enough for ya to eat, ye might as well wear it," Sheba said.

Suzanne looked to the side of the room. Sheba still held the soup bowl. Some of the soup dripped over the edge onto the floor.

"I just fell asleep before I got to it," Suzanne said still not fully awake.

"Sure. Ain't foolin', me, ye ain't." Sheba slammed the bowl down on a tray that held a plate of what looked like peas and cornbread. "Reckon ye'll be hungry enough at breakfast to eat whatever ya get."

Sheba took the tray and stomped out of the room, leaving the door wide open. Suzanne felt hope leap up in her but tried to keep it subdued. She didn't want any positive vibes leaking out to any of them.

"Don't get yer hopes up." Sheba reached into the room and pulled the door closed. "I just had to set this tray down. Ifin' you think that cold soup in yer face was bad, ye's got no idee what I'll do to ye if ya keep enticing my Purty."

"I'd rather bathe in that stuff than do anything to John Mark."

Sheba gave her an unpleasant smirk. "I done been around long enough to know, ain't no woman can resist that man."

The door closed with a loud bang. The lock's tumblers sounded like thunder rolling through the sky as Sheba locked the door. Suzanne lay back on her bed. The soup still clung to her hair. It stank. She stank. The whole situation was a putrid pile of pig crap. She never liked to admit defeat, but that point was nearing. She didn't know how much more she could take before she would give completely up.

Suzanne picked up the copy of the Bible where it had fallen when she went to sleep. As soon as she did, a militant feeling filled her up pushing all thoughts of giving up out of her head. She'd never felt anything like it, a heady mixture of stomach-knotting anxiety and raw hatred. Her fingers found the pulpy pages at the back that were the Book of Lot. The book flipped open to the first page with the genealogy on it. Suzanne ripped the page out. She dabbed her face with it, letting the soup seep deep into the paper. Then another page came out and was used to sop soup from her hair. She kept going until a small pile of balled pages lay at her feet and most of Lot was gone.

A laugh flew out of her mouth. Her militant feeling grew stronger. Her eyes shot to the rusty barbwire latticing the only window in her room.

"I've had my tetanus shot," she said as she walked to the window and looked out. The ground looked about twenty feet down. Her ankles would suffer from the drop, maybe even snap, but if they didn't, she'd get away and rescue would come. The barbwire blocked the opening on the outside of the glass. She pushed the window up. The old wood of the frame had swollen with time, and the wood sputtered and stuttered its way up. The short hairs on her back of her neck stood on end from the squeal. She hoped that no one heard it, but it would be hard not to.

Once she had the window as high as she could push it, Suzanne studied the frame where the wire attached. Bent fence staples held the wire in place. The u-bend in the middle of the steel nails rusted in the wood. Paint chips shimmied under her fingernails as she tried to dig the staples out. The sharp stab into the quick brought her fingers to her mouth so that the saliva could perform its strange curative magic.

Suzanne slapped the inside of the window frame. She wouldn't be able to dig the staples out with her fingers. The strands of wire looked tight, but she tried to wrap her hand in it. There was enough slack to get a fold of wire into her palm. She set her teeth as one of the barbs bit into her skin. The knuckles of her hand crackled as she made a fist, and with a quick jerk, one of the staples tore free from the wood. Suzanne let the strand of wire go. Blood trickled down the side of her hand from where the barb gouged a ditch into her skin. She wiped the blood away with her other hand and looked at her work.

A horizontal strand of the barbwire hung loose. Suzanne set her teeth again and repeated the process until all the horizontal barbwire strips were pulled free from one end of the windowsill. Bloody gouges pocked her hand. The wounds burned and itched. Fat drops of blood dripped from her hand to the floor. They pooled together like that of the blood from her dream. She imagined herself hanging by her heels bleeding out just like the trooper. It went away with a firm shake of her head.

"Stay focused. For the kids."

The kids would have to stay behind while she went for help. What would Solomon do to them when he discovered she'd bolted? Suzanne swallowed hard as she stared out the window at the darkening sky. A few birds flew to roost in the dark trees at the edge of a large pasture. Momma birds would fight to the death to protect their young. The kids would be fine. Solomon could do nothing worse than what he already had planned, and if she made it, rescue would be there by sun-up.

Renewed in her resolve, she gritted her teeth and wrapped the wire in her hand again, then whipped her hand with a quick wrist movement. Blood slung all over the wall. Solomon and the others would see it, but she didn't care. She'd be long gone by then. She worked hard not to cackle a crazed laugh as she wrapped the wire around her uninjured hand and tugged down on a vertical strand of wire until it ripped free from the wood, and several barbs sliced into the skin of her palm and wrist. By the time the window was free of the barbed wire latticework, Suzanne looked like the worst cutting emo kid she'd ever seen. All the wounds bled. All the wounds stung. All the wounds screamed: *freedom*.

She wiped her hands clean of the blood. Twin streaks of bright red stained her jeans. The air rushing into the room felt cool and carried the smell of a farm at night. Whiffs of hay mingled with the bad smell of manure. A whippoorwill cried out in the night. The song of the bird felt like a warning to Suzanne as she stuck her head out of the window.

Whip-her-will. Whip-her-will.

A pipe ran beside the widow to the ground. A glance up saw it attached to a gutter on the roof. Suzanne reached and shook the pipe. It wiggled back and forth, but the metal seemed firm.

Swallowing hard, Suzanne stuck her upper body out the window. She balanced herself with her hands as she brought one knee onto the sill. The knee rested between two barbs. The other knee rested close to a barb, and it poked the side of her leg. Once her balance was established, Suzanne reached out and grabbed the drainpipe with her left hand, twisting her body like a pretzel. With her left hand gripping the pipe, Suzanne reached and grabbed it with her right hand. Her knees slipped off the windowsill. The knee against the barb tore open with a jagged cut. The white edge of the frayed tear in her jeans soaked up the blood that gushed from the jagged slice. She dangled for a moment, feeling like her arms would give out on her before she could get any sort of footing. Her legs spun until they touched the old wooden siding of the house.

Suzanne looked down, took a big breath, and started to walk down the wall. Her cut hands slid down the almost-smooth pipe, but they sang in pain the whole time. Bits of rust and filth broke off and wedged themselves into her sores. Streaks of blood followed her down the pole, until the heels of her feet touched the soft ground at the bottom of the downspout. Suzanne got her footing. She looked up at the window she escaped from. A tatter from her blue jeans dangled out like a tress of Rapunzel's hair. The loose strands of barbwire hung over the window ledge like bachelor spikes daring someone to try to rescue the long-haired princess from the tower. Little did all those Prince Charmings know that the damsel had freed herself.

Whip-her-will. Whip-her-will.

The otherworldly sound of the bird made Suzanne focus. She wiped her palms on the front of her pants, leaving more bloody stains speckled with flakes of rust and moss. Nothing seemed to move in the house. Her stomach rumbled as she caught a whiff of the smoke coming from the cookhouse.

Suzanne pushed herself into the shadows where the porch met the rest of the house just as the cookhouse's door opened. The large frame of Sheba stepped onto the top step. She carried a large wooden tray full of various clay bowls. The light in the cookhouse was strong and cast out a long way. Suzanne feared that it might reveal her.

"Come on, Gomer," Sheba yelled. "Ain't got all night. Folks besides them strangers got to eat too."

Sheba walked down the steps, and a scarecrow of a woman followed. She too carried a tray laden with bowls. A young girl reached out and closed the door. The light snuffed out like a candle.

"What'cha reckon, Old Solomon, have us cook for tomorrow night?" Gomer, the scarecrow, asked.

"Reckon what that book tells him we's supposed to have at one of them feasts. I'm bettin' it'll be out of our best gatherings though."

"Sounds like ya don't trust what old Sol's up to."

"Hush, yer skinny mouth, or ye're goin' get us both whipped. Ya know better to talk about that kind of stuff, 'specially if Daddy Sol or Esau might be lurkin'"

"Sorry." Gomer looked down sheepishly.

"We best get on to the dining house before everybody gets riled up."

Suzanne watched and listened to the two women. Apparently, some of the Hassle clan besides Hadassah didn't agree with Solomon. As soon as Sheba and Gomer rounded the corner, Suzanne scuttled out of the shadows and into those cast by the tree used to whip people from. This shadow was thinner making it harder to hide. She hugged the trunk. The thick bark scratched her cheek as Suzanne laid her face against the tree. Her breath steamed lightly from her mouth and disappeared in an *S* swirl.

Whip-her-will.   Whip-HER-will.   WHIP-her-will. Whip-her-WILL-will.

The bird sounded closer and meaner. Suzanne broke from the tree and made a run for the pasture fence. The black forest loomed at the other end of the field. The moon lit the pasture well, but it left her no shadows to hide herself in. Suzanne didn't care. She sprinted to the fence and vaulted over, using her least wounded hand on the old wooden slates. Her feet hit the solid ground. Despite every aching, burning, or itching on her body, she ran as hard as she could across the field. The grass slapped her mid-thigh and hindered her some, but she kept up the pace. As she neared the middle of her trek, a covey of quail flew up in front of her. Without thinking, she screamed. It echoed through the empty night air.

Suzanne fell to her knees letting the hay conceal her. She felt furious that she'd given herself away so quickly. How long would it take them to check her room? She gasped for air. Another good sprint would bring her almost to the other part of the fence and then the woods. They would never catch her now. She had too much of a lead and getting those kids rescued gave her a better cause.

With a great gulp of breath, Suzanne hopped to a standing position and began sprinting across the field. The grass beat at her. It whistled as it brushed her pants. Her heart beat in her ears, and the long-drawn puffs of breath sounded like the steam from the old train at the zoo. Her vision narrowed to the spot she would launch herself over the fence at to disappear into the dark woods.

An explosion erupted from behind her. Suzanne became aware of her surroundings again. She glanced back still running. *Don't look back. You'll turn into salt,* something told her. As best she could see, several of the Hassles had clambered into the pasture after her. Another explosion and she realized one of them was shooting at her. She turned back to the front. The fence was only a few yards away now. Her side ached. The fence drew closer and closer. Another shot rang out in the night as Suzanne slammed both hands down on the top rail of the fence. A nail drove into her palm, but she barely noticed the pain on top of the rest. She clambered over the fence and found herself at the edge of the woods. Another glance back, risking the fate of Lot's wife, and she saw that they still chased her. Suzanne rubbed her burning side, but trotted off into the dark thicket of trees.

Whip-her-will. Whip-her-will. Whip-her-WILL-WILL.

16

Yea,
thorns will snarl thy progress,
but be of good cheer
The world will believe

BOOK OF LOT 16:33

DARKNESS ENGULFED SUZANNE, SLOWING her down in the woods. A little bit of moonlight filtered through the dying leaves and pine needles of the thicket. Limbs from wild privet smacked her in the face, and over-the-hill blackberry vines snagged her pants. She felt like she was running through living mud. The trees kept the noise of her Hassle pursuers tamped down. Every now and again, Suzanne could make out a yell from one pursuer to the other. She didn't even know if they were in the woods yet.

Then the sound of Agrippa yelling something in his high-pitched, slurred voice rang out. She could tell that at least he had entered the woods.

Suzanne pushed deeper in. The ground began to slope downward. Her calf muscles strained as she focused on going downhill. The slope became steeper. The leaves under feet became more slippery. At one point, Suzanne's feet slid from under her. She skidded five feet down the side of the hill before her feet hit a tree root poking up from the ground. Stunned, she took a brief moment to catch her breath and try to calm her heart.

Agrippa seemed to be the bloodhound for the group. He yelled something out again, this time even closer.

Suzanne clambered to her feet. She dug her fingers into the moist earth, stirring up the musty smell of rotting foliage and gaining the stability she needed to step over the bent root and continue trekking down the slope.

The slant began to flatten out. She was able to move faster with better footing. Now she heard the Hassles on the hill above her. They murmured and scuffled in the leaves. The lust to see their position pulled at her, but she wouldn't give in. Looking back had cost her time once. This time could be her pillar of salt time; she pressed on.

The ground underfoot became spongy. The smell of moss and dank mud wafted around Suzanne. She turned her strained hearing from the noises of the Hassles, who started down the slope now, to closer sounds. Water bubbled and danced over rocks near her. The noise of it trickling and laughing cleared her mind some. Above her, the canopy of oaks, elms, and pines broke up letting in more light. A glance forward saw a thousand moon diamonds shining off the water that rolled over small rocks. She walked to the edge and got on her knees. The water cooled her burning hands and relieved the itchiness of her wounded palms. She splashed the water on her face and felt a bit rejuvenated.

"She slid right here. Ifin' we's lucky she hurt herself and's a layin' just down from here," Agrippa's voice rang out clear and comprehensible. They were closer than she'd expected. Anxiety stretched at the muscles in her chest, causing slight pings of sharp pains.

She hopped up and plunged her feet into the cold water. It stopped just shy of her knees. Instead of trekking across to the other side, she turned upstream and walked against the current. The water swirled around her legs. Her shoes became heavy as she sloshed away. Her feet slipped, and she fell into deeper water. It came to her chest, but the water eddied here. She pulled at the water with her arms and kept walking. Now the sound of her movements were muffled.

Agrippa's voice echoed up the stream to her. "Here's her footprints."

"Don't see none on the other side," John Mark yelled.

"She must've taken to the water. Half of 'uns go downstream; me and the rest'll head upstream," Agrippa said.

Suzanne looked back, shocked and horrified at how well they could track her. She had to know how far she was from them. Three bobbing lights pierced the darkness several yards behind her. The stream made a strategic bend so that a clump of trees and brambles kept her hidden for now. Suzanne moved forward still pulling herself through the eddy current. She walked to the bank. It was shoulder high, but she sunk her fingers into the soft earth and gripped it like she was hanging onto a handlebar. She pulled up. Her feet dug into the soft bank below the waterline. Her shoulder muscles ached. She thrust upward with all her leg strength and hit the bank on her belly like a seal in a show at the zoo. Repositioning her hands, she clambered up the bank. Her wet feet splayed out for lack of good traction on the slippery leaves and muddy soil.

"I think I just seen her," Levi yelled.

Suzanne stayed on all fours. She scrambled until she hid behind a knot of wild privet wrapped with blackberry vines. Old straw and left over vegetation from a flood helped to fill in some gaps in the undergrowth. She watched her pursuers through the gaps. The light from the lanterns did little more than cast a wan glow on the Hassles. The back of Agrippa's head showed more than anything. He led the others up the brook. The water splashed.

"Get up here with that light," Agrippa waved his hand to his partner.

The front lantern-bearer went ahead of Agrippa. The light swung back and forth illuminating the banks and the trees along the brook. Suzanne couldn't tell anything from her distance. The light swept once more.

"She ain't gone that way," Agrippa said. "Shine it over yonder."

Both lanterns cast their beams toward Suzanne. She tried to lie flat so the flood washings would hide her.

"I just seen something up there," Agrippa said. "Swing that light back to that pile of washed-up straw."

Suzanne didn't wait for the light to shine back over her. She popped up and started running into the woods. The Hassles splashed behind her but didn't yell. She hoped they would have trouble clambering out of the deep pool like she did. The brambles tore at her pants and occasionally at her leg. Her calves stung as much as her hands from all the briar pricks. A low hanging branch slapped her in the face. Her hair tangled in the twigs. The sound of tramping feet came behind her.

"She done caught her hair up in that sweet gum," Agrippa stood just up the slope from her.

"Absalom, Absalom," Levi sang out.

Ignoring the hot, searing pain on her scalp, Suzanne jerked her head down and let several clumps of her hair be torn out by the roots. She ran as fast as she could through the undergrowth. Her wet feet and soggy shoes felt like lead weights keeping her feet pressed down. She turned back and saw Agrippa and the others gaining ground.

Never look back. The voice in her head spoke those words as the ground disappeared from under her feet. She toppled down a slope. Her elbow hit a root sticking through the ground. Another somersault sent her knee grinding into an outcropping of limestone. Suzanne felt the vertigo of head-over-heels tumbling when she slammed into something hard that she could only guess was a tree. Her head slammed forward and to the side. Something sharp and horrible pierced her cheek. Suzanne screamed in pain as other thorny pricks stabbed into her skin. She hung from the tree like Christ pinned up with a hundred needles.

Blood began to fill up her mouth. She tried to spit, but the movement made the thorn in her jaw tear at the side of her cheek. Her tongue brushed the tip of the wooden blade and felt the stick and how sharp it was. Suzanne started to choke on the blood and saliva mixture. She let it ooze from the corner of her mouth to give her some relief. Her eyes teared too much for her to see anything but the beam of lantern light that shined at her.

"There she is," Agrippa said. "Looks like she took a spill down into the hollar and landed in a honey locust."

"Looks likes she's bleeding awful bad," Levi said. "Reckon Daddy Sol'll mind that?"

"He ain't worried what she looks like, as long as she can breed. Reckon a couple of thorn pricks ain't going to stop that," Agrippa said.

All three laughed a snorty laugh. The light got closer to Suzanne as her pursuers clambered down the hillside. For the first time, she was almost happy the Hassles were around. The injuries to her body still hurt, she knew that, but shock from all of them at once seemed to tamp the pain down. Blood and saliva still oozed from her mouth. She felt a callused hand on her.

"Look's like she done got one of them thorns in her jaw," Agrippa said. "If you know what good far ye, ye'll hold still."

He put one hand on Suzanne's cheek and another on the side of her head just above the thorn that pierced her mouth. The calluses felt scratchy like the briars that whipped her earlier. His grip tightened then a searing pain ripped through her face. Blood streamed into her mouth like water over a spillway. She spat blindly. Through the new pain, she hoped it splattered on Agrippa. The next thing she knew, her whole body cried out with a new horrible agony, as the Hassles lifted her out of the thorns of the honey locust tree.

"Don't reckon I'm goin' to make ye walk," Agrippa said. "Ye can thank me later. Levi, tote her up the hill until we find John Mark. He can carry her back to the house."

Suzanne couldn't have answered if she had wanted to. She felt herself being lifted over Levi's shoulder. Her face hung down against his back. She opened her mouth to let the bloody saliva drip out. Her waist rested on Levi's boney shoulder. Her butt waved in the air. She was the caveman's prize being taken back to the bedding chamber, but right then she didn't care. Pain was all she knew, and all she could think of.

Suzanne lay on a cot. Her head rested on a rolled towel, and a bowl lay on her stomach. The weight of the bowl pressed down every time she breathed. A bright lamp of some sort blinded her. Its luminescence shined in her face. She couldn't move her head because of the pain, and closing her eyes did nothing to block the light.

Suzanne had blacked out somewhere on the way back from the woods. She roused only a few minutes ago. With nothing stirring around the rims of the bright light, she couldn't keep up with time. The air of the room seemed fresher than any she'd breathed since being hauled to Hassle's farm. *Am I in a hospital?* This thought passed. An emergency room would be full of noise and bluster. Policemen would be around her asking questions as soon as her eyes had fluttered to consciousness.

"Where am I?" She uttered the words as pain streaked across her face.

A chair creaked from somewhere behind her head. "Finally awake, are ye?"

The voice was old and creaky but pleasant and female. Suzanne tried to move her head to get a glimpse of the speaker.

"Don't be doin' that. I got'cha where I need ya. Ye start movin' around, and I'll have to work ye back the way I like, and ye'll be hurtin' more than necessary."

Suzanne felt a hand on her shoulder. It trembled just enough to notice, but not from anger or fear. The tremor came from age. The lamp over head moved down her body some and besides the green and red flashes in her vision, she could see. The old woman who'd looked after Lovell the first day stared down at her.

"Hadassie?"

"Stop talkin'. Ya goin' to rip that hole in yer jaw wider if ye keep it up." The bowl on Suzanne's stomach pressed down.

The sound of liquid being wrung out echoed to her ears. "I'm Hadassah. Can't stand being called Hadassie. Some of 'em call me Haddie. I don't mind that too much."

"What?"

"Told ye to keep quiet. Don't ya remember? I'm the one that takes care of the hurt, animal and person alike. Some folks call me a nurse, but I ain't never had no formal education in it. I piddle around with wild plants and such too."

Suzanne had heard this story before. She didn't believe very much of what Solomon said, but it definitely seemed that Hadassah had some dementia setting in. Cold water rushed down Suzanne's face as Hadassah squeezed a rag out over her head. The soft texture of the cloth felt nice as it rubbed along her forehead and down her uninjured cheek. The rag was put back in the water and wrung out again.

"This ain't goin' to feel so nice."

The water dripped on the punctured cheek. The little droplets made Suzanne cringe, then the rag pressed to it. Sharp stabs of pain went through her face as if shards of glass were being pushed around. Suzanne set her teeth, but it didn't help. She thought it might be making it worse. Tears began to well in her eyes as she clenched them as well. The torturous face-washing ended and the bowl on her stomach lifted off. Suzanne opened her eyes and watched Hadassah put the bowl just out of the light's range.

"Open up," Hadassah said.

Suzanne complied. The bright light was adjusted back to her face. Hadassah leaned over her, and it shaded some of the brightest light. Suzanne watched until her eyes crossed as Hadassah poked a long cotton swab into her mouth. The pain in her jaw sang out again, and a strange bitter taste filled her mouth. Then, the jaw seemed to numb. Hadassah pushed up on Suzanne's chin, like the dentist did when he wanted her to close her mouth.

"Well, that's about all I can do for that hole in yer jaw. It'll have to heal itself on the inside. The thing about mouths is they're good at that." Hadassah took Suzanne's arm and rolled it so her palm would be facing up. "Let's look at these hands." The old woman made a whistling sound through her teeth.

"What?" Suzanne said this through her clenched teeth.

"Just askin' for lockjaw, ain't ye?"

"Better than waiting for Solomon to do his dirty work, but I had a tetanus shot at the beginning of the summer."

Hadassah looked down at Suzanne with eyes the color of Solomon's, but these eyes were sympathetic. The old woman smiled and patted Suzanne's shoulder as she walked past. She came back with another metal bowl. This was smaller than the first.

"I reckon ye're wanderin' why I'm bein' so nice to ye." Hadassah dipped a clean rag into the bowl and wrung it out.

The smell of alcohol filled Suzanne's nostrils. She knew this would hurt. As soon as Hadassah put the rag on her cut and raw hands, the sores began to sting as if on fire. Suzanne let a long hiss out through her teeth.

"Don't take that as me bein' mean, now. It's the best medicine I can offer for now. It's mash liquor. Stuff's so strong, it'll burn out guts and germs alike." Hadassah took the rag away and rinsed it in the bowl. "I suppose that shocks ye—a Hassle bein' nice."

Suzanne tried to smile. This woman was being very nice, perhaps a little *too* nice. She began to wonder what would come next. Was Hadassah going to cut her foot off? Did the old woman intend to clean her up and then let Agrippa or one of the other Hassle men come in and have his way with her? As Hadassah started washing some throne punctures on her arms, Suzanne fought to get up off the cot.

"Settle down. Simmer down girl."

Hadassah pushed on Suzanne's shoulders to try to put her back down. The bowl of alcohol toppled to the wooden floor with a clang, and the pong of the liquid filled the room. She got to her feet despite the old woman's best efforts. Suzanne felt the roughness of the floor and realized she was barefoot. She looked down and saw that she was naked from waist down except for her panties.

"Where are my pants?" she asked.

"I had to take them off, to check ye over."

"Get them for me, now."

Hadassah shook her head. "If ye go out that door, Esau and Agrippa's waitin'. They'll grab ya up and take ye to some shed and give it to ye good. Only thing that kept them from doin' it as soon as ye got back from the woods was that Esau's a Sodomite, and I told 'em ye needed tendin' too to keep ye from getting' the lockjaw. 'Grippa didn't much care much about that either. Said it keep you from a yellin'."

For the first time since arriving to the farm, Suzanne felt hopeless. She felt the rush of adrenaline drain from her body as if someone had pulled the plug out of a tub. Defeated and exhausted, she let herself crumble onto the cot. Slumped over, with elbows on her thighs and hands cupping her head, she glanced up at Hadassah, despite the pain that pressing on her face caused her. Suzanne used it to keep her thoughts clear and focused. She wasn't feeling too trusting of the old woman and didn't want Haddie's niceties to make her neglect to see some foul intentions.

"Why would you do that?" she asked. "Why would you want to keep me safe?"

"Not all of us Hassles is the same, honey. Ye best remember that. Now lay down and let me finish cleaning ya up."

Suzanne lay back down. Hadassah poured out some more alcohol into her bowl and started cleaning her other arm. Then she moved on to the thorn and bramble wounds on her legs. Everything stung, but the pain somehow numbed her momentarily as she stared up at the ceiling, wishing she was somewhere, anywhere else.

"Solomon's all about God punishin' us for not bringing about the chosen one sooner. He thinks ye and them young'uns are going to save everything."

"You don't?"

Hadassah laughed a high-pitched cackle. "Ain't never been no angels ever visited this farm during the Civil War or otherwise. Our great whatever daddy was a nut. He made it all up to keep his young'uns from marryin' Yankees. Solomon done tried this before. Even bought some poor boy out of Mississippi from his no account daddy. Never worked out and of course he blamed the prophecy and—"

The door to the shack slammed opened. The cool night breeze wafted in. The bright light Hadassah used to work on Suzanne fluttered in the rush of air. Suzanne propped herself up on her elbows. Solomon walked in on his stick. He slammed the door as he entered.

"Don't be comin' in here disturbin' her tonight, Sol," Hadassah fluttered her arms out to him like a momma hen beating away a chicken snake.

"Shut up, Hadassie." The old man's words fell flat to the floor like lead. "I's just come to check on our little runaway."

Solomon pushed Hadassah to the wall and stood by Suzanne's cot. He shoved her back down flat and stared her in the eyes. His deep green eyes bore no sympathy whatsoever. He nodded his head as if approving something.

"Did a good job on yerself." The veins in the old man's neck strained at his skin. "What were you thinkin'? Is you tryin' to anger me? How's about God?"

With the sound of a raging bull, Solomon swung his cane at the chair near Suzanne's cot. She couldn't see it, but heard the wood shatter from the impact. The old man stepped away from her. The sound of the solid wood of the cane making contact with a metal surface rang out through the room like the peeling of a bell. Glass shattered. The smell of alcohol permeated the room again. The sounds of destructive rage made its way around the room until Solomon came up to her on the opposite side from where he'd started his tantrum.

"Suppose ye look a bit rough, but how's this?"

Suzanne felt his rough callused hand touch her leg just above the knee. He moved it up her thigh as Suzanne tried to crawl out of her skin. A finger wiggled its way underneath the elastic leg band of her panties. He flicked at the edge of her pubic hair. She closed her eyes and poked her tongue to the thorn prick. The old man chuckled as he moved his finger deeper into her pubic delta, and Suzanne bit her lip until it bled. Tasting the metallic quality of blood told her she should hurt, and she focused on that.

17

There is a balm in Gilead
To make the wounded whole

NEGRO SPIRITUAL

SUZANNE DIDN'T KNOW WHAT happened. She expected Solomon to brutalize her right there on the cot in Hadassah's shack, but nothing happened. Her eyes opened just a slit, enough to see Solomon paused over her with the point of a pair of scissors against his throat.

"I suggest ya get yer fingers back where they belong, and ye get out of my house," Hadassah said, pressing the tip into the loose flesh of Solomon's neck.

He retracted his fingers back outside Suzanne's underwear like a child extracting his hand from cookie jar after getting caught trying to sneak one out. "I wasn't gonna do nothin', Haddie."

Hadassah kept the scissors to his neck. He moved away from Suzanne, but the nurse followed him. They walked to the door.

"I'll remember this," Solomon said. "Ye best keep that in mind."

Hadassah pulled the scissors back. "I know ye won't forget, but just remember nobody else will take care of ye and yern."

Solomon stormed out, slamming the door behind him. Suzanne propped up to get a better look at Hadassah. The old woman put the large pair of scissors back into the pocket on her apron.

"Thank you."

"For what? Ye's in my care. I ain't gonna let nothing happen to someone I'm seein' after."

"At least let me help you clean up the mess he made," Suzanne said. Somehow the idea of tidying up gave her a feeling of superiority over the old man.

Hadassah pushed down on Suzanne so she would settle back. "Lay down and get some rest. He ain't goin' let this pass that easy. Get ye a good night sleep while ya can."

Suzanne laid back and closed her eyes. She felt on fire and had to do something to help with the burning. Sleep wasn't going to come like this.

"How bad?" Suzanne asked.

"What?"

"How bad do I look?"

Hadassah made a *humph* sort of laugh. "Well, ye look better than ya will tomorrow when it all starts to bruise and pus over worse. Ye just survived an encounter like that with Solomon and yer worried about how ye look? " She huffed again.

Suzanne noticed that her mouth, at least on the inside, seemed to feel a lot better. The wounded area was still numb.

"Mouth oughta be goin' numb about now." Hadassah sorted through some items. She tossed things aside and made clattering noises. "No-vo-cane. Don't know how Sol got a hold of it, and don't care. Works better than anything I got when people get mouth sores."

Suzanne laughed to herself at the childish way the old woman said the word. Hadassah knew what she was doing, and it was a lot more than basic first aid. Suzanne sat up and watched her as she fumbled on a metal cabinet.

"Do you know how my kids are?"

Hadassah stopped her rummaging and looked back over her shoulder. She turned back to a small pan she was looking through. Her hand came up with a large syringe still sealed in the plastic packaging.

"I know about 'em," she said.

"And?"

The old woman ignored her, walking to another metal cabinet on which sat a large glass jug with a metal screw-on lid. She laid the syringe down on the cabinet and unscrewed the jar's lid.

"Hadassah, I asked you about the kids?" Suzanne spoke a bit louder and crisper just in case the older woman had hearing problems.

"No reason to raise yer voice." She stuck her hand into the jar and fumbled with smaller vials. "I can hear ye just fine and dandy. I ain't answerin' 'cause yer hurt bad enough as is."

She brought out a vial the size of a shot glass. Hadassah held it close to her eyes, smiled and sat it on the cabinet top.

"Is it that bad?" Suzanne couldn't keep the panic from her voice.

Hadassah grabbed the vial and syringe as she turned and moved to Suzanne. "How much ya weigh?"

"One twenty-five or so."

The old woman nodded her head. She unwrapped the syringe, tossing the plastic to the floor. She popped the top off the vial. With a smooth motion she pulled the cap off the needle with her lips, and inserted the needle through the rubber on top of the vial. The liquid transferred up the syringe to a particular hash mark. Suzanne could see it but had no idea what the measurement was. Hadassah pulled the needle out. It looked long and a bit thicker than Suzanne was used to. A drop of the serum beaded on the stick's end.

"What is that? I told you that I had a tetanus shot not long ago."

"I'm sorry. Penicillin. Just in case something nasty got in yer body from all the gouges and whatnot. I keep a supply here mostly for the animals. That's why this needle's so big. Roll onto your side. Ye'll need to take this in a big muscle."

Suzanne didn't move. Hadassah took the rag she had soaked in alcohol and waited. She motioned for Suzanne to roll over.

"There's no way." Suzanne crossed her arms like a kid making a very important point.

"It ain't goin' hurt ye any more than just the stick," Hadassah said. "Are you 'lergic?"

"No, I'm not, but I've had nothing but trouble since I got here. Now you want me to trust you just because you cleaned me up a bit and swabbed me with Novocain. I don't think so."

"In case ye can't tell, I ain't like the rest of these jackasses. Ye think I'd put them scissors to old Sol's neck if I weren't tryin' to help ye? I take care of the sick, animal and person. I'm the midwife. Been birthin' babies my whole life. Ifin' I was like the others, ye'd be dead by now."

"Why won't you tell me about the kids?"

"Cause I want ye to calm down. Ifin' it'll get ye to take this shot then I tell ye. Solomon's almost got 'em where he wants 'em. Another day or so, and they'll be beddin' everything ready to make babies. The best thing ye can do is take this shot, and take this night's rest. That's all I can gets ye."

Somewhere outside a man screamed. It was high pitched and full of terror. As the voice broke, Suzanne recognized it as Lovell. Somewhere out there, he was in extreme horror, pain, or both. She looked at Hadassah, but old woman cast her eyes to the floor.

"At least yer young'uns won't have got through that."

"What is that?"

"A powerful mixture of jimson weed, morning glory seeds, and mash liquor. I don't use any of that together. The seeds alone will make a body crazy for hours. Sol wanted the concoction."

"And you made it for him? I thought you said you were on our side."

Hadassah shrugged. "If I hadn't mixed it up, there's no tellin' how much Sol would have put into it. Probably been enough to kill a horse much less poor old Nathan. That shouldn't cause no permanent harm."

"Beyond altering his thoughts or causing him to trip out." Suzanne thought about what the old woman had said. "Wait, who's Nathan?"

"That man Solomon got me to make that concoction for."

"His name isn't Nathan."

"Ain't it? Could've sworn that was it." Hadassah shrugged her old stooped shoulders. "Mind's slippin' a bit. Been noticin' it for a spell now. I do know there's still time to save them kids. I just said they's *almost* ready. Old Sol didn't want to fool with givin' them that drink. I don't rightly know what amount would be safe for young'uns. He wants them most."

Suzanne stared into nothing. The kids were almost ready. Lovell had completely broken after the whipping, and there was no telling what shape he'd be in after drinking that cocktail. He screamed again, crying out about giant spiders. Her muscles tightened at the thought of what could be happening to him. Suzanne sighed. She was alone, tired, and hurting. Hadassah was right—the best she could do for everyone was to take her medicine and get a good night's rest while she could. She rolled over on her side and pulled her panties down to reveal the upper part of her buttocks to Hadassah. The alcohol swab went on cool. The prick stung, but nothing as bad as the pains she already had that night. The swab went over her bottom again.

"Thank you," Suzanne said.

"I've been arguin' with Sol for years that he's wrong. All this beddin' with yer family bound to bring trouble, but he's just as hardheaded as any man. I almost got away, but in this area, ya can't do nothing when yer name's Hassle. So I come back to play doctor."

"Tell me about how you learned to nurse."

"Me and Sol got away during the big war. I joined a Christian group and went to England. I drove an ambulance and helped patch up people. Solomon, he got put in the marines and sent to the Pacific. He's got all sorts of stars and ribbons for killin'. He loves to talk about the things he did to those poor slanty-eyed boys." Hadassah shook her head. "Thank God, I never had the blood come on me. Only God knows what might've happen to me then."

Hadassah walked to a cabinet hanging on the wall. She got a quilt out of it and brought it back to Suzanne. She tucked the quilt around her.

"Sol would've done kilt me ten times over, ifin' I didn't keep everybody fit." She sighed, staring off into nowhere, stretching and rubbing her back before turning back to Suzanne. "Let's try to get ya to sleep."

The old woman blew out the flame in the bright lamp. The room fell into a soft dimness. Suzanne closed her eyes and willed herself to sleep. She never slept well on her back, but rolling to her preferred sleeping side was not an option. Her cheek still hurt too much for any thought of that. She heard Hadassah settle into a cot somewhere behind her.

"Did you treat Warren after he was whipped?" Suzanne whispered.

"Yeah. Whippin' can be a horrible thing, Miss Clay. Few people, men or women, are strong enough to keep their convictions when they get a horse whippin'." Hadassah let out a long sigh. "Trust me, I've endured a few myself."

"That's horrible, why?"

"Told ye that Sol would've done killed me if he had another nursemaid, but since he don't and I won't train nern, he'd whip me. It's been a while though."

"I'm sorry."

"All in the past, Miss Clay, all in the past."

"Suzanne, please call me that. You've been so good to me that I might as well let you use my first name."

"Thank ye much, Suzanne. Now get ya some sleep. This is bound to be the last good night ye get."

Suzanne closed her eyes again. She listened to the noises of the night. Crickets chirped out in the distance. Pigs and other barnyard animals made their nocturnal noises. As she drifted off to sleep, the whippoorwill started up again from a distance. Lovell cried again so faintly that Suzanne paid it almost no attention as she slipped off into a sleep of pure exhaustion.

When the door burst open with a loud slam, Suzanne was startled out of a deep sleep, maybe the deepest of the night. Her sleep-hazed eyesight made out the outline of Solomon standing in the doorway. The morning sun glared so much it made her eyes water. She noticed that her eye on the side of her jaw wound was swollen shut.

"Get up," Solomon said. "Ye's had enough of a good night's sleep."

Suzanne eased to a sitting position. Her body ached all over. Her head swam. She touched the side of her head and felt the fever coming off her swollen eye and cheek. Solomon stepped into the shack and closed the door behind him.

"What do ye want?" Hadassah walked up from behind Suzanne and stood beside her. "I ain't done nursing her yet."

"By the looks of her, ye should've put her out of her misery."

Suzanne stood up. The quilt over her bare legs fell to the floor as she caught her balance. As the blanket bunched up at her feet, she remembered that all she wore were her panties. A sudden rush of embarrassment overtook her. She tugged at her shirttail trying to cover herself.

"Well, that's a welcomin' sight," Solomon said. "I'd have more than imagination if I'd my way last evening."

Suzanne saw the lustful look in Solomon's eyes. They

narrowed like he was trying to get a good look at her legs and process it into memory. She squatted down to pick up the blanket and wrapped it around her waist.

"Ye can see she ain't decent." Hadassah pulled the long pair of scissors out of her apron pocket. "I'd hate to remind ye of how ladies should be treated, by makin' ye one."

Suzanne laughed. It was a chuckle that she hid as a cough. Either way, her face roared its objection of being stretched too much. Solomon showed his disapproval of the laugh with an evil glare. He stepped up to Hadassah and poked his finger into her drooping chest.

"Have her ready by lunchtime. I don't want no excuses. We's got a full day today, includin' a lunchtime baptizin', and I want her there." Solomon pulled his finger back. "And I'll be needin' another two bottles of that elixir ye made up, sooner the better."

"That man's done had two bottles of the stuff. I don't know what it might do to him," Hadassah protested.

"So far, it's done exactly what I wanted it to. Besides a case of the screamin' trots, he ain't had no ill effects."

Hadassah dug in her medicine cabinet and brought out two little bottles full of the stuff Suzanne watched Lovell drink after being beaten. She handed them to Solomon. "Any more, it'll kill him. I'm almost sure of that."

Suzanne became acutely aware of the reality of what Solomon had been force-feeding Lovell. She felt scared for his safety again. After the events of the night, she'd forgotten how many feelings she had for him. The last thing she wanted was for him to be poisoned. Even brainwashing would be better than that. At least then he would still be alive.

"T'won't need any more than this."

Solomon pocketed the bottles. He looked at Suzanne again. She could feel the lust radiating off him like the heat coming off her injured jaw.

"I thought lust was a sin," she said.

"So's bein' a whore." Solomon reached out and groped her breast hard. "Take the mote out of ye own eye before tryin' to get the speck out of mine."

Hadassah opened and closed the scissors hard and loud. Solomon fidgeted, let go of Suzanne's breast, and headed back to the door. He left without saying anything else. She, however, felt dirty, very dirty. The feeling of his hand twisting her breast lingered. It bothered her that the touch wouldn't go away and, worse, she felt his finger twirling her pubic hair again.

"I guess we need to get ye somethin' to wear, and let ye get cleaned up," Hadassah said. "I'll go get some hot water from the cookhouse. Reckon they'll be windin' down breakfast by now, but there'll be plenty of hot water. Ye can wipe yerself off."

"Thank you."

Hadassah left Suzanne standing in the shack. She let the blanket fall back to her feet. The cool morning air swirled around her bare and scraped legs. It felt refreshing and clean. Deep down she wished she could let the fresh air swirl through her body and force out all the sludge the Hassles caused.

18

He that believeth and is baptized
shall be saved;
But he that believeth not
shall be damned

MARK 16:16

SUZANNE STARED OUT THE windows in Hadassah's shack. The morning light softened all the colors of autumn. The morning seemed muted as well. Animals grunted and snorted in their usual barnyard way, but now they sounded like they were all the way to the edge of the woods. Only the smell of smoke curling up from different houses filled Suzanne's nose.

"Feelin' any better after gettin' a bit clean?" Hadassah asked coming into the shack.

Suzanne turned to the old woman, half startled. "Yeah."

Hadassah fanned a long blue dress out. It hung in the air and flapped like an unfurling flag. "Brought this to ye. Ain't much to look at for city folk, but ya won't have to walk around wrapped in a quilt."

Suzanne pulled the quilt draped over her shoulders tighter around her. She'd forgotten about it. Hadassah walked across the room and laid the dress on the cot. Suzanne turned back to the window as Hadassah started knocking around behind her. Metal bowls and other things clanked as she shuffled them around. Suzanne took one more deep breath of the morning-fresh air and went to the cot. The quilt dropped to the floor as she picked up the dress. The material felt rough in her hands, but was a pleasant color of blue, almost cobalt. She studied the stitching. The dress looked like something from *Little House on the Prairie*, but the tailoring was top quality.

Suzanne stepped into the dress and pulled it on. She reached behind her neck and fastened the button. The collar of the dress stood high on her neck, almost touching her jaw line. The fabric felt even rougher against her body with no undergarments to separate her more tender skin from the clothing.

"I must look like something else in this get up."

The old woman turned around. Her heavy brown dress lacked the high collar that Suzanne's had. "Well, it ain't the dress that's ruinin' yer looks," she said. "That *face* is somethin' else."

"I figured. I probably look like a witch from a children's book." She walked to a mirror on the wall. Her face stared back swollen, and discolored. "I'm even green in places."

"That'll go away in a few days," Hadassah said. "Let's put some salve on it."

Hadassah held up a bowl with a wooden spoon in it. Suzanne walked over to her. The old woman swabbed her finger in the goo and started wiping on Suzanne's face. The salve neither burned nor cooled. It just felt heavy. She closed her eyes and let Hadassah slather her with it.

The door slammed opened. Hadassah's finger jabbed a sore place on Suzanne's arm. She started up with a jolt, opening her eyes and letting out a cry of pain and fright. Agrippa stood in the doorway. He grinned showing the misshapen teeth in his mouth.

"Ain't got time to tart yeself up," he walked inside. "We's got places to be."

"She ain't tartin' up, 'Grippa. I's doctorin' her sores with a salve."

He shook his head. "Ain't time for that either. Daddy Sol's called the family together. We's havin' a baptizin'."

Suzanne didn't like the sound of that. She thought about the kids and how they might have given into the Hassles last night. "Who?"

"Ye know him. Now get up and get ready to go."

Suzanne stood and walked toward Agrippa. Hadassah tried to stop her, but she pulled away from the old woman's grip. She stopped in front of Agrippa. He snatched her arm with a tight grip and dragged her toward the door.

"You don't have to squeeze my arm so hard. I won't try anything."

"Can't trust ye. Already run off into them woods, didn't ye?"

"Look at me." Suzanne ran a hand over her face. "I've learned my lesson."

Agrippa led her down the steps onto the hard-packed ground and let go of her arm.

"Aight, but don't try nothin' funny, or I'll kill ye. Understand?"

Suzanne nodded. A line of people passed by as she and Agrippa walked away from Hadassah's shack. Every one of them had bright orange hair. Each was speckled with deep brown freckles. A round faced boy with wide set eyes and a flat nose smiled at Suzanne as he passed. He gave her a slight wave with his short stubby hand. She recognized the telltale signs of Down's syndrome. It didn't tell of inbreeding as much as it did of parental age. He kept smiling sweetly, and Suzanne returned his wave, as an older bent man took him by the arm and pulled him along.

As she and Agrippa stepped into a widening area of the farm, Suzanne got her first good look at the Hassle community. Long buildings made from gray boards stretched along one side of a wide dirt road. Each building had two doors at the end. The other side of the road was lined with smaller shacks of the same material. The road dead ended at a large log church building. The throngs of Hassles gathered in front of this building, but none went inside. Agrippa and Suzanne stopped at the edge of the crowd.

"Aren't we going in?" she asked.

"Don't baptize on the inside," Agrippa said. "Ain't enough room."

Suzanne looked up as the church doors opened. Amanda and Christopher walked down the steps and turned to face the church. Next Heather came out by herself. Then Ty walked out. His left eye was bruised and swollen. Ty spied her. He cut through the crowd to her.

"What happened to you, Ms. Clay?" he asked.

"I fell down. What happened to you? Did they do that to you?"

Ty cut his eyes to Agrippa. "I fell down, too."

"Are you the one being baptized?" she asked.

"No, they said that they needed to teach me one more thing before I could be baptized."

"Do you want to be baptized?"

"Not really, but I thought maybe I should just to make them happy," Ty answered.

Suzanne looked at Ty. She rubbed his shoulders and

thought about the bleeding shreds that Lovell's back had been in after his lesson. Ty smiled at her. She tried to smile back, but the pain in her mouth was too much. More commotion brought her focus back on the church building. Sheba walked out carrying a copper bucket. A bit of water sloshed out onto the small porch. She stood to the right side and sat the bucket at her feet. Esau walked out next. He bent low to get through the door and carried a copper ladle in one hand and a copper chalice in the other. Then Solomon walked out in a long white robe with grapevines embroidered down each side of the front. Each purple grape looked like a place where blood seeped out from small pin pricks. He smiled a large beaming smile that showed his horrible yellow teeth. Beside him stood Lovell, whose smile was just as broad. A boy, who looked a little older than Ty, came out of the church behind Solomon.

"That's Jonathan," Ty pointed like a kid excited to show someone a new friend. "He's been our Bible teacher."

Suzanne nodded. Jonathan carried a glass salt shaker and a small cooler. The Igloo cooler was the first modern thing Suzanne had seen since being brought to the Hassle farm. He sat the cooler down to the side of Solomon and opened the top of the salt shaker.

"Brothers and sisters, sons and daughters, nieces and nephews, today is a happy day for our family," Solomon said over the low din of the crowd. The murmuring stopped. "We's gettin' another new member by baptism assigned by our Father Lot."

The crowd clapped softly. Suzanne glared at the porch. Lovell kept his face frozen in a broad grin, but his eyes didn't match. A small familiar glimmer seemed trapped there. It was dull and tarnished, but she saw it. Maybe it was just wishful thinking, she hoped not. Solomon patted him on the shoulder. Lovell unbuttoned the blue chambray shirt he wore and took it off. He handed it to Sheba. She folded it over her arm as he lay down on the porch floor with his hands placed under him at the small of his back.

"Jonathan will now make Warren Lovell our cousin by salt," Solomon said.

Jonathan knelt over Lovell and poured a large amount of salt into this hand. Suzanne had trouble seeing over some of the crowd, but it looked like the salt was sprinkled thickly around Lovell's navel. Once his hand was emptied of salt, Jonathan dusted both of his hands off over the navel and stood.

"Now the fire from Heaven, like in the day of the destruction," Jonathan said, in a deep smoky voice.

Solomon opened the cooler. He took an embroidered napkin from his robe's pocket. He reached into the cooler with it and brought out a large hunk of ice. He handed it to Jonathan who held the chunk with the napkin. The boy knelt back over Lovell. Suzanne lost sight of what he was doing to Lovell as the crowd leaned forward for a better look. Lovell yelled out in pain, but Jonathan kept over him.

"What's he doing to him?" Suzanne asked Agrippa. She tried to keep the fear out of her voice.

"Nothin' to worry 'bout. He's just getting the sign of Lot," Agrippa answered.

"What's that?"

"Ye'll see."

Jonathan stood and gave the ice back to Solomon who tossed it into the cooler. Lovell rose to his feet, an angry red ring puffed up around his navel. Suzanne realized it was a deep salt burn, probably enough to leave a lasting scar. It looked almost like the birthmark she had mistaken for a scald mark a few nights before.

"Warren Lovell, ye have received the Mark of Lot. Do you wish to be baptized into his family?" Solomon asked.

"Yes." His body trembled just a little. Suzanne figured it was from the pain of the salt burn and probably some reaction to all that junk they'd been making him pour down his gullet. She blamed the flat, artificial look on his face on the same thing. Only his eyes looked anything like what Lovell usually was. A small bit of life remained there, but not much.

"So be it." Solomon took the copper chalice from Esau. He dipped it into the copper bucket at Sheba's feet. "I baptize you in the name of God and our Father Lot."

Water ran down Lovell's face and plastered his bangs to his forehead as Solomon turned the chalice upside down over his head. The old preacher handed the chalice back to Esau and took the dipper. He filled it with water as well.

"Now to quench the fire of Heaven."

Solomon poured the water over Lovell's navel. He wiped over it with his hand. The remaining water washed over Lovell's crotch, darkening his pants as if he had peed himself.

"Thank you, Daddy Sol," Lovell said, with what sounded to Suzanne like a forced sincerity.

"Go my child, be fruitful and multiply," Solomon responded. "Now yer first communion."

He handed Lovell a bottle of the jimson weed liquor. Lovell took it and swallowed as if it were nothing more than sacramental wine. Then Lovell bowed to the crowd who started to whistle and clap. Esau and Sheba took their ceremonial objects and reentered the church. Lovell walked in after them followed by Jonathan. Solomon looked out over his family.

"Tonight, we eat the Feast of Salt for our new family member and our new salvation. God's punishment is at an end. We will rule the earth."

He turned and walked into the church. The doors closed, and the crowd began to break up and wander away. Suzanne spotted Hadassah walking away shaking her bent head. She wanted to run to her but couldn't leave Ty. Solomon planned on flogging the boy next, and she wouldn't let him from her sight now. She took him by the hand.

"Ty, no matter what, stay as close to me as you can," she whispered to him.

"Yes, ma'am."

Christopher, Amanda, and Heather walked back to Suzanne and Ty. Agrippa circled them like a vulture waiting to dine on rotting flesh. Each of the students hugged Suzanne, but no one asked what happened to her.

"Are you kids okay?" she asked.

"We're fine," Amanda said.

"Have you seen Rachel or Eric?" Suzanne asked.

"Yes," Heather said. "We ate supper with them last night. That's when Rachel said she was having a baby."

"Eric said Solomon told him that he was going to give me and Heather a baby," Amanda said. "I don't want a baby right now though, Ms. Clay."

"Don't worry. That's not going to happen," Suzanne said.

"Don't be tellin' these young'uns not to believe Daddy

Sol," Agrippa said finally standing still. "Ye keep fillin' up their heads with lies, and Daddy Sol'll get rid of ye like he did that darkie. They ain't never goin' figure out what really happened. Esau let me cut his face up real good with broken glass."

"I'd like to see him try that with us." Suzanne stared straight into the harelip's beady green eyes. She didn't blink, but he did. A twinge of guilt over the trooper's death twisted around her spine. "I'm not afraid of him or you."

"I'd like to see *ye* say that to *him*."

Agrippa grabbed her by the arm putting pressure on one of puncture wounds from the honey locust tree. It singed with pain, but she set her teeth and didn't let it show. Suzanne jerked her arm free from him.

"You can show us where we're going, but I'm tired of being pulled around everywhere like a dog on a leash."

Agrippa snarled as best his split lip would let him. "Fine."

He walked toward the house. Suzanne motioned for the kids to follow, and she brought up the rear. Things had been happening *to* her too much, now she intended to make things happen. Time was running out. The feast marked the beginning of breeding. Suzanne remembered that from her readings.

19

Suffer the little children
to come unto me.

MARK 10:14

SUZANNE LAY ON THE small bed in a cramped little room with her eyes closed. She had taken a nap while the kids milled around, but now she listened to them. They had no idea she played 'possum.

"Do you think that Ms. Clay is all right?" Heather's soft voice was so reminiscent of a little girl.

"She said she was," Ty said. "Said she fell down."

"That's what they told you to say," Christopher said. "After he hit you all over, that Agrippa told you to say you fell down."

"I don't think she's lying. She's a grown up. They don't have to lie about that kind of stuff."

"I don't think we're going to get out of here," Amanda said.

"Don't be stupid, Amanda. Ms. Clay won't let us down," Ty said.

Suzanne rolled over onto her back and let out a sigh to give the kids a hint that she might be waking up. She didn't want to embarrass them if they realized she had been listening. A groan came out by accident as she stretched out. Her stiff muscles hurt with pangs of pain and low aches.

"I think she's waking up," Heather said.

Suzanne sat up and tossed her legs off the side of the bed. She stretched her arms over her head. It felt both good and unbelievably painful at the same time. She even yawned, which stretched the puncture wound in her mouth and made it burn like she'd swished Tabasco sauce.

"Are you kids okay?"

They nodded yes. She looked them over. Each bore worry lines over their youthful faces. Ty's seemed the worst because of the bruises and swelling. She figured she looked much the same to them.

"Did I miss anything while I was asleep?"

Ty shook his head. "No, we kind of dozed off too, for a little while." He looked apologetic. "I'm sorry. I should've stayed awake to keep watch."

"That's okay, Ty. We've all had a tough last few days. Sleep will keep us ready for whatever we have to do."

He smiled and seemed more at ease. The door to the room flew open as Sheba stepped inside carrying a plate with a loaf of cornbread. She shoved it toward Christopher. He reached up with shaky hands and took the plate. Sheba walked out without saying a word. Solomon stepped in after she had left. He carried a tray with tin cups and a pitcher. He handed it to Heather, who placed it on the floor.

"I had an idee that y'all might be peckish. We'll be havin' our big feast tonight, and I don't want y'all eatin' like hogs. This bread and water should get ye over 'til then," Solomon said.

"How nice of you to deliver it yourself." Suzanne used every bit of sarcasm that she could.

"Don't flatter yerself too much, Miss Clay. I just didn't have anythin' else goin' on."

Solomon looked her over. She felt his eyes wash over her body like a cold rain penetrating the thin clothing that

Hadassah had given her to wear. A look of contempt crossed his lips. "Ye look like manure."

One of the kids snorted a laugh. It was the kind of humor only children would find funny. Ty shushed whoever it had been. Suzanne smiled at Solomon as best she could.

"It'd be hard for me to look much better, considering things."

"We can't have our prize sow lookin' like that at the feast. Ye'll bathe yerself and put on something better than one of Hadassah's old rags."

"A new outfit would actually be nice," she said. "How out of the ordinary."

"Listen here, I ain't takin' no more lip off ya. I'd soon as have ya strung up and gutted than bed ye to any of my children so keep yer graces. Understand. The bathing is for purification much like our feast."

Hate flared on Solomon's face, and Suzanne nodded her understanding. She never let her eye contact slip from his, though.

"I'll have someone fetch up some hot water, and then they'll get ya for yer bath." Solomon looked at the kids. "The rest of ye try not to get too much dirtier. I reckon young'uns don't care about looks as long as all the bits and pieces work and feel good."

Solomon honked a laughed and left, locking the door behind him. Suzanne let out a long puff of air. She hadn't realized she had been holding so much back.

"What did he mean?" Heather asked.

"Guys, I shouldn't have to be the one to tell you this, but they plan on having sex with us, so they can have more babies,"

Suzanne swallowed the lump of disgust in her throat. "When you do this without a person's permission, it's called rape, and it's illegal."

"So we don't let them," Ty said.

"The problem is they can take it. At least from us girls," Suzanne said. "It's a bit harder with guys."

"What do you mean?" Christopher was so childishly innocent.

Suzanne sighed. "Things just work a bit different, but I think I can help us all."

The kids listened to her as if she read their favorite book. Suzanne explained some basic self-defense techniques that they might use to keep from being taken advantage of. She used the simplest language she could and tried her hardest to make sure they understood without depriving them of too much of their fleeting innocence. The kids seemed to understand and even asked a few questions. The whole ordeal exhausted Suzanne more than she could have imagined. She eased back down on the bed. The kids sprawled out the floor nibbling on the dry pone of cornbread and sipping the water. They didn't say anything.

Suzanne lay a long time, or it seemed to be a long time, with her eyes closed. They burned, and she wished that she had a cool wet cloth to put on them to help with the fire. The kids hadn't spoken since the conversation. Every now and again one of them would shuffle on the wooden floor, and Suzanne would know that they were still in the room and awake. The bright light that had been in her eyes when she had lain down again was dimmer. The afternoon set in and soon the feast would begin. The smell of food cooking in the cookhouse wafted into the room. If she hadn't eaten some of the cornbread, she would have been very hungry, but the gritty pone satisfied her enough and thoughts of their impending evening took away whatever appetite remained.

The lock on the door clicked. Suzanne sat up and turned towards it. She opened her hot eyes and blinked out some tears as the door opened. Agrippa stood there. A grin spread his lips wider than his cleft palate ever could.

"Daddy Sol told me to git ya for a bath," he said.

Suzanne didn't try to hide the disgust from her face. "He sent *you*?"

"I'm the only one able. Everybody else's got a part in the feast. I'm just to keep guard around the farm, and to help ye get clean." Agrippa held up his arm.

A calico dress was draped over his forearm. It looked thicker than what Suzanne wore, so she felt some relief in the fact that she might have a better dress. He raised his other hand which held a bar of homemade lye soap wrapped in a rag of old white flour sackcloth.

"Well, is the bath ready?" Suzanne asked.

"I wouldn't come to get ye if it weren't."

Suzanne stood and walked to the door. "Kids, I guess the feast will be in a little while. Just do what they tell you, and I'll see you in a bit."

Ty jumped to his feet. "I'm going with Miss Clay."

"I don't think so, young'un," Agrippa said.

Suzanne would have liked to have someone else with her, but Ty didn't need to see her in the altogether anymore than Agrippa did. She smiled at the young man.

"Ty, I need you to stay here with the others and make sure they're safe. Is that okay?"

Ty nodded, but she could tell he was not happy with the decision. She mussed his hair and followed Agrippa into the hallway. He locked the door and pointed to a room at the end of the long corridor. It was the only one with an opened door, and light streamed into the hall. It took a moment to realize it was the room she had escaped from. Agrippa pushed her forward. The room was lit by an overhead lamp and two more lamps, one on a table, the other on the cabinet holding a washbasin. The large wooden tub still sat in the room. A thicker curtain hung over it from a removable metal holder. She would be able to wash without Agrippa seeing everything. This gave her some comfort.

Agrippa closed the door behind them and locked it. He laid the dress on the table near the lamp and then tossed the soap and rag into the tub. He grinned at Suzanne.

"There ye go."

Suzanne looked at him. He stared back.

"Can you turn around until I get behind the curtain?"

"No."

Suzanne sighed and started to unbutton the dress she wore. She tried her best to keep the front up as she did this, and tried to pretend like Agrippa wasn't watching the whole time. His face appeared to have a wolfish lust on it. To him this must be the equivalent of a striptease, Suzanne thought. She turned her back to him and faced the curtain of the tub. The dress fell from her body. She stepped out of it and into the tub pulling the curtain to as quickly as she could. The water felt lukewarm and wonderful on her feet. She stooped and grabbed up the soap and rag. Rubbing the rag over the soap and wringing it out before standing erect, Suzanne started washing her face.

The bruises and cuts were tender to the touch, and she didn't put much pressure on these points. Then she moved down her body. She took a chance to glance out at Agrippa. He stared at her and jiggled his groin with his hand. He was getting off.

"So, what is it that you have to do tonight instead of coming to the feast?" Suzanne asked.

"Watchin' the road." Agrippa stammered over his words. "Daddy Sol thinks some more cops might be comin' to see what happen to that darkie. I told him wasn't no such thing goin' happen. We made a good job on that car. Nobody would know it wasn't a wreck."

"That doesn't seem fair." Suzanne finished with the soap. She dropped it into the water with a splash. "You should get to celebrate too."

"That's what I thought, especially since I can make children, but Daddy Sol said no."

"Is John Mark going to be on look out too?"

"Course not. Daddy Sol, don't make him miss nuthin'. Ye'd think he was Daddy Sol's own boy the ways he treats him." Agrippa sounded jealous. "I ought slice up his purty face like I did that darkie trooper's."

Suzanne stooped and rinsed the soap first from her face then from the rest of her body. She took her washrag and wrapped her right hand in it. The water cooled and drizzled down her arm. She opened the curtain to the back of the tub and climbed out.

"Do you have a towel or something? I need to dry off before I put my clothes on."

She looked around the curtain and saw Agrippa looking around for something. While his back was turned, she walked to the window. It was still open, and a cool breeze drifted in.

"Hey, ya ain't tryin' to escape again, are ye?" Agrippa said.

Suzanne leaned on the sill. She arched her back and looked over her shoulder. A million pinups in magazines had struck the same pose. Agrippa looked at her with more lust in his eyes than Suzanne thought a human could show. He also held a quilt in his hand.

"This air feels so good on my body. It's got my nipples all hard. I bet old John Mark would love to be in your place right now. He's been trying his hardest to win me over since I got here, but I'm here alone with you. What do you think about that?" Suzanne couldn't believe she said that, but it worked.

"Reckon it's good." Agrippa licked at his lips and walked to her.

He held the quilt open. Suzanne turned her head to look out the window as he placed the quilt around her shoulders. The edges spread out enough to hide any arm movements. Just what she had hoped for.

Suzanne grabbed a strand of barbwire with her right hand. She took the edge of the quilt on her left and twirled. The quilt wrapped around her and at the same time she jerked the strand of wire free. The rag kept her hand from further injury.

She looked Agrippa in his face. He almost panted. The front of his dungarees bulged out, and he couldn't keep his hand off the bulge. Suzanne made an obvious look at it and smiled.

"Why don't you let me help you with that?"

"Aight."

Suzanne sashayed around Agrippa. He tried to turn to keep facing her. She shook her head with her lip poked out like she was disappointed.

"Haven't you ever had a reach around?" she used a low sexy voice. Agrippa shook his head. "Turn your back to me. You'll love it."

"Make it rough. I like it rough." Agrippa did as she said.

"Don't worry; it's going to be rough."

Suzanne let the quilt fall from her shoulders. She undid his pants and let them fall around his knees.

"Bend over a little and rest you weight on the windowsill," she said.

He obeyed. Suzanne pushed against him to help pin him to the window. He giggled with delight. She took the free end of the barbed wire strand in her left hand. Swiftly, the garrote went over the harelip's head. He didn't notice until she tugged the wire around his neck, and the barbs bit into his flesh. Agrippa tried to fight against her. She had him pinned well and with his pants around his knees he couldn't push away with the legs because he would become entangled and fall. Suzanne pulled as hard as she could. Her left hand began to bleed as the wire cut into the skin.

Agrippa gagged and hacked. He reached up with his dirty hands and tried to claw at her face. A time or two he hit a bruise. She winced but never let her pressure on the wire go and began sawing it back and forth. The muscles in her arms began to burn and ache. Her biceps quivered and hopped like a muscle spasm. Agrippa's knees gave out on him, and he crumpled to the floor. His gagging now garbled with blood. Suzanne knelt down with him. She kept the wire as taut as she could still sliding it back and forth little by little. One last spasm came from Agrippa in an attempt to inhale, then he went limp. His tongue lolled out of his mouth and dark crimson blood splattered on the floor.

Suzanne let the wire fall from her hand. Trickles of blood ran down her freshly washed arm. Rivulets of darker blood ran down Agrippa's neck from the gash the wire had made. Suzanne rested for a few minutes, waiting for her muscles to quit trembling. Adrenaline and fatigue weren't the only thing that made her shake. She'd never killed anything outside of the odd mosquito. Even if Agrippa wasn't much better than one of those annoying insects, he was a human. She looked at this body slumped on the floor. At that very moment, she felt no better than the Hassles. They did horrible things and justified it the whole time. If anyone asked her why she killed him, her justification would be self defense, but murder was murder. She hated herself for what she had done, and what she was about to do. Probably in the not so distant future, a whole new set of actions would increase her self-loathing.

Suzanne took a deep breath and then caught Agrippa under the arms to drag him to the tub. She hefted him into the water head first. The white, slightly frothy water turned pink then red with his blood. Suzanne finagled the corpse until he folded up into the tub. She pulled the curtain around it.

Puddles and streaks of blood marked the floor from the deed. Everything within her felt numb. She'd never been in a fistfight, but now she had nearly sawed a man's head off. She shook the thought away and used the quilt to mop up the blood. Satisfied that she had cleaned up most of the evidence, Suzanne went to the basin and pitcher. She took the rag still wrapped around her right hand and washed off her bloody arm and palm. Then she used the rag as a bandage for her bleeding hand.

Suzanne got dressed. The garment was a bit big and looked like a sack on her, but that didn't matter. She tried to open the door. It was locked. She needed keys—she had forgotten about that during the struggle with Agrippa. Going to the tub, she set her jaw, averted her eyes from the gore, rolled up her sleeves, and plunged her hands into the bloody water, finally finding the keys in his pocket.

Suzanne snuck out of the death room and locked the door behind her. She didn't figure anyone would miss Agrippa until much later or even tomorrow. She would let herself back into the room with the kids, and after all the feasting the night had to offer, she would use the keys to get everyone away. It was almost too easy.

20

And ye shall feast on the bounty;
ye shall lay with others
And know them
to bring about the new generation.

BOOK OF LOT 20:14

NOT LONG AFTER SUZANNE had come back into the room with the kids, the smell of food started wafting to them in a constant stream. She didn't know what kind of strange foods might be there, but it definitely smelled like a scrumptious feast in the making. It even smelled like baked sweets might be in order. She hadn't seen anything close to a dessert since she had gotten there. Suzanne felt almost giddy. It was like being a kid on Christmas Day. The kids looked at her strangely.

"Why are you so happy?" Ty asked.

"Am I?"

"You're smiling, Ms. Clay," Heather said.

Suzanne noticed the twinges of pain that burned around the edges of the stab wound in her cheek. She touched the rims of her mouth to confirm that she was smiling. After doing what she had done, how could she be so happy?

"I *am* smiling. I don't know why. Sometimes when we're under a lot of stress, we do things that don't match our feelings."

The kids nodded like they understood. The problem was Suzanne *was* happy. She could almost feel the freedom of getting back to town. The lock on the room door clicked. It swung open. The lanky teenage boy from the baptism—Suzanne remembered Ty telling her it was Jonathan—stood in the door. His red hair lay plastered to his head, split down the middle revealing his smooth freckled forehead. A few festering zits shined on his chin. If Suzanne had seen him anywhere else, he would have gone unnoticed as a typical teen guy, except that he was missing an ear. She hadn't noticed that at the baptism.

"It's time to go to the feast," he said.

His voice was deep and almost sultry. Suzanne found it unsettling. Her giddiness faded away as she looked at him.

"Who are you?" Suzanne asked.

"He's Jonathan," Ty said. "He's the one that's been teaching us about his Bible. I told you that at Mr. Lovell's baptism."

"Our Bible," Jonathan corrected. "Ya're part of the flock now, or will be."

The boy sounded too much like Solomon for Suzanne's taste. She thought her plan after killing Agrippa was too easy. This boy would probably be the wrench in her gears.

"How did ya get back in here?" Jonathan asked Suzanne. "Y'a're the one called Miss Clay, ain't ya?"

"I'm Ms. Clay, and Agrippa let me back in after I bathed."

The boy eyed her with his deep green eyes. They narrowed to slits as if he were straining to read her very soul. He was even more like Solomon than she had first thought.

"Where's he now?"

"How would I know? He kept ranting about having to keep watch tonight instead of being at the feast. He's probably started his sentry job," Suzanne said.

"Sounds like him to be complainin'. We all has our jobs to do. He always thinks he gets the short end of everythin.'"

Jonathan fluffed his hands in the air, meaning for the kids to get up. "We don't want y'all to be late. Y'all's kinda of the guests of honor. That's a least what Daddy Sol been callin' ya."

"So, he's your father too?" Suzanne asked.

"In name only, ma'am." Suzanne stopped half standing. Politeness came from a Hassle's mouth; maybe things would work out after all. "He's trainin' me in his footsteps. I'm the next preacher for the family."

Suzanne stood the rest of the way up, as the kids rose to their feet. The skinny, gangly boy standing in front of her looked anything but evil enough to carry on Solomon's ways.

"Well, let's get this over with," Suzanne said.

Jonathan let the kids into the hall first, then Suzanne. He walked behind them as they headed down the hall to the grand staircase. All the doors along the hall were closed this evening, leaving the narrow hallway dim. Only the glowing lamplight from the ground floor lit the way. The smell of the different foods mingled and seemed to hang just at nose level. She hated to admit it to herself, but Suzanne really was hungry. She wanted to feast. The kids started down the stairway. The sound of applause rose from below. Suzanne took to the stairs. The whole lower floor of the house was filled with tables and chairs. Every table had chargers of food on them. Everything imaginable from a farm like this was present. It appeared that every Hassle stood there clapping as the guests of honor descended to the feast.

When Suzanne and the kids reached the ground floor, Esau ushered them to Solomon's side. He stood at the end of a grander table than the rest. It was engraved with grapes and other fruits. Solomon wore the robe he donned at the baptism. Lovell, Rachel, and Eric stood on his left side. The two children looked like they always did, but Lovell looked pale. His skin took on a waxy look in the candlelight, and his eyes seemed more distant. The spark she'd noticed at the baptism was even duller now. It disappointed her, but after all she knew he was being put through, it wasn't surprising. Suzanne and the kids stood to his right. She was the farthest away. All eyes were on them.

For the first time, Suzanne saw how many members of the Hassle family were present. The sound of the clapping was intense. It almost overwhelmed her. The clan tonight appeared to be two hundred strong. The group at the baptism would have been about a hundred she thought. The rest of the family must have been staying in those long shacks. The few distinct faces she could make out from the shadows explained why she hadn't seen these Hassles. They were more deformed than Agrippa, Esau, or Jonathan combined.

Suzanne spotted a pinhead, with a small patch of orange hair at the top of his pointed head. The little Hassle with Down's syndrome swayed in and out of the shadows. A few others had distinctive facial features that spoke of genetic anomalies, but she didn't know what they were.

"A few words before our feast," Solomon said, bringing Suzanne's attention back to him. "This is the first time we've ever had this feast, and there's a reason. The prophecy from our Father Lot ain't never been fulfilled until today."

Murmurs rumbled through the audience. It seemed to Suzanne that the entire clan hadn't been informed of what was happening. This didn't surprise her. She would have been surprised if half of the gathered clan even understood what Solomon was saying.

"We eat tonight the Feast of Purification. Our Father Lot's wife was turned to salt for her disbelief in God. He turned her into salt to clean her soul. Salt purifies all," Solomon said. "I asked Jonathan to read the scripture for us before our meal."

Jonathan came up from the crowd. He carried a Bible opened to the back. Suzanne recognized the pulpy insert that was the Book of Lot.

Jonathan cleared his throat. "Book of Lot, Chapter 20: A time will come to pass when ye my children will be barren and none shall come from thy loins. This be the time of impure blood. For as my sons, Ben-ami and Moab are my sons and grandsons, so will be some of ye. Yea, thy might be thy own cousin. As it be, man must have clean blood." He paused and cleared his throat again. The boy's voice was deep and soothing, but it trembled as he spoke. Suzanne recognized that he must not speak in front of this many people very often. "At that time of barrenness, I shall send ye one who will save my children. She shall have the name Rachel, and shall bring in new blood. This blood will purify and make ye fruitful. With the new blood will come the great Whore, the bringer of the New Jerusalem. She will be mother of many and make the new Zion rise and the seals to be broken."

Solomon put his hand on Jonathan shoulder. "As many of ye know, if not all of ye, my daughter was named Rachel by her mother. I's known since her birth that this day would come. Now, my dear daughter is with child, the child of one other than our family."

He patted Jonathan again. The boy turned a pulpy page and picked up with another verse.

"Same book and chapter, verse twelve. 'At that time, those who are fruitful, those who bleed regularly or produce the white seed shall be presented with other lambs. These lambs shall bare new sheep for my flock. First shall come a ram converted by the Fire of Heaven. He shall first plant his seed in the new ewes to insure their fruitfulness so as thy seed shall not be wasted. When those ewes carry their young to the time of birth, then ye shall know these new sheep and be fruitful. These are the words of thy Father Lot. And ye shall feast on the bounty; ye shall lay with others and know them to bring about the new generation. There shall be salt in all the food of thy feast to purify ye for the mission of God and thy Father Lot. Eat and drink deep. Ye who are fruitful are the blessed. May the love of your Father Lot be with ye even until the end of time.'"

Jonathan closed the book. He had reached the end of the insert. Suzanne had peeked at the end when she had her own copy of the Book of Lot. It was the way she read most every book. She always needed to know the end of the story. Now, Solomon dismissed Jonathan with another pat on the back. He smiled and opened his hands before the assembly.

"Brothers, sisters, nieces, nephews, sons, daughters, and cousins of all sorts, celebrate. For those who can make children eat at the table to my left. The rest choose where ye will," Solomon said. "Eat, drink, and be happy for tomorrow we begin a new life, and those who shan't be with us shall die under out feet."

A meager group of the red haired congregation broke off from the rest and went to the table on Solomon's left. A sheet of paper hung from the front of this long table. Written on this sheet of paper in a shaky childlike script was: The Fruitful

Table. The last thing Solomon said kept turning over and over in her mind.

"What do you mean?" she asked him.

"About what?" Solomon asked almost innocently.

"Die under your feet."

"Rachel's baby's the Savior. Father Lot has told me that those who won't believe must be kilt." Solomon smiled.

"Just of your family?"

"We's ready to bring death to the whole world, starting tomorrow," Solomon smiled. "Eat big and thank God ye's with us, Miss Clay."

Suzanne felt her jaw drop. How had she stumbled into a situation where someone was trying to use her and her students to bring death to "disbelievers"? This was still all too surreal.

Sheba started picking up the plates at the far end of their table. She put food on them and passed them back out. She moved down until she got to Suzanne.

"What'cha wantin' to feast on?" Sheba asked.

Suzanne didn't like the look on Sheba's face. "Whatever you want me to have, Sheba. I've lost my appetite."

"I think ye ought to have nothin'."

Solomon shot an angry look at Sheba. "I don't care what ye think. Get Miss Clay a nice variety of our bounty. Why should she miss out on your God-given talent?"

He put his hand on her bare arm. The dress sleeves were still rolled up from when she fished the keys out of Agrippa's pocket. She felt the hardness of his calluses. Even his finger-tips seemed to be callused.

"I hope that Sheba's not been too mean to ye. I might not like ye, but I don't want anyone else bein' ill toward ya,"

Solomon whispered in her ear. "Yer still part of the prophecy, and yer still divine. For that reason, I keep ye alive."

A wave of realization crashed over Suzanne. She rolled Solomon's hand over. His fingertips looked like the pads on a dog's foot. There wasn't a fingerprint.

"You were the ones that messed up my school," Suzanne said.

"And threw that rock through yer window, while ye were havin' yer whore relations with that soldier," Solomon whispered. "Ifin' yer talkin' about my fingers, it's a family trait. Soon all of ye will have them. A little fire will harden those fingertips right up. That's the way we'll know not to kill ye when we start the divine war. Ye'll also receive the mark of Lot on the belly button to show ye've been converted." He took his hand away. "I thought ye were supposed to be smart, Miss Clay. It took ye long enough to figure all that out. I even told ye we were the ones making the calls."

"I've been having a bad week," she answered.

Sheba slammed a plate down in front of Suzanne. It brimmed with all sorts of food. Suzanne nodded her appreciation and started to eat, forcing a bite into her mouth. Solomon patted her on the shoulder and walked away. She decided that she needed to eat because it was going to be a long night.

The food tasted very good. It had all been fried, and heavily salted. Suzanne thought there was too much salt, but then she remembered that Solomon had said the food was salted for purity. She became very thirsty. Her mouth turned into a desert. She looked for a cup, but they didn't have any. Sheba came back around. She slammed a tin cup down in front of Suzanne.

"Suppose yer getting' a bit dry by now," she said. "Ye'll just have to wait 'til I's get back with some water."

Sheba snorted like a pig. She moved down the line, placing cups in front of the others. Salt from the food got into Suzanne's mouth wound. It started to burn. Suzanne dropped her fork. She started to swab the wound with her tongue. The pain of probing hurt, but it helped to relieve the stinging of the salt. She looked down the length of the table. Sheba started at the other end pouring out the water.

Before Sheba made it past Lovell, the pitcher flew from her hands. It hit the table spilling water all over and then clanked to the floor. Sheba followed the pitcher. She hit her head on the table as she crumpled into a heap. The crowd at the tables turned and looked at her. Suzanne stood up so that she could see. Sheba frothed at the mouth and convulsed. She became rigid then loose. Her body contorted into pretzel positions that a woman of her size shouldn't be able to get into. Finally, she began to flop on the floor like a fish. Her eyes rolled back into her head showing only the whites. Many in the crowd gasped. A few moved toward her.

Solomon stood. "Let her be. The Devil's upon her. Let him finish, and he will go away."

"No," Ty said. "She's having a seizure. I have them sometimes."

"Shut up boy," Jonathan said as he approached the table. "The Book of Lot makes mention of this. Our Father Lot says it's when the Devil's upon some'un."

"Ty is right," Suzanne said. "That's nothing but a medical issue. No demons are causing it."

"Shut ye mouth, whore," Jonathan said. "Yer blasphemies

won't be tolerated."

"You should hold her down so she doesn't hurt herself," Ty said.

"And risk gettin' a devil myself. Yer dumber than I thought," Jonathan said. "It'll pass, just watch."

"Out of my way." Hadassah's familiar voice rang out of the crowd.

Suzanne watched Hadassah part the crowd. She knelt by Sheba. The contortions seemed to be slowing. Hadassah took a wood tongue depressor from her apron pocket and shoved it into Sheba's mouth, pressing the tongue down. Solomon pounded his tin cup on the table to bring order. The commotion in the room quieted. Suzanne looked at the old man.

"As it be written, Devil be gone from our sister. Find another to jump in and find them at the nearest crossroads. Devil, Devil in my eye jump on the next that passes by," he said.

Sheba made two more hard convulsions. The last contraction caused her bladder to void. The front of her dress darkened with urine, and the room started to smell of her foul bodily fluid. She roused and propped on her elbows. Hadassah took the depressor out of her mouth. Sheba's dazed look testified to the post-seizure confusion.

"What happened?" she asked.

"A devil came upon ye," Jonathan said. "Daddy Sol cast it from ye to the nearest crossroads, as is written."

"Ye had convulsions from yer palsy," Hadassah said.

Sheba clambered to her feet. She rubbed her head and noticed that she had wet herself. Suzanne thought she saw a blush rising in her face.

"I reckon I should go lay down," she said.

"Tis the best to do," Solomon said.

He then called on two stout Hassles to help her up the stairs to her bedroom. Everyone went back to the feast like nothing happened including Hadassah. Another Hassle brought up a full pitcher and finished pouring water into the cups. Suzanne swallowed half her cup in a gulp, just briefly swishing it about in her mouth to clear out the salt residue.

"Why did they think that the Devil was doing that to Sheba?" Ty asked Suzanne.

"Because they aren't educated like us," she said. "If they don't understand something medical is happening, they blame it on the Devil."

"Why?"

"People have done that many times through history, but when it comes to Solomon, he doesn't want to know any better," Suzanne said.

"Why didn't Mr. Lovell argue it with them?" Ty asked. "He's seen me have a seizure."

Suzanne thought the boy might have realized the change in Lovell, but he must not totally understand. "That's not really Mr. Lovell."

"What do you mean? It looks like him."

"Look at him again. Does it really?"

Ty looked over at Lovell. He seemed to study his face. As focused as his stare was, nothing would get past him.

"He does look different," Ty said. "He looks funny like when they baptized him. A zombie look."

"He always looks like that now. It's what Solomon and Jonathan want us all to look like. Do you understand?"

Ty turned back to his plate. He toyed with a pile of string beans. Suzanne looked past him down the table. The other kids ate and talked to themselves. She figured that Ty could tell them everything himself. He would know how to best tell them how evil the Hassles were; if they hadn't figured it out already. Her scan went past Heather, the last of the kids, to Solomon. He wasn't eating but stared straight out in front of him at the crowd. Suzanne looked over at the Fruitful Table. They all sat on one side of the table, and most stared up at her and the kids. They all looked like dogs after a female in heat.

A hand rested on her shoulder. Suzanne looked up into the face of Solomon, smiling down at her again. She was getting the special attention tonight. Did he know about Agrippa?

"I hope everythin' at this here feast was to yer suitin'."

"It was surprisingly good. A little salty, but that was the point of it, right?"

His smile deepened. "Ye seem to git some of this, don't ye?"

"I'm not as stupid as you seem to think I am." Suzanne locked a hard stare into Solomon's eyes.

"I never thought ya were. Quite the opposite Miss Clay. I reckoned ye to be too smart for yer own good, and so fer, I's been right." Solomon patted her wounded cheek.

A sharp stab of pain spread throughout her mouth and face. Suzanne clenched her teeth, but never let her glare break with Solomon's eyes. The thin taste of blood trickled onto her tongue. She'd caught a bit of her lip in her teeth and sank down on it. The pain meant little considering, but the taste of her own blood kept things level.

"So when does this breeding begin?" she asked.

"Soon, but not tonight. Tonight we feast and enjoy this revel," Solomon said.

"I thought the Bible taught against reveling."

"Aye, it do, but not on important feast days such as this. Eat, drink, and be happy."

Solomon walked away. He raised his hands and started swinging them like he was directing an orchestra.

"There's a land that is fairer than day." Jonathan began to sing.

The whole room burst into a cacophony of *In the Sweet By and By*. Suzanne never heard such a warbling in one room. Then people started to get up and dance. They flailed their arms around and hit their heels hard on the wooden floor. She kept her eyes darting back and forth across the crowd. The whole group seemed swept up in some religious ecstasy. It grew greater as the hymn switched to *When the Roll is Called up Yonder*. Her eyes fell on Lovell, as he downed another last bottle of the jimson weed and morning glory seed concoction. As the song talked about laboring from dawn until the setting of the sun, she felt like the sun in Lovell's eyes was about to set as well.

21

Through many dangers,
toils and snares
I have already come

AMAZING GRACE

SUZANNE STOOD IN THE middle of the slave shack she and the others had been locked in the day of their arrival. Shadows cast by a single candle danced around on the walls looking like so many black phantoms. The window stood open letting the cool evening air blow in. Nothing seemed to stir outside. Only the crickets and random tree frogs chirped in nature, but not many of those sang tonight. Suzanne figured the temperature would be dropping low and so the singers in the night choir would be nestling in for a cold night and not wasting their energy singing.

Suzanne circled the dirt floor trying to decide where to sit. She noticed that a pallet of several quilts had been laid out on the floor. The patchwork covers appeared new. Each patch looked bright and untainted with dirt or other soiling. Suzanne walked closer to the pallet to get a better look at the artwork on the quilts. The twitching candlelight behind her made it hard to make out the pattern. It almost looked like a mosaic.

"Could they have made a mosaic?" she asked herself aloud.

Nothing answered except the croaking of tree frogs. Before she could answer herself, the pattern came into focus:

the figure of a young woman resting on all fours. An older male figure with a fully erect penis mounted her from behind. Another young naked woman draped herself over the back of the old man. She bore a cup in her hands. The bodies of the human figures were made of pink fabric from many different garments, but the mosaic was an orgy.

"Oh my God."

Suzanne stepped away from the quilts. She looked to the window. The rusted barbwire still latticed the opening, but a pair of two-by-twos were nailed crisscross over the wire. *They thought about me escaping that way.* She went to the door. The only handle was a bent piece of metal. She tugged on it, but the door didn't move. Suzanne knew it wouldn't. They had her locked in as usual.

She walked to the back wall and stood there. It had started. Solomon lied to them all. He planned for the breeding to start tonight. Suzanne patted the boards on the wall behind her. She listened to see if any creaked or popped, a sign of weakness. Nothing answered her back. She kicked one of the boards with all her effort. It didn't budge.

"Might as well quit that," John Mark said from outside the door. "Ain't but one way out of there now, and it's through this here door."

The door opened. The flickering candle revealed Esau and John Mark standing in the doorway. The shadows played on the peaks and valleys of their faces. Sinister skull-like faces looked back, a death's head staring with penetrating green eyes. Suzanne gasped as the thought that both of them might be her match came over her.

"Don't git yerself worked up. We ain't here for no humpin',"

John Mark said. "I told ye that Esau was a Sodomite. Daddy Sol's forbidden me from touchin' ye."

"Then who?"

Suzanne hated the idea of having Esau or John Mark raping her. Esau moved to one side. Lovell stepped into the room. The candlelight played a similar effect on him as it had the Hassle men. He looked even more like a half-dead version of himself. His eyes looked out with no zeal, just flat staring. The spark that made him Warren Lovell was gone. Suzanne never imagined eyes could have a matte finish, but his new ones did. They weren't the same as before at the dinner though. Even without the sparkle, they had a real quality to them.

"The soldier of prophecy," Lovell said.

"Warren," Suzanne said.

John Mark let out a laugh. It shook Suzanne to the core. It was an unearthly sound like air passing over the top of a glass bottle. The door closed, and she heard it being locked. Lovell walked toward her. She moved to the side away from the pallet and toward the door. He started unbuttoning his blue chambray shirt.

"Warren, we don't have to do this. We can just tell them we did it."

"What would be the use of that? This ain't for fun. It's for makin' young'uns." His face looked like Lovell, but his voice was not his at all. The words strained a bit coming out as if he were trying to block them or deflect something.

His shirt was off, and now he worked on his pants. He had them unbuttoned and started pulling them down. They were off before Suzanne could reach the door. The naked Lovell grabbed her by the arms. He tried to kiss her. The pressure of his lips made her mouth hurt. Suzanne struggled to tear free from him. His grip that was so strong the other evening when they had made love was equally so now but came without any of the tenderness she had experienced then. Suzanne tried to plant her knee in his groin, but he positioned himself as if expecting this.

"Come on, baby," he said his voice more familiar as he hugged her and tore at the buttons on the back of her dress. "We've done this before. Remember?"

Suzanne struggled more. The dress ripped and buttons popped off. She felt her back exposed to the air.

"I made love to Warren Lovell, not you."

She remembered the tenderness of that night. Lovell had eased her to the floor and cradled her head under his arm. It had been a slow act full of passion and desire, a slow burn, a simmering of passion between the two of them. Deep kisses had filled them both to the brim with sexual pleasure before it all exploded in fireworks of sweet, fairytale love making. She had never remembered a time quite like it.

In the slave shack, there was no tenderness. Lovell jerked down on her dress. It ripped some more and crumpled to the floor. She stood naked before him. Every scratch and prick from her run through the woods showed pink and red in the candlelight. Lovell let her stand there. He stood erect and ready. She tried to cover herself with her hands, but he knocked them away.

"No point in that. I've seen it before."

He grabbed her breast and groped it hard, pinching her nipple between his thumb and forefinger. The pain shot through her like electricity. She swung at him, opened palm and made contact with his mouth. She drove his lip into his teeth as best she could. A trickle of blood rolled down his chin. It was thin and bright red. He wiped it away.

"Stupid whore, can't you hear the angels? Can't you hear them telling us this is God's will?"

Lovell grabbed Suzanne by the hair. He wrapped his hand deep in her locks until his knuckles rested on her scalp and pulled. Suzanne followed. Her scalp was still tender from having jerked out a large chunk of hair during her escape attempt. Lovell kept fondling her breasts with his free hand.

Lovell twisted around behind Suzanne. Her scalp burned from the new strain on her hair. He pushed down on her shoulder.

"Get on all fours, like the creature ye are."

He tugged her hair and put a knee in the small of her back at the same time. She did as he ordered. There seemed to be little other choice. Her knees hit the softness of the quilts. Her hands rested there as well. She took comfort in feeling the quilts; nothing else would be this soft.

The next thing Suzanne felt was the pressure and pain of being violated.

Suzanne lay crumpled on the quilt pallet. She thought Lovell had left as soon as it was over, but she wasn't certain because she wouldn't lift her head to look around the room. Time seemed unreal. Everything seemed to be moving at the speed of light and the speed of a snail simultaneously. Her blood rushed through her body with so much force she heard it in her ears like the rumbling of water over a falls. Her tears and gasped sobs hung in time almost paralyzed. She lay motionless, not quite in a fetal position but close. Somewhere between reality and horror, she stared with blind eyes at the wall. The motley black shadows cast from the candlelight danced around. The only benefit she found was that nothing hurt. All the pain she acquired since being among the Hassles had numbed her body along with her mind.

From somewhere too distant to know, Suzanne became aware of a voice. A familiar, friendly voice called her name. She knew that she'd gone over the edge. Voices whether you had been raped or not weren't a good sign. The voice kept coming and grew stronger and clearer. Suzanne recognized it.

"Come on, girl," Hadassah said.

Suzanne felt callused hands on her body. She cringed and almost struck out. Looking up she saw the old green eyes of Hadassah looking down at her. The crone held open what looked like a robe.

"I don't know if I can stand." The words were snorts and sobs. Suzanne almost didn't understand herself.

"Sure ye can. Take my hand."

Suzanne grabbed Hadassah's hand. She clambered up. Hadassah threw the robe around her naked body. Suzanne, wobbling on her unsure legs, put it on properly. It felt soft like terrycloth. She felt warm and secure as if in her own robe in her own house.

"Let's get you over to my cabin. I'll see how bad things are."

Suzanne followed the old woman. She didn't question anything nor even think about it. Hadassah carried a lantern rigged to only cast light ahead of them. The walk from her prison shack to Hadassah's cabin was a short one. Suzanne was happy for that. Every part of her body hurt now. The numbness wore off shortly after they stepped out into the night air. The robe around her helped to block the chill, but the ground felt hard and cold to her bare feet. Little rocks smashed into her tender soles.

"I'm going to have bruises on the soles of my feet."

Hadassah closed and locked the door. She walked past Suzanne and trimmed a lamp that only glowed softly. The room grew much brighter as the lamp grew in strength.

"Everything that's happened and yer worried about bruised feet?" Hadassah asked. "Get up on my table."

Suzanne sat on a wooden table. The back adjusted up and down, and two stirrup-looking devices were on the sides of the other end. Hadassah adjusted the back so it reclined in a sitting position. She eased Suzanne back. Then she swung the stirrups around.

"Put yer legs in these."

Suzanne looked at her. She heard the old woman's words, but couldn't or wouldn't comply. She hadn't figured out which one yet.

"I ain't goin' to do nothing bad to ya. I just need to see what's happened."

Suzanne placed her right leg up. A long string of seconds played out before she put her left leg into the stirrup. Her legs trembled. Hadassah pulled a stool up and poked her head between the stirrups. Suzanne started to cry.

"Please stop."

Hadassah sat up. She nodded her head. "Put yer legs down."

Suzanne let her legs fall free of the metal contraptions. Hadassah patted her on the knee as she got up from her stool.

"I know it's tough," she said, "but nothing looks too bad down there. He must've taken it pretty easy on ye." Hadassah handed Suzanne two white tablets and a glass of water. "Take those."

"What are they?"

"Aspirin. Ain't the best thing in the world fer what happened to ya, but at least they'll help ease some pain."

Suzanne took the aspirins. They tasted more bitter than most other aspirins she had taken. They seemed to melt faster too. She eased the tension out of her body. The room was bright and warm. That gave her some comfort.

"Mine and Solomon's youngest sister was raped," Hadassah said after some time had passed in silence.

"What?" Suzanne asked. She had dozed some.

"Her name was Martha. Our daddy had let her go to public school down in Marquisville. She had to walk a mile to catch the bus. Back then it wouldn't pick ye up here at the house. One day a Negro came by. He snatched her up, and raped her."

Suzanne looked at Hadassah. Tears pooled in the old woman's eyes. She wiped them with her shirtsleeve as she walked to a cupboard at the other end of her cabin.

"She got pregnant and had a half-negro baby."

"What did your family do? They aren't the most open-minded bunch." Suzanne expected Hadassah to tell her that they killed the baby.

"Solomon lost his mind, which wasn't that much of a stretch even back then. He found that darkie and gutted him like a hog. That's why he hates darkies so much. Martha died a few days after having little Rebecca. The baby came out backwards, ye see. One of the worst birthin's I ever did. Solomon raised the baby like she was his. He trained her in *our* ways. She was a smart one too, even went to college."

"Where is she now?"

"Solomon won't let her live up here with us. He said she's got God's will to do." Hadassah sat some clothes on Suzanne's stomach. "Get dressed."

"But where is Rebecca?"

Suzanne sat up. She unfolded the dress that seemed a bit more modern than the calicoes most of the Hassle women wore. She dropped the robe off her and stepped into the dress. Hadassah helped her button it up the back.

"She just ain't here. Solomon don't tell me everything, but I'm sure she's been workin' with him to get y'all up here, along with Nathan. She's usually up to no good."

"You said Nathan again," Suzanne said. "Who is Nathan?"

"The boy Solomon bought in Mississippi. He's around here somewheres. Just saw him."

"I was raped," Suzanne said, looking down at herself in the blue checked dress. The weight of what happened just then coming to her as the soft cotton lay against her naked flesh.

"That's right." Hadassah patted her on the shoulder, and seemed to come back from her dotage.

"By a man that I thought I loved."

"He ain't who you thought he was. Solomon made sure of that." Hadassah turned Suzanne to look at her. "I need ye to listen to me. I got to tell you about my niece. I shouldn't 'cause Solomon'll kill me, but—"

The door to the cabin burst open. The wood on the frame splintered from the force of the blow. Suzanne screamed and almost fell backward over the nursing table. Solomon stepped inside followed by Esau who dropped a large chunk of wood as he did so. It had been his battering ram. The old man bore an evil smile on his face. Each of the yellow teeth looked like those of a vicious jack o'lantern.

"I think ye've said enough, Hadassie," Solomon said.

"I ain't said enough. I's gots lot more to say."

"And that's yer problem. Ya don't know when to shut up."

Solomon walked to Hadassah. He pushed Suzanne against the table. Her buttocks plopped onto the flat table-top. As he passed her, he took up his cane like a baseball bat. Suzanne tried to grab him but came up fruitless.

"Just put that thing away, Solomon. Ye ain't goin' to kill me. Who'd tend to everybody?" Hadassah backed away.

"She's a trained nurse. Went to college for it, among other studies. Plus, ye's losing yer mind, old woman."

The old man's words seemed to dance out of his mouth as he backed Hadassah into a corner. Suzanne tried to jump up and help her nurse, but everything had gone numb again. Even her eyes wouldn't close as Solomon bludgeoned Hadassah in the stomach. He did this four more times across her legs and pelvis before the old lady slid down the wall.

Solomon walked past Suzanne, leaning on his cane just like he had when he walked in. He stopped and put his finger on the end of her nose. He pushed down on the tip and let it go.

"We found 'Grippa," he hissed. "Ye best hope that man's seed took, or I'll skin ya alive like a catfish."

Solomon curled his fingers into a fist. He walked back to the door and patted Esau on the arm. "I think we'll let her stay here with old Hadassah. Some time with a carcass might do her some good."

Esau snorted and followed Solomon from the cabin. He pulled the burst door closed. Suzanne heard them nail boards across the doorway. She looked at Hadassah crumpled in the floor, bleeding. A small pool of rich purple blood expanded out from her legs. Suzanne jumped from the table. She went to Hadassah. The blood felt slick on her bare feet. The old woman's breath rattled.

"Listen girl, Solomon ain't let them kids be raped like he did ya, not yet. He was hopin' that the rape would break ya." She coughed and grimaced. "Get my keys, and get them kids."

Hadassah held her side. She closed her eyes but still breathed shallow, pained breaths. Suzanne reached into Hadassah's dress pocket. She found the key ring there. The keys were nothing more than to a few padlocks and a large iron skeleton key.

She walked to the basin that Hadassah kept full of water. Suzanne washed her hands free of blood. Then she poured water from the basin's pitcher on her feet to clean the blood from them. She replaced the pitcher and walked to the cupboard that Hadassah took her dress from. The cabinet was made of cedar and smelled sweet. She rummaged in the nest of clothes until she found a pair of shoes. They looked like house shoes of some sort, but they were better than nothing. Suzanne put them on.

She opened the window and started to climb out of the cabin. Something stopped her. It wasn't fear. She was so afraid that she had quit noticing that. Something else told her to wait a while. She needed to let the night get a little deeper and then go get the kids. Some of the Hassles might still be moving around. If she got caught, then there would be no hope for anyone. Suzanne closed the window, went back and sat on the nursing table, and waited. She listened to Hadassah's labored breath. Time was important. If she moved fast enough she might be able to save the old woman as well.

22

Go down Moses,
way down in Egypt land
Tell ole Pharaoh,
to let my people go

NEGRO SPIRITUAL

NO LIGHT CAME FROM the old plantation house. The night was dark as well. The moon hid behind thick clouds that promised rain. One of the few things that made Suzanne feel like a country person is that she could smell rain before it started to fall. Tonight smelled like rain. The rich gamey scent of it energized her. It promised cleansing, and that's what she need, what she wanted.

The night air washed into Hadassah's cabin. Suzanne kept watch toward the house. Nothing moved outside for a long time. She had no idea for how long, but suddenly the time seemed right to get going. Suzanne walked to the open window and climbed out into the yard. She carried Hadassah's large pair of scissors. It was the only large sharp object she could find.

Suzanne faltered when her feet touched the ground outside the window. The darkness of the night pressed in around her. It pressed so hard, she lost her breath. Bent double, Suzanne panted trying to catch as much oxygen as she could. A voice with a high tinny quality yelled from deep in her brain. *You can't do it. You'll fail.* The voice came from the night; Suzanne knew it. Solomon controlled the night. He controlled everything. He was some strange, evil wizard who controlled everything and everyone like so many puppets.

"No." She said it aloud. She said it to break the silence and get rid of the voice.

The tinny interior voice shut up. Suzanne caught her breath. Her lungs felt rejuvenated. She pushed off the side of Hadassah's cabin. Her footfalls echoed across the yard. The sound exaggerated in her ears. She just knew that someone would hear them and be on her before she made it to the back door of the house, but no one came.

Suzanne slid to a halt at the edge of the back porch, closest to the cookhouse. The smells of the feast still seeped out into the night. The smell that soothed earlier in the evening now burned Suzanne's nostrils with its stench. It reminded her of Solomon. She saw his face leering at her, his yellow teeth bared in a carnivorous grin. In her mind, he watched Lovell rape her. Solomon gawked at the act. He let his tongue loll out from lust.

She readied herself to enter the house when a hand clapped down over her mouth. A scream escaped her but was muffled in the meaty palm. The other arm wrapped around her waist and picked her feet up off the ground. Suzanne screwed her eyes around to get a look at her attacker as all the wounds in her face on the body burn and seared at the same time. She kicked at the solid, muscled shins as hard as she could. Even though the hand over her mouth didn't seem big enough, she imagined Esau had her and would finish her off for killing, not one but two of his brothers.

"Stay quiet," John Mark whispered in her ear. "If ye don't make no noise, neither one of us is going to get in trouble."

He moved her away from the main house to behind the cook house. Several piles of wood were stacked in triangular patterns near the building's back door. A heavy splitting ax stuck out of a stump, and a smaller hatchet rested on the top of one of the piles. Suzanne took it all in. The terror of the moment gave her some strange type of slow motion attentiveness.

John Mark's breath was on her neck, and his lips hovered near her ears. "If ye scream, Daddy Sol is going to know ye've been wanderin' around up to no good. He ain't real happy right now, and when gets real unhappy, he kills stuff. Ye understand?"

Suzanne nodded. She got the point completely. John Mark took his hand away from her mouth, turned her to face him, and shoved her against a pile of wood. He unfastened a few buttons on his shirt and slipped it over his head. His muscles were well developed almost like those of a model. It amazed her. She could only imagine the ego-boosting effect of living around the rest of Hassles must have had on John Mark. He hitched her dress up to her waist.

"I figure I can get in a good rut, because Cousin Warren done made it with ye. Ifin' ye get pregnant, Daddy Sol'll never know it might be mine. Ye ain't gonna say nothin' cause he'd kill ya and ya baby."

Suzanne felt John Mark press his weight against her as he tried to find the port for his desire. Her arms remained free. She pushed herself up and stretched out for hatchet that rested so tantalizingly close. John Mark chuckled a little and scooted up higher following after her. She thought he must think she was playing with him. He paused, and she knew he'd found what he was looking for. Before anything else could happen, she snatched the hatchet and swung it blindly over her head. The hard, blunt end struck something solid. John Mark's weight lifted off her.

She stood, keeping the hatchet ready. The Hassle held his hand over his eye. A stream of blood ran into his face, and his manhood dangled from his pants. The sight of the stiffness of human flesh pointing at her sent a rage through Suzanne. She didn't yell, but struck out with all the force she had. The blade of the hatchet caught John Mark in the soft part of his throat just under his Adam's apple. She pulled the small ax back. It made a wet popping sound as it left his throat. Blood spurted out into the night as John Mark grasped for the wound in his throat. An airy gasping sound escaped from him. Suzanne brought the hatchet down against the side of his skull. The blade, kept sharp for chopping firewood no doubt, wedged into his cranium with the ease of a hot knife going into butter. He jerked and his knees buckled under him. As he collapsed, Suzanne lost the grip on the handle. Her hands were covered in blood. That horrible feeling that she'd encountered when she'd killed Agrippa came back to her as she watched John Mark twitch on the ground as he died. She couldn't believe this was her life, that this is what she had to do to survive.

After scanning the grounds to see if the commotion woke anyone, Suzanne pulled the hatchet free. It would make a much better weapon than the scissors. She gripped it and headed for the house. Other things had to be done before the night ended. As she passed the corner of the cook house, she noticed a rain barrel. The water felt cold as she submerged her hands to clean them of the gore. It made her feel a little calmer as she headed to the house.

The steps onto the porch didn't register in Suzanne's mind. The next thing she knew she stood inside the house just behind the grand staircase. The house creaked. Suzanne ducked into the darker shadows of the already dark house. The air held all the tension of a thunderstorm. She waited for the bolt of lightning so the crack of thunder could loosen things. The clouds could only hold back so much rain before the deluge. Suzanne kept to the shadows with the hatchet drawn up ready to strike out. She stood there for what seemed like hours. No one came by, and no more creaks groaned.

Suzanne kept the small ax in attack position and moved out from behind the stairs. She didn't know where the kids were, but thought the best place to look was in the bedroom they had been in before the feast. The first stair popped under her weight. Suzanne stopped and waited.

Nothing happened.

The second and third steps were silent. The fourth step moaned. She stopped again.

Nothing happened.

She took the next few steps two at a time. The step to the landing cracked. Suzanne stopped and stood looking down the dark hallway of the second floor. There was no hint of light beyond a very dim glow the cloud-covered moon supplied through one open door. She listened. Sleep sounds came from most of the rooms. A small knot of fear tightened in her stomach. The only thing that protected her from the onslaught of the Hassle hordes was a few closed doors, a pair of scissors, and the hatchet. She waited.

Nothing happened.

Suzanne crept down the corridor, stopping at each door until she found the one that she had been sequestered in with the kids. She pressed her ear to the door. Someone snored softly on the other side. Suzanne imagined that Ty sounded like that when he slept. Something about him made her think that he, of all the kids, would snore.

She pulled the keys out with her free hand and fumbled until the skeleton key was dominant. Before she tried to unlock the door, she jiggled the doorknob, and to her surprise found that the door was unlocked. She put the handle of the hatchet in the pocket of her dress. It weighed it down, but she didn't want to frighten the children. She took the scissors out just in case a Hassle waited on the other side instead of her kids. Suzanne pushed the door open. The hinges squeaked from lack of oil. She stepped inside, stopped, and waited.

Jonathan hopped to his feet.

Suzanne backed away. The young Hassle had been lying on a pallet near the door. He was guarding the others. Suzanne swallowed the lump of a scream in her throat.

"How'd ye get in here?" Jonathan asked.

The icy fear that held her in place with its frigid hand melted away. The keys fell to the floor with a loud jangle, rousing the kids. Ty was the first to lift his head.

"What's happening?" he said slurred with sleep.

"Blasphemy," Jonathan said.

Before Jonathan could say anything else, Suzanne slashed him across the face with the opened scissors, slitting a gap at the hinge of his mouth. He clawed at the scissors as Suzanne made another swipe and then another. Blood sprayed across the room. Heather and Amanda made the squeaking noise of a scream caught in their throats by total horror. Jonathan tried to speak, but the words gargled out in bubbles of blood.

Suzanne kept swinging the scissors until Jonathan fell to the floor. His blood pooled across it. Everything seemed to take forever, but only seconds elapsed. Suzanne became aware of it as the fog of her rampage lifted. The kids, *her* kids, stood around her. They were slack jawed. Suzanne became aware of the room, of the house, and of the noise of the sleepers awakened by the commotion.

"We've got to go," Suzanne whispered in cold flat tones. "Now."

She hurried into the hallway, dropping the gory scissors and taking the hatchet back out. The kids came out behind her. She ran them down the hall as the doors to the bedrooms started to open. They stood at the bottom of the stairs when Suzanne heard him.

"My boy, she's done killed my boy!" Solomon sounded more wretched than Suzanne had imagined possible.

For a moment, she stood stone fast, grasping the hatchet that still dripped with John Mark's blood so hard her knuckles ached. The hammering of running feet across the second floor hallway brought her to herself again. Suzanne ushered the kids out of the house through the French doors. She turned back into the house and saw Solomon near the top of the stairs. He locked eyes with her and hurried his pace down the stairs. Suzanne grabbed a kerosene lamp off the shelf near the door, spying a pack of matches beside it. The oily smell of kerosene filled her nostrils as she smashed the lamp on the floor. Solomon took pause as she struck one of the matches.

"Don't even think about it," he said.

"Light her up," she said, remembering what one of the Hassles had said back at the bus.

Suzanne dropped the match on the floor. Flames spread out like orange shag carpet. She rushed out the doors as more of the floor welcomed the flames as it fed off of years of oil used to keep the timbers free of termites and other vermin. On the front porch, she looked around and spotted the old Chevy parked where she first met the Hassles.

"Run, get in that truck," she yelled at the kids. They looked at her dumbfounded. "Just do it."

Heather, Amanda, and Christopher bounded down the steps and across the yard to the truck. Ty didn't move.

"What about Eric and Rachel?" he asked.

"What about them?" Suzanne pushed on the boy to get him moving, which he did, in short fumbling steps.

"Aren't we going to get them?" Ty ran across the yard now. Suzanne kept up.

"I don't think we can."

"Stop her. Kill her if ye have to," Solomon yelled from the door of the house.

Suzanne jerked open the door to the truck. The kids were already sitting in the cab. Ty clambered into the bed. Suzanne turned the ignition, and the old beast of a truck roared to life.

Suzanne popped the clutch and shifted down the gears. Gravel, dirt, and bits of grass slung up from the back tires as the truck moved forward. She switched on the headlights. The dimmer was on the floorboard. She tapped it with her foot, and the night filled with the light of the truck's high beams.

"Where's Eric and Rachel?" she asked not really knowing why. She'd just as soon as leave them as help them.

"They have their own cabin," Heather said.

"Do you know where?"

The girl nodded.

"Well? Where?"

"Behind the house, go behind the house," Heather said.

Suzanne whirled the truck around. She drove straight at the group of Hassles running across the yard toward the burning house. The lights washed them out. Several of them held their arms up to keep the light from blinding them. With the truck bearing down on them, the group had to jump aside to keep from being hit. Suzanne kept the accelerator pushed down hard as she turned the corner of the house. More debris from the ground tossed into the air. She ignored Heather as the girl tried to direct her to Eric and Rachel. The truck pulled up to Hadassah's cabin. Suzanne jumped out of the cab. This distance wasn't far from the swarms of Hassles, but most were too distracted by the burning house to notice she had stolen the truck. She figured the horde thought Esau drove it for some water to help douse the flames that ate away at their ancestral home place.

"Ty, put the tailgate down and come and help me."

Suzanne heard the boy follow her orders. She whacked the boards holding the door closed with the hatchet. It broke after two strong chops. The door swung limp on its broken hinges. Suzanne ran inside, and Ty followed.

"Grab Hadassah under her arms. I'm going to get her legs, and be careful because she's hurt bad," Suzanne said.

She and Ty hefted Hadassah up. They carried her quickly to the truck and laid her out in the bed. Hassles of every size boiled out of the bunk houses. Most moved slowly from being jerked out a deep sleep. Hadassah groaned but didn't rouse from the stupor of her shock. Suzanne and Ty got back into the truck. A quicker Hassle grabbed Suzanne's door and tried to keep her from closing it. She chopped his hand with her ax as she shifted the truck into drive. The Hassle howled in pain and slid down the door while being dragged a yard. Heather pointed out Eric and Rachel's cabin, and Suzanne steered the careening truck that way. A group of Hassles ran toward them. The truck bore down on them. A tall lanky Hassle slammed into the hood and rolled off.

The truck slid to a stop in front of the second shack up from Hadassah's. Suzanne shifted into neutral. She scurried out of the Chevy, still holding the hatchet. Her hands ached from the death grip kept on it. Another group of Hassles rushed past toward the house. Suzanne's heart paused for just a moment imagining if they suddenly turned on her like birds in flight. Instead, they kept hoofing it. She could hear the noise of the fire as it engulfed the old plantation.

"Can you drive?" she asked Ty as she hurried around the truck.

"I've done it a long time ago, grampy's tractor."

"Get in the cab, and wait. Tell the others to get into the bed and be careful of Hadassah."

Suzanne jerked the door of the shack open. The cabin was lit by a single kerosene lamp. She saw the form of Rachel and Eric lying on a bed.

"Get up!"

The two roused, but didn't move.

"I said get up!"

Rachel and Eric got to their feet. Suzanne waved them to the door with the little bloody ax . They didn't protest but followed her direction.

"Get in that truck and don't cause me any trouble."

The kids ran out of the cabin and crawled into the truck. She took a look around and knocked the lamp to the floor as she ran out. The sound of fire racing across the floorboards to incinerate the spilled kerosene was the last thing Suzanne heard before she put her foot on the truck's running board. A hand grabbed her by the elbow.

"Where are you going?"

She turned to see Lovell holding her arm. He smiled at her but still owned his changed eyes.

"Let me go."

"I can't let you do this. You can't get away. Daddy Sol sent me to stop you. You were paying too much attention to everything else to notice me."

"They're coming," Amanda yelled. "There's a bunch of them coming!"

Suzanne screamed from so deep inside her she felt like her throat would rip open. She swung the hatchet at Lovell. He backed off once he saw the bloody blade, but it sliced into his arm. Lovell swung around, hitting her arm with enough force to knock the weapon from her hand. She kicked him hard in the gut with a force she didn't know she had, making him stumble and fall to the ground, before climbing into the truck and slamming the door.

"Drive!"

"I can't drive this. It ain't nothing like grampy's tractor. "

"They're almost here!" Heather screamed.

"Come here, you whore!" Lovell slammed a bloody hand on the window.

"Sure it is. Just push in that pedal beside the brake and pull the gearshift back at the same time and hit the gas," Suzanne tried to keep her calm in the chaos.

Ty did as he was told. The truck lurched and then sped forward at whiplash-inducing velocity. Suzanne looked into the side-view mirror and saw Lovell tottering off balance. A larger group of Hassles chased them.

Ty turned the truck between two shacks, going the wrong way. A pair of Hassle men clambered down a set of stairs, the truck nearly hitting them.

"Turn around and go back the way we came," Suzanne said. "The main road is back that way."

Ty whirled the truck back onto the path they had made through the dying weeds. Flames now shot out of the door and windows of Eric and Rachel's cabin. They passed the house and the place where the truck had been parked. The headlights lit up the road that cut through the woods to the highway. Its engine whined from being in the wrong gear.

"This isn't the best way to learn how to drive one of these, but hit the clutch again, the pedal by the brake, and shift the stick back and toward me," Suzanne said.

Ty did this, causing the truck to lurch and almost die. The gears ground with his clumsy shifting, but the truck kept heading down the road. Suzanne looked back. The taillights cast an evil red light on the road behind, but no one followed.

"Where ya takin' us?" Rachel asked.

"To town," Suzanne answered.

"W-what for?" Eric asked.

"I don't know yet. I'll decide that when we get there," she pushed her sweaty bangs from her face, smearing a little blood on her forehead.

"You can't do this. This is God's will," Rachel said.

"It might be the will of your god, but my God's will is to keep you safe and alive," Suzanne said. "Don't try anything either. I don't want to tie you up, but I will."

Eric and Rachel turned to look out the windshield. They stank. The whole bunch of them stank. Suzanne just now became aware of the smell. The close confines of the truck's cab did that. She even smelled. The scent of blood hung on her. She looked at her hands. Blood splatter ran up her arm, and her hands trembled. She turned and looked out the window. Her reflection looked back. The swollen eye and lacerations on her face looked wicked in the dark reflection. Her whole face looked like a skull staring out from some creepy Halloween decoration. She swallowed hard and started to count. They would be on the highway soon and in town after that. She needed a clear head, and counting had always helped to do that.

23

'Twas grace that brought me
safe thus far
And grace shall lead me home

AMAZING GRACE

THE CHEVY STALLED AS it pulled off the dirt road to the Hassles' farm and onto the pavement of the county highway. Ty looked at Suzanne. His eyes darted around, and his mouth hung open. He turned the ignition over, but the motor just ground and sputtered.

"What's happened?" his voice brimmed over with anxiety.

"The truck stalled," Suzanne answered. "Calm down. It's not that big of deal."

"But they're behind us," Ty said. "They'll catch us."

Suzanne looked into the side mirror. The taillights illuminated the road until it disappeared around a curve. No one was within eyeshot. She figured if the Hassles were after them they would be far enough back that she could change places with Ty.

"Let's switch places," Suzanne said. "I'll drive us the rest of the way into town."

She got out of the truck. Ty did the same. They crossed paths in the glow of the headlights. Suzanne got behind the wheel, shifted the gears into neutral and turned the ignition. The engine groaned and growled but didn't catch. Ty slammed the passenger side door as he got in. Suzanne jumped. Her bones felt like they were trying to get rid of her skin and take off running ahead of them. A yip escaped her mouth.

"Sorry," Ty said.

"That's okay. I'm just a bit jumpy." Suzanne put the truck into gear and then back to neutral. She tried to start it again, but it still wouldn't catch. Ty looked at her, his eyes wide with worry. Everyone else had somehow fallen asleep. Suzanne was glad of that. She didn't need the others starting to panic. Enough of that emotion tightened around her for them all. Another attempt and the engine caught, but sputtered out.

"Are we out of gas?" Ty asked.

Suzanne looked at the gauge, terrified the needle would be resting on the red E, but the needle stayed just past the half-full mark. She shook her head at him. Another try brought the engine roaring to life. Suzanne pumped the gas pedal. The engine raced. She shifted the gears hard, not letting off the accelerator. The truck bucked, tossed up loose flint gravel, and tore off down the road. The tires squealed once they touched the pavement. The truck fishtailed as Suzanne got control of it. All the hubbub roused Rachel and Eric.

"What's g-going on?" Eric asked.

"We're heading into town," Suzanne said, "to get some help."

"Don't worry," Rachel patted Eric on the arm. "Daddy Sol will get us before anything else happens. He ain't goin' let nothin' happen to me or our baby."

Suzanne whipped her head around to the filthy little girl. The stench coming off her and the others almost made her ill. Something else made her uncomfortable. She'd wanted to leave Rachel back with the Hassles. Suzanne cared about the other kids and even Hadassah, but Rachel seemed more evil than even Solomon because she didn't care about all the chaos that she had caused.

"We'll see about that," Suzanne had lost her ability to contain her contempt.

Rachel stared back at her with hate brimming in her eyes. The dim light from the dashboard made the shadows deep in the girl's face. She looked like a twisted, impish version of her Daddy Sol. Suzanne felt a new wave of disgust wash over her as they passed a sign declaring they were in the Marquisville police jurisdiction.

All the traffic lights flashed amber as Suzanne drove through the abandoned streets of downtown Marquisville. The sprinklers shot water across the lawn of the courthouse. The coppertop dome of the building looked dull in the moonlight. The street lamp that lit the parking lot of the Marquisville Baptist Church flickered on and off as if hiding its light under a bushel.

The old green beater turned off Main Street onto Church Avenue. None of the lamps on this street worked. Only the headlights from the truck cast light on the road. Suzanne pulled into the parking lot of the sheriff's office. Two brown and white cruisers were parked near the door, but all the lights in the office were off. A placard that read *Please Call 911 for Assistance* hung on the door.

"Are they closed?" Ty asked.

"I think so," Suzanne sighed.

She knew the county only had so many deputies, but

closing the sheriff's office at night seemed unbelievable. She wished she had her cell phone. The city had removed all the pay phones to save money.

"They're closed," Ty verged on panic. "Daddy Sol is going to get us, isn't he?"

Suzanne twisted her head to Ty. She narrowed her eyes to slits at him. "No, he's not, and don't call him that. He's not your daddy, Ty." She reversed the truck into the street. "We'll go to the hospital."

The truck sputtered as Suzanne shifted into first gear, but kept going. They drove back down Church Avenue toward Main Street. Suzanne could only imagine what the ER staff would think when she walked in with the kidnapped kids, looking like she'd been used as living voodoo doll. They would call the cops and the news. There would be so many interviews the nurses wouldn't be able to do their work.

"Nurses," Suzanne said aloud.

She slammed on the brakes. The truck screeched to a halt. The sound of bodies slamming against the cab reminded her that the kids and Hadassah were still in the bed of the truck. She'd almost forgotten, just like she'd forgotten what Hadassah had told her about Solomon's favorite niece being a nurse. Suzanne drove onto Main Street heading away from the hospital.

"Where are we going?" Ty asked. "The hospital is the other way."

"The school," Suzanne answered.

"The police will be at the school?" Ty asked.

"Not right when we get there, but when we go inside we'll set off the silent alarm. That will call them there."

Ty nodded like he understood, but she knew that he didn't. Suzanne drove back past the courthouse through all the flashing amber stoplights until she turned onto Euclid Avenue, where the school was located. The flag in front flew at half-staff. Only the light in the hall by her office glowed from the windows. She drove around the side to the back of the school. The headlights lit a set of metal double doors that led into the back of the gym. Suzanne stopped the truck and got out. She left the lights on but put the keys in her pocket.

"You guys stay here," she said to all the kids as she stepped away from the truck.

Suzanne walked to the doors and pushed on them. They didn't budge, and she wasn't surprised. After everything that had happened, the superintendent would have insisted the school be locked down like a bank vault, but not everyone knew about the girl's locker room window.

Suzanne walked around the side of the gym. The light from the truck dimmed to a pale yellow glow. She had enough light to see the window she'd been meaning to fill out a work order on all year. Blue paint coated the inside of the glass pane so no one could look inside.

Suzanne pushed in on the top of the window. The bottom poked out enough for her to get her hands under the lip of the frame. She pulled hard, and the window creaked open with a harsh metal-on-metal noise. The gap between the window and sill gave Suzanne enough room to wriggle into the building. She slipped under the window and slid into the school head first. The cold tile floor of the girl's locker room greeted her hands as she entered. Once her feet had crossed the windowsill, Suzanne stood up and started waving her arms about like she swatted off an angry hive of bees. With any luck, the motion detector took notice and set the alarm off.

The showers dripped, and the noise echoed through the empty locker room. Suzanne felt her way along the wall of the dark room. Her hip knocked into a sink, but she made it to the door. It swung open. She stood in the hallway between the boys' and girls' locker rooms. The hall ended at the back door. Suzanne hurried to the door and pushed it open.

Suzanne sat behind the secretary's desk staring at the janitor's closet door across the hall. Eric and Rachel were locked inside. Suzanne couldn't think of anywhere else to put them so she could keep an eye on them. Ty, Christopher, Amanda, and Heather slept in Ms. Dodge's office. It had been cleaned of all the filth during their time with the Hassles. Suzanne and Ty had gotten Hadassah into the nurse's office near the library. The old Hassle rested on the examination table. She looked something a kin to a scarecrow tossed around in a wind storm, half deflated with limbs in all directions. Her already pale skin looked gray. She whimpered softly. Suzanne wished she'd tried to find some of the old woman's herbs that might help dull the pain.

Even though the red light that meant the alarm had been tripped flashed from the control panel, Suzanne dialed 911. She wouldn't feel safe until someone assured her the police would be there soon.

"911, what's your emergency?"

"This is Suzanne Clay, and I'm in Marquisville Middle

School. Can you send the deputies over?"

"Principal Clay?" the dispatcher asked.

"Yes."

"The alarm at the school came in about fifteen minutes ago. I called for Deputy Rusty Cardiff to respond. He should be there within about fifteen minutes. He's the only deputy on duty, and he was all the way up in Leesville."

"Fifteen minutes?" Suzanne's eyes widened in disbelief and looked up at the clock on the wall. It read 1:27 AM. "I can wait that long."

"Hold on, Ms. Clay. Where have you been?"

"Kidnapped."

"And the missing kids?"

"Kidnapped with me. I've got them here at the school." Suzanne thought of Hadassah. "I'm going to need an ambulance too, but I don't want them taking her to Marquisville Hospital."

"Who's injured, and how bad?"

"None of the kids that I know of, but an old lady. Both of her legs are broken, and there may be internal damage."

A familiar voice spoke in Suzanne's other ear. "What old lady?"

Suzanne looked over to see Ms. Dodge standing in the doorway. Her hair looked barely combed, and her eyes were puffy from being awakened from sleep.

"Thank you," Suzanne whispered into the phone, then hung up. She turned to Ms. Dodge. "One of the Hassles."

"One of the Hassles?" Ms. Dodge asked. "Where have you been?"

"Solomon and his family took me and the kids hostage."

Suzanne stood and came around the desk, embracing Ms. Dodge. "They tried to brainwash us."

Ms. Dodge broke away from Suzanne. "You brought one of them with you?"

"Yeah, but she's not like the rest. Her name's Hadassah, and she's in the nurse's office."

"Where are the kids?"

"Ty, Christopher, Heather, and Amanda are in your office. Eric and Rachel are in the janitor's closet." Suzanne pointed to the closed door next to the open door of Ms. Dodge's office. "It's the only door I could lock and keep an eye on. I didn't need them running off."

Ms. Dodge hurried across to the janitor's closet. She unlocked the door. When she opened it, Eric and Rachel lay on the floor asleep and in each other's arms. Ms. Dodge looked back at Suzanne with a smile on her face.

"Ain't that sweet," she said.

"Yeah, if she didn't insist that she was pregnant," Suzanne said. "That just kind of makes it twisted."

"Get up, you two," Ms. Dodge knocked on the door jamb.

Rachel and Eric stirred. They sat up and stretched out. Each stood up still stretching. Eric came out of the closet first. Ms. Dodge directed him into her office. Rachel came out, yawning and rubbing her eyes.

"You get in there with the others," Ms. Dodge said to her.

"All right, Rebecca," Rachel walked past Ms. Dodge into her office.

"What did you call her, Rachel?" Suzanne asked.

"Rebecca," Rachel said.

"That's Ms. Dodge to you," Suzanne snapped. "I don't

care what kind of trouble you've gotten everyone into or how pregnant you are or you think you are, you aren't an adult and will give your elders respect."

"She's right," Ms. Dodge said. "No student calls me by my first name."

Suzanne stepped into the hall and pushed the closet door closed. "You should've reprimanded as soon as she said that."

"You're right. I'm just tired."

Suzanne put her hand on Ms. Dodge's shoulder. "Trust me, I understand."

Before Ms. Dodge could answer, the front doors rattled and a hard, meaty banging came on the glass. Suzanne felt the sensation of her skeleton trying to jump out of her body again. Even Ms. Dodge jumped at the noise. Both looked at the door. The Bryces stood on the other side with their faces pressed to the glass. Mr. Bryce's nose was upturned like a pig while Mrs. Bryce's nose pressed down, flattening out.

"What are they doing here?" Suzanne asked Ms. Dodge. "Did you call them?"

"No."

Mr. Bryce banged on the glass again. Ms. Dodge walked and opened the door for them. The Bryces walked in, both in pajamas. Mrs. Bryce's hair was in fat bristled rollers. Ms. Dodge pushed the door closed behind them.

"Where's my boy at?" Mr. Bryce asked, as acidic as ever.

"He's in Ms. Dodge's office," Suzanne said. "With the others."

"Get him out here," Mr. Bryce said.

"Aren't you even worried if he's all right?" Suzanne asked.

"Oh, yes," Mrs. Bryce said. "How is my baby?"

"M-momma?" Eric stepped out of Ms. Dodge's office.

Mrs. Bryce grabbed her son up and hugged him hard. She pinned his arms to his side and covered his grimy face with kisses. Mr. Bryce reached in and pulled Eric away. He shook him hard. Suzanne stepped up to stop him.

"Where have you been?"

"With R-rachel and her family."

"Why?" Mrs. Bryce asked.

"B-because I love her."

Suzanne saw the look of disgust cross the Bryces' faces. She felt the same way but hoped she was able to keep look off her own face.

"She's having my b-baby, t-too."

"What?" Mrs. Bryce's voice went up an octave. Mr. Bryce chuckled out his disbelief.

"I'm afraid it might be true," Suzanne said.

"We're not having it," Mr. Bryce became serious. "They'll have to prove it. I'm not paying child support for some bastard that kook Solomon says is my boy's."

"D-don't say b-bad things about Daddy Sol."

"*Daddy Sol?*" Mrs. Bryce said. "What have they done to you?"

"They brainwashed him. The Hassles have a cult and tried to brainwash us all." Suzanne pointed to her bruised and pierced face. "This is what happened if you resisted."

"I think we should all wait in my office until the deputy gets here," Ms. Dodge said. "I'm sure he'll have lots of questions."

"I think that's a good idea too," Suzanne said.

Mr. Bryce kept his eyes narrow and his mouth drawn

tight, but nodded his agreement. Everyone went into the counselor's office. The room seemed smaller with so many people crammed in there. It smelled horrible as well. Suzanne forgot how bad everyone looked and smelled until then. She wished she could forget it again.

"How long until a deputy gets here? We overheard the call that the kids were here." Mrs. Bryce looked up at Suzanne. "We got an emergency scanner to keep up with the news after Eric ran off and the whole bus thing."

"He should be here any minute," Suzanne looked at the wall clock that read nearly fifteen minutes since she'd called 911. The front door jangled. "That must be him."

"I'll let him in." Ms. Dodge got to her feet.

"I'm glad all this will be over soon," Mr. Bryce said.

"'Bout time too."

The voice Suzanne knew too well, and the words hit the floor like falling lead weights. She cut her eyes to the door not bothering to turn her whole head. Solomon stood framed in the doorway, leaning on his crooked stick and smiling his hateful smile.

24

Ye are my children.
Ye are the Children of Lot

BOOK OF LOT 1:1

THE AIR SEEMED TO evacuate the room as Solomon stepped inside. He leaned on his cane. His lips curled in a malicious grin. Suzanne felt like gasping for breath but didn't. She focused her mind and kept her breathing normal. The others weren't as able. Heather sucked in great sobs, and Chris whimpered.

"Daddy Sol, I knowed you come and get us," Rachel said.

The girl's eyes were bright like two backlit emeralds. Eric perked up as well. He smiled a large white-toothed smile.

"I knowed it too," he said, but from him, the grammatical mistake seemed forced.

"You're not going anywhere with him," Mr. Bryce's voice was clipped, and the words bore force behind them.

"I don't reckon ye's got a say in that," Solomon said. "Eric is my son now. He's part of the Hassle family. Show him, my boy."

Eric smiled and lifted his shirt. His belly button had a red scab formed over it. It was the mark of Lot.

"That means he's mine."

"Like hell he is."

Mr. Bryce squared off with the old man. Solomon smirked. Suzanne couldn't believe her eyes when she saw the confidence in his face. The old man meant to have everyone back just like he had it.

"I grow tired of ye, Mr. Bryce. Esau, relieve me of this burden."

Solomon stepped aside, allowing Esau to lumber into the room. Things became more claustrophobic as the room filled with Esau's bulk. The already scarce fresh air all but evaporated. Mr. Bryce started to quiver with rage. His head vibrated, and he flushed as red as the fire alarm pull just on the other side of the office door. He let out a screeching war cry. All his soul seemed pumped into that scream. Mr. Bryce charged at Esau. He tucked his head down to ram his skull into the wall of flesh. Suzanne motioned for the kids to get against the walls. Mrs. Bryce and Ms. Dodge did the same.

Mr. Bryce's head slammed into Esau's stomach. The large man exhaled a puff of air and bent in the middle. The force of the blow knocked him back through the door. Mr. Bryce followed. He charged again, and rammed his head back into Esau's gut.

"Come on," Suzanne muttered. "Keep it up."

Mr. Bryce pulled back and made to ram Esau again from a shorter distance. The impact was not enough. Esau grabbed Mr. Bryce around the waist, lifted him up, and held him over his large woolly head. Mr. Bryce kicked down against Esau's head. He snorted. Suzanne had never met a giant, but she thought that Esau's snort must be what one sounded like if they were real. One of the kids hollered from fright. Heather sobbed louder. Ty covered his ears. Mrs. Bryce, who had moved to see the fight, covered her eyes. Esau turned the smaller man around his head like a propeller. Mr. Bryce began to scream with rage and fear. Solomon released a deep laugh of victory. Sheba and Lovell chuckled at the sight from the hallway as if they were watching a professional wrestling match instead of a murder. As the last of the horrible screech echoed down the hall as he threw Mr. Bryce against the closet door. The whole wall shook.

Suzanne took a step towards Mr. Bryce, but she was stopped dead in her tracks by a sickly cracking and popping from his body, as not one but a plurality of bones snapped simultaneously. She'd never heard anything like it. Her stomach turned over.

Mrs. Bryce rushed from the room. She knelt beside her husband and wailed. The words coming out were incomprehensible. All Suzanne knew was that she begged for her husband's life, if he still had one.

"Get her away." Solomon came out of the office door. "Let Esau finish him once and for all."

Sheba snatched Mrs. Bryce and held her in a bear hug. Mrs. Bryce struggled and kicked at Sheba, but the Hassle woman was too much of an immovable force for Mrs. Bryce to succeed. Esau stepped up to Mr. Bryce, nothing blocking him from finishing what he had started. He drew his large, booted foot up, and stomped down on Mr. Bryce's head. Suzanne couldn't grasp the sound of his skull collapsing, much less when Esau kept stomping him four or five times. Blood pooled around the entrance of Ms. Dodge's office. The kids quit making any noise. Not a sob came from their mouths nor a whisper. Eric stood at the edge of the door looking into the hall. He stared at his father's body. Mr. Bryce's head was nothing but a lump of broken bleeding flesh with his brains splattered on the walls and floor.

"D-daddy," the boy whispered. Then he broke into tears. He crumpled to his knees on the floor.

Solomon put his hand on the boy's head. "Don't worry. Yer a Hassle now."

Eric looked up at the old man and in the voice of a small terrified child said, "I d-don't want to b-be a Hassle."

Solomon shook with rage. He drew his hand over his head and backhanded the boy across the face. Eric fell over from the force of the blow. His cheek bore a deep red hand-print on it. Suzanne felt something break loose from deep inside her.

"You will not do anything else to these children." She stepped up to Solomon as stone solid as the words she had just uttered.

"What?" he growled. "I reckon I'll do as I please. I's the patriarch of this family same as Lot was of his. I's the bearer of the glory of our Savior, and no sass-mouthed whore is goin' to stop me."

Suzanne snatched Eric up and pushed him back into Ms. Dodge's office. Her clenched fists throbbed. Blood roared in her ears, and she became aware of the beating of her heart like war drums in the distance. Now she stared into his eyes, deep into the void of humanity they bore.

"Kill her," he said as if saying little more than thank you for a passing compliment. "God knows hisself all the evil she done brung onto us."

"Stop right there." A voice came from the glass door as it jiggled hard.

Suzanne looked up and saw Rusty standing with one hand on the door handle and his gun drawn and pointed toward

Solomon. She backed into Ms. Dodge's office, hoping that Rusty wouldn't hesitate to shoot through the glass.

He hesitated.

Solomon grabbed Mrs. Bryce and pulled her in front of himself. Rusty kept his revolver drawn and pointed through the glass door.

"Shoot," Solomon smiled at the deputy.

"Step away from the woman," Rusty yelled through the door. "You don't have to involve them."

"Ye'll just have to shoot."

Suzanne watched from the door of Ms. Dodge's office. Sheba, Lovell, and Esau turned to face the entrance door as well. Suzanne waved for the kids to come to her. Eric was the first to her side. He slipped his hand into hers and squeezed, looking for comfort. The others lined up behind him. Ms. Dodge stood behind Rachel with her hand on the girl's shoulder.

"Come on, while they're distracted, we'll go through the classrooms and try to get out through the library," Suzanne whispered.

"No," Rachel said. "We ain't doin' no such thing."

"Ms. Dodge, please help me."

Ms. Dodge put her hand over Rachel's mouth. "I'm sorry sweetie, but it won't be just a minute. Cooperate."

"Come on." Suzanne crept out into the hall.

The kids followed her. She opened the nearest classroom door, inhaling the refreshing gust of cool air that puffed out into the hall. The kids went inside, Ms. Dodge following with her hand still over Rachel's mouth. Suzanne trailed them, closing the door with little noise. She fumbled with the lock and secured it.

Light from a dusk-til-dawn lamp filtered in through the windows. The desks were arranged in rows so the middle of the room had a long walkway across. A door to the next room stood in the wall. Several classrooms were on the hall toward the intersection that led to the library. Each opened into the other.

"All right, let's get across to the next room. Just keep going until we get to the cross hall. We'll get into the library. You can let her go, Ms. Dodge."

Ms. Dodge took her hand from the girl's mouth. "Now behave, Rachel."

"Daddy Sol!"

"Stop her," Ty said. "Shut her up. Shut her up, already."

Ms. Dodge reached to cover Rachel's mouth again. The girl pulled away and ran to the door. Chris tried to stop her, but she tripped him. He skidded across the floor and hit the wall just under the blackboard. Heather came around to try to catch Rachel, but toppled over Chris who stayed sprawled on the floor. As Rachel reached the door, Eric tackled her from behind at a full run. They both went to the floor.

"I'm s-sorry, R-Rachel, but we can't go b-back with them."

Suzanne walked to the teacher's desk. She opened a drawer and rummaged until she brought out a roll of masking tape. She walked over to Rachel and Eric.

"Thanks." She took Rachel by the arm and stood her up. "I don't want to do this, but you've given me no choice."

Suzanne freed an end of the tan tape. She took Rachel's hands and started wrapping the tape around the wrists. After a few rounds, Suzanne tore the tape free from the roll and secured the end onto the rest of the tape.

"Daddy Sol, Esau, Sheba, help us. Help me!"

"Shut up," Suzanne muttered.

The kids looked at her. She shook her head as she tore off a strip of tape long enough to put over Rachel's mouth. Suzanne looked at Ms. Dodge. The counselor shook her head disapprovingly.

"We've got no other choice, Becky. She won't cooperate." Suzanne felt a twinge of guilt wrap around her intestines. She paused and forced back the burning tears that threatened to fall as she spoke. She struggled to keep her voice from cracking. "I've done things that you can't imagine. This isn't anything compared to that."

A pounding rattled the door. Suzanne looked up at Ms. Dodge. She motioned for the counselor to go into the next classroom. She whispered to lock the outer doors that connected to the main hallway as they passed from one room to the other. Ms. Dodge hesitated but then hurried away. She and the kids disappeared through the doorway that led to the next room. The door shook again from a heavy knock. Suzanne figured it was Esau banging.

Rachel squirmed and tried to yell from behind the tape, but only a high-pitched squeal of a sound came through. Suzanne grabbed her by the back of her shirt and pushed her forward. They entered the seventh-grade math classroom. The desks all faced the door. The white board still had a few easy level pre-algebra problems on it. The light in the room was dimmer than the other one because it was farther away from the outside lamp.

"Keep moving," Suzanne closed and locked the door behind her. "Ty, keep up with Rachel, please."

"Yes, ma'am." Ty grabbed hold of Rachel's shirt and pushed her forward.

The door to the classroom behind them burst open with a loud bang. Suzanne pushed Chris and Amanda, who dawdled around the room toward the next door. Ty and Rachel disappeared into the dimness of the next room. Suzanne stopped at the next door after entering the eighth-grade English classroom and locked it. A large yellowing poster of Mark Twain stared at her from the far wall. She mused that Tom Sawyer might enjoy her situation right now, if the scamp thought being raped by murderous hillbillies was exciting. The light came in just enough to make it across the room without ramming into a desk. Ms. Dodge stood at the door across the room. Suzanne knew that they would be in the next hall just a few steps from the library as soon as they went through that door.

"Come on." She pushed past the kids and Ms. Dodge, opened the door, and poked her head into the hall enough to look both ways. The fluorescents overhead hummed their disquieting tune like a million thirsty mosquitoes.

"Everyone into the hall, and then to the library."

Suzanne rushed into the hall. Heather and Amanda hurried out first. Eric and Chris followed and disappeared into the inset where the library door was. Ty pushed Rachel through the door, and Ms. Dodge brought up the rear. The door from the first classroom to the seventh-grade math classroom crashed open. Suzanne pushed Ms. Dodge toward the library and closed the door to the English classroom. Another door crashed open. Suzanne knew that little was going to keep Solomon from what he wanted. She and Ms. Dodge hurried into the library as the door from the English classroom into the cross hall ripped open.

25

A good tree cannot
bring forth evil fruit,
neither can a corrupt tree
bring forth good fruit

MATTHEW 7:18

SUZANNE LOCKED THE LIBRARY door. Only a narrow vertical window latticed with wire gave a view into the hall. She walked into the reading area of the library. The air smelled of dusty books. A large cutout of the Cat in the Hat stood against the circulation desk. These elements should have been calming, but she thought she could hear Esau's footfalls nearing the door. The kids stood in a circle around Rachel. Ms. Dodge stood behind the circulation desk.

"So, we're going out a window?" Ms. Dodge asked.

"No." She pointed to the end of the bookshelves. "Kids, there's a closet over there." A wooden door stood in the wall. "It's big enough for you all to stay in there."

"I c-can't," Eric said. "I'm t-too scared."

The main door to the library rattled hard. The wood popped. Esau snorted like an infuriated bull.

Suzanne took Eric by the shoulder and pushed him toward the closet. "This will be over soon. Just go in with the rest, and stay quiet. Ms. Dodge and I aren't going to let anything happen to you."

"B-but that's n-not t-true," he whispered back.

"Of course it is. I'm not going to let them get you if I can help it," Suzanne said, realizing that she couldn't promise the

Hassles wouldn't get the children back, but she was going to die trying to keep that from happening.

Eric pulled her down so he could put his mouth to her ear as she opened the closet door. "She's one of them."

"Huh?"

"Ms. D-dodge is a Hassle."

She looked into the boy's eyes. There was no guile in them, only truth. She swallowed hard against the little knot of fear that the idea of Ms. Dodge being one of them gave her, and patted him on the shoulder. "Kids go on and get in that closet. Don't make me tell you again. You too, Eric. It'll be okay."

The library's door popped again. Esau whistled.

The kids filed quickly into the closet. Ty let each of them into the closet then closed himself in with them. Suzanne hurried to the closet door. She jiggled the handle. It was locked.

"Don't come out or do anything until me or a police officer says so," she said to the door.

"Yes, ma'am," Ty said back.

"And turn off the light. They'll see it from under the door."

She looked down at the bottom of the door. The light seeping from the crack between the door and the floor blinked out. A chalkboard on wheels was pushed in the corner. Suzanne rolled it in front of the door. The lyrics from John Lennon's *Imagine* were scribbled on it. The yellow lettering looked too fresh, so she smeared the chalk with her arm. Satisfied that the writing looked like it had been on the board a while, she scurried to a window in the far wall. She flipped the latch up and pushed open the window. Esau had stopped pummeling the door. She shot a glance up at the small window and saw nothing but the wall across from the door. He must have gone to get the others.

"You think that'll fool them?" she asked Ms. Dodge, trying to hide her newfound disgust for the woman.

The counselor looked at the window. "It might, but if they're as determined as they seem, I don't think anything will stop them from getting what they want."

Suzanne heard the voice of Solomon echoing down the hall toward the library. She trotted to the circulation desk and stood behind it with Ms. Dodge. She scanned the opening in the desk for anything she might use as a weapon.

"They'll be coming any moment now," Suzanne said.

"It should've been sooner," Ms. Dodge said, "but Esau had to go and get the others before he busts in. He's big, but he's not the smartest one."

Suzanne acted like she hadn't heard Ms. Dodge talk about Esau as if she knew him personally. Instead, she held her hand out to the counselor.

"What's that for?" Ms. Dodge asked.

"Sisterhood."

Ms. Dodge took it, letting her fingers wrap around Suzanne's hand. The tips of Ms. Dodge's fingers felt hard and callused. They felt like Solomon's had earlier at the feast. Suzanne pulled her hand away from Ms. Dodge's.

"What's the matter with your fingers?"

"What do you mean?" Ms. Dodge rolled her hand over and looked at them.

Suzanne took notice too. Each finger was tipped with a hard callused pad of skin. How she had never noticed it before, she didn't know. Ms. Dodge balled her hand into a loose fist.

"I'm told it's a family trait," Ms. Dodge said. "I wouldn't know. I never knew my father."

"Because a black man raped your mother."

"Oh," Ms. Dodge sounded surprised. "Have I told you this before?"

"No, your Aunt Hadassah did."

"I – I don't have an Aunt Hadassah. You're nuts or something." Ms. Dodge stepped out from behind the circulation desk and headed toward the door.

"Going to help them, Rebecca?"

"Help who? I don't know what you're talking about." Her words took on the staccato of hyper nervousness.

"Solomon hurt Hadassah. He hurt her badly."

Ms. Dodge stopped halfway between the circulation desk and the door. She turned and looked back at Suzanne. A different look came from her eyes. They narrowed and became sinister, as sinister as any look Suzanne had seen from Solomon.

The door moaned again as something very meaty slammed against it.

"Good. She deserves to die. Daddy Sol should've killed her a long time ago. I told him that I could take care of family, better than she could," Ms. Dodge said, her voice suddenly falling into a bravado echoing the Hassle clan. "All she ever did was try to stop the prophecy. She hates us. She hates her own family."

"She seemed like she loved you and your mother. She told me about how it broke her heart when your mother got pregnant from that rape, and how sad it made her when your mother died giving birth to you."

"Aunt Hadassie always tried to get me to leave the farm. She told me I could be anything I wanted because I wasn't tainted like the rest of them." Ms. Dodge's eyes shot daggers toward Suzanne. "If I wasn't *tainted* like the rest of them, then why couldn't I have children?"

Suzanne thought for a moment. "I don't know. Sometimes things just happen."

"I can't have no babies because I'm a Hassle as much as Esau, Sheba, Daddy Sol, or your lover, Cousin Nathan. Hadassie just wanted to live her dreams through me."

"Cousin Nathan? Do you mean Warren?"

"Of course I mean Warren, you ignorant whore. Daddy Sol bought him off a drug addict down in Mississippi, to raise for this very moment. He even made him join the military so he would be a soldier. I taught him from the time he was a child so that he could blend into the world until the time came." Ms. Dodge tried to get past Suzanne. "Hold on!"

The door to the library rattled on its hinges as Esau pounded on it. Suzanne reached under the desk and grabbed hold of a wooden-handled letter opener. She brought it out and held it at her side. The door shook again. The reinforced structure designed to help in tornado situations seemed be keeping the storm of Esau at bay.

"Let us in," Solomon yelled. "Don't make us break this door down, too."

Ms. Dodge moved to go for the door. "I'm coming, Daddy Sol."

Suzanne came around the circulation desk. She flipped the letter opener so the knife end pointed away from her body. "Don't move, Becky. I'll kill you if I have to."

"Hogwash." Ms. Dodge smiled. "Look at you, you're nothing but a pincushion." She moved closer to the door.

Suzanne moved fast. She'd didn't run, but it didn't feel like walking either. She felt like she flew to Ms. Dodge's side. The counselor shoved Suzanne hard to the right trying to evade her, but Suzanne stood firm. The door banged again, and wood splintered.

"Another knock like that, and they'll be in here. Might as well let me open the door and save that repair bill." Ms. Dodge smiled, making her clean white teeth shine.

Suzanne had trouble seeing a Hassle in Ms. Dodge, but knew it was the truth. She had an even harder time imagining that Lovell had just manipulated her to exactly this moment. Ms. Dodge pushed her again and made a break for the door taking advantage of her momentary distraction. Suzanne caught her balance, drew the letter opener up and pivoted. The blade tore into Ms. Dodge's arm, and she grabbed hold of the gash.

Suzanne was on her. "I told you I'd kill you to save these children."

The letter opener plunged into Ms. Dodge's neck. It gashed a jagged tear across her throat as Suzanne pulled it through her skin like the seal of an envelope. Ms. Dodge crumpled to the floor holding her hand over the tear. Blood spurted from between her fingers and onto the off-white cinder block wall. She made a gurgling noise as she tried to speak.

"What was that? I couldn't hear you." Suzanne felt vindictive and guilty at the same time. She couldn't stop the sinister smile from forming on her face as she gazed down at Ms. Dodge. How much of this had Ms. Dodge been responsible for? Did she identify Marlene as the "Yankee" on the bus? Did she make those phone calls to Suzanne's house? How many lies had she told Suzanne? What had been Lovell's part? What lies had he told?

The library door crashed open. Suzanne wiped her hand across her face leaving a streak of deep red blood. Its ferric smell filled her nose, and her mouth tasted as if she were sucking on a penny. The red fire alarm pull was on the wall not three inches from her. Suzanne looked over her shoulder and saw Esau charging into the library, followed by Sheba. Both looked as wild as she must have with a war paint of blood on her face. Lovell and Solomon came in last.

"The winder's open," Sheba said. "Bet them brats done run off."

"Take a gander," Solomon said. He looked at Suzanne and then to the crumpled bloody mass that had been Becky Dodge. His face melted from a smirk of triumph to a frown of despair. "Rebecca." He wailed her name.

Suzanne had never heard someone wail in grief. It unnerved her more than killing Ms. Dodge had. Solomon shook. He's knees knocked together, and Lovell caught him before the old man hit the ground.

"What's the matter, Daddy Sol, never seen a dead person?" Suzanne said. The vindictiveness toward the old man felt justified, and no guilt over it prodded at her.

"Kill her! Rip her head off her shoulders and piss down her throat. Rape her to death if ye want. I ain't got no more need for the whore, prophecy or no." Tears rolled down Solomon's cheeks.

"Nothin' make me happier, seein's as what she did to my Purty," Sheba said turning from the window.

Esau and the fat woman advanced. Suzanne gripped the

blood-slimed handle of the letter opener tighter as she reached for the alarm pull. Her fingers hooked over the lever, and she tugged. The room erupted into the high-pitched siren of the fire alarm, and strobe lights attached to the siren speakers began to flash. She clenched her empty fist and stood ready.

26

A time to love,
and a time to hate

ECCLESIASTES 3:8

ESAU STOPPED HIS CHARGE at Suzanne. He clapped his meaty hands over his ears and started to run around in a tight circle. His whistle boomed louder than the screaming siren. It was a sound of intense pain like she'd heard the first day she'd met the Hassles.

Suzanne remembered the reaction he'd had to the high pitch of pig squealing, but she never expected him to turn into such a child. Esau fell to his knees and curled up into fetal position. He kept his hands clamped tightly over his ears.

"Get up ye great lump of pig dung!" Solomon yelled, stomping his cane on the ground, his voice barely audible over the siren. "That noise ain't goin' do nothing but make yer ears hurt. Get up and get her."

Esau stayed curled in the floor. Suzanne moved toward him. She was almost over him, when a small rolling cart filled with books toppled over. The clattering startled her even with the screaming of the fire alarm. Sheba lay across the cart, her whole body heaving to and fro. Frothy slobber bubbled out of her mouth. She flopped off the cart with enough force that the metal frame skidded across the floor.

"Get up, Esau. Be a man, not some snot blowin' baby!" Solomon roared, but Esau made no effort to stand.

Lovell charged Suzanne. She had almost forgotten about him. She swung the letter opener at him, forcing Lovell to back off and favor the gash on his arm she had made with the hatchet. It appeared he had sewed it up with a thick white twine. She swept the blade at him again. Her teeth clenched, and her lips pulled back into a snarl. Everything seemed to be gone from inside her. She felt nothing. Numbness wasn't even present. Suzanne couldn't remember ever feeling completely hollow in her life, but now her heartbeats echoed through the chasm of her insides.

"Give me the letter opener, Suzi," she read Lovell's lips. His voice was too soft to boom over the squeal of the alarm. "I'm not going to hurt you. It's me, Warren."

Suzanne swung the letter opener again, this time at his face. She moved in a circle trying to position herself for a sprint out of the library door. She glanced at Esau hissing and spitting on the ground like a wounded animal. Lovell took advantage of her momentary lapse in attention and grabbed her free arm. She jerked back, but his grip was too strong for her.

"Got'cha." He mouthed.

Suzanne looked into Lovell's face. His eyes bulged from his head, and the veins in his neck distended. A tight, almost pained, smirk stretched across his lips. Lips that were thin and pale. Black bags hung under his eyes. He looked more like a crazed maniac than the man she thought she loved.

Solomon said something too low to register over the din. Suzanne looked up. The old man had crawled to Ms. Dodge's side. He petted her bloody face, caking his fingers with gore. He heaved with sobs. Lovell jerked Suzanne's arm, slamming her into his chest. He reached for the hand with her letter opener.

"We won't be needing that."

"All right."

Suzanne used the little bit of leverage she had and all the force she could muster to stab the blade into his shoulder. Lovell let her go and took a few stumbles backward. He grabbed the slimy wooden handle. A dark maroon circle spread over his shirtsleeve from where the blade stuck out.

He yelled as he pulled the thin blade out of his muscular shoulder. Bits of dark red gore splattered on the floor, and the wound bubbled blood from it. Suzanne took her chance. She ran as hard as she could to the open door. The hallway flashed with the shadow and brightness of the strobe light. The alarms weren't set synchronously, so they echoed down the hall at different times. The air felt cooler. Suzanne hadn't noticed how hot she had become in the fight.

She took only a moment to notice this before sprinting down the length of the hall back to the L where she could run to door where Rusty had been. The Hassles had turned the lights out when they left that hall, so the only light came at a constant pulse from the fire alarm. Suzanne thought about the hundreds of scary movies she'd seen with just such a scenario. At least she wasn't wearing heels. She ran down the hallway. The outside door let in the glow of the steady parking lot lights into the hall. Suzanne focused on that light.

Something lay in the middle of the floor not far from the door to the main office. It wasn't Mr. Bryce. His corpse still lay splayed out where Esau had killed him. As she drew closer, Suzanne made out the color and style of Mrs. Bryce's clothes. No blood seemed to come from her. Maybe she wasn't dead. Suzanne made it to the first classroom they had escaped to.

The junction to the side hall that led to the lower grades came up quickly. Mrs. Bryce's body was close enough for Suzanne to get a detailed look. She didn't seem to be breathing. Suzanne glanced to her left as she passed the hallway junction. She registered a dark shadow.

The force of the blow stunned Suzanne. She was only aware of moving sideways across the hall. Her shoulder throbbed in agony as it slammed into the cinderblock wall. A poster of Garfield came free and fell over her head. It blotted out the light, except for the tiny twinkling dots dancing in her vision. All the scrapes, scratches, and bruises complained about being battered again.

"Caught you," Lovell said.

Suzanne felt his weight on her side. She tried to shift, but he had her well pinned.

"My army football team won our division championship," he whispered in her ear like it was sweet nothings. "That's why I'm so good at plowing you."

Suzanne wriggled her right arm loose and pushed the poster off her head. The door to freedom was tauntingly close. A few more steps and she would have been free. Suzanne almost cried. The void of emotion that had blissfully descended only minutes before was now flooded to the point that she felt physical straining at the edges of her brain.

"Now I'm going to take you someplace and show you something I learned in Afghanistan."

Lovell stood. Suzanne breathed in full. The new, cool air, helped stave off the panic she thought would overtake her. She tried to get to her feet, but Lovell twisted his hand into her hair. He started to pull straight up on it.

THE CHILDREN OF LOT

"Warren, don't," Suzanne tried with all her effort to keep it from sounding like a plea.

"I guess you should have thought about that before you stabbed me, again."

Lovell jerked her hair, harder. The roots burned as they began to tear out of her already tender scalp. She hurried to get her feet under her and stand. Lovell started walking to the main office. He took long strides backward so that he could keep his tight grip on her hair. Suzanne walked as quickly while trying to keep as much pressure off her scalp as she could. He pulled her into the office.

"Is your door unlocked?" he asked.

"I've got no idea. Why?"

Lovell pulled her to her office door. He opened it. Bursts of bright light lit the room up like vivid flashes of lightning, but no siren squealed in her office. He dragged her in, not turning on the lights. "This strobe light effect is going to be kinky."

"Warren, don't do this."

"Isn't like we've not done it before." He let go of her hair. "Ain't like I've got a choice. This is all I'm meant to do. God put me on this Earth and had me sold to Solomon to help fulfill his prophecy. 'And she that will save my people, shall be mated with a soldier who was bought like a bull for the cattle.'"

Suzanne stood straight. Her back was to the open door. She took a step back, ready to turn and run. Lovell grabbed her by the arm, jerked her to him, and turned her to face the desk. He pushed down so her backside stuck up in the air. Suzanne wiggled her arms from under herself before he could press down on her. She felt the tail of her dress go up over her buttocks. Hadassah didn't give her any underwear, and her butt was naked to the world.

"How inviting. I never showed you how we would give it to the Afghan women that we suspected of working with the Taliban. I thought it wasn't appropriate for ladies like you. I guess I was wrong."

Suzanne stretched out over her desk trying to get her fingers on the edge of the center drawer. She wriggled up, making her naked backside rise.

"You getting antsy for it? Just give me a second."

Suzanne's fingers slipped over the wooden lip of her center drawer, as the sound of Lovell unzipping his pants filled her ears. She pushed the drawer open as far as she could. Lovell's pants hit the floor, the buckle on his belt jingling. Suzanne dug her fingers into the drawer, prodding for anything. Lovell's fingers entered her, probing. She bit her lip as he pushed his pinkie into her rectum, but kept two in her womanhood.

"The shocker," Lovell laughed, "but that ain't the only shock you're going to get tonight, whore." With his free hand, he jerked on her hair. Her hands shot up from the drawer in reaction to the sharp burning of her hair reaching the tearing point. "Especially if you keep digging in that drawer."

Suzanne had felt what she had been looking for. Lovell pinched hard on something he must have been looking for too. A sweet pain like too much pleasure shuttered through Suzanne. She bit on her lip hard and bucked as best she could. He let loose of her hair, and she plunged a hand back into the drawer. She dragged a box cutter across the bottom of the drawer with a finger until she wrapped the others around it. He kept grinding away at her most sensitive area until her stomach started to turn over. With a push up with her elbows, she jerked the razor from the drawer. A flick with her thumb sent the blade out, and she bucked again like she was in ecstasy. Lovell only held her with his inserted digits. Suzanne slid up with her knees. Lovell pulled his hand away.

"What's the matter, don't like it no more?" He kept a lecherous tone in his voice.

"No, I just want to be on top. I want you to go as deep as you can while I'm sitting on it."

"Sounds like fun." He smacked her on the buttocks.

Suzanne rolled over and sat up quickly, swiping at Lovell with the razor knife. The blade cut across the top of his wrist as he lifted his fingers to smell them. He yelled and reached for her. His pants still hung around his ankles. He tottered and fell toward her. Suzanne scooted off the desk as Lovell fell onto it. His good arm was under him, so he tried to lift up with his injured shoulder, but it faltered on him. She put her knee into the small of his back and pressed her weight against him.

"I told you I like it on top."

"This isn't any fun."

"Where are Solomon and Esau? Are they still in the library?"

"I'm not saying anything."

Suzanne reached around Lovell's neck with the tip of the razor against his Adam's apple. "Still going to play mute?"

"They were still in the library when I left. Esau was still crying in the floor." Lovell paused. "Please don't kill me. I wasn't going to rape you to death. We were just going to have some fun."

Suzanne hesitated with the blade at his throat. Not a week ago, she had made love to him on her living room floor. Now she had him bent over her desk with his pants around his ankles, a box cutter to his throat.

"We've had some good times. I just needed some more of what you gave me tonight," he said.

"You raped me tonight." Suzanne hissed, starting to cry. "I didn't give you anything. You took it."

"You're mine to take when and where I like. Solomon gave you to me when he bought me years ago. You're mine."

"I'm not something to be given. Are you even there, Warren Lovell?"

"Hassle. My name's Nathan Hassle. I am a child of Lot just like Daddy Sol and the others. Warren Lovell was the name of my first birth before I was bought."

Suzanne's blood ran cold. She slit his throat and let him bleed out on her desk while she held his head back by his hair. The man she thought she loved was already dead.

27

Cometh the wrath of God
upon the children of disobedience

EPHESIANS 5:6

SUZANNE FLOPPED INTO ONE of the vinyl chairs in her office used for guests. The box cutter still rested in her hand. She looked down her body. The blue dress Hadassah had given her was black, soaked through with others' blood. She felt sticky. She felt sick. The coppery smell of all the blood made her light-headed. Her stomach turned, and she lurched forward, vomiting on the floor. Her sick mingled with the blood already congealing on her once expensive rug. The inside of her mouth stung with the stomach acid brought up with the vomit. Her insides felt like they were full of black sludge. She needed to be cleansed.

A water fountain with cool clean water stood in the hall just outside her office, drawing Suzanne's thoughts. Her knees wobbled as she stood and straightened. She stepped over Lovell's legs, nearly tripping. Her vision took on a soft quality. The walk from her office to the fountain seemed like a hazy dream. She found the fountain, an oasis she needed. The water chilled Suzanne as it crossed her lips. It cooled her burning mouth and quenched her thirst. For the first time in a week, she felt satisfied, and things became clearer to her.

The fire alarm still screamed. The strobe lights still flashed the only light in the hallway. Suzanne realized that

Rusty and probably more deputies or police were just on the other side of the door. Her freedom was only steps away. She could burst through the doors and run until she couldn't go any farther.

Freedom.

The closet—the kids were still in the closet with the Hassles hunting them like ravenous wolves. Suzanne stepped away from the water fountain. Her leaden legs lifted slowly one at a time. She walked through Mr. Bryce's blood and over Mrs. Bryce. The metal door handle felt cold on her hot hand as she pushed it open. The early morning air rushed around her crisp and clean, bringing the dusty scent of October with it.

"Freeze," Rusty yelled from somewhere in the parking lot. Suzanne's eyes hadn't adjusted to the light from the street lamp yet. "Drop the weapon."

Suzanne lifted her hands and realized she still toted the box cutter. She let it go, and it clattered on the pavement. Rusty stepped up from her side with his pistol drawn and aimed at her.

"It's me, Rusty, Suzanne Clay." She turned to face the deputy head on.

Rusty dropped his gun lower but still kept it in a ready position. "What the hell happened to you?"

Suzanne glanced down at herself again. Somehow from her office to the outside, she'd forgotten how gory she was. "I know I look like Carrie on prom night, but I'm okay. It's not my blood."

"Where are the kids?" Rusty asked.

"In the library. Locked in a closet." She looked around. Only one police car sat in the parking lot. "Where are the others?"

"I'm it. I didn't bother calling for back-up, and I told the fire department not to show up. I was sure there wasn't a fire."

"Why?"

"I got a personal grudge against them. That one called John Mark's been foolin' around with my wife. I caught them in the act and tried to kill him, but he slipped away. I'm not the smartest one, but I'm not dumb enough to march up to their place to get him. I've just been biding by time. My wife's pregnant. It's not mine, either. I want these durn Hassles all to myself." He craned his neck to look around and narrowed his eyes. "So where are they?"

"In the library, I think." Suzanne felt a bit sorry for Rusty. "You don't have to worry about John Mark any more. I took care of him with a hatchet to the head."

The deputy nodded with a satisfied look. "Let's go."

Suzanne shook her head. "I can't."

"You've got to. I don't know my way around the school, and if they're hiding, you'll know all the good spots." Rusty went to pat her on the shoulder but stopped and pulled his hand back. "I'm sorry."

Suzanne drew in a slow haggard breath. "Okay. Here's what's in there. Mr. and Mrs. Bryce are dead and lying in the hall right at the door." Rusty nodded. "There's a lot of blood, so don't slip." He nodded again. "Lovell is dead in my office. I had to kill him. He was one of them, and he tried to rape me, again, and I think he would have killed me."

"It's okay. I knew he was friendly them, at least with John Mark. I'd seen at bars around. I just figured Mr. Lovell didn't know any better. Sorry about that," Rusty said. "What about the Hassles?"

"The last I saw them, Sheba was having a seizure. Esau, the big one, was curled up in the floor from the noise. He can't take loud noises. That's why I tripped the fire alarm."

"So I was right there wasn't a fire?"

Suzanne shook her head. She tried to keep everything in a smooth progression but couldn't remain focused. "Anyway, the old man was the only one left able to do anything. When I left him, he was crying over Ms. Dodge. She was his niece."

"His niece?"

"Yeah, I think she helped orchestrate the whole thing. I killed her too." Suzanne blinked. She did so consciously because she thought she hadn't for a while. "Am I going to jail?"

"Right now, Suzanne, we need to get the kids."

Suzanne nodded. She turned and headed back into the school like nothing had happened. If her mind had been working right, she'd have recognized that she was in shock. Rusty followed her. He had his pistol drawn up ready to fire when needed, but let her stay in the lead until they came to the junction of the side hall where Lovell had blindsided Suzanne. Rusty eased around the corner sweeping his arms side to side making sure the side hall was secure.

"Don't hesitate," Suzanne said as they walked past the junction. "Shoot them as soon as you see them, or they won't give you a second chance."

"Let me worry about that." Rusty sounded as cocky as ever.

Suzanne grabbed his shoulder and swung him around to face her. "Listen to me, you Barney Fife wannabe, I'm the one who've they beaten, tortured, and raped. I'm the one who knows what these freaks are capable of. Shoot them as soon as you see them." She pointed back behind her. "They've got no regard for us or anyone. Didn't you just step over those two bodies? The Bryces got in their way. They'll do the same to you if you give them the chance."

Rusty swallowed hard. Suzanne could tell he didn't like getting his orders handed to him.

"All right." He tried to shrug her hand off his shoulder like an irritated child.

Suzanne stared into his eyes for a moment longer, then let go of his shoulder. She left a bloody handprint on his brown uniform. Rusty glanced at the stain and grimaced. Then he turned and started down the hall again. The strobe light gave only a tantalizing glimpse into the first classroom on the hall. The door lay broken on the floor. Shadows hung over the corners. Nothing moved. Suzanne and Rusty moved down to the next room. The door to the seventh-grade math classroom was closed. Rusty motioned for Suzanne to open it. She jiggled the handle, but it didn't turn.

"It's locked," she said. "We locked it while we were getting away to hide."

"Can't take that chance. Back up."

Suzanne stepped away from the door. Rusty drew his leg up. He kicked the door hard with the flat of his foot. The door creaked and popped but stayed in place. He kicked it again. The door gave way and swung open. Rusty stepped just inside. He looked both ways. Suzanne peeked in as well. No one hid in there, either. Rusty stepped out, and they moved to the next door, the last one on the hall before the junction with the library's hallway.

This door opened without even turning the handle. Ms. Dodge hadn't locked it; she'd cracked it for easy entry by the Hassles. Fortunately, Esau had chased them through the classrooms. Suzanne felt an odd sense of relief. Rusty made a sweep of the room. It too was empty.

"They must still be in the library," he said, stepping back into the hall.

"Or out the window and back to their farm," Suzanne said, with a glimmer of hope in her voice. "With or without the kids."

Rusty turned the corner of the hallway. He pointed his pistol straight ahead of him. He braced the weapon with both hands. Suzanne stepped in front of him again. The short walk from the junction of the hallways to the library door slogged on forever like she was making her way through knee-high mud. The sirens screamed faster down this hall. The others echoed through the school. Suzanne started to develop a headache from the noise and flashing lights. She rubbed her temples.

"What's wrong?" Rusty whispered. "Do you see something?"

Suzanne shook her head. "I've got a headache, but I don't hear Esau carrying on either. He was making all kinds of racket after the alarms went off."

"Let me get ahead of you." Rusty pushed by her. "Is the next door the library?"

"Yeah."

They crept forward. Suzanne kept casting glances behind them. They hadn't looked in the gym. What if Esau and Solomon had gone there instead of leaving? They could be creeping up behind them for an ambush. She looked back in front of her as Rusty stepped into the doorway. The library lights were out. Only the flashing of the emergency lights lit the room.

Rusty put his back to the nearest wall and walked in with his gun pointed to the reading area. Suzanne followed and shimmied against the wall as well. The room was empty except for Ms. Dodge's body still lying crumpled against the wall and Sheba lying underneath the window. She didn't move. Rusty walked to Sheba. He squatted, still keeping an eye on the room. Suzanne scurried to the light switch. The room filled with the comforting fluorescent light. The siren quit squealing at the same time, but the strobe light kept flashing.

"The siren shuts off automatically after so long," Suzanne said. "What about Sheba?"

"She's dead."

Suzanne walked over to Sheba's body. The Hassle's face looked blue with tinges of purple at the edges of her lips. Her mouth hung slack enough to see inside her maw. Sheba had bitten her tongue in half while she seized and choked on it. A frothy mixture of slobber and blood dried on her chin. The fat woman's eyes stared glassily at the ceiling.

"Aren't you going to close her eyes or something?" Suzanne asked.

"That's only in the movies, Suzanne. We don't really do that."

Suzanne nodded, unable to take her eyes off Sheba. She moved closer to the open window. Before it could register clearly, Suzanne felt her hair jerked up, and her scalp burned again. Something pulled her toward the window. For a blurry, panicky moment, Suzanne thought Sheba had jumped up and gotten her.

"Rusty!"

Suzanne grabbed at the hand that held the back of her hair. It felt broad and meaty, Esau's hand. He'd sprung a trap. She tried to contort to see him, but it pulled more at her sore scalp.

"Let her go," Rusty emphasized each word.

Suzanne looked at the deputy. He straightened up, pointing his pistol at her and Esau. The hammer clicked back. Suzanne pulled hard to her left. Her hair stretched to the extreme without tearing out from the roots.

"Shoot him." She pawed at the giant hands pulling her hair through the window.

"I might hit you."

"I don't care. Shoot."

Seemingly in slow motion, Suzanne mouthed the word *please* to the deputy as she saw the muzzle flash and felt Esau's grip let go before she heard the shot. Without the tension of the giant pulling on her, Suzanne fell to her left. Her left arm hit the floor, but it kept her from hitting her head. Two more shots rang out before she got to a sitting position. She looked out of the window with just enough time to see Esau fall over backward, a red hole in his forehead and two reddening roses on his shoulder and his chest. As she stood, the giant Hassle hit the ground. It sounded like a tree crashing to the ground after being sawed down.

"Where's Solomon?" Suzanne asked.

Rusty stepped over Sheba and leaned out the window. He looked in both directions. "Don't see anyone else." He came back in. "But it's too dark to see very far. The old man probably left that big son of gun to finish us off while he ran back home."

"Maybe." Suzanne wasn't quite convinced Solomon would give up that easily.

"Where are the kids?"

Suzanne walked to the far wall. She pushed the mobile chalkboard out of the way and knocked on the door. No one answered. They had listened to her.

"Ty, it's Ms. Clay. I'm here with Deputy Cardiff. It's okay to come out."

"No."

"It's safe. I promise."

"I want to hear the policeman, too," Ty said.

"Didn't you hear the gunshots?" Suzanne asked.

"I heard that siren too. Why haven't the firemen come?" Ty asked.

Rusty started walking to Suzanne and the closet. He held his pistol to his side. "It's okay, kid. I'm Deputy Rusty Cardiff."

Rusty stopped just at the side of the circulation desk. Suzanne heard the lock on the closet door twist. It swung open. Ty came out followed by the other kids. Each one's hair plastered to his or her forehead from sweat.

"It got hot in there," Chris fanned himself by pulling the front of his shirt out and fluttering it.

"D-deputy l-look out." Eric pointed to the circulation desk.

Suzanne turned as Solomon stood up, swinging his heavy walking stick at Rusty's knees. The deputy toppled to the floor. His pistol came free and slid across the floor.

"Y'all thought me just an old fool, did ye?"

He swung his stick down at Rusty like an ax hitting him across the back. The deputy huffed out breath but tried to lift up again. Solomon cracked him on the side with his stick.

Suzanne stood paralyzed. The glimmer of hope that filled her when Esau fell like so much dead wood disappeared into the ether. Now, she had nothing to cling to. She'd lost hope too many times over the last few days. Everything emptied out of her, even her will to resist, except for a small distant voice that yelled deep in her mind to charge.

"Young'uns, I reckon we can be getting' back to the farm just as soon as I take care of Miss Clay."

Solomon kicked Rusty in the ribs. The deputy lay there not moving. The old man stepped over him and toward Suzanne. He drew his walking stick across him like a bat.

"When I was in Iwo Jima, I learnt that when ye crack somebody's skull, it sounds just like hittin' a muskmelon with a baseball bat, 'cept muskmelons don't scream."

The evil smile he was so prone to show came on Solomon's face. It contorted into the visage of a devil, not a far cry from what the old man was. His eyes turned to slits, and dirty nubby teeth showed. Suzanne stood firm, unable to move. She now thought it was more suicidal ideation than total fear. Maybe she wanted to die and just get everything over with. It would be so much easier to just let Solomon kill her than live with all the scars he had and would cause later on. Fighting back seemed futile against her total exhaustion.

"Stop." Ty said with the authority of a man who knows he's strong.

Suzanne looked at the boy. He held Rusty's pistol out with both hands aimed at Solomon.

"Put down that BB gun, boy. You ain't goin' to shoot nobody." Solomon kept advancing on Suzanne.

"I said stop."

A demonic snarl contorted Solomon's face. He roared like an animal, bringing his stick up to deliver a death blow. He charged Suzanne. She gasped waiting for the stick to burst her skull, but nothing happened. Solomon stopped only a foot from her. His mouth hung loose. Suzanne had heard the shot. Solomon blinked. Another shot echoed through the room. Solomon's knees buckled, and he crumpled to the floor. His stick came loose from his hands and flew to his side, landing with a loud clatter a few feet away.

Suzanne looked at Ty. He kept pulling the trigger of the revolver even though it only clicked, emptied of its live bullets. She reached out and pushed his arms down. Ty quit shooting air.

"It's okay. You got him," she said.

"I had to do something." Ty stared at Solomon's crumpled body. "He was going to get you. I'm not going to Hell for it am I? Sol told us the Bible says not to kill."

"There are exceptions," she patted his back.

Ty nodded and dropped the pistol on the ground like it was some cheap dollar-store toy. He looked like any other kid again. Suzanne laughed and cried at the same time as she let herself sink to the tile floor. Her legs wouldn't support her anymore.

28

O they tell me of a home
where no storm clouds rise.
O they tell me
of an unclouded day

AMERICAN HYMN

SUZANNE SAT UP AS her nurse walked in, carrying a little plastic cup filled with pills. She smiled as she took the medication from him. Three pills sat in the cup, a blue one, and two white tablets.

"What are these?"

"Paxil, Xanax, and an antibiotic," the nurse answered.

When he grinned, dimples formed in his cheeks. Suzanne thought about how much she liked men with dimples in their cheeks. She tossed the pills in her mouth and swallowed them down with orange juice left over from breakfast. The larger of the two white pills lodged in her throat. The bitter flavor of antibiotics washed though her mouth. She took another big gulp of juice, finishing off the container.

"Got one stuck," she said.

"Those big ones are hard to swallow." He took a stethoscope from around his neck and listened to her heart, then to her breathing. "How's the pain today?"

"I'm sorer than anything else."

The nurse nodded and jotted down her answer on his clipboard. "Did you sleep okay last night?"

Suzanne looked at him. She slept only because they had given her some sleeping pills, and she had nightmares the whole night. Solomon kept chasing her down the hallways of the school. The halls never ended. They went on into infinity, and Solomon never tired no matter how far they ran.

"Fine."

"Don't lie, Ms. Clay," the nurse said. "The doctor is planning on releasing you today, either way."

"Horribly. I had nightmares all night, but I couldn't stay awake long enough to shake them off because of the sleep medicine."

"They gave you Ambien for sleep. Sometimes that makes people have more vivid dreams than they would otherwise. I'll see if we can't get Trazadone put in place of that before you leave." The nurse made another note on his clipboard. "Just to let you know, all your tests came back fine. You don't have any STDs or major infections. The only thing that hasn't resulted yet is the pregnancy test, but it would be too soon to know that anyway."

"I've been steady on the depo shot for a long time now. I'm pretty sure I'm safe from that." Suzanne smiled. The ulcer in her mouth from the thorn wound stung a bit. "So when is the doctor going to let me go?"

"As soon as I report your morning assessment to her."

"Believe it or not, I don't want to eat another lunch in this place. Go tell her I'm fine," Suzanne smiled.

"Sure thing, Ms. Clay."

Suzanne settled back onto her pillows. The television was on *The View*. She'd never cared for the show, but the only thing else on was Andy Griffith or infomercials. The hospital blocked most every channel except the local and religious channels. The women on the screen chattered about some new movie out with some new hunk of a star that Suzanne had never heard of. When they showed him, she was sure he was jailbait.

A knock came at the door. Suzanne roused as Rusty and another uniformed officer came into her room. Rusty had a black eye.

"Suzanne, this is Detective Stephens with the Marquisville PD. He needs to ask you a few questions, if that's all right."

Suzanne stared at them. Yesterday, two state investigators had stopped by to ask questions about a missing state trooper, Henry Nalls. She told them about Esau killing a black state trooper, but she didn't know what happened to the body. They thanked her. She thought all the questioning would be done.

"I've answered just about every question I can think of to answer."

"Probably so," Stephens said. "I've only got one though."

"Shoot."

"Are you willing to press charges against the Hassles for kidnapping you?" he asked.

Suzanne laughed. It came out without her meaning for it to. She shook her head. "The ones that did it are dead. There's no one to blame, except the fine citizens of this town for not insisting the lazy police do their jobs and try to find us. I suppose I should just let that go though."

"Ma'am, there are about 200 Hassles at that farm. Every one of them is guilty," Stephens raised an eyebrow at her as he jotted notes.

"I'm pretty sure that some of those 200 are too mentally challenged to know any better. Plus, believe or not, they weren't all bad. Solomon's sister, Hadassah—I'm pretty sure she's in this hospital somewhere—is as good as gold." She shook her head again. "Just let the rest of them be. Without their Daddy Sol, they'll probably die from starvation anyway."

"Are you sure, Suzanne?" Rusty asked. "They've done some horrible things to you."

"Thanks. I didn't realize that." She paused giving the deputy what her students called, *the stink eye*—sarcasm that should be easily understood by even someone like Rusty. "Make the health department and mental health get out there and treat them. That'll be enough for me." Down deep inside herself, she knew that would be satisfactory to her.

The nurse pushed into the room past the two police officers. He held two pieces of paper in his hand.

"I've got your release papers, Ms. Clay," he said. "I just need for you to sign them."

She snatched them from him and snapped her fingers for a pen. He handed one to her.

"Don't you want me to tell you about them?" he asked.

"Nope."

Suzanne signed the papers and handed the back to the nurse. She tossed the bedclothes off, revealing she was already wearing jeans. She got up out of bed and slipped a pair of shoes on.

"I don't want any of the complimentary toiletries and whatnot," she said to the nurse. "Have you got my scripts out there at the nurse's station?"

"Yeah."

"Let's go get them."

"I need to call for a wheelchair," the nurse said. "It's regulations."

Suzanne pushed him between the two officers. "I know, but I've been helpless long enough. I'm walking out of here on my own two feet."

In the hall by the nurse's station, her nurse reached over the desk and grabbed up a small square slip of paper. It had a doctor's name and address across the top. He handed it Suzanne.

"Thanks. I wish you the best," she said and started down the hall.

"Ma'am, about the charges," Stephens said to her back.

"I already told you." Suzanne threw up her hand and walked off the unit.

Suzanne walked up the stairs to the third floor of the hospital. Next to the courthouse, the hospital was the tallest building in Marquisville, with three floors. The thought of riding on a cramped elevator was too much for her. She'd never been claustrophobic, but the ability to escape seemed a prized talent at the moment. The door from the stairwell to the third floor's main hall screeched open when she pushed it. Scratches on the door frame told of how the door must have been sticking for a while.

The third floor looked more cheerful than the unit she had been on. A large nurse's station took up the center of the hall with rooms on the two wings from it. At the end of each wing, smaller nurse's stations were positioned. Bright paintings hung on the walls. It was a good place for the kids to be. Suzanne walked to the main nurse's station. A woman wearing royal blue scrubs looked up. Her badge said she was the unit secretary.

"Can I help you?" she asked.

"I'm looking for Ty Arthur's room."

"He's in," the secretary glanced down at a paper list, "Room 333. Down that way."

Suzanne walked in the direction the secretary pointed. She found the room's door wide open. Ty sat up in bed watching the television that hung from the ceiling. He had a flat screen TV in his room. The third floor was definitely better. Suzanne looked at it. Scooby and the gang seemed to be dealing with ghosts in an ice cream factory. She tapped on the door.

Ty looked at her. "Ms. Clay."

"What?" said a woman's voice from the bathroom.

"Ms. Clay's here," Ty said.

"Can I come in?" Suzanne asked.

Ty nodded. "Yeah, but you'll have to sit on my bed. Momma's got the only chair."

"That's fine. I've been sitting all morning." Suzanne stepped into the room. "I'll stand."

The door to the bathroom opened, and Ty's mom walked out wiping her hands on her pants. She smiled and stuck her hand out to Suzanne, who shook it. Ty's mom's hand was still damp.

"I just came to say good bye," Suzanne said, "and to thank you, Ty."

"We should be thanking you, Ms. Clay. You saved all our kids," Ty's mom said.

Suzanne stared at the floor. She counted the blue specks on the cream background to keep back the tears. When the burning at the edges of her eyes stopped, she looked up.

"Not all of them."

"But you tried," Ty's mom said, "and you saved my little man."

"Momma, please. You're embarrassing me." Ty grinned and seemed to blush.

"Don't be embarrassed." Suzanne mussed his hair. "Mommas are supposed to think that about their sons, even when they're as big as you. I'm serious when I say thanks. You saved my life."

"What else would I have done?"

Ty's question was innocent. Suzanne realized that he had to save her. He didn't know what else to do. She smiled at him and nodded.

"So, how long are you going to be in here?" Suzanne asked.

"Don't know," Ty answered.

"The doctor and the lady they sent from the mental health center think that all the kids need to be evaluated at Children's Hospital. To make sure that nothing *goes wrong*," Ty's mom used air quotes. "We're just waiting for his bed to open up."

"That sounds like a pretty good idea. I'm heading to a place like that myself as soon as I leave here."

"You'll be at Children's Hospital with us?" Ty asked.

"No, I'm going to a place in Atlanta. They specialize in helping women who've had things happen like I have. They'll make sure that I'm good as new, or as close to it as I can get."

"So you are leaving as principal?" Ty's mom asked.

"I couldn't go back if they offered me the job. Too many bad memories now. I'm not even going to get the stuff out of my office. Let them deal with it."

She looked at the wall clock. It was almost lunchtime, and she was determined to not eat another meal in this hospital.

"I guess I'll be going," she said.

"Please don't go," Ty said. "We'll miss you."

"I'll miss you too, but I've got to. I've got to get myself fixed."

Ty nodded and smiled. His mother shook Suzanne's hand again. Suzanne hugged Ty then walked back out into the hall. The rest of the kids were up here, but she couldn't bear to visit with them. Talking with Ty had almost broken her back down to uncontrollable crying.

Suzanne walked past the nurse's station. She waved to the secretary and then went into the stairwell. It smelled musty and like old rusty metal. She walked to the ground floor and out the front door. Wal-Mart sat across the highway from the hospital. The parking lot was full of cars. The sun glared off the windshields making the whole parking lot glow like a light bulb. She shielded her eyes and started walking down the sidewalk away from the hospital and toward the Greyhound station. For just a moment, she thought about how many Hassles might be in the world. Hadassah had said Solomon had kidnapped people before. How many times might that have been? Suzanne let those thought go.

Her ticket to Atlanta waited at the desk in the bus depot. Everything she owned was in her house, and it would stay there for a long time. Suzanne couldn't go back there just yet. Everything seemed scary, except the idea of getting to Atlanta and treatment. She walked past the civic center. A sign announced the Fall Carnival. The religious folks of the town thought that Halloween was satanic and had insisted that the school rename the old Halloween fair, the Fall Carnival. They didn't know evil. She'd looked the devil in the face and survived. Now she thought about looking God in the face and reevaluating her place in the cosmos. She'd have time.

The long silver bus rolled into the depot as Suzanne stepped up to the door. The beacon in the windshield said "BHM/ATL." She walked into the office, got her ticket, and boarded the bus. Half an hour later, she watched through the windows as they rolled past the courthouse. The copper dome shined in the sun, like a star. The bus passed the bank, and she caught her reflection in the mirrored windows of the building. Then the town petered into a few houses with large yards. They crossed the bridge of Lafayette Creek, and Marquisville lay in her past.

Suzanne looked forward at the plush seat ahead of her. She'd lucked out that no one sat beside her. She spread out, truly relaxing. The bus swayed back and forth as it went toward a new home and an unclouded day.

We hope you've enjoyed the story. Please help us share this story with other readers by letting us know what you thought with a review on either **amazon.com** or **goodreads.com**.

Thank you kindly,
Montag Press Collective

Vic Kerry lives in Alabama with his wife, seven dogs, and cat. By day, he is a mild mannered psychotherapist. By night, he's an over-wound adjunct psychology instructor, fueled by too much sweet tea. Whenever he can catch a minute, he's a horror writer. Everything else seems frivolous to mention, but he is also a narcissist, day and night. Vic has an MFA in writing popular fiction from Seton Hill University and is haunted by the ghost of his dearly departed cat, Possum H. Puss Lovecraff. That sums him up perfectly. You can like him or friend him on Facebook or stalk him through Twitter (@DarklyVicKerry) and his blog (www.vickerry.wordpress.com)

Tree Black
Connor De Bruler

It's hard being a trans woman. Harder still in North Carolina. Sandy Pogue knows this first-hand. Along with her Cherokee boyfriend Yona Bridger, Sandy manages to eke out a simple but happy life until inevitable circumstances force them to pack up and skip town.

As they try to carve out a new life, Sandy and Yona find themselves in the clutches of a bizarre cult of kidnapped women and demonic children. What is Yona's connection to this mysterious group of backwoods zealots, and can he help Sandy avoid a fate worse than death?

More than just their two lives hang in the balance as they hack a bloody swath through the ancient countryside, trying to reach the safety of the light through the TREE BLACK.

*In **Tree Black**, de Bruler introduces the most amazing new heroine to blast onto the horror scene in ages. Swinging her hatchet through the heads of demon possessed hillbillies, Sandy is a cross between Hedwig and Evil Dead's Ash Williams. A fully realized and dynamic character instead of a boring clichéd archeytpe, Sandy strikes blow after brutal blow for outsiders everywhere.*

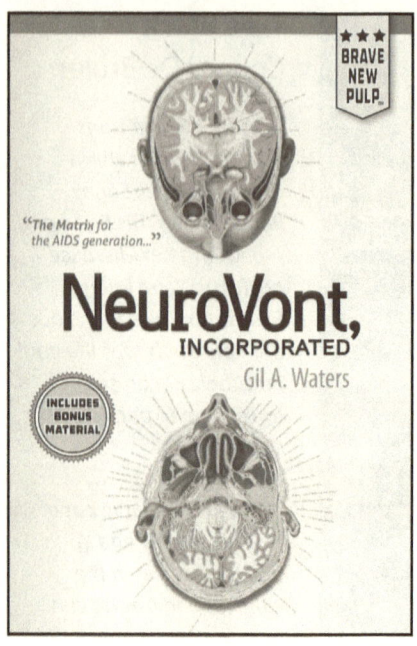

★ ★ ★
BRAVE
NEW
PULP™

"The Matrix for
the AIDS generation..."

INCLUDES
BONUS
MATERIAL

NeuroVont, Incorporated
Gil A. Waters

**Sex, drugs, and . . .
post-corporeal
transmigration?**

*Rik was stuck in a dead-end
office job, relying on copious
amounts of weed to make it
through each day. His affair
with the boss was the only
highlight in his otherwise
miserable existence. Then
a terrorist group released a
vicious, highly contagious
virus—and everything
changed.*

*When Rik becomes infected, he finds himself on the run from a government
that ruthlessly hunts down anyone who might be sick. He soon learns that
narcotics dull the symptoms, and that sex with another infected person gets
him higher than he's ever been. He hooks up with a beautiful ex-government
agent, Dez, who is also infected. Together, they seek sanctuary in a mysterious
underground organization: NeuroVont, Incorporated. What they find will blow
their minds…*

*Gil A. Waters' brisk and spare future perfect story imagines a world where
getting infected means that you are chased by the government as bio-
terrorists, and the only people that can help do so through an underground
network of sex- and drug-fueled safe houses. As a beacon of hope,
NeuroVont, Incorporated turns the cryptic anonymous corporation into
a safe place where people in trouble can disappear to discover the true
meaning of the infection that's sweeping America in the near future. The
writing is light and cheery as Gil Waters keeps the sex, drugs, and jokes
zinging faster than the five ball bonus on the best pinball game ever.*

The End of Jack Cruz
A.A. Garrison

The movies never prepared him for this, even the ones that ended badly.

Jack "Colonel" Jones is suddenly alone in the world. After surviving a plague that decimates the U.S., and perhaps the entire human population, he is left in a junky's nightmare where hard drugs are the only remedy for an ongoing virus and dead bodies are his only companions. Sick and desperate, he meets a savior who goes by the name Jack Cruz.

Jack Cruz is a hulking behemoth with a giant pistol and stockpile of post-apocalyptic supplies, but he also has a mysterious past and an increasingly disconcerting obsession with the death and decay that surrounds them.

As Colonel's suspicions rise, and he begins to feel complicit in the wrongdoings of his post-apocalyptic roommate, Colonel must grapple new the questions: Can you be moral when there are only two people left on earth? Can there be sanity? And who decides? Is Colonel just paranoid, or are his fears justified?

As the stakes heat up and the intensity flares, Colonel must find out the truth and decide – when your only companion in the world might be a murderer, and there is no one left to kill, is surviving worth it?

Hanging Fields
Steven Maxwell

A fierce and shocking account of lost souls in a violent working-class town where, for some, cruelty and betrayal are the only means of survival.

The soldier is home. Back from the desert with a brutal secret, his life begins to collapse, his mind starts to unravel, and his family is afraid of him. Menacing calls and texts say they know what he did, while stalking cars threaten far worse.

Buried in a sadistic world of dog fighting and military drugs, cult abuse and execution videos, he's engulfed in a paranoid rage so intense it endangers those around him. Yet why do the people in his life pose a greater danger to him?

Steven Maxwell has created a tiny British masterpiece in the world of unemployed hoodlums, single mothers, and returning war vets. Haunted by a society that rejects them and finding solace in a world of online snuff videos, computer video games, and the constant hum of horror videos and real life crime news stories, two half brothers try desperately to regain some sense of control over their lives. Unable to deal with the many layers of despair coating the bottom of British society, both brothers careen towards each other as they try to find something to believe in and something to hold on to, something which turns out to be their mutual hatred for each other. Reminiscent of classic youth-gone-wild teensploitation stories from the early 60s, Mr. Maxwell deftly relocates the desperate downward spirals of those archetypal young men into today's world of ubiquitous cell phones and near constant texting, creating a timeless tragedy for today.

Hooks & Slaughterhouse
Alana I. Capria
Illustrations by Rita Okusako

"Once upon a hollowed out moon, my liver withers..."

The Bloodless girl is haunted by confusing memories of her cannibalistic worm mother. Did the Bloodless girl bury her worm mother in salt? Where have all the worm siblings gone? And how did the Bloodless girl end up on a curving rural road that leads to nowhere and everywhere?

The Bloodless girl can't remember. All she knows is that dust fills her arteries and the worm mother is gone. Accompanied by a skeletal pumpkin and devil tree, the Bloodless girl journeys through the New Jersey backwoods in search of a hilltop slaughterhouse that is the key to regaining her blood and learning the truth about the worm mother's disappearance.

www.ingramcontent.com/pod-product-compliance
Lightning Source LLC
Chambersburg PA
CBHW032135270626

47172CB00008B/42